Children of Dynasty

Christine Carroll

Jewel Imprint: Ruby
Medallion Press, Inc.
Florida, USA

Dedication:

Always, to Richard.

Published 2005 by Medallion Press, Inc.
225 Seabreeze Ave.
Palm Beach, FL 33480

The MEDALLION PRESS LOGO
is a registered tradmark of Medallion Press, Inc.

Printed in the United States of America

Library of Congress Cataloging-in-Publication Data

Carroll, Christine.
  Children of dynasty / Christine Carroll.
     p. cm.
  ISBN 1-932815-42-2
  1. San Francisco (Calif.)--Fiction. I. Title.
  PS3603.A774575C48 2005
  813'.6--dc22

                              2005016459

ACKNOWLEDGEMENTS:

Thanks to my agent Susan Schulman, for her tireless and patient support, and to all the wonderful folks at Medallion Press who made this possible — Helen Rosburg, Connie Perry, Wendy Burbank, and Leslie Burbank, to name the ones I know best.

And appreciation to all those who helped me with suggestions or just plain inspiration along the way: author Robert Vaughan, Jim Harris, the students of the Rice University Novel Writing Colloquium, in particular Karen Meinardus who edited the entire manuscript, Marjorie Arsht, Kathryn Brown, Judith Finkel, Bob Hargrove, Elizabeth Hueben, Joan Romans, Angela Shepard, Jeff Theall, and Diana Wade. And Rita's girls Babette DeJongh, Susan Nickson, Betty Pichardo, Susan Sandler, and Jesica Trapp. The members of West Houston Romance Writers of America are a constant source of information and wellspring of enthusiasm.

Two persons who are no longer with us were pivotal: the late Venkatesh Srinivas Kulkarni, author, teacher, and beloved friend, and the late Rita Gallagher, author, teacher, and woman of consummate style and grace.

CHAPTER 1

$\mathcal{M}$ariah Grant hugged her slender body against the deepening chill of the San Francisco twilight. Behind her, music and party chatter drifted out through the French doors of Davis Campbell's Seacliff mansion. Perched on the brink of a precipice, the stucco-walled edifice boasted three wings, handmade clay roof tiles and a two-story wall of glass overlooking the Pacific. Mariah's view from the terrace swept from the Golden Gate Bridge south to the trackless sea, while a line of ships headed for the expanse of open ocean. Their purpose and motion made her wish she were bound for some exotic port, to be anywhere but in the home of her father's most bitter rival.

Only a month had passed since she joined the family company and, due to her dad being under the weather tonight, she represented Grant Development alone for the first time. Her hope this evening was to meet Senator Lawrence Chatsworth, former head of the Bay Area Regional Planning Commission, a man whose influence had opened doors for many.

Though she might feel confident invading the Campbell domain for business reasons, she had trouble setting aside her personal feelings. She expected Davis Campbell's son Rory to be here, she counted on it, but the prospect of seeing the man she'd once loved made her chest feel hollow.

As the sun sank into the molten ocean, a salt breeze stirred her hair. She knew she should go back inside and look for the Senator, but instead stood compelled by the rugged San Francisco terrain, achingly familiar, yet now more precious for having spent her college years at UCLA, and four more working in Southern California. Virtual exile from her father, but it had been necessary both to pay her business dues and heal the wound inflicted by Rory Campbell.

Fixing her eyes on a deepening ochre sky, she steeled herself to rejoin the party. All the key players in the Bay Area developers' community were here. Hundreds of guests crowded the elegant high-ceilinged rooms, drinking premium liquor and vying for information to help their interests or hinder others.

Before she could turn back toward the house, a hand brushed her forearm. "Mariah."

Startled, she turned and looked up into warm brown

eyes. Six-foot-two inches of well-built man in a tailored tuxedo, Rory Campbell brought back all the memories she'd tried to forget.

"It's been too long." His voice sounded familiar, deep, and even though she could no longer replay that seductive tone in her mind, her heart remembered. Treacherous images swirled of being in his arms when she was eighteen and innocent.

Rory's gaze traveled from the straps of her gold sheath down to the curve of her waist. In the San Francisco boutique, the dress had seemed the perfect revenge, but now she wondered if it revealed too much. With a coolness she didn't feel, she looked up at wavy, black hair above dark angled brows, high cheekbones, and a square jaw softened by a sensuous mouth. The scent of his aftershave wafted to her, bringing back a bygone summer when she'd sprinkled the fragrance on her pillow so she could dream of him. He'd been a slim blade of youth then, with a gaunt face composed of angular planes. Tonight, he wore an aura of self-confidence that declared the heir to Davis Campbell Interests had come into his own.

"How did eight years get away?" he asked.

"You were married for seven of them." She failed to state that his rush to the altar indicated how little she had meant to him.

He looked pained. "You know Elizabeth and I . . . that I'm single?"

She studied the sea cliffs. "Your divorce made the news."

Last fall when she was visiting her dad for Thanksgiving, the lead story in "On the Spot," the city's video equivalent of the tabloids: "City's most eligible bachelor once more at large."

"The paparazzi are relentless." Rory looked annoyed. "Ten minutes after you joined your father's company, the word was out."

Through the French doors, Mariah spied Davis Campbell's tall frame cutting a swath through the party crowd. "And for the past few months you, too, have been with your father." Her tone hardened. "You swore you'd never work for him."

Rory's mouth twisted. "I remember saying I wanted to run white water raft trips."

They'd played that kind of "what if," sailing on the Bay where sunlight sprinkled diamonds over the water.

"We thought we'd do whatever we wanted when we grew up." Though Mariah knew he'd recently turned twenty-eight, Rory spoke with the sadness of a much older man.

To remind herself, and him, how he'd once caved in to his father, she looked a challenge at him. "What happened to your dream of being your own man?"

"The same thing that happens to so many with a legacy." Though his words rang with finality, his dark expression conveyed something like regret. "At least you're where you've always wanted to be, training to run Grant Development. You said that was your dream, and here you are."

When she was a little girl, her father had taken her to construction sites. While he took notes on his aluminum, weatherproof clipboard and talked with employees, she watched with a child's single-minded fascination. Dreams of a future where she saw her creations take shape had consumed most of her life.

Rory glanced over his shoulder at the crush inside. "I'm surprised you came tonight."

"Dad was a bit taken aback when we both got an unprecedented invitation from Davis Campbell. Then he decided it must have been a business courtesy." Reluctant to mention her father's health lest it get back to his rival, she finished, "I came alone."

Speaking of her father, she realized that the wall of glass on the rear of the house exposed her standing with Rory. If the ever-active grapevine paired them, Dad would be sure to hear and be hurt by his daughter's indiscretion.

"Would you be here if you'd known the invitation was from me?" Rory spoke with a trace of what could not be hesitation, not in the "the city's most eligible bachelor."

Mariah went still inside, afraid of trusting too much in his statement. She had trusted him once before, and look where that had gotten her.

"Why would you invite me?" She tried to sound casual.

He smiled for the first time. It softened his features, making him more like the youth she'd known. "Maybe when I heard you'd come back to town I got curious."

"Curious." She too, had wondered how they would react to seeing each other again. "If you did invite me, why include my father?"

Rory's eyes twinkled. "Asking you both seemed less obvious."

Like his smile, his teasing tone took her back. When his

gaze took another tour from the top of her head to the tips of her strappy gold sandals, goosebumps prickled her skin.

"You're chilled." He shrugged off his jacket and draped it around her.

She wasn't sure she wanted the remembered intimacy of wearing his clothes, but with bowed head, she let him cover her shoulders with the coat. His hand brushed her collarbone, left a tingling spot on her skin, and she wondered if it were her imagination that his fingers were unsteady?

Before she could stop herself, she looked up. In his eyes, she found the same smoky look that had so often preceded a kiss. With a flutter in her stomach, she realized how easily he could have her back under his spell.

She tried looking away, at the flagstone, the railing around the turquoise swimming pool, but it was no good.

"Mariah." Rory tipped her chin up so she met his eyes once more. Rather than lower his mouth to hers, he studied her in silence, as though measuring his next words. "You ever think 'what if?'"

Closing her eyes, she rode a wave of pain. Why couldn't she be immune to him after so many years of silence?

"Admit it," Rory's voice was soft. "You remember, too."

Memory held it all, from the times she had raised her face for his kiss to his vow that nothing would come between them, not school, long distance, or their parents. Did she feel his breath, a faint stir of air before her?

Before she could decide, Davis Campbell's imperial tone intruded. "Rory!"

Her eyes snapped open.

Rory stepped back, and turned from her toward the French doors where his father stood.

Davis must be about fifty-eight now, her father's age, as they had been classmates at Stanford. A complimentary scatter of silver threaded his thick, black hair, but he still carried his tall frame proudly. Though undeniably good-looking, his predatory expression chilled her enough to draw Rory's jacket closer around her. Behind him in the great room, his big game hunting trophies festooned the walls.

Davis fixed on Mariah, his dark eyes as hard as she remembered, reminding her of the night he'd caught her and Rory making love on his yacht. Drunk on freedom and the heat of their bare skin, neither of them heard the tap of footsteps on the dock until it was too late.

Though the sea breeze cooled the terrace, the memory of shame heated her.

"What are you doing in my home?" The man she blamed for destroying her dreams glared down at her.

Shaken by the recollection of Davis's unleashed rage upon catching his son with John Grant's daughter, Mariah nonetheless drew herself up. "I was invited."

Davis's scowl deepened; now he would demand she leave. She wondered if Rory might object and admit he was the one who had wanted her here.

To her surprise, Davis put on a calculating expression. "Our guest lists are long," he said at last, dismissing her with a wave of his hand.

Mariah gave Rory an uncertain glance. Had he been playing games about inviting her?

"I told you to visit with Senator Chatsworth," Davis growled at his son.

It was happening again, as it had years ago. Expecting Rory to do his father's bidding, she said coldly, "Your jacket," and held it at arm's length.

Rory took it with a deft motion and slipped it on. Yet, even as her spirits sank, he gave his father a defiant look and took her elbow. "Come and meet the Senator," he urged.

Her instantaneous reaction to his touch reminded her not to risk getting hurt again, but it suited her evening's mission to allow him to lead her through the French doors.

Inside, Rory bent to kiss the cheek of a petite woman. "Mother. You remember Mariah Grant."

Eight years ago, Kiki Campbell had been an attractive, rather plump woman. Now, she wore the ascetic look of a woman who dieted religiously. Her red hair was obviously the result of salon visits, and though her face wore the faintly surprised look that comes with plastic surgery, Mariah suspected she really was astonished to see John Grant's daughter with her son.

With a gulp from her half-empty wineglass, Kiki said, "Love your dress." An out-of-place giggle suggested she'd had enough to drink.

Mariah studied Kiki's lime green bouffant dress, fashioned for a woman half her age. "You look nice, too," she said gently.

Behind his wife, Mariah saw Davis enter from outside, his alert gaze assessing and lingering on the gathering's beautiful, elegant women. Kiki noticed, too, and for an instant her green eyes rested on her husband with what could only be yearning. "On the Spot" routinely implied that she endured his philandering, just as the gossip rags suggested that Rory, too, discarded women like used tissues since his divorce.

Despite that Mariah had agreed to come in with Rory, this reminder of his marriage and the news stories about his recently playing the field made her turn away as though she had business with someone. The next feat was making it happen in a crowd where she knew so few people.

No one familiar was in sight, yet she left Rory and his mother with purpose in her steps. Fortunately, she spotted a man standing next to the buffet of jumbo shrimp, lobster, and caviar, his face familiar from development industry magazines. Takei Takayashi, a hearty middle-aged man with the compact muscles of a linebacker, watched her approach with alert dark eyes.

"Hello, I'm . . ."

"Mariah Grant." Takei's broad face broke into a smile. "You're the image of your mother." His California accent suggested he was American-born, but he dipped his head in a series of traditional Japanese bows.

"How are things at Golden Builders?" she asked. A fleeting glance told her that Davis Campbell was taking in their conversation.

"We're now the third largest in the Bay Area." Somewhat

importantly, Takei adjusted a silk tie patterned with colorful crested cranes. "I figure on overtaking Grant next and then going toe to toe with Campbell." His smile softened his challenge, and she recalled that, in spite of their rivalry, he was a friend of John Grant.

Mariah nodded, though the much smaller Golden Builders was in no danger of overtaking either of its major competitors. She couldn't imagine why he would think so, except a man was entitled to dream.

Recalling that Rory had worked as an architect at Golden for seven years, she spoke before she could stop herself. "Why did Rory Campbell leave you?"

Takei sobered. "It was time he took his place in the family business, learning the kind of things his father's showing him on the executive floor. You also must identify, after paying your dues in L.A."

"That's true." In southern California, she'd been busy if not happy, running hard in pursuit of her dream to return in triumph.

Rory appeared at her elbow and greeted his old boss. Then he touched Mariah's arm. "There's an opening with the Senator now."

She studied Lawrence Chatsworth, who was shaking hands with Davis. A high-energy man, the Senator's pale sharp eyes were always moving. He wore his light brown hair a bit long in back, perhaps to appeal to baby boomers.

"Excuse me," she told Takei and went with Rory.

When he presented her, Chatsworth said smoothly, "A

pleasure, Miss Grant. I don't know your father well, but I was sorry to hear his company isn't doing as well as it once did."

Mariah tried to hide her shock by keeping her chin high. "Where did you hear that? Grant Development is doing fine."

Davis gave a soft chuckle that set her on edge, and she believed she knew where the rumors had gotten started. Takei must have heard them, too.

Looking at the Senator, Davis said, "It's a shame you didn't know the buzz on Grant wasn't true, Larry. Maybe you wouldn't have passed the word in Washington."

Mariah nearly gasped, but managed to press her lips together. From the corner of her eye, she saw Rory's head snap up.

Chatsworth sipped at his drink and mused, "But you know what they say, Davis. Where there's smoke, there's fire."

"True," Davis returned. "And even if we were wrong, there's no place for apologizing in this tough world."

Rory murmured at Mariah's ear, "So he always says."

Davis gave him a black look.

The Senator focused his spotlight on Mariah. "So, what does Grant have in the works to pull things back up?"

Her mind raced. There were several large tracts of ranch land coming up for bid in the late summer. She knew that her father had his eye on at least two of them with Pacific frontage. And as surely, she knew that mentioning any interest in either of them in front of Davis Campbell would be foolhardy. Better he go to the bid table ignorant of which contest

John Grant intended to enter.

"I can't discuss our plans," she parried.

Davis shot a sidelong glance at the Senator, and Mariah gave up any thought of further conversation with the powerful politician. His allegiance was clear.

"I see someone I must speak to," she said with as much coolness as she could muster.

Walking away, she was once more aware of the sea of unfamiliar faces that surrounded her. To hide that she was meeting no one, she searched for and found the powder room off the main foyer. The decorator's gem of a bath with solid gold fixtures underscored the difference between Davis Campbell's ostentation and the simpler way her father preferred to live.

A gilt-framed mirror over the alabaster sink showed her color was high. Taking deep breaths, she smoothed her blond hair, wind-blown from the terrace, over her shoulders. Then she washed her hands and pressed a damp paper towel to the sides of her neck. Noting the décolletage of her small breasts in the sequined dress, she tugged at the neckline and blushed at the folly of wearing it to make Rory see what he'd missed out on.

Could it be true that he'd invited her tonight? A flush darkened her already pink cheeks at the memory of his steady regard when he spoke of them being prisoners of their inheritance. Yet, if Davis had been the one to include her on his guest list, as he'd implied, he might have hoped inexperience would loosen her tongue. Prying questions delivered so casually from the Senator could have been engineered to start her bragging about Grant's plans. Then Davis would know where to place his chips against his rival when the next package of raw land came up for bid. The question was whether Rory would have begun his own sly exploration had they not been interrupted on the terrace. If her own dedication to her family company was any yardstick, his allegiance to DCI must run deep.

Freshening her lip gloss, Mariah debated leaving, but she refused to be driven away so early in the evening. The last thing she wanted was for Rory's father to believe he'd gotten the better of her.

She returned to the party, head high and smiling.

As she moved from group to group, she saw that Davis kept up with her movements, watching those with whom she spoke and often drawing near enough to eavesdrop. In turn, she noted the people he cultivated. A young and eager state representative, a florid older gentleman who was current head of the Bay Area Regional Planning Commission, and there was Thaddeus Walker, Grant Development's usually lugubrious, big-eared banker at First California. Mariah moved closer, but was unable to hear what he and Davis discussed with such animated camaraderie.

She also watched Rory. Standing easily on the balls of his feet, he seemed to fit here in his father's house. Could he be trusted, or had he grown into a man cut from the same cloth as Davis and the Senator?

As if he felt her looking at him, Rory turned and met her

eyes with a peculiar emphasis that seemed to charge the air. After a moment that had her breathless, he took two glasses of champagne from a caterer's tray and came toward her. "Thirsty?" Pinpoint bubbles of effervescence welled in the crystal flute.

Torn between suspicion and the rekindled magnetism between them, she reached for the stem. "I suppose I should thank you for the fine food and wine, that is, if you did invite me."

Before she could take the glass, Davis appeared beside them with a striking twenty-something beauty who snagged it ahead of her.

Mariah recoiled.

Sylvia Chatsworth, the Senator's daughter and the latest woman linked with Rory in the tabloids, lifted the champagne and drank. In her twenties, with a spill of sleek black hair over bronzed shoulders, she had what Mariah's high school art teacher would have called "good bones."

While Davis beamed as though he'd found a match for his son, Sylvia kissed Rory, missing his mouth and leaving a smudge of crimson on his cheek.

He swiped at his face. "Mariah . . ."

She had had enough. As violent as her reaction to seeing him again was, she must put a stop to this. He might have the gift of transforming a woman's bones to putty, but she refused to get caught in the Campbell web again.

"Lovely party," she announced coldly, looking toward the mammoth carved doors where she had come in from the front courtyard. With a false smile curving her lips, she walked blindly through the foyer toward the exit.

From behind, she heard Rory call for her to wait. For the barest instant, she hesitated, but too many unanswered questions sent her on into the spring night.

The day after the party, Mariah drove through the Sunday evening rain to the Stonestown neighborhood where she had grown up. The older, but pleasant, district lay south of Golden Gate Park and east of Ocean Beach. Once rolling sand dunes, the terrain now marched up and down gentle hills where modest stucco homes built with post World War II financing lined quiet streets.

Parking in front of her father's bungalow, she was struck once more by the contrast between the simple way he lived, plowing every spare dime back into Grant Development, and Davis Campbell's lifestyle. Her jaw set as she prepared to break the news about Campbell and Chatsworth's scheme to defame him.

Dodging raindrops up the walk between double rows of pampered rosebushes, she let herself into the house and pocketed her key.

In the narrow hall, she paused beside a wooden chessboard to study the move her father had made since she was last there. This set was dedicated to an ongoing match that only moved forward when she dropped by home. When she was in L.A., this had lain dormant for months. Of course, then they had played on the computer, sending moves back and forth by e-mail. Mariah studied the board, lifted a knight, and moved it two spaces forward and one to the right, a little closer to her father's king.

From the hall, she followed the familiar mouth-watering smell of marinara sauce to the kitchen. Golden oak cabinets glowed and produce spilled over white marble countertops.

"You didn't call." John smiled from where he was stirring the contents of a saucepan. "I hope I have enough pasta." He wore his usual at-home uniform of khaki slacks and a worn out blue dress shirt, the ceiling spotlights accentuating his shock of silver hair.

Setting her keys and purse down, she stretched to kiss his cheek. "How are you feeling?"

"Fine as can be." He appeared well rested, his gray eyes alert and clear.

"You do look better than you did Saturday," she tempered, checking the sauce, and finding a generous amount of Italian sausage.

He saw her gaze. "Fat's where the flavor is."

The familiar sight of him stirring a pot touched her heart, reminding her of days when he cooked, and she did homework at the kitchen table. Now he asked her to make a salad with cherry tomatoes and peppers and to boil salted water laced with olive oil.

While she was washing lettuce, he held out a spoonful of sauce. "Taste."

"I don't have to. It needs more sugar."

"Wrong." He grinned. "When I saw your car pull up, I added some."

Turning back to the stove, he took an experimental sample of his creation and added another pinch of salt. "Now, tell me about last night at Campbell's. I expected you to call earlier."

Mariah rummaged under the cabinet for a cutting board. "Quite a turnout, and an amazing place. I didn't realize the Campbells lived so high."

"Who all was there?"

She sliced tomatoes. "Well, of course I didn't know many folks."

Not wanting to spoil her father's appetite after he'd gone to so much trouble, Mariah managed to entertain him with details unrelated to Davis Campbell for the time it took to get the meal ready.

John carried plates heaped with linguini and sauce to the butcher-block table. As they sat down, he beamed at her proudly. "You don't know what it means to finally have you at Grant Development."

"You don't know how glad I am to be here." This past winter when she'd finished work on the Desert Hot Springs Convention Center her father came down for a tour. In the grand ballroom beneath a crystal chandelier, he took both her hands. "It's time."

He twirled pasta with a spoon. "With you here, we'll beat out Davis Campbell and be the biggest in the Bay Area."

Suddenly, the blend of basil and sweet tomatoes wasn't as appetizing as before.

Though she hated to break the news during dinner, she put down her fork.

"Dad."

His face sobered.

"There's something you should know."

Briefly, she told him the rumors circulating about trouble within Grant Development, and that both Chatsworth and Campbell appeared to be fueling them.

John shoved back his half-eaten plate. "Davis had been against me for almost thirty years, so there's no surprise there." His voice was grim. "But it disturbs me that he's got the Senator in his pocket."

The memory of Sylvia Chatsworth's possessive certainty of Rory made Mariah's stomach ache. "I think maybe it has something to do with his daughter and Rory Campbell." She couldn't keep an acid note out of her voice.

Her father gave her a sharp look. "Did you see him at the party?"

"I saw him," she admitted. "For the first time in eight years."

Although John had never taken the inflexible stance against Rory that Davis Campbell had against her, he'd obviously felt relief when she was safely in Southern California and Rory married to another woman.

Now he studied her, his face troubled. "I've always thought you should live your life the way you wanted . . . but you don't want to see him again."

The part that stung was that Mariah did want to see Rory. Even as everything in her knew it would be a mistake. "He's with Sylvia Chatsworth, Dad," she protested. "You don't have to worry."

He ran a hand through his silver hair, a sure sign he was concerned. "You and I are the same. We've never moved on from our first loves."

He glanced toward a gilt-framed photo of her mother on the counter. It could have been a picture of Mariah, with a smooth line of jaw, blond hair falling over her shoulders.

"Catharine was even more slight than you. Like a pale bisque doll near the end." He touched a fingertip to the cool glass, as though he could reach the sweet soft corner of his wife's mouth if he moved his hand in just the right way. When he rubbed his palm over his own face, Mariah imagined he was aware of the loose flesh and wrinkled skin.

She touched his hand and saw a sparkle of tears matching her own. Memories of her mother were hazy; golden eyes like her own, a soft touch while being tucked in, playing tag in the spring grass.

John cleared his throat. "I came home, one of those perfect sharp blue days, and saw her with you out on the lawn. She said you'd set a record at twenty steps. The two of you in the afternoon sun were the most beautiful thing I have ever seen."

Mariah had always figured he remained in this house because it held so many memories. "Why do you single out that day?"

"When we went inside, the phone rang. It was her doctor, asking us to come in again after her routine physical."

Ovarian cancer, swift scourge of the youngest women, had stolen Catharine from them when Mariah was but three. When the loss came back to her, it was in bits and pieces; the hospital's antiseptic smell, crying and being carried out of the memorial service, the mound of flowers turned sodden in the rain.

"After the call, I tried to kiss her and rekindle the spark, but the fine light was gone." John's eyes rested on that far-away day. "Light has never held that quality for me since."

Seeing his sadness undimmed by years, Mariah tried to ignore a familiar twinge of pain. Whenever she wondered if the kind of joy her parents had shared would come to her, she was forced to admit her father was correct. No one had ever moved her like Davis Campbell's son.

Rory had been right last night, too; she had wondered "what if" so many times she'd lost count.

And, as the rain made rivulets down the kitchen window, she did so again.

*T*wo hours later, Mariah busied herself straightening the living room of the apartment she rented in a Marina District Victorian. After stacking the same magazines for the fourth time, she sank onto her new wicker sofa. Though she stared at the ivory and green swirls in the matching rug, she saw a long-ago June morning . . .

Eighteen-year-old Mariah discovered from the Sunday morning *Chronicle* that John's rival Davis Campbell kept his racing boat on a Sausalito pier. A photo showed him holding aloft a silver cup, not even the newsprint blurring the sharp intensity of the man. He looked at his trophy with the same expression he'd used over the years to examine Mariah, an avarice that always made her uneasy.

Studying the photo, she caught sight of a younger man beside Davis, a fit and slimmer version of the yacht's captain. She had never formally met Rory Campbell. Nonetheless, despite the lack of introduction, she was utterly smitten with him. Two years ago, she had watched this bronzed youth with flashing limbs destroy an opponent at a tennis party. In the milling aftermath, while she waited at courtside to attract his attention her father had announced abruptly that they were leaving.

Mariah set aside the newspaper, and, tiptoeing so as not to wake her father, left a noncommittal note. Then she drove his Pontiac across the Golden Gate Bridge to Sausalito.

When she arrived at the marina, an unforecast squall played an eerie piping chime, beating the sailboat halyards against their masts. Fog streamed into the harbor, pleasure boats sat idle at the piers, and the houseboat community was battened down. For a moment she hesitated, but with this weather, she should be able to look over the yacht without being discovered.

Once on the pier, she had no trouble locating the knife-like vessel *Privateer*. A towering mast stretched up into the mist, and at least fifty feet of sleek hull shone bright even in the gray light. Water drops beaded the rich teak deck trim.

"Come in out of the rain," said a male voice from aboard.

Even with her tennis shoes' traction, Mariah nearly lost her footing on the slippery boardwalk. Steadying herself on the boat's wet aluminum rail, she turned to see who had spoken.

A tall, narrow-faced man stood in the shadowed companionway. Dark eyes peered at her from beneath the brim of his ball cap.

Instinctively, she pulled her damp denim shirt tighter around her. Caught flat-footed on the owner's pier, she steeled herself and hoped Davis Campbell would not recognize her since she'd grown up. "I was just admiring your boat." She tried to smooth her wind-tangled hair.

"*Privateer* is my Dad's," confessed a voice she now recognized as far less commanding than Davis Campbell's.

Mariah nearly sagged with relief, but her heart began to race. Hadn't she hoped to run into him, without daring to admit it?

"I'm Rory Campbell," he said. A rough blue cotton shirt over loose khaki shorts complimented his taut body.

When he reached a hand to help her aboard, his skin felt callused against hers, a suggestion he knew his way around the yacht's winches and lines. Reluctant to break the spell by telling him she was a Grant, she tempered with, "Mariah." The rain came down harder, blowing beneath the canvas bimini over the broad cockpit.

"Come below," he urged.

Though she compromised by taking a seat on the ladder down to the cabin, drops still splattered her. Rory reached to close the Lexan hatch, his chest only inches from her face. She caught his scent, a pleasant aroma like geranium petals warmed by the sun. Strung tight at his nearness, Mariah was nonetheless disappointed when he turned away.

In the spacious galley, he lighted a brass lantern and suspended it from a hook over the table. Thus illuminated, the teak-lined cabin was as large as her father's living room. Rory filled a kettle and put it on the stove, ferreted out teabags, and set out mugs with *Privateer* on them in gold letters. Waiting for the water to boil, he leaned against the counter and sent her a swift appraising glance.

She shivered.

"You're cold." He unbuttoned his shirt, revealing a nest of crisp hair and rosy brown nipples drawn tight against the cabin's chill.

Embarrassed by the flush that warmed her cheeks, she hugged herself to hide her breasts' inevitable reaction to his splendid bare body.

He came toward her, a lithe animal on a stalk, and draped the shirt over hers. Once more nervous at him standing so close, she threw out the first thing she thought of. "Do you go to school?"

"Stanford. Business, that I may be worthy to wear Davis Campbell's crown." He gave a sardonic bow.

"You sound bitter."

"You'd be, too, if your father expected you to follow his footsteps without a thought."

Mariah had never considered anything other than taking over for her dad someday. The love for building came to her naturally; it didn't make sense that, as his father's son, Rory would want anything else. "What would you rather be?"

"An architect, an archaeologist . . ." He waved an

impatient hand. "I only know I've never been given a choice." The kettle whistled. He poured, dunked teabags, and fished them out with a spoon. "You don't get to pick your father."

He handed her the cup, and their hands touched.

"My father is John Grant," she confessed.

"I thought so," Rory said evenly. "Mariah's not a common name." In the rain-scattered light, his eyes held hers. She felt her pulse flutter at the base of her throat, but in the embrace of his shirt, she felt inexplicably safe.

He set his cup aside. Very carefully, as though she were a wild thing, he lifted her hair and spread it over her shoulders. She sat still and told herself she should be afraid here alone with Davis Campbell's son. Yet, she could summon only a buoyant elation. Rory seemed different from what her dad told her of his father. Honest rather than scheming.

She wasn't sure which of them closed that infinitesimal space, but his lips on hers had the softness of a remembered dream. The briefest graze and he drew back.

Mariah cherished the sense he was also feeling his way. With trembling fingers, she touched his smooth-shaven cheek. Its warmth, and the dear dimple in the crease beside his mouth undid her. He pressed his lips to hers again, tasting of tea and a sweetness that intensified her yearning. Though a little voice whispered she didn't even know him, his kiss argued that he knew everything about her.

While rain streamed over his father's boat, the Stanford man seduced a girl who wanted to believe.

Sitting on her apartment sofa, Mariah had to admit he

hadn't really seduced her. Having dreamed for years of the young man she'd seen playing tennis, she'd been half in love with him before he even spoke to her. Ready to cancel her plans for UCLA and attend a Bay Area college, prepared to defy her father and turn her life upside down . . . for she'd imagined them as star-crossed lovers defying their families' enmity.

How blind she'd been not to see she was on a collision course with her destiny at Grant Development. How fortunate she had managed to learn her lesson. For the past eight years, she'd been a woman who cut to the bottom line, trusting nobody. Men had come and gone in her life while she kept her emotions in check and made sure she was the one in control . . . Until last night, when she learned how tenuous her rein on feeling was.

Getting slowly to her feet, she decided she needed a sounding board. While in L.A., she'd missed her best friend Charley Barrett, but on her return to the City, he'd talked her into renting the place downstairs from his.

She went up and knocked at his door, using a secret code developed during their tree-house days. Outside the rain-streaked hall window, the streetlight was shrouded in fog, far different weather than L.A.'s relentless sunshine.

Charley opened his door, blue eyes smiling into hers. "Mariah!"

Mid-twenties like her, he stood tall and skinny. A mass of freckles decorated his face below a mop of unruly red-brown hair he'd inherited from Tom Barrett, her father's right hand man.

"You nearly missed me." Charley's rain parka was in his long-fingered hand.

"You're going out?"

His grin widened, revealing a chipped tooth Mariah knew came from a tumble off his bike. "Got a poker game with the guys. High stakes."

His boyish enthusiasm was that of someone much younger. As kids, he and she had both talked of going to college, but ADD and dyslexia had limited his options. Though he now worked as a construction laborer for Grant Development, the disparity in their positions had not diminished their friendship.

Charley checked his watch and shifted his weight from one lanky leg to the other. "With this weather, I'm gonna be late."

His insistence on going out to play cards worried her, for his father Tom had once had a gambling problem. Though she considered asking him not to go, she kept silent, trying not to mother him.

As for herself, Mariah didn't know whether to be disappointed or relieved at not being able to visit. Charley knew all about the heartbreak she'd suffered with Rory. When it had happened he'd struck the right balance between sympathy and telling her she'd been an idiot to go for the wrong guy. Now she wondered if he might think her foolish when he heard how powerfully she'd reacted to the man who'd once dumped her.

Rising on tiptoe, she kissed Charley's cheek. "You run on.

I haven't got anything that won't wait for another evening."

He ran down the steps two at a time and slammed out of the foyer.

She stood on the landing for a long time, studying the relentless rain.

Rory rammed his Porsche through the gears on the way to his father's house. Lightning flared, and the gutters ran full. Heading back to the scene of last night's party, he wondered what he'd been thinking to invite Mariah. Curiosity, he'd told her, but after eight years, he'd expected she would be out of his system.

Nonetheless, on the terrace he'd immediately recognized the woman with spun-gold hair, and spiraled back to that long-ago summer, reverted to a raw kid raging with hormones . . . Seeing Mariah again had brought back the heady feeling of possibility, a sensation he thought he'd lost. Now, as he guided his 911 through puddles into the mansion's drive, Rory wondered again what life would be like had he not made the boyish decision to give her up so easily.

Beneath the porch's overhang, he brushed water from his sleeves and rang the doorbell. Years ago, he'd found out his key no longer fit the lock, but refused to admit he'd noticed.

Beyond the sidelight, Anna, in her usual uniform of dark dress and severe coif, opened the door. "Mr. Rory!" she said with a smile.

Once inside, he headed for the family room. In the two-story space, an Alaskan brown bear stood on hind legs, lips drawn back in a snarl. A rhino's head hung above the fireplace, while a full standing lion with a black mane guarded the French doors.

Rory entered, his wet shoes squeaking on the slate floor.

His father emerged from the depths of a wing chair, his Oxford-cloth shirt open at the neck.

"Where's Mom?" Rory asked. He'd always known there was something missing in his parents' marriage, but usually when he was invited to dinner, he found them together.

Davis's expression darkened, but before he could speak a door closed in the rear of the house. Someone came in from the garage, rapid footsteps pattering across the stone.

"Good evening, gentlemen." His mother paused in the hall archway, her flaming hair backlit by the foyer chandelier.

Davis turned on his wife. "Where have you been?"

"Out." She smoothed her pantsuit, frowning at some damp spots.

"Where?"

Rory went to the windows. Dusk was falling early, darkening the sea.

"Where I've been is none of your business." Kiki's tone dripped ice water in a manner Rory had never heard before.

"I'll make it my business," Davis threatened.

"Why would you care where I've been?"

His father suddenly laughed. "I don't care; I just hope

you're preserving appearances."

Rory hated hearing this. Though the gossip rags frequently suggested that infidelity was the way of his family, he liked to think things weren't this bad. The saddest part was he thought his mother still cared for her husband and hungered for some sign he returned it.

He was sure of it when her defiant expression crumpled. Apparently close to tears, she said softly, "My bridge club went to afternoon tea at the St. Francis."

Anna appeared in the doorway to announce dinner.

While the family suffered through the strained atmosphere and a meal of roast quail, wild rice, and baby peas, Rory thought that things hadn't always been like this. As a child, he'd dogged his father's steps with worshipful adoration, looking up to the man who taught him to sail and took him to construction sites. When he grew older, he continued to admire his father, until he realized he was expected to grow up to be exactly like him. That was when, despite his desire to be a builder, he determined to make it his own way.

Last night, Mariah had pointed out his inconsistency in going to work for DCI after vowing never to do so. He wondered if she could understand how times and circumstances changed. A few months ago, his mother had come to him and argued the case for his joining the family business.

"You know I can't tell if Davis's ideas are brilliant or demented. He's getting on in years. You owe it to yourself . . . and to me . . . to look out for the family interests."

He'd been forced to consider it. With Father growing

older, working together might be a last chance for the kind of relationship Rory had dreamed of as a kid. And, though his long-suffering mother laid on the guilt, what cinched it was his boss's suggestion that only at DCI could Rory learn things Takei could not offer in his smaller company.

So, he'd come into the business wary, yet at the same time eager. And for a while, he'd begun to believe his fears were unfounded. His father had been reasonably pleasant to work with, and if he were running around on his wife, Rory had seen no signs of it.

However, in the past month Davis had undergone a change. More driven, shorter-fused, he had treated Kiki with the kind of outright cruelty Rory had witnessed this evening. He also seemed especially focused on beating out John Grant, as if their rivalry were fresh instead of many years old.

When the family meal ended Kiki left them alone. Davis ushered Rory toward the library. Eight years ago, after driving a shamed and shaken Mariah back to the city from the yacht basin, dropping her off in front of John's house without Rory having a chance to speak to her alone, his father had led the way to the same austere room lined with shelves of unread books.

"What were you thinking," Davis had shouted, "taking up with John Grant's daughter? If you got that little slut pregnant, don't even think of running off to Nevada. I'll make sure any marriage is annulled."

Rory figured he could do it with the local judge in his pocket. Nonetheless, he fought back. "I'm not a kid. It's not your place to dictate my personal life!"

"I'm your father, and that's as personal as it gets. If you ever want to run DCI . . . "

"That's your plan."

"Or work anywhere in this industry, you'll stay away from Mariah Grant."

Rory had known there'd be trouble if their fathers found out they were seeing each other, but this was worse than he'd imagined.

"Why wouldn't you want to merge our companies?" He dangled the carrot. "Think of the power."

"I'll do business with anybody but John Grant." Davis's face looked stony. "You put his daughter out of your mind."

If only it were that simple. Mariah was his haven from the world and believing she felt the same kept him fighting.

"I don't need your money or your company. I'll change my major."

"I'm paying the university."

"I'll get a scholarship."

"A word from me, and the Stanford committee, or any other school, would lose your application." Davis paced like a caged coyote. "You think you don't need money? If you're parking cars would John Grant's daughter look at you twice?"

The windmill he jousted overwhelmed Rory. Even if he were willing to throw away his birthright, Mariah would still wear the albatross of Grant Development. Despite her youth, he could see her commitment to running the company would never falter.

With that decision eight years in the past, Rory was again in the library, determined to remain cool whatever happened.

His father went to the sideboard and poured single malt scotch without offering one. Then he moved toward his throne, an imposing high-backed chair of smooth reddish wood mined from South Africa's ancient railroad ties. Years of habit dictated Rory take the opposite seat. Tonight he stood.

"I'm sorry you had to hear that between me and your mother." Davis's tone was familiar, political, as he cupped his drink in both hands, and swished it around.

Rory forced a shrug. "I've heard you fight before." He paused. "Well, not like that."

Davis's expression sharpened. "Are your negative feelings about marriage based on our troubles?"

"Some are." But an image of Elizabeth's chocolate brown eyes, her face etched in lines of sadness when they had decided to end it made him go on, "Have you forgotten I'm divorced?"

Davis played deaf. "You know what an advantage marrying your mother was. The Mainwearing position helped assure DCI's place in this city."

Several times since Rory's divorce, his father had pointed out a woman, discussing her potential advantages as though contemplating a corporate merger.

"Don't even think of going there," he cautioned.

"I'm afraid we have to." Davis gave a tight smile. "Son, I'm talking about Sylvia Chatsworth. I know you've been seeing her."

Rory could not deny that for the past few months, Sylvia's black gaze had intrigued, but his father's matchmaking made every instinct in him seize up. "I don't love her."

"You don't marry for love but for the right reasons," Davis plowed on.

"Sylvia and I have had good times, but I won't make her my wife." He grabbed the decanter, fumbled with the stopper, and poured a splash of single malt. "Marrying Elizabeth on the rebound was a disaster." In the years between, he'd strengthened his walls, been unable to give Elizabeth what she deserved.

And Mariah . . . Rory drank to keep the words inside.

Seven years ago, he'd told her he loved her. That boy had fallen for her with his whole heart, bought the white house and the picket fence myth, mixed up somehow with believing he and Mariah could build a corporate empire together. Now, his failed marriage, and the poor state of his parents' union, had made him a far different man.

He wasn't sure what love meant anymore.

The political fundraiser was in full swing when Rory escorted Sylvia Chatsworth to the top of the Marriott. Beyond fan-shaped glass walls, the towers of the Bay Bridge marched toward Oakland. Tall buildings cast sunset shadows on the San Francisco streets where conventioneers and taxis mingled to their mutual advantage.

Rory already regretted keeping the date with Sylvia, arranged before he'd seen Mariah again, and before his father had tried shoving him toward the Senator's daughter. He checked Sylvia's vermilion leather coat and moved into the main room, savoring the fact that his parents were out of town for the weekend.

"There's the heir to Grant Development again," Sylvia said in an ugly voice, but his radar had already detected Mariah from across the crowded room.

He wished even more that he'd come solo.

She stood near the bar, a petite woman who could have looked fragile. Yet, the set of her proud head gave away her strength, that of a finely wrought saber. Rising young District Attorney Lyle Thomas, a burly blond who might have descended from the Vikings, rested a predatory paw on her arm. The man stood big enough to put Rory in his place if he gave in to a sudden irrational impulse to knock that hand off Mariah.

Even through his suit coat, Sylvia's lacquered nails dug into his forearm. Rory felt certain that in her low-cut leather sheath she had every man in the room aware of her wide-set, generous breasts. Black hair made a smooth fall over her bare shoulders. Yet he thought she came up wanting beside Mariah's trim figure in a tasteful black velvet tunic, her golden hair caught up at the nape of her slender neck.

After drinks and a buffet supper, an enthusiastic crowd greeted Sylvia's father, the featured speaker of the evening.

"Good evening, ladies and gentlemen." With a sharp

sweep of the room, Senator Lawrence Chatsworth managed to look at each person. "I recognize all my many friends here this evening, and I can't begin to tell you how much your support means."

Takei Takayashi led a round of applause.

While Chatsworth warmed to the topic of national security, Sylvia slid a hand onto Rory's thigh and whispered, "Bored yet?"

"Of course, but we ought to stay awhile."

The fact was that he couldn't have been dragged out of here. Repositioning his chair, he checked how Lyle staked his claim on Mariah and studied the pale shadow at the hollow of her throat. When he'd thought of seeing her again, he'd imagined the same girl, just a few years older.

But she was not the same; Mariah was more vivid than he recalled, more passionate . . . and suspicious, the way she'd asked if he invited her to the DCI party. Yet, how could he blame her? In her version of events, eight years ago he'd married another woman completely without warning. That Mariah had refused to talk to him for months before he exchanged vows with Elizabeth was no excuse in her view. Hell, they said peoples' memories were so poor that even eyewitness accounts were unreliable. How could either of them be expected to have an accurate, much less dispassionate version of events? Especially after time had faded their colors and muted their sounds.

While Rory studied Mariah, their glances suddenly met and held. Her faced remained in placid lines, yet her eyes revealed something deeper . . . a stark baring of what also ate at him, and had grown sharper since the last time he saw her. He nearly got up and went to her, but managed to stay in his seat when she turned away and smiled at something Lyle said.

Rory's reserve lasted until he applauded a speech he hadn't heard, and in the hubbub of chatter and pushing back of chairs, Mariah rose and walked alone to the wall of windows.

"I have some business with Miss Grant," he muttered to Sylvia and got up. A poor excuse, but it would have to do. The remembered curve of Mariah's cheek seemed a magnet for his palm.

When he drew closer to her the rest of the room receded; the spotlights dimmed to little stars. Outside, downtown had donned its night sparkle; one of the Bay Bridge towers glimmered, and an approaching fogbank blotted out the others.

Mariah appeared to study the skyline.

Rory cleared his throat.

She turned and said, "What are you doing over here? Aren't you squiring old 'Larry's' daughter to keep him doing favors for your father?"

At her uncanny aim, he flinched. "I'm not involved in any so-called favors."

She shook her head so vehemently that her hair brushed her velvet-clad shoulders. "You thought you were clever at the party, talking about the past to soften me up, so I'd spill company secrets."

There, he saw it again in her eyes, a flash of intensity like a stab of sunlight reflecting off water. Despite people start-ing to look their way, he found himself taking her arm. The memory of her pained expression on the terrace when he had asked "what if", made him confess, "I talked about our past because when I saw you again I could think of little else."

Mariah jerked away. "Save your sweet talk for Sylvia."

"It's not talk. It's the truth." Emotion rising, he took a chance that their shared history still had the power to cause her pain. "Tell me you don't feel the same . . . without lying through your teeth."

Spots of color rose in her cheeks. "It doesn't matter how I feel. It never has." She took a half step toward him, and he imagined he could feel the force of her anger. "Tell me you haven't been dancing to your father's tune all your life . . . without lying through your teeth."

Walk away, he thought, as they both did eight years ago. The hell of it was he didn't want to.

Rory moved closer, and Mariah retreated until the window wall was cold against her back. "What are you doing?" she asked.

"Proving I don't always do what my father would like." His voice sounded husky. "You should have figured that out when I invited you to the party."

"There are plenty of reasons I could have been invited. Only one is sentimental."

"I invited you because I wondered how it would feel to share the same room with you again. Oh, I admit I believed I wouldn't remember the way the sunset brightened your hair."

She cut in. "I remember a lot of things. I remember you married Elizabeth."

"Are you accusing me of leaving you?" He sounded incredulous. "Your roommate at UCLA told me a dozen times you wouldn't talk to me after Father . . ."

"Called me a slut and a whore?" Her raised voice was drawing an audience. "How fitting we each have own version of reality. The plain fact is, no matter what we once wanted, our fathers destroyed it before we were born."

Rory stepped back as though he'd been slapped.

Letting the glass support her, she watched his rawboned figure march toward the table where Sylvia Chatsworth waited. How dare he be angry? She was the one who should be upset at him for bringing up the past when he was involved with another woman.

After months of fall semester at UCLA with an ache in her chest that wouldn't go away, Mariah had told her roommate she'd take Rory's next call. A week passed without him trying again. She decided to phone him, but he'd told her he planned to live off campus with fraternity brothers, and his name wasn't in the listings. A dozen times, she picked up the receiver to dial Davis Campbell's house. A servant would answer; she'd pretend to be someone else.

Another week went by. A look at her school calendar said the Thanksgiving holiday was next Thursday. She'd go home, find Rory. Tell him she loved him, that they could make it without their families.

The Sunday before Thanksgiving, the *San Francisco Chronicle* carried Rory's wedding announcement. Mariah found it when she got home to Stonestown on Wednesday night, opening the kitchen trash to drop in a soft drink can. Wrapped around some vegetable peelings was a photo of Rory with a woman she recognized as his childhood friend Elizabeth, their pictured faces darkened by tomato juice. While her father watched TV in the living room, she slid down the side of the counter to land in a heap on the kitchen floor. Hugging her knees with her arms, she hoped the sounds of a late night talk show muffled her sobs.

Rory had never been worthy of her trust.

On the drive to her fashionable North Beach townhouse, Sylvia was quiet. Too quiet, Rory suspected, but he enjoyed the silence. As they approached her building, she pulled a remote from her evening bag and opened the street level garage.

Inside her place, he watched her go into her kitchen and pour two glasses of Caymus Reserve Cabernet. Rory stood near the door, determined not to stretch out on her buttery leather couch this evening.

Sylvia brought him wine and ran the daggers of her nails through her hair, a gesture he'd previously found provocative. Tonight, he thought it looked practiced.

"Now, tell me about you and Mariah Grant," she demanded in a no-nonsense tone.

"I told you I had business with her."

"Monkey business." Sylvia drank without apparent appreciation for the wine. "I know you almost married her once."

He set his glass on the counter. His long-ago interlude with Mariah had been hushed up, the only time John Grant and Davis Campbell had agreed on anything.

"Where did you hear that?"

"You remember that dinner Daddy threw last month? Where I was talking with your mom?"

"I saw the two of you together and wondered what was afoot."

"I made the mistake of telling her I was thinking of snagging you." Sylvia's head was high. "She said I'd better hurry because Mariah Grant was back in town."

He sighed. After his divorce he had thought Sylvia perfect for him, a wild spirit who didn't want to light. That had been true awhile, but now he realized his mother was right. He took a single regretful sip of Caymus, trying to think of the best way to break this off.

"I saw the way you looked at Mariah," Sylvia accused, "like she was some goddess."

Her expression was of genuine hurt, but it was nothing like the mix of promise and pain in Mariah's eyes.

"Sylvia, I'm sorry," he said. "You and I both know this isn't working."

Her chest heaved, the soft-looking leather gapped to

expose the rounded tops of her breasts. That the sight no longer moved him reinforced his need to get out of here.

He started toward the door, having to pass her on the way. She blocked his path, the bright sheen of her eyes beginning to burn at him. He sidestepped her and continued his retreat.

"Get out!" Sylvia shoved at his back. "Everybody in this town knows you're best at exit scenes."

Rory went down the stairs to the parking garage, and her door slammed. Through the panel, he heard a crash and the sound of glass breaking.

Maybe there could have been a better way to extricate himself, but it was done. His father would have to give up his dreams of matchmaking.

Out on the street, cars cruised past, the North Beach weekend nightlife heating up. He could go to a bar or club, but the thought of the meat market scene disgusted him this evening. Instead, he drove his Porsche toward the Golden Gate and across the brightly lit span. Then on darker winding roads, he let speed, precision, and focus free his mind.

An hour later, he was sitting at the brink of a cliff at Point Reyes. The headlights illuminated a rising mist, beckoning him into the infinite night. It reminded him of when he was a kid, and his father pointed a flashlight at the heavens, saying beams of light traveled forever in the void of space.

All those foolish little boys with flashlights, victims of a cosmic conspiracy that had them thinking they were signaling someone . . . rather than alone in the universe.

Just over a week since he'd seen Mariah at April's end, and, despite her cool reception, he'd felt the click of connection, a sense of being no longer alone. Beside the sea cliff, Rory closed his eyes and admitted time had not healed the raw wound of their past breakup.

Nor would more time bring relief.

CHAPTER 3

$\mathcal{M}$ariah drank bitter office coffee and stared at the morning sun's reflection in the mirrored building across Market Street. On her desk lay a sheet of paper headed "Notes for Monday Meeting." The rest of the page was blank.

Seeing Rory at the Marriott had shaken her more than she cared to admit. Lyle Thomas, with his enthusiastic penchant for gossip, had pointed out that Rory and Sylvia were "a match made in heaven, or at least somewhere over their heads." Considering the amount of money involved in some of the deals made in the city, Mariah could understand how men might use their adult children as pawns.

So was Rory involved in his father's machinations or was

he ignorant of "favors" as he claimed? Could a man fake the emotion she'd seen in him on his father's terrace and again last night? His declaration that he'd been trapped in remembrance was the most disturbing, for she, too, had thought of little else since they'd been reunited. At the most inopportune moments flashes of memory kept surfacing; fantasies of the two of them in a secret hideaway, a country inn where no one knew or cared that Grant was with Campbell.

Mariah trashed her empty foam cup, put on her charcoal wool suit jacket, and left her office. Down the hall, she entered the nerve center of the company, with teak paneling and table, the latest teleconferencing equipment, and big screen projection TV.

The first arrival, Arnold Benton, had already taken a seat in a leather swivel chair. The colorless man in his early thirties gave her a disapproving glare that suggested she take the next shuttle back to L.A. Then he bent deliberately to study a page full of notes, revealing the bald spot in his thinning pale brown hair.

"Morning," Mariah said to the top of his head. She hoped that in time working for her father's company would become less awkward.

"Hey, you," Grant's second-in-command Tom Barrett greeted her from the doorway. The big shaggy man with a recalcitrant shirttail and unruly reddish hair no barber could tame reminded Mariah of a well-loved teddy bear. He winked, his blue eyes as bright as his son Charley's. "I'd have taken a bet you'd beat me here."

Arnold made a small sound that might have been a snort of disgust.

In the next few minutes the conference table filled with Grant Development's heads of engineering, law, public relations, human resources, and construction. Though over a hundred employees worked on the lower floors, it was up to the management team to coordinate, and they did so each Monday morning.

Mariah's father entered last, a weekend of rest having softened the lines around his eyes. Once he sat at the head of the table, the meeting began.

As Grant's financial officer, Arnold Benton droned at length about the status of two hundred million in construction loans with First California Bank. The gist was that he had everything under such wonderful control that it bored him. Mariah had seen the technique in L.A., the young executive in need of the further challenge of promotion.

When it was her turn, she thought of her blank sheet of notes and reported, "The Bayview Townhomes project is on budget and schedule." She hoped to get by with that, but Arnold inquired as to some numbers that necessitated a trip to her office for them.

On her return to the conference room, she was shocked to hear him saying, " . . . Mariah and Campbell at the Marriott . . ."

As he apparently saw Tom's eyes shift to her in the doorway, Arnold broke off.

Her face warmed as every eye turned to her.

John's usually equable expression had been replaced by an edgy look. Throughout the rest of the meeting, she chafed at the fact that the subtext of every encounter here was that she was her father's daughter.

Before John adjourned the gathering, he turned to Mariah. "Could I see you privately?" His voice was soft, but she felt sure everyone heard.

It seemed to take a long time for everyone to file out. Tom threw her a sympathetic look while Arnold appeared barely able to contain his glee. As soon as the door closed, her father rose, slid a hip onto the table, and looked down at her. "What's this about you and Rory Campbell?"

"What about him?" The heat was back in her cheeks.

"You heard Arnold."

"I did. Is this the seventh grade?" She hated that the Campbells still had the power to drive a wedge between her and her father.

"It's a far cry from school days." He looked chagrined. "I so hoped you and Arnold would get along. He's our most promising young executive."

"Considering that most of them are over fifty, he's your only young manager. Except for me."

"You are young yet," John said. "This is the big league, Mariah, and Rory works for the competition."

"I'm aware of where he works." Her voice matched the tautness of his. Why was her usually reasonable father unreasonable over the Campbells? "Dad, you don't act this way about Golden or any of the other competitors. Takei

Takayashi has beat you up on bids over the years, and you two play golf at least once a month."

"Campbell is different," John insisted. "I saw the look on your face when you spoke of running into Rory at the party." A muscle worked in the side of his cheek. "Are you seeing him again?"

Bitter laughter burst from her. "One thing I can assure you. I am not seeing Rory Campbell."

Her father stared at her, the hard look in his gray eyes foreign. She met his gaze without flinching, for she'd told the truth. Finally, he softened. "All right, daughter."

Leaving the conference room, she noted a baleful glare from Arnold, who was in the hall.

When she got to her office, the phone was ringing. She stepped across the green carpet of the executive floor and answered, "Mariah Grant."

"Bad time?" Rory asked without identifying himself. Back in the old days, they'd called and just started in talking.

She nearly dropped the receiver. "What are you thinking to call me here?"

"Be kind." He spoke softly, and she wondered if he was at DCI. "Here I sit, quaking in my boots because I mustered the nerve to dial your number."

She couldn't forget watching him escort another woman home. "Did you and Sylvia have a nice weekend?"

"Jealous?" He sounded hopeful.

"Don't flatter yourself," she blustered, though she re-called too well her flush of outrage at the way the Senator's daughter had advertised her claim on Rory with ostentatious little touches.

"Forget Sylvia." His tone was urgent. "Have lunch with me."

A pulse began to pound, low inside her. Despite assuring her father she wasn't seeing Rory, she stretched the phone cord and closed her office door. Leaning against it, she imagined the two of them in a secluded restaurant booth.

A light on her telephone blinked. The call came from her father's office.

"Come on, Mariah," Rory said.

"Lyle Thomas told me all about you and Sylvia," she returned. "He's been catching me up on who's who in the city."

"Nobody dishes the dirt better than the D.A.'s own."

"It wasn't dirt. He's promised to show me around, introduce me to people."

"You're going out with that guy?"

She wasn't, but if he wanted to two-time her with Sylvia, let him think she had other things going. "I'll see whomever I please."

"How about seeing me?"

She checked her office clock. "I have to be over at Grant Plaza in a little while," she evaded.

From her window, she could see the rising steel and concrete of the forty-story construction, already dominating the neighborhood north of the Moscone Convention Center. When it was complete, Grant Development would occupy the fortieth story penthouse.

"The elevations are going to be beautiful." Rory spoke

with the appreciation of a fellow builder, but where did he get his information?

"What do you know about Grant Plaza?"

"For Christ's sake, there was a big article in the *Chronicle* six months ago. Didn't your father send you a copy?"

She was silent, noting that Dad had apparently given up on calling her.

"I guess I can't blame you for being wary of me, but I told you before, I'm not involved in corporate spying." He sounded sincere.

She envisioned the little comma of shining hair that drooped over his forehead. The one that gave the polished man an air of innocence.

"Have lunch with me," he asked again, quietly. "We'll go someplace where lots of people will see us together." He stated it like a vow, the way he'd once promised forever. Something in his voice made her want to believe.

She was tempted, but . . . "I've already been chewed out this morning for talking to you at the Marriott."

"So, now it's you who's afraid of Daddy?"

The challenge she'd thrown him about dancing to his father's tune sounded different on the receiving end. Maybe it wasn't as easy as throwing convention aside, especially as she'd given her word she wasn't seeing Davis Campbell's son.

"This is insanity," she told Rory. "I've got to go."

Yet, when she put the phone back into its cradle, she kept her hand on it for a long time.

After a light lunch at her desk, Mariah set out for Grant Plaza. Though she walked briskly, when she turned the last corner and caught sight of the rising spire she stopped on the sidewalk. A man behind her nearly stepped on her heels and muttered something about her not using her brake lights.

Still, she stood gazing up at the partially completed edifice backlit by a crystal sky. The girders and floors were complete, the main electrical conduits in place, and the glass going in. Once the wind no longer swept its uninhibited way through the building, the interiors could be started.

When someone else bumped into her, she shook free of her reverie and hurried on to the site. There she grabbed a hardhat from the main trailer and headed out to find the supervisor.

A group of workers stared at her. A big man with a black beard, his hammer hanging from his belt, murmured, "Mariah Grant." Her name passed from man to man.

Someone nudged her.

She jumped and turned to find Charley Barrett grinning down at her. "You're a celebrity."

"Hardly." Mariah laughed. "You win the pot last night?"

"Hardly."

"I take it you two know each other." Cassie Holden, one of the city's few female supervisors, fixed them with direct eyes in a sun-beaten face. The close-cropped gray curls peeking from beneath her hardhat said she'd paid her dues.

Charley turned to his boss. "Mariah and I grew up together. Partners in war . . ."

"He throws a mean clump of green onions," Mariah agreed. "Sent more than one soldier on the opposite side in tears to tell his mother."

"Partners in crime, too." Charley chuckled. "Remember when we knocked out the big window at the dry cleaners with a bottle rocket? I never saw so much broken glass." She'd escaped with him to Stern Grove, a city preserve near John's house, and hidden out in the redwoods until after dark.

"Shhh." She put a finger to her lips in mock embarrassment.

Cassie smiled as the three of them waited for the construction hoist. With a creak and groan, it arrived.

Inside the cage, a glazier with bunched muscles watched over several window panels covered in protective paper. He dipped his head to Cassie. "Special order of smaller panes for the top floor corners. The crane operator's busy."

"Go ahead, Andrew," Cassie agreed.

Charley stuck out a wiry arm and stopped the metal gate. "You can drop me at twenty-seven."

Mariah stepped forward, but he put out a hand. "Weight limit." Flashing a smile through the wire mesh, he pushed the button to ascend. "My place tonight. Pizza."

"Okay." She'd tell him the latest episode in the saga of her and Rory. Rather than thinking her foolish as she had feared, Charley had listened to the stories of the DCI party and the Marriott with sympathy.

While the hoist rose smoothly up the outside of the building, Mariah craned her neck to follow it. Nothing she imagined could begin to touch the majesty of building a skyscraper.

Above, the car started to slow near the twenty-seventh floor when a sudden sharp crack sounded like a rifle shot. In the same instant, the purring whine came to a halt.

"What's that?" Mariah squinted up into the midday sun.

The elevator began its descent slowly, but within a second, she realized it was accelerating. A high-pitched whine began, and the frame started an ominous rattle.

"Run!" Cassie ordered.

Mariah tore her gaze from the falling cage and tried to move, but the air seemed to turn to a thick liquid that she swam through. Through the din, she detected the shrill note of screaming. A nearby aluminum shed, set up as a break room, offered the only shelter, but the door was on the opposite side. Out of time, she dove for the space beneath where the shed was propped on cinder blocks.

The loaded hoist smashed into the ground level steel plate. Despite the wire mesh enclosure, shrapnel flew. Although Mariah rolled herself into the small space under the shed, something struck over her left eye.

For what felt like a long time, a cacophonous rain of chunks and splinters hit the ground around her. Her heart raced, so hard she felt sick.

An unnatural silence fell. She listened for the workers' shouts and imagined everyone staring open-mouthed at the wreckage. In disbelief, she raised her hand and traced a sticky warm wetness on her face. Though the vision in her left eye was blurred, she made out a litter of twisted metal and glass at the base of the building.

Blood spattered the steel frame ten feet in the air.

Rory sat at his drafting table, reviewing a computer plot of an elevation. Normally, he loved envisioning a building he'd conceived, but this afternoon he'd lost focus. As he'd told Mariah, it had taken all his nerve to phone her. Like a fool, he'd thought if he were willing to ignore his father's wishes, she'd do the same.

His office door opened. "Did you hear?" His secretary babbled.

"Slow down and tell me." He braced for war news or a report of a terror attack.

Her round face pink, she twisted her hands in her floral print skirt. "The hoist at Grant Plaza fell . . . killed some people."

"Good Lord." Mariah had said . . .

Leaving his suit coat behind the door, Rory ran through reception and stuck his hand into a six-inch gap to reopen a crowded elevator. The passengers stared owl-eyed. When the car stopped in the lobby, he shoved out through the revolving doors and onto the street.

He ran, heedless that his dress shoes weren't Nikes. Sweat broke out, and his shirt clung to his back. He ducked around a vending cart selling hotdogs, passed a line of elementary school children on a field trip, and dodged businessmen carrying briefcases. When he turned a corner and saw Grant

Plaza on the skyline, he stared at his goal, only to be jerked back to reality by a bicycle courier's angry shout.

After six blocks, he rushed up to the site and found yellow police tape around it. Without slowing, he lifted the plastic strip and went under. Somebody yelled, but no one stopped his getting to the main construction trailer.

Rory yanked open the door and found a group of hard-hatted men in a heated discussion. One with a black beard was saying, "Zaragoza went up to weld just before, but nobody's seen him."

"I saw him on the ground after," said a blond youth. "Must have come down the stairs."

The group dynamic perceived an outsider, and they fell silent. A dozen pairs of eyes focused on Rory's disheveled state.

"Help you, sir?" asked the fellow sitting at a battered desk.

His chest heaved. "I'm a . . . friend of Mariah Grant. Supposed to meet her here."

The man shook his head.

Something clutched in Rory, and he reached to support himself on the doorframe. "She's not . . ."

"No," the bearded man said, "but she was pretty close when the elevator came down. Got some glass . . . " He gestured toward his eyes.

"They said somebody died," Rory got out.

"A laborer and one of the glaziers."

"That's rough," he said, letting a moment of silence elapse. "Got any idea where Mariah went?"

The man behind the desk looked sympathetic as he shook

his head.

Outside the trailer, shards of glass, plywood, and metal spread over a wide area. Though the bodies had apparently been removed, the police lines were drawn tight. Several TV vans with satellite antennas lined the curb; one marked with the logo of the sensationalist "On the Spot."

Seeing the hallmarks of disaster, Rory wondered how many times he had ridden a hoist and felt triumph over the elements. Today, some poor souls like him had risen into the afternoon sky; only their number had been up.

A breeze off the Bay dried his sweat, making him shiver. Everything seemed at a distance, from the growl of city buses to their diesel fumes. The sunlight looked garish; a pea soup fog would be a more fitting shroud for the workers who'd lost their lives.

As Rory turned his back on the bloody ground, his sense of relief over Mariah began to evaporate. The man had implied she'd been cut. Was she at one of the hospitals getting stitched up? What if she'd been disfigured, or lost an eye?

He speeded his steps away from the site, determined to find her.

In the hours since the hoist had fallen, time had lost its meaning for Mariah. It was near midnight when she opened the front door of her apartment house. Bone weary, muscles aching from her frantic dive under the shed, all she wanted was the solace of oblivion.

Though she'd managed a shower at the company work-out facility and changed into tights and a sweatshirt, she still felt dirty. Over her left eye, a throbbing cut felt stiff beneath gauze and punctures on her forearms sported Band-aids.

Yet, not all her wounds were physical. She knew she must be pale as a ghost, and her heart ached for her father. His face had borne a grayish pallor as he chaired a nightmar-ish after-hours management session. Saying he'd rather be alone, he had refused her offer to come home to Stonestown with him.

Now she wished she'd insisted, for Charley wasn't up-stairs watching the news or reading before going to bed. Only last night, she'd heard him stirring around, home from an-other of his card games. He usually told her he won, grinning and waving a sheaf of bills that might have come from his paycheck — years ago his father had perpetuated that fiction before he joined Gambler's Anonymous — but today Charley had told her he'd lost.

She shuddered and tried not to imagine his and glazier Andrew Green's final moments. Routine though the hoist might have been for workers who were there every day, Char-ley had told her he never tired of riding to the heights. Rising smoothly up the tower, he must have been as curious as she at the snap of the parting cable . . .

Only it marked the end of his and Andrew's world.

How difficult it was to believe he'd never flash his trade-mark grin again, and even more impossible to imagine Tom

Barrett and his wife Wendy already immersed the nightmare of making arrangements. Charley couldn't be gone. He must be asleep, the way she wanted to be.

Her breath caught.

Her friend wasn't sleeping, but lying on a slab at the mortuary. The electric essence that was Charley had departed; she'd known when it she saw his crystal blue eyes gone opaque.

Keys in hand, Mariah approached her apartment, making a note to call the manager about the burned out bulb over her entry. Though preoccupied as she reached to unlock her door, she saw a darker shadow in the hall and realized it was a man.

Her heart leaped.

"Didn't mean to scare you." Rory pushed off the wall.

She bit back the scream rising in her throat. While thankful it wasn't a criminal lurking in her hall, she wondered if she was up to dealing with Rory this evening.

"I heard about the accident." His voice bore a hoarse quality, as though he'd been shouting. "Are you all right?"

She struggled with her lock. "I'm fine."

"Like hell you are." He placed his hand over her shaking fingers, inserted her key, and swung the door wide. She brushed the wall to find the switch and flooded the room with light.

Rory looked as haggard as she felt, in wrinkled jeans and a black DCI golf shirt that proclaimed his allegiance. Deep shadows lay beneath his eyes, bruise-like. "May I come in?"

She should send him away, for nothing either of them

could say or do would change their situation.

"Please," he said softly, without pleading.

With her usual frame of reference upside down, she gestured him inside.

He shut the door behind them. "Where's your liquor?"

She waved toward a kitchen cabinet and made her way to the living room. Soft cushions on her couch took her into a welcome embrace.

Rory poured two glasses of amber liquid and brought one to her. Taking it, she swallowed raw whiskey around the hard place in the back of her throat.

He frowned and gently touched the bandage above her eye. "That was close."

"Eleven stitches." The quaking in her grew worse when she recalled how she and Cassie had nearly been on the hoist.

Rory sat beside her. "Did you know the victims?"

"Not Andrew Green." She drank again, coughed. "But Charley Barrett . . ."

"The fellow who went sailing with us."

She nodded. In June of that long-ago summer, the three of them had cruised beyond the Golden Gate to toast the limitless lives ahead of them. "That's him . . . was him." She swallowed. "My best friend in the whole world."

"Charley was a good man."

"Tom's a good man, too, who shouldn't have to go through this." If there were anybody to blame, it might make it easier. She took another burning drink, and a seed that had been planted when the hoist crashed germinated. "I'll bet your father's glad."

Rory surged to his feet. "Look here . . . I can't control what he thinks."

"*We* can't do anything about our fathers." Her glass trembled. "Don't we settle that every time we see one another?"

He moved swiftly, taking Mariah's drink and setting it aside. He pulled her to her feet and gripped her shoulders. "To hell with our fathers. When I heard about the accident, I ran through the streets to Grant Plaza like a wild man. I had to know you weren't hurt or . . . I crashed the police barricade, went into the trailer . . ." His voice broke. "I only knew people had died."

His anguish penetrated her haze. He gathered her to him, her face against the side of his neck, the smell of his skin familiar, yet new. They were both alive and Charley . . .

Rory's mouth came down, crushing hers so she felt his teeth behind his lips. The desperation that had been in his voice a moment now before flavored his embrace.

For a wild instant, response flickered in her, a sense of "what if." Should she twine her arms around his neck and give in to this treacherous tide of feeling, it would be all or nothing, the way it had been with them from the start.

Then his intensity became too much for her, after all she'd been through this day. All she could imagine was to lie down in the dark and find her way to a sleep where she wouldn't dream of blood and broken glass.

She pushed at his shoulders.

His lips softened on hers, then were withdrawn. "What

am I doing? You need rest."

Even so, he drew her back against his chest. Beneath her ear, she heard the pounding of his heart, the way it must have been when he raced through the city streets. But could she trust he was his own man and not his father's?

"You need to go." Her tears were coming, and if she cried in his arms, she'd be lost.

Rory smoothed her hair and set her away from him. Torn by the temptation to call him back, she watched him leave his untouched drink on the table and let himself out.

She curled into a ball of hurt. Salt stung her eyes and cheeks . . . how cruel that she and Davis Campbell's son had been placed by accident of birth on their fathers' chessboard.

Yet, tonight Rory had said, "To hell with our fathers."

CHAPTER 4

Charley Barrett's closed casket sat against a marble wall surrounded by banked floral arrangements. Mariah vaguely remembered the mortuary, a venerable city tradition, as the place family and friends had paid their respects upon her mother's death. Her father did not speak of Catharine, but looked around the viewing room with its green damask drapes as if it were familiar.

Around Charley's casket stood a clutch of men wearing dark suits and women in black. Some approached to study the bronze box while others did not, but everyone conversed in hushed tones. Beneath a translucent alabaster fixture, Tom Barrett stood slumped in a wrinkled pinstripe, his usually clear blue eyes red-rimmed. Though clean-shaven, a rash of bumps said he'd made a mess of it.

Mariah's father moved toward the taller man, and they clasped hands. "God, Tom. Your boy . . ."

"John. Of all the rotten luck . . ." Tom trailed off, taking his old friend into a bear hug while the rest of the mourners pretended not to notice two men sobbing out loud. When they broke apart, both Tom and John wiped unabashedly at tears.

Tom hugged Mariah in turn, lifting her cleanly from the floor. Her ribs compressed, and her breath came out in a rush before he set her down.

With a thick finger, he touched the framed photo atop the casket. The camera had caught Charley laughing, his arm around the neck of his Golden Retriever, Luke. Sunlight glinted on the dog's smooth coat and on the young man's bright hair.

"I'm sorry it had to be Charley," Mariah said. It must have occurred to Tom that if she and Cassie had taken the hoist first, his son would be alive. "Such an unfair twist of fate."

"Fate?" With a glance around, Tom bent to her. "That may not have been an accident." His words were soft, yet struck with force.

"Who'd want to hurt Charley? Or one of our glaziers?"

"It was almost you on that elevator."

Mariah's stomach churned.

"Promise you won't gamble with your safety," Tom insisted.

Surely, he didn't think there had been foul play. He must be grasping at straws, a father's attempt to avoid admitting the senseless nature of the accident. The single detective assigned to the case viewed the matter as an equipment failure, as did she.

Turning away from Tom, she saw her own father's concerned face and realized he'd overheard. "I promise I'll be careful," she said to mollify both him and Tom.

Wendy Barrett, a bird-like woman who moved in fits and starts, came and hugged Mariah. She returned the embrace, shocked by the older woman's pallor. Usually fit and healthy from daily tennis, Wendy seemed to have shrunk by inches.

It made Mariah ache inside. Charley's mother had watched out for him and her when they were preschoolers. As they grew older, she'd chaperoned after school hours, driving them to club meetings and ball games. One of the fondest memories was of a crisp fall day when Wendy called her and Charley to the back porch with a plate of homemade caramel apples.

"I'm so sorry that you were there . . . that you had to see . . ." Wendy glanced toward the closed casket.

Mariah was trying to forget the bloody flesh, the protruding bones, telling herself it had nothing to do with Charley.

Wendy pulled a wad of tissues from her jacket pocket and offered one. Mariah took it and dabbed at her eyes.

In the midst of blowing her shiny nose, Wendy suddenly straightened. "Oh, no."

Mariah followed her gaze to the viewing room door.

Beneath a recessed spotlight, Davis Campbell and his wife made their entrance. The owner of DCI bore an emotionless expression on his hawklike features, his mourning suit somehow blacker than every other man's. Though Kiki's dress matched her husband's somber suit, her red hair made a beacon.

Wendy flushed and fiddled with her crying rag. "Why did they have to come?"

Mariah touched her arm. "It's what people do."

Wendy moved to her husband's side, and the battle lines were drawn. Tom Barrett stared at Davis with what looked like hate, but there was something else. It almost looked as if the big man were afraid. Mariah's father joined the Barretts, standing shoulder to shoulder with his friends to accept Davis's smooth political greeting.

Mariah stayed back, watching the ritual exchange until some sixth sense made her look again toward the door.

In a dark suit like his father's, with an appropriately muted tie, Rory was every inch the scion of DCI. Though his eyes passed over Mariah without pause, she noticed a subtle change in him, a delicate sharpening of every feature. Seized with the desire to adjust the scarf on her coatdress or tame the errant strands of her hair, she forced herself to remain motionless. He might have come to her apartment under cover of night, but here they were on display. Speaking publicly in any but the most cursory manner would wound the Barretts as well as her father.

Nonetheless, his sweep of the room complete, Rory's gaze fixed on her.

It brought back the night of the accident. How many

times since had she relived his kiss? She'd told Wendy the Campbells were here out of social obligation, but something in the set of Rory's head said he'd come for her.

Sure enough, he started toward her as though he didn't care what anyone thought. Though her breath caught in her throat, she stood her ground, waiting.

Before he could reach her, a blinding glare washed in from the hall. A video unit and TV lights preceded a hatchet-faced man with caramel skin who announced into his wireless microphone, "This is Julio Castillo, reporting for 'On The Spot.'" The reporter approached Tom Barrett. "How much will you sue Grant Development for?"

Tom's face went red.

"Are you planning to go soft on the company because you work for them?"

Wendy shoved the reporter's shoulder. "We're not talking to you!"

Mariah moved, but her father beat her to it, pulling the bereaved mother behind him.

Recognition dawned on Castillo's taut features. "It seems we have the privilege of interviewing John Grant."

"No comment." John's face was closed.

"Now, sir," Castillo went on. "This is your opportunity to defend yourself and your company's safety record."

John set his jaw and stared right through the man with the microphone.

Castillo continued. "It's my understanding that the glazier, Andrew Green, leaves a wife and twin baby girls . . . Is it true Grant was negligent?"

Mariah reached her father, seized his shaking arm, and turned on the reporter. "How dare you invade a time of grief with your accusations?"

Tom grabbed Castillo and gave him a shove. "Get out."

Off balance, the reporter stumbled over the wire frame of a floral arrangement. With a hand out to catch himself, he knocked Charley's picture off the casket. Glass shattered on the marble floor.

Rory moved, acutely aware the video was still recording. John Grant's pale face and an angry-looking Mariah stood out in the crowd as he cut through to the cameraman. "Turn it off."

The wiry man ignored him.

"I said . . ." Rory stabbed a finger at his chest. "To turn it . . ." Another impact of index finger on breastbone. "Off."

The red light went out, the camera lowered.

Rory saw his father staring at him, but they'd come to pay their respects, and respect it would be.

He looked down at Castillo on the floor, bent, and grabbed him by the lapels. "Get out of here with your talk of lawsuits or you'll be sued for lies and slander."

Castillo flinched, and the watchers seemed to hold their collective breath.

Rory released his hold. When the reporter regained the

confidence to start swearing at him, the full impact of what he'd done struck. His next foray into the limelight with "On the Spot" would not be pretty.

Stepping back, he gave the fallen man space to get up. As though a spell had broken, a melee of speculation broke out. Grumbling to save face, the crew gathered their equipment and left.

Rory put out a hand and rested against the wall to catch his breath. From the other side of the room he felt his father's dark gaze on him. He reached to adjust his loosened tie, and someone tapped him on the shoulder.

Hoping it might be Mariah, he turned to find John Grant with his hand extended. "Nice work, son." The older man's gray eyes were sincere in his drained face.

This taste of approval from an unexpected quarter almost convinced Rory the consequences of his action might be worth it.

He pushed himself upright. "Thank you, sir."

Mariah watched in disbelief as her father and Rory shook hands. She would never have expected DCI's heir apparent to defend Tom and John, and, by implication, Grant Development. From the astonished look on his face, she didn't think he quite believed it either.

While John moved to help calm Tom and Wendy, she and Rory faced each other in the midst of the crowd.

He jerked his head toward the door. "Let's get out of here."

"I . . ." She glanced around to indicate their public status.

"It's simple. I walk out. You follow me."

She couldn't go with him. Yet, she wanted nothing more.

"I'll be waiting." He walked away, his back straight. Accepting congratulations for the rout of "On The Spot," he worked his way toward the exit. His progress was easy to follow; his patrician head stood out above the others.

Mariah turned away from the door as though she'd forgotten she had even spoken to Rory. Kneeling, she picked up Charley's picture, taking care not to cut her hands on the glass slivers stuck in the frame. Gently, she placed the photo back atop the casket and looked again at Charley's likeness. Irreverent and brash, if he were here he'd tell her to grab life while she could.

If that meant to walk out of this room, it was her prerogative.

In the deserted hall, her heels echoed on the ancient marble floor. Hearing measured footfalls ahead of her, she rounded a corner and confirmed her partner in stealth was Rory.

"There." He gestured toward the entrance to a darkened chapel.

Inside, gilt and dark wood framed a large Crucifix on the front wall. Murky, stained glass windows lined the outside walls. The only light came from a lamp left on over the speaker's lectern. The air smelled faintly of incense.

Once the door closed behind them, Rory drew Mariah past rows of empty pews to a spot against the back wall where no one looking in could see. There, he propped his hands on either side of her. "Are you all right?"

Within the shelter formed by him and the wall at her back, she felt better than she had in days. "I'm making it." She kept her tone even. "Thanks for helping out in there."

"I've been in Castillo's sights, myself."

"You will be again."

He shrugged. "Along with you and Grant Development. The press won't let the accident go without sensationalizing it."

"We've been running the gauntlet from home to office for days," Mariah agreed.

His brow furrowed. "Any theories how that elevator managed to fall? I thought they had redundant safety mechanisms, rack and pinion . . . and why didn't the emergency brake work when the cable failed?"

On top of Tom's worries, Rory's words brought back the clutch inside Mariah. Despite it, she said, "Our engineer says these things happen. OSHA will insist on an independent lab report."

"Do you think it's possible someone's out to get Grant?" Rory mused.

"Other than your father?" she blurted.

His stunned look made her realize how that sounded. "I mean . . ." she trailed off.

His silence was louder than an outburst. At last, he said, "Given what you're going through, I'll let that pass." He drew a deliberate breath. "I'm talking about something else. When I was in the Grant Plaza construction trailer, I heard the men talking about a welder, a guy gone missing?"

"I haven't heard that." She made a mental note to find out.

"Ah." He looked as though he wanted to say more, but subsided again into silence.

After a moment, he touched the bandage over her left eye so gently she barely felt it. "Take care of yourself. Since I can't."

Though he wasn't pressing her against the wall, he was close enough that she dared to imagine him taking one tiny step closer. Glancing up, she caught him looking at her mouth.

The gossip columns said he was a notorious skirt chaser, but she felt safe, and alive with the strumming tension between them. It might be in the worst possible taste to feel this way when Charley lay dead, but she'd heard losing someone brought out the survival instinct. Maybe the Irish had it right, a wake with music, dance and drinking. Before she knew she had made a decision, Mariah raised her hand and placed her fingertips against Rory's lips. The shaking that had troubled her for days had gone.

He exhaled softly. "I know this is not the time or place, but . . . later." The last word was rich with promise.

From outside the chapel came a racket of heels on the stone floor. A filtered female voice reached them. "I'll show you where we have the services."

"Come on." Rory grabbed Mariah's hand.

They exited the other side of the chapel before the first door opened. In the hall, the lights seemed too bright.

"Let's go someplace," Rory urged.

"I can't. I drove my father."

"Then tomorrow. We'll go sailing on the Bay."

"You must be out of your mind."

"Then go crazy with me." His eyes were dark velvet.

"The funeral is at ten in the morning."

"And we'll both be there." He grimaced. "But watching them put Charley in the ground isn't my idea of a proper tribute. He'd rather that tomorrow afternoon we were out on the water, thinking about the time he was with us."

She shook her head. "I'm not going on your father's . . ."

"We're taking my boat." He grabbed both her hands. "I want to show it to you."

"I don't know, Rory . . ."

Yearning surged. Concern over family feuds and real estate seemed petty when life could end so randomly. She thought of Tom Barrett's gambling and knew each choice, no matter how small, was a dice roll, like letting Charley and Andrew Green take the hoist first.

Was she ready to roll her own dice?

CHAPTER 5

El Camino Real was the street where San Francisco buried her dead. Monument companies, their lawns covered with sample tombstones, did business cheek by jowl with private Italian, Jewish, and Chinese cemeteries, as well as the larger multi-ethnic memorial parks.

Mariah stared out the side window of the limousine on the way to Charley's grave. Today was another of what her father called a perfect, sharp blue day. He and she rode with Charley's parents, both Tom and Wendy red-eyed from weeping.

The procession entered Cypress Lawn Cemetery through a granite archway. Marble mausoleums marked the resting places of the wealthy, while fields paved with flat stones stretched away toward the edges of the hillside park. The limousine pulled up near the highest point of the burial ground where a crowd waited beside the open grave. Rumpled crimson carpet ineffectively camouflaged the irregular mound of earth.

Mariah and her father emerged from the car, and he offered his arm. Placing her hand above his elbow, she wondered who needed to lean on whom. After four terrible nights of silence from Charley's empty apartment, it was beginning to sink in that he'd not be back.

Approaching the graveside, she caught sight of Rory standing straight and alone, sunlight gleaming on his hair. Though she'd seen him only last night, her heart quickened. Thankfully, she didn't see his father.

Mariah and John took a seat with Tom and Wendy beneath a canvas awning. The laden pallbearers placed Charley's casket on a dais above the vacant vault.

The reverend, a beanpole of a man in a long black robe, began speaking sonorously of saying farewell to Charley at his eternal resting place. "And so we commit his body to the earth, and his spirit to Heaven. The Lord is my shepherd. I shall not want."

The cold from the metal chair seeped into Mariah as the assembly joined in reciting the Twenty-third Psalm. "He maketh me to lie down in green pastures, he restoreth my soul."

Across the lawn, a life-sized angel in flowing marble robes knelt atop a headstone. The sculptor had eschewed the usual ethereal and unmoving portrayal. Rather, this angel had been dragged to earth. Her long white wings hung limply, brushing the ground. Her head bowed in what looked more like despair than prayer. Stone tears marked her pale cheeks.

Mariah swallowed, a hard ache in her throat, for in a plot near the angel lay her mother. Carved onto a granite headstone alongside his wife's was her father's name.

"Yea, though I walk though the valley of the shadow of death . . ."

From somewhere behind her, she recognized Rory's deep voice. "I will fear no evil."

But she was beginning to be afraid. Of Davis Campbell's machinations, of the voracious appetite of reporters like Castillo for "On The Spot," of the look in Tom Barrett's eyes when he suggested she might have been targeted to die.

When the service ended, Mariah joined the receiving line between her father and Tom, greeting men and women who were mostly strangers. All the while, she waited for Rory.

When he got to Tom, she heard him say, "I hadn't seen Charley in years, but I'll miss knowing he's there."

"Thanks for what you did last night, Campbell." Tom sounded grudging. "Those 'On The Spot' people are scum."

Rory moved to stand before Mariah, compassion and sorrow in his dark eyes. She took an instinctive step forward into his arms. Though by now she'd hugged a dozen people she didn't know, casual yet intimate connections forged by common grief, Rory's embrace was different. Warmth, not of desire, but of comfort, seeped through her. The same sense of relief she'd not been ready to accept the night of the accident. Drawing a shuddering breath, she felt how tightly wired she was and tried to relax. One of his hands rubbed between her shoulder blades.

"I'm sorry, baby," he whispered.

Fresh tears for Charley welled. Rory's arms tightened. With her cheek against his wool lapel, she caught her father's gray gaze.

Despite John's obvious disapproval, when Rory set her away from him she wasn't ready. Perhaps he wasn't either, for he bore an expression of frustration like the one she was trying to hide. Drawing a business card from his jacket pocket, he pressed it into her hand. "My cell number's there. If you decide to go sailing, call. I'll be at my place until around noon."

Rory stepped away to face her father. Mariah watched the two men shake hands briefly and with less warmth than the evening before. "Sir," Rory said before turning away.

Her fingers clutching his card, she watched him leave without looking back at her. Only then did she glance down at the crisp white paper with black lettering: *Davis Campbell Interests*.

When the receiving line began to break up, it was too soon. For once the last car was out of sight, the gravediggers' backhoe would cover Charley's vault with earth.

Her father took her arm and drew her away from the open hole. Without discussion, they both turned their steps in the direction of the Grant family plot. At the base of the headstone on her mother's side rested a sheaf of white roses wrapped in florist's paper. The offering was as familiar as the granite's texture, for whenever the previous flowers began to wilt a fresh bouquet replaced them.

John bent and touched a creamy petal, then straightened and bowed his head.

Mariah ran her gaze along the words carved below "beloved wife." "Catharine Mariah Stockton Grant," she murmured.

He must know she had heard it a thousand times, but, "We named you for her middle name, also her mother's name."

Mariah might be the end of the line; if she continued as she had for the past eight years, devoted to career and loving no man, there might be no more passing on of family names.

She came out of her reverie to find Grant's director of public relations April Perry at her elbow. Copper-haired, with a porcelain complexion and prime time television makeup, April wore a bright blue dress that looked out of place among the mourners. She had not attended the funeral, staying behind at the office this morning.

"What are you doing here?" Mariah asked.

"There's a pack of news crews camped out at Grant," April said. "Not the usual one or two lurking reporters. I couldn't reach your cells."

John reached to his belt to turn his electronic leash back on. "After 'On The Spot' failed to run that footage from the funeral home last night, I was hoping things were settling down."

April looked troubled. "I guess they want to make hay

out of the service being today."

"I'm surprised that Cypress Lawn security kept them out of here," Mariah said.

John sighed. "We'll have to show our faces sooner or later. How about if we go and get it over with?"

Wendy clutched Tom's arm. "Not you."

"Not you today either, Dad." There wasn't any use in putting it off, but she thought he needed at least the weekend of rest. "What if we all check into a hotel until Monday morning?" she suggested.

"How about the Nikko?" Tom agreed. The tall white tower with its modern décor and exclusive Japanese restaurant was a common stop for Oriental travelers. "We locals ought to be able to hide out there."

The mention of hiding out made her think of Rory's invitation. From their position on the hill, she could see blue ocean, hazy in the distance. Charley would never again see the rippling of the bay or a sail's billow, but for her, life, motion, and the man she once loved beckoned.

A few minutes later, after the limousine had returned to the Barrett's house, she told her father casually, "I'm going to run by my place for an overnight bag. I'll see you at the Nikko later."

"Watch out for the press," John cautioned.

She flashed a grin. "What can they do to me? If I see them I'll say I have 'no comment'."

Leaving the Barretts, she did drive toward her Marina District apartment. Though it was eleven thirty, she thought there'd be time to change into sailing clothes and pack for the weekend at the Nikko before phoning Rory.

Turning into her street, she saw two TV vans parked in front of her house.

"Full court press," she muttered, slamming on the brakes.

With a fast U-turn she headed back the other way. She couldn't tell if they'd seen her as she went around a corner.

Rory's business card lay on the seat beside her. She managed to read and stab out the number for his cell phone on hers. On the fourth ring, he answered.

"The press are camped out at my place," she told him. "I'm not sure if they saw me."

"Listen carefully." He was all business. "I'm at my townhouse. On Vallejo, up high, on the right."

She checked her rearview mirror and saw a white van with roof-mounted satellite equipment a few lengths back in the other lane. Speeding up, she whipped her car around the first turn on the way to Vallejo.

"Where should I park?" she asked Rory.

"I have a two-car garage. You drive in, I'll close it."

All the way to Vallejo, the news crew stayed with her, so close that she was able to identify the "On The Spot" logo. They were right behind her when she drove into the open garage and watched daylight disappear with the lowering metal panel.

Rory waited in the doorway from the garage into his townhouse. Instead of the suit he'd worn to the cemetery, he'd changed to casual navy pants and a red long-sleeve pullover.

Mariah left her car and followed him into his kitchen to see how he lived. The place was bright, decorated in a nautical theme of white and dark blue. No sign of a bachelor's dirty dishes in the gleaming stainless steel sink.

The doorbell rang. She jumped.

"You're safe here." Rory's protective tone both surprised and warmed her.

She followed him into his living room, decorated in the same white and dark blue, with red and gold accents. "Did you choose all this?"

"I did." He grinned. "I let Elizabeth keep pretty much everything and started over." On a mirrored shelf in his dining room, he pointed out an array of tall ship models. "I put those together myself."

"They're wonderful."

The doorbell rang again, and the sound of heavy knocking came from around the corner in the front hall.

Trying to ignore the would-be intruders, Mariah continued to look around. On an end table beside the couch was a picture of Rory at age five or six. In the cockpit of a sailing vessel, the small determined boy stuck out his skinny chin and manned a wheel taller than he was. Behind him, Davis stood watch, a father's softness in his eyes.

Rory moved to stand beside her. "It's strange. Sometimes I can't deal with him, yet . . ."

A wave of longing for things to be different swept over her.

The news crew kept exhorting someone to come to the door.

"What if they don't leave?" she asked.

Rory arched a brow and moved closer. "We can stay here." His expression suggested he was all too aware they were alone with the world locked out.

Before she could react, he bent and touched his mouth gently to hers. How well she knew the shape and texture of his lips, yet how different this kiss was from ones they'd known long ago. Then, he'd been urgent and eager, rushed by the single-minded passion of youth. Now she sampled a more complex recipe.

How easy it would be to get lost in this, but she managed to remember. "I need to get to the Hotel Nikko. My Dad and the Barretts are going to stay there this weekend."

"I thought you'd let me take you sailing," Rory said with obvious disappointment.

She gestured toward the front door. "Won't 'On The Spot' follow us?"

"I can outrun anything they've got in my Porsche. Come on, go with me." Taking in her black suit, he said, "I'll find you some sweats or something to wear."

Mariah's determination wavered. Her father and Tom were the best of friends. They and Wendy would spend the afternoon and evening in discussions of people she didn't know, the way generations failed to cross-communicate.

"Please," Rory entreated. "Think of what you need right now . . . and what I need."

Sausalito hadn't changed much. A few more bungalows and townhouses on the hillside above, a few more galleries and shops than when Mariah first came to Davis Campbell's yacht.

Midday sun cast sharp shadows between the close-packed stucco buildings, flowers rioted in window boxes. Waves slapped at the breakwater, sending up a salt tang to mix with aromas of cooking seafood and other delicacies.

As Rory parked his Porsche in the marina lot, Mariah's sense of unreality increased. None of this fit the expectations she'd had waking up this morning for a funeral.

Although she'd changed into workout clothes and shoes from a gym bag in her car, she had trouble keeping up with Rory. He hurried past a fountain surrounded by pigeons, making a beeline for a little Italian market. When he apparently recalled that her short legs were no match for his stride, he waited for her with a rueful smile.

Inside the shop, colored peppers and garlic hung in strands from the ceiling, red ripe tomatoes and bright oranges overflowed bins, and wooden shelves groaned under the weight of canned goods and olive oil tins. Despite her lack of appetite the past few days, the mingled aromas of spices and fresh-baked bread made Mariah's stomach growl.

With interest, she watched Rory select a thick crusty boule, then hold up Fontina, Brie, and vintage Chianti for her approval.

Walking toward the marina took her back to the day they'd sailed with Charley. Even more of a rowdy kid then,

Charley had been like a younger brother going along on his sister's date. Through misty eyes, she smiled at the houseboats and the forest of sailboat masts.

When she and Rory stepped onto the dock, the music of the shrouds grew more melodious, a blend of pitch as lines beat against the hollow tubes of the masts. About halfway down the pier, Rory indicated a sailboat with a royal blue hull and white decks. No ostentatious yacht like his father's, it looked older than the other vessels, lifting and lowering with the swell. Its teak trim had faded to a gentle gray.

When she stepped on the rail, the boat didn't move. It only dipped a fraction of an inch when Rory joined her aboard.

"Pearson Rhodes '41," he said with pride. "Built in '65, back when they didn't know the strength of fiberglass. Her decks are this thick." He held up his thumb and forefinger two inches apart. "She's fast, too. I like the zip of a smaller boat than *Privateer*."

"What's her name?"

Rory looked thoughtful. "That's a puzzle. When I bought her earlier this spring her name had been painted over. I haven't had a chance to decide on one." He cocked his head and grinned. "I could always call her 'Mariah.'"

Her heart thudded at the suggestion he'd put her name on his pride and joy in foot-high letters, but paint was cheap, and perhaps he'd made the same offer to Sylvia Chatsworth.

At her lack of reaction, Rory's smile disappeared, and he turned his attention to unlocking the companionway slide. She sensed his withdrawal and felt ashamed of what she'd thought, but couldn't figure out what to do about it.

Mariah put the sack she carried onto the deck, waiting for instructions. It might go against feminism, but one thing she recalled about sailing was that the captain made the rules. "When you have your own boat," Rory had told her long ago, "you'll be in charge."

Remembering details as they went along, she helped him prepare to cast off. Together, they removed blue canvas covers from the sails and brought up cockpit cushions along with lifejackets.

The engine started with a roar, exhaled a cloud of blue exhaust, and subsided to a gentle putt-putt as Rory backed out of the slip and steered toward the Bay. Once in open water, Mariah took the helm while he clambered forward to raise the mainsail. It caught the wind, and the boat heeled.

Untying the sheets from the huge jib sail wrapping the front stay, Rory threaded color-coded lines back to the rear winches. He unfurled the jib and called for her to shut off the engine.

Immediately, the loud laboring was replaced by the smooth hiss of water against the hull.

Mariah inhaled the sense of peace that surrounded them, yet noted the bustling of ferries and windsurfers leaping wave crests, their colorful sails and wetsuits contrasting with the blue water.

Over the next hour, she fell back into the old rhythm of tacking, changing directions against the wind. "Ready about," Rory would say, while she loosened the sheet that held the jib taut. Then "Hard alee." Amid flapping chaos, the jib and main swung to the other side of the boat while she climbed across to sheet both sails in firmly.

The Pearson glided soundlessly under the Golden Gate Bridge, its vermilion metal towers rising in majestic contrast to the cerulean sky. Huge tankers and container ships ploughed in and out of port. Their wakes gently lifted and lowered the sailboat's hull, yet crested against the bridge supports with startling violence.

In a sheltered area on the north side of the bay, Rory sailed in lazy circles while Mariah laid out bread, cheese, and wine. Going below, she located stemmed glasses wrapped in dishtowels to keep them from breaking in rough seas, and brought them on deck.

"Too deep to drop anchor." Rory steadied the wheel with his knee while he pulled the cork.

Mariah took the bottle from him, catching a whiff of the wine's sharp-edged bouquet, and poured. The first glass she handed to Rory. The second she filled and took into her hand.

"To Charley," Rory said before she could.

"To Charley." She swallowed the tart crimson liquid around the lump in her throat.

Reflected in Rory's sunglasses, Mariah saw herself pour wine into a third glass. He came to her and wordlessly put his hand over hers on the stem.

Was that an echo of Charley's laugh or a sea bird's cry? In her mind's eye, her friend appeared once more, long limbs, freckled face, and mischievous eyes. A vivid image that time must inevitably fade.

In fitting farewell, she and Rory poured wine upon the water.

On the sail back, Rory kept the boat close-hauled against the wind, showing Mariah what it could do. He brought a yellow foul weather jacket from below for her, but even with the coat on her face and hair were soon dripping from the spray. He liked that rather than complaining or flinching, she laughed with each dousing.

His sense of exhilaration lasted almost all the way to the marina. Then he began to have the sense of time running out. Just before they pulled into the quiet water of the harbor, he lost a battle with himself and leaned over to kiss her. The quick buss tasted of salt on their chilled lips, but it was also a memory. He'd also kissed her on that perfect long-ago sail with Charley, before bringing the boat to the dock.

When he nosed the Pearson into its slip, it was nearly four o'clock. The sun shadow of the hill above Sausalito covered the harbor as Rory and Mariah worked together to put everything back in its place. With the sails covered, life vests and cushions back below, they washed the salt from faces and hands and dried their briny hair on thirsty cotton towels.

Even without makeup, with her hair brushed back and caught in a clip, Rory thought Mariah looked wonderful. In an effort to prolong the afternoon, he suggested another trip to the Italian market, this time for a warming cappuccino.

When they approached the counter, the proprietor recognized them and asked how was their sail. With a wink, he told Rory his "missus" was "most beautiful." Mariah immediately appeared engrossed by the tubs of gelato in the freezer case.

Rory reached for his wallet and counted out bills. The man's innocent assumption burst the fragile bubble he'd constructed around him and Mariah today, reminding him that despite a raging obsession there could be nothing for them. No normal progression from an afternoon sail to dating on the town, no getting down on one knee with the diamond ring . . . he'd tried all that with Elizabeth and ended up in divorce court.

Their drinks in hand, Rory led the way to a table on the exterior patio where they were the only customers. Sipping hot sweet coffee, he studied Mariah and found that despite his resolve to avoid getting burned again, he was once more playing "what if." With her hair drying from dark gold to wheat and her cheeks sun-warmed, she made him want to protect her from the roving press, from sorrow over Charley. The last thing he wanted was to take her back to the city.

"Drive down the coast with me," Rory decided aloud. "We'll spend the weekend at Big Sur."

Mariah gasped. "I can't," she said automatically. "Dad expects me at the Nikko."

Rory unclipped his cell phone from his belt and held it out. Her own was in her purse in the Porsche's front luggage compartment, the charger at home on her bedroom dresser. "Tell him you're with a friend," he said. "He'll be glad you have something to take your mind off things."

In the interest of harmony, she decided to drop the issue of her father. Rory might feel the same involuntary negative response she did at the mere thought of Davis Campbell. Instead, she gestured at the still-damp, salt-stained legs of her workout pants. "I don't have a thing to wear."

He dug in his pocket and tossed a credit card on the table. "We'll buy whatever we need in Carmel." Reaching across, he took her hand. "Haven't you ever wanted to go someplace on the spur of the moment?"

She had thought about it. Inevitably, it had been with a darkly handsome man who looked a lot like Rory Campbell.

His fingers persuaded, stroking a light rhythm on hers.

To keep things in perspective, she pulled away. "Let me think."

"Don't think." He recaptured her hand and brought it to his lips. With the tip of his tongue, he teased the space where two fingers joined, a butterfly's touch with a deep, roiling impact. "Just feel."

She took her hand away again, thoughts swirling . . . of conflicting interests between their companies, Davis Campbell's ire, and her father's disappointment if he knew where she was.

"No thoughts of the future or the past," Rory proposed.

"Just an escape to a fantasy world where we can do whatever we want."

"That'll be the day." She rose and turned away. Standing in front of the low wall surrounding the patio, she heard the scrape of his café chair on the tiles. Surrounded by the scent of potted flowers, she detected the spicy addition of his after-shave . . . just before his hands spanned her waist.

Though she couldn't see his eyes, she imagined their expression. Seductive and pleading, yet with a pride that said he was no beggar. Desire swirled and gathered at the base of her stomach. In the two weeks since she'd seen him again, she'd relived their past with a sense of hopelessness, like biting on an aching tooth. Now, for the first time, she permitted herself to imagine making love with him again.

"Trust me," he whispered near her ear. "You won't be sorry."

It was too soon for trust between them; she could not forget his past betrayal. But her knees went weak with the same primal reaction she'd always had when his breath warmed her neck.

In an uncanny display of mind reading, he said, "If you don't trust me, trust your instinct."

He reached back to the table, picked up his cell phone, and held it before her eyes.

As if in a dream, she saw her hand lift and take it.

Yes, said the Nikko operator, John Grant was registered. The line began to ring.

He wouldn't be there. It would ring and ring and then she'd tell Rory she couldn't go.

"Hello," said her father.

"Dad." Mariah took a hesitant breath and glanced at Rory.

"Don't say no," he said urgently.

He was right. "No" wasn't good enough anymore. Neither of their fathers had any business telling her and Rory how to live.

"Mariah?" John asked. "Where are you?"

Once more, she paused. She could truthfully say she was with a friend, but that set a precedent for a secret affair, something she had no stomach for. Though he might be let down, even angry, Dad deserved the truth from her rather than from an "On The Spot" story about her going to Rory's townhouse.

"I'm with Rory. He rescued me from the press this afternoon."

"When will I see you, then?" he asked tightly.

"I know you don't approve, but you were right about there being something between me and Rory. Maybe you saw it before I could admit it to myself." She spoke into her father's silence. "With all that's happened this week, the accident, and Charley . . ." She swallowed. "Rory and I are going to drive down to Big Sur for the weekend."

CHAPTER 6

On the drive down, Mariah had trouble believing she had told her father where she was going. All he had said was, "I hope you know what you're doing, daughter," but the resignation in his tone had her wondering if she should ask Rory to turn the Porsche around. It wasn't too late to get back to the city by sunset.

For it was in this night's darkness that she would truly cross the threshold. She knew from her experiences in the past eight years that going to bed didn't constitute commitment, but with Rory, it would be different. Although the storm of feeling that had surged through her at his touch had subsided, images of them together kept flashing as if on a screen.

Of their past . . . the incandescent glow of the first time they'd made love. In the vee berth in the prow of *Privateer*, looking up at silver raindrops on the Lexan forward hatch, feeling the canvas cushions rough beneath her bare back, she'd given herself to him. Given and taken with a fresh, unfamiliar hunger, been filled and fulfilled, fierce joy seizing and transporting her until she felt she exploded into glittering shards. She sparkled and shone despite the gray day, all the while she felt herself floating somewhere above the bunk. Finally, softly, the pieces of her landed, gradually reassembling into someone that did not even resemble the old.

At least that's what she had believed. Could she now truly set aside his marriage to Elizabeth, and believe he was not his father's man?

Even as the thought formed, she recalled Rory's premise. No thoughts of the future or past, an escape . . . that was what she had bought into when she took his cell phone and called her father. With a sinking feeling, she feared she had made a terrible mistake.

Yet, she recalled the deep intensity in Rory when he'd asked her to trust him, and if not him, then in herself. If she asked him to take her home, she would never know where their fantasies might lead.

When they passed Fort Ord with its huge dunes buffering the shore, Rory lifted his hand from the steering wheel and placed it on her thigh above the knee. His thumb moved over her yoga pants lightly, but she felt the touch as though her skin was bare.

As always, his slightest caress sent the familiar deep warmth that flushed her chest, tightened her nipples into peaks, and set up a melting glow at the base of her stomach. And her images shifted from past to future . . . to this night when they would finally be together after eight lonely years.

Fire winked back at Mariah from the jewelry store window in Carmel's shopping district. Of the collection of opulent gems on black velvet, she had eyes only for the show-piece, a rare pigeon's blood ruby. The oval center stone was clear, the purest of reds. Triangle-cut side diamonds glittered and flashed.

The kind of piece a woman sported in her fantasies but would never buy for herself.

She caught the quick look Rory gave her before he left her in the spring dusk and went inside the brightly lit jewelry store. Through the glass, Mariah saw him gesture the sales-woman to the front window. Pinpoint spotlights gleamed on his dark hair and reflected off the sunglasses he'd shoved on top of his head.

With a glance around the street to make sure no news crew trailed them, Mariah followed him inside. "What are you doing?"

The saleswoman shoehorned into a leopard print skirt rummaged in the front window and offered the ruby ring. "Three point five carats in the center stone, the finest natural color from Burma. The side diamonds are E color, VVS1, one point two carats total weight."

The ring was breathtaking. Rory turned it in his hands and asked for a jeweler's loupe. Squinting, he studied the stones at ten-power magnification.

He couldn't be thinking of buying it? The new jeans, leather jackets, toilet articles from a modern day apothecary, along with the mystery purchase he'd made from a fine lingerie store . . . all had been in the spirit of their weekend getaway. This was something else.

Lifting her left hand, he slipped the ring onto her finger where it fit as if it had been custom made. From his breast pocket, he withdrew the credit card they'd been trying to wear the numbers off. "She'll keep it on."

The saleswoman produced a tiny pair of manicure scissors and cut off the tag dangling from a silk thread. Though she held the scrap of cardboard so the price was not visible, Mariah knew the ring must be very expensive.

"Rory, no," she said.

He had decreed they were not to think of their shared history or an uncertain future. Therefore, it was her misfortune for noticing he'd slipped the ring on her third finger, left hand. He might be having fun playing make believe, but in every store, she'd imagined they were a couple out shopping on a Friday evening, with a home and a life to share.

Palming the credit card, the saleswoman seemed to think of something that needed doing in the rear of the store. Left alone with Rory, Mariah looked up at his shining eyes and almost believed he shared her vision.

But . . . "You mustn't do this." Each time she looked at the ring, she would wish its meaning were real.

Something swelled in his chest as Rory took her hand with the ring on it. "We can do anything we want. We've left the world behind."

"The bill will come next month." Mariah's troubled golden eyes held his.

"My fantasy is to buy you this," he insisted. She'd been so happy earlier, laughing while they tried on clothes, playing peek-a-boo while he made his secret purchase of something special for her. This ring was special, too; he'd seen her pupils dilate at the sight of it.

She did not renew her protest but stared at their clasped hands.

"Please," he said. "I want to." He could see by her face that there was something he wasn't getting across.

Another moment of hesitation and her gaze seemed to penetrate his skull.

At last, she spoke. "All right, Rory . . . if it makes you happy."

This was all wrong. From her rapt expression upon seeing the ruby, he'd figured it would be a hit. Feeling at a loss, he called the saleswoman and finished signing the charge slip. He passed the empty red velvet box lined in white satin to

Mariah; she stowed it in her purse.

Outside, he walked with her down Ocean Avenue. The Friday evening bustle was in full swing, people gathered at patio tables for drinks and dinner. They could have a meal here in town rather than waiting until they reached the inn on Big Sur, shop more . . . what could he do to put the magic back in the evening?

There. Beside the steep front steps of the landmark Pine Inn, he spied a young man with a white sidewall haircut selling flowers out of a bucket.

Grabbing Mariah's hand, Rory detained her to make a transaction, a single long-stemmed red rose. He presented it with a smile, hoping to get back the euphoric mood that seemed to have gripped her as well as him while they shopped and wandered through galleries.

Leaving the lights of the merchant district behind, Mariah walked ahead of Rory downhill past ivy-covered fences until the street ended at Carmel Beach. Kicking off her new sandals, she hooked them with two fingers and set off though a grove of cypress with heavy needles. Beyond the steep hill of powdery sand, salt mist and the long curve of the bay beckoned, glassy swells rolling in and breaking with loud hollow booms. She followed the slope down onto damp, packed sand and stopped at the verge.

As an expiring rush of wave washed her bare ankles, she

asked herself why she wasn't floating on a cloud. Here she and Rory were on the perfect romantic getaway, he had bought her a beautiful ring, not wedding jewelry, but a start. Yet, she could tell by the unsettled feeling in her chest that a fantasy weekend wasn't enough. She wanted to be able to believe in him, the way she once had.

Rory approached and stood tall and lean beside her, his own shoes in his hand as he sucked in his breath at the chilly water. "Tell me what's the matter."

Another comber crested and broke toward the shore, sending them both backing away from the incoming tide. They stood on the packed sand together, and she imagined how they must look to the older woman walking by with her Greyhound, a pair of lovers wordlessly taking in the beauty of night falling over the sea.

When they were once more alone with the surf, Rory nodded toward the ring she wore. "When I saw you looking at that, I wanted you to have it. I'm sorry it was the wrong thing to do."

Watching a breaker crest and collapse, she fingered the rose stem and tested a thorn with her thumb. "You talked about make-believe. Well, my fantasy isn't about jewelry or flowers."

"Mine is," he insisted. "I never bought you flowers when you deserved a garden. I never gave you a ring."

As she had before when Rory spoke of the past, Mariah closed her eyes. An afterimage of Pebble Beach Club's sparkling lights danced on her lids. "Please," she pleaded, "don't say things like that."

Unless you mean them.

Rory turned away before she could see his expression. "Shall we go, then?"

They walked in silence up to his car. She wondered if he would head back toward San Francisco or continue south to the country inn he'd told her about . . . if he also felt torn between backing out before they could hurt each other more and wanting to go forward?

They approached the intersection with scenic Highway 1, and he put on his turn indicator to go to Big Sur. The town lights illuminated his profile as he dealt with traffic and joined the weekend exodus south.

The roller coaster road mirrored Mariah's emotions. The Porsche's headlights revealed arched concrete bridges spanning gorges that appeared bottomless in the night. Cliffs loomed, deeper shadows against the dark sky. Inside the leather cocoon of the passenger compartment, she and Rory were as isolated as two people could be. And though together at last away from prying eyes, their silences spoke louder than the words intermittently exchanged.

The road wound down into a valley where trees overhung it. A rustic wooden sign said they entered the Ventana Wilderness. Rory turned onto a smaller road and began a steep climb, leaving the ocean below. Finally, with a spatter of gravel, they stopped in the drive of the inn.

Mariah looked out through the windshield, acutely aware of the gold band circling her ring finger.

Rory cut the engine. "Having second thoughts?"

She'd imagined them together like this so many times . . . always in her version, they'd been pledged to each other.

"How about thirds?" She swallowed. "Oh, Rory, what are we doing here? We can't just escape from everything without thinking about it."

He took her hand and rubbed his thumb over the smooth metal of the ruby ring. "We can sure as hell try."

Mariah should have been starved, but she ate lightly of succulent sweet abalone and grilled artichoke, with vintage local Riesling. Rory put away a rare filet of beef, mixed green salad, and a deep red Cabernet.

Over a dessert of fresh strawberries and luscious brandied cream, Rory finished his story of a recent sailing excursion. "It was the first time I raced her and won. All because I was able to loft the spinnaker before the other guy at the downwind mark."

Although Mariah hadn't been in a sailboat race since their summer together, she could picture the triangular racecourse, sleek hulls flying huge colorful sails as they drove for the finish line.

"I'll take you as crew for the next one," Rory said.

His words sent a gust of hope through her, but she merely smiled and told a story of snorkeling kelp forests, golden fronds swaying in cerulean water. She wasn't ready to believe that hiding out with her in a remote inn would translate into defying his father openly. Nor was she certain she'd done the right thing in telling her father she was with Rory.

Dinner wound down, and Mariah became more aware of the bracelet of illumination that lighted the way across the mountainside to their secluded bungalow. With butterflies beginning in her stomach at the thought of the broad bed, she spoke of blue flowers in a window box. Was the mellow, aged brandy better than the more aromatic younger version? Did she want decaf espresso or high test?

When they left the restaurant, their distance from the city was underlined by the waning moon's light, not too bright to subdue a blanket of stars. She looked up into the sky and wondered how many times she had studied the few stars visible in L.A., thinking that somewhere Rory gazed up, too. There were too many sparkling gems in the firmament tonight to single out a wishing star, but she sent up an entreaty for what was happening between her and Rory to be real.

They entered the deep forest, their feet making no sound on the soft mixture of earth, needles, and bark. Redwood scent rose on the damp air, and small lights cast shadows amid the towering giants. In deference to the stillness, neither of them spoke. Yet, her thoughts whirled down corridors past and present. She'd never been able to resist Rory, not as an innocent, and not within the circle of his arm tonight.

He stopped on a wooden bridge where a small stream's music defied the silence and his arm came around her. Looking down at garden lights sparkling on the water, she said in the same light tone they'd used during dinner, "I'm glad we came. This place is lovely."

He pulled her tighter against him. "Stop it, Mariah."

At the emotion in his voice, she began to tremble.

"Quit making small talk." His hands roamed her back. "Quit pretending to act casual."

"You said in Sausalito that we weren't to think."

"I know I said not to think, but that was crazy. If I'm honest with myself, and with you, I have to admit I've been obsessed about this, one way or another, since I saw you again."

His urgent tone led her to expect the crushing embrace he'd given her the night of the accident at Grant Plaza. Instead, he turned her to him slowly, barely brushing her lips with his.

It was like coming home, their connection immediate and vital. Had she ever known a man whose breath melded so sweetly with hers? Sliding her hands up into his hair, she caressed the back of his neck with the boldness she'd dared at eighteen. At this simple touch, she felt him shudder.

Their kiss deepened, escalating from exploration to his tongue seeking hers with bold authority. He snugged her closer and let her feel what she was doing to arouse him. Joy surged while the melting warmth in her expanded. Wicked images warred with propriety; he would make love to her here in the dark woods, up against the wooden rail . . . someone could walk down the path at any moment.

Rory kissed the side of her neck then moved his lips to the hollow at the base of her throat. Her head tipped back, and she gasped at the pleasure needles shooting hot and cold through her.

"Admit it, Mariah," he whispered. "There's never been anybody who did it for us like each other."

The last of her reservations fell away like water tumbling to the pool below. There was no telling where they would end up, but she would seize this moment, this now.

The thin high tone of a cell phone made them jerk apart.

"Dammit!" Rory reached to his belt and unclipped the small device.

Another tinny ring sounded out of place in the deep forest.

What would be his answer to the real world's summons? Did Sylvia Chatsworth wonder why he was late coming over? Had his father discovered through some clairvoyant sense that his son was AWOL?

On the third ring, Rory flipped the phone off the bridge. With a gulping splash, it sank into the dark pool.

When they arrived at their secluded bungalow, housekeeping had prepared a love nest. In the entry floored with black granite, spiky ginger and bird of paradise graced a crystal vase. On the granite bar top, an iced bottle of champagne rested beside a brandy bottle with appropriate balloon glasses. Chocolate and assorted cheeses promised to satisfy a late night appetite.

Rory went to the hearth and put a match to the pre-laid fire. Then he reached for the bag containing the mystery purchase he'd made in Carmel. "I hope you like it."

In the top of the sack, Mariah saw black velvet. Smooth and plush in her hand, the floor-length robe unfolded as she drew it out. "It's fabulous." Opening the sash, she uncovered the lining of crimson silk.

He grinned. "Sedate, but with a bit of wickedness beneath."

True to the spirit of being wicked, she took the robe with her into the bath. Staring at her reflection in the mirror, she found a woman transformed. Her eyes appeared huge, soft. Golden hair spilled over her shoulders, making her look like the younger woman who had gazed into the glass in the master head aboard *Privateer*, the last time she and Rory were together like this. The night Davis had discovered their secret, she'd brought along a silky robe from home. Brushed her hair and gone out to find Rory turning the cabin into a candlelit fairyland . . . an idyll that lasted until the tread of his father sounded on the companionway stairs.

Brushing aside the nagging sense that running away from the city had solved nothing, she focused on the fervor in Rory's voice when he told her there'd never been anyone for him like her.

Slowly, she took off her clothes and wrapped herself in Rory's gift. The silk was the same hue as the ruby sparkling on her finger, black velvet an elegant foil. She picked up the brush Rory had bought her in Carmel and tamed her hair. With care, she removed the Band-aid covering the cut on her forehead. The reminder of the accident, still lined with sutures, reminded her that life was precious and ephemeral, and if she dared tonight, hers for the taking.

Feeling like an infatuated teenager, Rory waited for Mariah on their private fenced patio with a sunken Japanese-style bath. Barefoot on the slate tiles and naked under one of the hotel's white terry robes, he swirled a snifter of brandy and imagined the dark ocean, more than a thousand feet below. On impulse, he opened the gate and saw a small path, no more than a tantalizing swath of flattened grass, leading away into the Ventana wilderness.

Tomorrow the high country beckoned, with spring hills green and wildflowers in bloom. He and Mariah would walk for hours . . . and talk. Did she still like peanut butter crackers? What movies could she quote? He couldn't remember her favorite color; was it red like his?

Breathing the scent of evergreen from the nearby woods, he closed the gate. The bath steamed in the deep forest night, its heat inviting. He decided to wait for Mariah.

A smile curved his lips, and his stomach tightened, his sex stirring with anticipation. He'd told the truth this evening beside the stream where his cellular phone rested in peace. No one had ever made him feel this peculiar mix of thrill and ache.

Not his well-loved wife Elizabeth, with whom he'd had affectionate sex that left him warm yet not quite satisfied, or any of the women he'd tried on and discarded publicly courtesy of "On The Spot." His first few months of the divorce crazies still had the power to make him ashamed. And not Sylvia Chatsworth.

No, it was Mariah, his first, and the only one he could imagine being with tonight.

Clad in nothing but the silk and velvet wrap Rory had given her, Mariah opened the sliding glass door to the patio. She felt a swell in her chest at the sight of him, bronzed skin against the white of his robe, his hair curling over the collar.

She started to speak, but he put a finger to her lips. "Let's not spoil it with talk; things go wrong when we talk."

There was much unsaid between them, yet he was right about the minefields awaiting them should they start discussing reality. Reinforcing her decision not to think but to feel, she accepted the pact by pressing her finger to his lips in turn.

He sipped from the snifter and held it while she drank in the exotic aroma and fiery taste of brandy. Bending, he set the glass on the rim of the bath, glanced toward the steaming pool at their feet, and with eyes on hers, loosed the belt of his robe.

Her breath caught.

Terrycloth slipped from his shoulders and slid down his body.

He was as beautiful as she remembered, the planes of

his face sculpted by shadows. No, more so . . . with the slender strength of a rapier. His long line of torso still tapered to narrow hips and compact rounded buttocks, but now he looked stronger, more substantial. The whorl of hair below his navel pointed the way to his sex, rising powerfully from a dark thicket.

A flush of heat suffused her.

His eyes acknowledged her approval while letting himself down into the dark oval of water. He ducked his head and came up sleek and shining. Although silent, everything about him bespoke his need, from the set of his mouth to his hand, raised dripping from the bath to beckon.

A momentary hesitation, and she loosed the tasseled sash and spread the velvet open. With shaking hands, she pushed the robe from her shoulders. As silk slipped over her hips to pool on the tile, she heard Rory's audible breath. Though she wasn't as reed thin as she'd been at eighteen, appreciation warmed his gaze.

Over cool stone, she stepped to the edge and let the warm pool take her into its embrace.

Water swirled as Rory moved with a suddenness that surprised her. His lips, wet from the bath, took hers urgently.

Her mouth opened beneath his as it had on the forest bridge. For a long moment, they explored anew the texture and taste of each another. Then he drew back, reached for the brandy snifter and dipped a finger. Very slowly, he moved his hand toward her while she drew in her breath at what she believed to be his destination. Sure enough, he touched the liquid drop to the tip of her bare breast.

With a gasp, she brought her hands up to grip his head, guiding his kiss to her taut peak. He teased and tantalized, his tongue hotter than the bath water. When she was aglow with need, he lifted his head and reached for more brandy.

She beat him to it. Bending, she flicked her tongue over his tight brown nipple, licking at the pungent liquor. It was his turn to hold her mouth hard against him while she reveled in her power to make him moan low in his throat, "Mariah."

The sound of her name uttered in that profoundly sensual tone sent sparks running along her nerves. Deep and low inside her, an aching void grew. This was the feeling she'd known eight years ago each time he started making love to her. Then, as now, there had been no words, just the soft exhalation of need that grew sharper with each passing moment.

Rory reveled in sensation. This was the urgency he'd known with her in *Privateer*'s berth, when he'd shoved aside a pile of life jackets to make a place for them their first time. Never in his young life had such a wild current surged. Perhaps the forbidden aura surrounding John Grant's daughter had driven him to make the first move, but once he tasted her sweetness and saw it metamorphose to passion, he was hooked.

Tonight, made impatient by his pounding blood, he climbed from the pool and extended a hand to help her out. She emerged with water sheeting silver over her breasts and down the curve of belly. Her hips had the right fullness, her breasts were small and perfect, pink-tipped the way he thought a woman should be. Without breaking their grasp, he scooped up his robe and used the terrycloth to scrub beaded droplets from their bodies.

Moving swiftly, he led her inside where firelight played over the quilted bed comforter. He'd take her down now, bury himself in her warmth . . .

But that wasn't right. He was no longer an importunate youth who'd gone after what his body desired with no holds barred. Tonight, he wanted to explore with subtlety. No rushing his fences, no quick hot coupling, despite that he could barely deny this urgency.

Drawing a slow breath, he sat on the edge of the bed and pulled her against him, his arms around her waist. He laid his cheek against her stomach reverently.

Mariah stood between Rory's thighs, more aware of her body than she had ever been. This tingling in her breasts and between her thighs held the promise that slow exploration might take her to heights past unions had failed to scale. Breaking their vow of silence, she said, "You can't know how many times I've imagined this . . ."

"But I can."

She met his gaze of desire and danger; swept back to the first time they'd met and kissed on *Privateer*, alone in the rainy harbor on Davis's forbidden refuge. Tonight, present and past fused. His hands were everywhere and she met him. She used her palms as sensors, rediscovering his skin, smooth over solid muscles.

Rory lowered his mouth to her breast. When he circled its tip with his tongue, an electric connection to her sex made her whole body shiver. She moved unashamedly against him.

He drew back and gave her a heavy lidded look. Her hand found the steel of him sheathed in velvet skin, tightened her grip on his hardness, and tugged him toward her.

Rory glanced toward the bathroom. "I'd better . . ."

He moved lithely from the bed, and Mariah lay back, watching firelight play on the walls and ceiling. They had all this night, and the next . . .

He returned with a foil packet that he placed on the nightstand, and a small vial. When he opened the tiny bottle and passed it under her nose, the sharp spice of ginger root filled her head. With a nudge, he indicated for her to turn onto her stomach. "Let me touch you," he said thickly.

If she had thought their play with brandy erotic, she'd not imagined him straddling her behind, his hardness against her. If she tilted her spine at the right angle, if he moved his hips just so . . .

But they'd taken it too quickly when they were young. Like firecrackers in a string, each caress had begotten another until she and Rory exploded and lay spent. Tonight, though she ached to be filled by him, hot and urgent, she wanted even more to prolong each exquisite sensation.

Rory poured pungent oil into the hollow at the base of her spine, thick warmth spreading like honey over her skin. He bent to spread the aromatic liquid, his hands hot on her flesh. Stroking smoothly, kneading, he eased knots in her muscles that she hadn't known were there. With each pass, she drew in her breath.

He moved lower, tracing the contour of her ribcage and defining the curve of her buttocks. Closing her eyes, she lay taut while Rory traced ever-narrowing circles. At last, he reached the slick core of her that needed no oil. Feather light, he explored her silken folds while she choked back a cry. As though she were an instrument he played, his fingers kept up their gentle strumming until she forgot everything and arched against him, ripe to bursting.

They continued their play, banking the embers until it seemed they must burst into flame. She was ready to plead for fulfillment, but instead she found the vial of oil on the bed and held it up. "Now you."

He shifted his weight off her and lay back. She rose on her knees, poured oil into her palm, and rubbed her hands together to coat them. All the while, his intent dark eyes, alive with firelight, followed her every movement.

She touched his stomach, and he gasped. When her hands moved lower, he gave a ragged groan. Taking pleasure in giving back, she made a game of stroking him, first lightly and then with firmness, varying rhythms according to the expression in his eyes.

He put his hand on hers and stilled it. "I want it to happen inside you."

"Then make love to me." She moved to lie beside him.

His hesitation lasted the barest instant, but it was enough for her to wonder if she'd chosen the wrong words. He hadn't said he loved her, not in eight years. But as he moved to poise above her, his eyes searched hers as though wanting them both to be certain.

She could appreciate that; she had loved an eager young man, yet was aware it was too soon for declarations between them this time through.

He brought his mouth down on hers and pressed his sex against her stomach, thrusting up lightly. Desire lanced through her belly, as he whispered at her ear, "Don't think."

"I'm not," she lied, but when his tongue traced the contour of her earlobe and he blew lightly on her neck, it became the truth. She had to have Rory, deep and hot inside her, must find relief for the fever that gripped them both.

Her hands helped to sheath him.

"Mariah." He touched her, spreading her moisture.

Finally, with a ragged breath, he slipped into her. Their fit was immediate and urgent. Exquisite torture, far more intense than anything she could remember. For a long moment, he went still in her, and she savored the length and breadth of him. Then, slowly at first, he slid over her. Answering, she moved in concert, heightening her own sensation.

Their rhythm became more urgent. The room seemed to grow warmer, her fingers slipping on Rory's sweat-slick body. His heat transferred to her, a fine sheen of perspiration blooming between her breasts. Too long denied, they spiraled higher until the sweetness became unbearable.

Her hands on his back slid around until she held him against her with both arms, straining, reaching with him . . . until sensation broke in a cascade of piercing explosions that shook her to the core. Rory's mouth covered hers as he moaned his own shuddering release.

"My God," he gasped.

Breathing hard like him, she savored his weight. She could feel both their hearts hammering.

As she began to realize there was enough air to breathe, she felt a warm daze descend. For a long moment, she and Rory lay twined, until he rolled over to lie on his back. Stretched side by side, they reached and clasped hands as though they would never let go. For a fleeting instant, she believed that it was so.

But she couldn't think now, not with this impossible sensation of both floating and bone deep lassitude. For an instant, she was out on the water sailing, as they had been this afternoon, then back on the broad bed, lying limp as though drugged. Snippets of dream flickered like the firelight as she struggled to keep her eyes open.

It was no use; her lids were like drops of lead. The last she remembered Rory kissed her and covered them both with the sheet.

CHAPTER 7

*N*aked, Mariah pushed back the curtain in the front room of her childhood home in Stonestown. Instead of a vista of comfortable houses and the stand of redwoods in nearby Stern grove, a roiling sea smashed and battered the land. She peered in disbelief through the square of glass and saw a high comber spend itself on the porch steps.

She had to wake Dad so they could go someplace safe. But first, she had to cover herself. If he saw her without clothes, he would know she'd been with Rory.

A search of the hall closet turned up empty hangers where her father's coats should be. She decided to try her old room, throw on anything to cover her betrayal.

Turning into the hall, she stumbled into a bronze coffin with the lid propped open. Everything in her recoiled, but she forced herself to look inside.

There, in his best blue suit, lay her father on a satin lining. His pale face wore the unmistakable pinched look of death. Stumbling back, she found row upon row of shriveled flower arrangements filling the living room. Darkened, dry petals gave off a moldy stench.

From the front of the house, a smashing sound preceded the cascade of broken glass on the hardwood floor. A three-foot wave washed in, swept up the coffee table and tumbled it into the television with a crash. Green water swirled, deepening and reaching like a cold whip around Mariah's waist. It dragged her down so her head went under, but not before she saw it slosh into the coffin.

Fighting her way to her feet, she screamed, a slash of pain in the back of her throat.

The wave receded, washing her across the room, and throwing her hard against the front wall. She struggling to regain her footing and looked for her father.

Impossibly, the coffin was gone.

Rory appeared in the hallway to the bedrooms, dressed in black.

She gasped and cried his name.

He reached his hand and urged her toward him.

Sylvia Chatsworth came out of Mariah's childhood room. Wearing the black velvet robe Rory had given Mariah, turned inside out to reveal crimson silk, she ran a caressing hand through Rory's hair and handed him a Scotch on the rocks.

Mariah tried to run, but her legs were useless stumps. Another wave washed in and piled up in the hall. The last she saw of Rory and Sylvia they were chest-deep in swirling water, embracing and looking at her with mournful eyes.

Struggling out of the land of nightmare, Mariah fought off the bed covers. Sweat coated her nude body, the sheets felt sticky. Opening her eyes, she found dawn light wedging in through an open sliding door.

Chest heaving, she sat up and realized she was alone in the big bed. Thick mist lay over the Ventana wilderness. Damp nipped her nose. "Rory!" she cried.

"Out here," called his deeply familiar masculine voice.

Her heart pounding from ghoulish images, she saw him soaking in the sunken bath. With steam rising, he blurred as though he occupied another dimension. Last night's lovemaking now seemed as indistinct and far away.

They had both been sucked into the illusion that the Porsche was fast enough to outrun reality. But their world had followed them, creeping down the coast and up the mountain to surround them like the fog.

She swung her legs off the side of the bed, found her robe, and wrapped herself from neck to ankles. She went to the door and stepped out, her feet cold on the slate tile. "I dreamed my father died."

"No!" Rory cleaved out of the water in one smooth motion. He stood naked and dripping before her, every woman's dream.

Though tempted to slide back into their weekend fantasy, she couldn't do it. "I need to go home and check on him. We have to leave now."

His hands were wet on her velvet-clad arms, the damp soaking through. "It was a dream." He tried to gather her against his bare chest.

She resisted. "I'm sorry, but it feels so real."

Rory nodded toward the bedside phone. "Call him."

Almost stumbling, she made it inside and raised the receiver in a shaking hand.

Hotel Nikko's operator told her John Grant and Tom Barrett had checked out the night before. No one answered at home or at Tom's house. Cellular customer Grant was "out of range," as were Tom and Wendy. It was far too early to think her father and Tom were at the office on a Saturday, but she tried there.

While she made the calls, Rory slipped on the inn's white terry robe and paced, his sinewy feet leaving deep prints in the thick pile carpet. His hands shoved his black hair into disarray. When she placed the phone back in the cradle for the last time, he turned to her. "He's all right. You know he is."

She fought tears. "I wish I did. But Dad and I have always been so close; maybe the dream was a sign he's in trouble."

Though Rory came and gripped her shoulder, urging her

to believe she was overreacting, the image of her father's pale and lifeless face seemed too real.

Rory drove the Porsche hard on the northbound curves of the Big Sur Highway. By daylight, the rugged mountain coast showed off its splendor, jade cliffs slashed by veins of white quartz, turquoise swells of sea . . .

This wasn't what he'd expected from this morning. He and Mariah should have made love, breakfasted in bed, made love again, and showered together, soaping each other's backs. Instead, they'd crammed their newly purchased belongings back into the Carmel shop sacks and hit the road.

Passing back through the appealing seaside village, he wished he'd tried harder to talk her out of cutting their weekend short. He didn't want to take her back where news crews pursued her and John Grant hid out from the press in a hotel. Rather, he yearned to keep her safe with him.

Unfortunately, that was the stuff of fantasy. On Monday, it would be back to Grant Development for her, and DCI for him, where a slow poison ate at the joy and pride he'd had in his work at Golden Builders.

One thing he did know. First, both he and Mariah had to tell their fathers in no uncertain terms that they were going to see each other. Maybe he'd sworn off love, seeing it as the equivalent to handing a woman a blade to slice him with, decided on bachelorhood to keep out of a hopeless situation like his mother was in . . . but if he and Mariah did not explore the "what if," as he'd called it, they would compound their past mistake of breaking up. As for conflict of interest between Grant and DCI, though it would detract from the pleasure of sharing his work with her, he and Mariah could make a vow not to talk shop.

No, he didn't know where this was headed, but after last night, Rory knew he wanted her in his bed . . . and his life.

Two hours later, as Rory pulled onto Vallejo Street where he lived, Mariah wished she could have kept her part of their pact to escape. Though he had been quiet on the drive, she could tell from the aggressive way that he accelerated and braked that Rory was upset at her caving in to doubts.

In his garage, he helped transfer her things to her car. The packing done, she turned to him.

"Thanks for . . ." For sailing, dinner, a night in paradise? Things other couples took for granted. Blindly, she reached to open her car door.

He put a hand out and pulled her to him. She couldn't really feel him through her new leather jacket.

"Oh, God, Rory, what's going to happen to us?"

He took her in his arms and squeezed her so tightly she believed he was as desperate as she. "All I know is this isn't the end. You've told your father, and I'll tell mine."

Getting into her car, she blinked back tears. "I just pray

Dad's all right."

He tapped at her side window, and she lowered it. "Let me come with you."

She looked up at him and saw what must be truth in his gaze. What different roads might they have traveled if he had taken this attitude eight years ago? She didn't want to leave him, but a confrontation with her father was something she needed to handle alone. The only way to make amends was to brew her and him a good strong cup of Oolong, to sit with him on a bench in his well-tended garden and talk.

Mariah shook her head. "I'll handle it. We'll need to discuss . . . things."

Rory cupped her cheek, stroked her skin with his thumb, and stepped back to let her go. "After you see him, call me. Instead of this hiding out, let's turn the tables and go someplace the columns will see us together."

Buoyed by Rory's wanting to be seen in public with her, she pulled out of his garage. However, as she searched the Saturday afternoon traffic for a news van, she felt the weight of trouble once more descend. She, her dad, and Tom might have evaded the media's questions for a day, but the Fourth Estate would not lose their taste for blood overnight.

Sure enough, as she turned off Vallejo onto Mason she noticed a dark sedan distinguished by a flaking paint job on the hood pull in behind her. Something in the way the driver looked at her vehicle, an intentness, put her on guard. Perhaps he was a reporter, out cruising without a satellite crew. On the other hand, Tom's suspicions about the accident came back to haunt her.

A narrow-faced man in his late twenties or early thirties, she inventoried, dark hair pulled back from his face as though he wore a ponytail. The car was an older model Taurus.

She sped up, changed lanes, and took the next turn onto Broadway. He followed.

Without signaling, she made another turn onto Stockton and headed into Chinatown. This time the guy, if he were pursuing her, missed it.

In the heart of the Oriental quarter, slow traffic caught Mariah. Half a dozen times, she braked for jaywalking pedestrians. Horns honked, and fists were raised. Forced to a crawl, she lowered her window to cool her heated cheeks. Succulent aromas of seafood and rich sauces blended with salt air and car exhaust. Souvenir shops displayed porcelain tea sets and exquisite paper lanterns. Open-air markets sold live tilapia, shellfish on ice, and whole ducks suspended by their feet. It was difficult to believe she could be followed through this bustle, but she kept glancing behind her.

Finally, she managed to cut around several blocks. Wondering now if she'd imagined the whole thing, she zigzagged a few more times. When a check of her rearview mirror said she was clear, she turned south toward Stonestown.

As she drew closer to her father's, she wasn't feeling as good about her stalwart stand that she and Rory were going to be together. Rather, a wave of guilt lapped at her. She could have called home last night, tried to smooth things over, instead of shopping, dining, and hot tubbing. Parking in the drive, she thought how difficult facing him was going to be, her only excuse that she'd been under Rory's spell when she made that quick, cold call.

Straightening her shoulders, she got out of her car. A peek in the garage window told her Dad's wasn't there. With a frown, she checked the time and found it half past ten. On the way to the front door, she plucked the Friday and Saturday *Chronicle*s from under the arborvitae.

Inside, the high-pitched wail of the security system greeted her. She silenced it by entering the date of John's marriage to Catharine. The quiet sense of the house, dust motes floating, confirmed that she was alone.

Without pausing to look at the chessboard in the entry, Mariah went into the kitchen, lifted the phone and dialed. Cellular customer Grant was still out of range. No one home at Tom and Wendy's. She tried John's direct number at Grant Development, Tom's line, and the one in the conference room. When there was no answer, a renewed prickle of unease touched her spine.

She went to the sink and drew a glass of water. The ruby Rory had given her sparkled in the sun coming through the east window over the sink. Not an hour since she'd seen him, and already she felt an aching void. This rising certainty that something had gone wrong with Dad compounded it. No one could have reached her, for she'd put her purse and phone in Rory's trunk when they went sailing.

She called Tom Barrett's cell. He answered on the second ring, sounding worse than he had at the funeral. "Where've you been, Mariah? I tried to call."

"My phone wasn't on."

"I knew you'd want me to find you," he plowed on. "I even called Kiki Campbell last night and got Rory's cell number."

The sound of the ringing phone, so out of place in the forest darkness, returned to jar her. "You called last night?"

"Around ten."

Her creeping dread intensified. "Where are you?"

"Cal State Med Center, out smoking in the courtyard."

Her heart a trip hammer, her palm suddenly slick on the phone receiver, she heard her voice speak with surprising clarity. "Something's happened to Dad."

"God, Mariah, an hour after he talked to you yesterday, he had a heart attack."

As she barreled down Highway 1 past the Stonestown Galleria, Mariah deserved a dozen speeding tickets. She tried to keep her mind on driving, but an image of her father in a coffin floated between her and the rest of the world.

Tom waited for her outside the closed double doors of the ICU, his expression grave. "He's all right," she insisted.

"He's in surgery. A few minutes ago he took a turn for the worse, and they decided to crack his chest."

Taking her arm, Tom guided her to a waiting room where families sat vigil amid scattered newspapers and foam take-out boxes.

Mariah sank into a chair. "This isn't right. People have heart attacks and come home the next morning. They use that balloon thing to clear out your arteries."

Tom didn't answer.

Once at home, she'd turned on a medical TV show as a surgeon dumped a load of ice onto a human heart to stop it. With the chest covered in plastic sheeting and the ribs pulled apart, it hadn't seemed to be happening to a real person. Yet, beyond those swinging doors, the chest she'd been cradled against as a little girl lay cleaved in two. The arms that had swung her high bore taped-in needles. His lips lay slack, those that had smiled at her ten thousand times. Each time she'd taken for granted ten thousand more.

Hours passed. She kept upright through determination and vending machine caffeine. Tom went periodically to join the banished smokers outside, wreaths of cigarette smoke surrounding the joyless gathering. This was too much for him . . . and for her. First Charley, and now this.

Dad had to live.

Always when they were parted, she had a feeling he was out there somewhere, asleep or awake. Now, with his heart stopped, or God forbid, because the doctors had lost the battle, thinking of him felt like sending a message into the void.

Day crept into evening. Each time Mariah consulted her watch, she became more convinced it was running backward. The ruby from Carmel began to remind her of blood.

She pulled off the ring and put it in her purse.

The silence between her and Tom was by now deafening.

Though neither spoke of Rory, she felt like a pariah. If there were a higher power that lent an ear to human suffering or some pattern to fate, then she must make a bargain before her father was taken.

"Let him stay here," she thought with bowed head. "If he lives, I promise I'll never see Rory again." Painful the penance might be, but not too great a price to pay.

At half past ten, a slight, dark-haired doctor with liquid eyes came in wearing blood-spattered greens. He went to Tom, who introduced Dr. Patel.

"Your father is in recovery," the doctor said. "For the moment, he's critical and I won't mince words. If he makes it though the next few days, he'll have a long rehabilitation ahead."

With a sidelong glance at Tom, she had to ask. "Can you tell me what might have brought on his attack?"

"If I could tell you, I'd be a god. A heavy meal, a hormone fluctuation . . . "

"Anger?" Mariah asked.

Dr. Patel smiled gently beneath his silky dark moustache. "Every family member I meet asks, but who knows what happened last night to put things over the edge? All I can tell you is his arteries did not get plugged overnight."

"Thank you," she murmured.

The doctor left her with Tom, who wiped his tear-stained cheeks and turned to her. "I know why you were asking."

"Please," she whispered.

He shook his shaggy head, rebuke in his normally

smiling blue eyes. "Girl, I don't know what you were thinking . . . a Campbell."

Hot tears welled. Now that Dad had come through surgery she must make good on her pact with fate. "It was a terrible mistake," she told Tom. "I won't see Rory again."

Late Sunday night Mariah let herself into her apartment, weighted with exhaustion. She had only felt able to leave the hospital because her father remained unconscious. A red light blinked on her answering machine, reminding her that Rory had asked her to call yesterday; he'd planned on dinner. Now, it seemed as though she'd had that conversation in an alternate universe.

Unable to bear hearing his voice if he had called, she walked into her bedroom and closed the door.

When her head finally rested on the pillow, she expected to close her eyes and see horrific images of surgery. Instead, she saw the man she'd called "Daddy" when she was small.

Even then, his hair was prematurely salt and pepper, giving him a distinguished look that made her proud of him at grade school functions. In the evenings after homework, they played Chinese checkers, or in summer, badminton on the back lawn. When she reached the seventh grade, he taught her chess.

In high school, she won tournaments, finding most opponents no challenge after playing her father. In addition to the board at home in his hall, since she was at Grant Development he'd set up a game in his office so she could go in, see what move he'd made, and counter. Their first match had gone on for weeks when both were caught up in projects.

But it wasn't about games, or their mutual love for building. After Catharine died, it had been the two of them against the universe.

If he died, how could she go on?

Once more, she regretted her defiant impulse in flaunting her renewed relationship with Rory. Dad had only her best interests in mind when he warned against Davis Campbell's son.

Yet, closing her eyes, she saw Rory at his boat's helm, smiling while spray wet his cheeks and curled his dark hair. His voice echoed in her head.

When I heard about the accident, I ran through the streets like a wild man . . . I never bought you flowers when you deserved a garden. I never gave you a ring.

Her hands made fists on the sheets.

Across her bedroom, the glow of a streetlight illuminated the empty jeweler's box the ruby ring had come in. She got out of bed and found her purse, rescued the ring from rubbing against dimes and quarters, and placed it on the velvet cushion. Even as she closed the lid, she wanted to slide the gold band on her finger where Rory had placed it.

Yesterday, he had said it wasn't over.

Getting back in bed, she envisioned them together, lying close with his bare chest pressed to her back. He would come to her if he knew what happened; hold her so she wouldn't feel alone.

But she must not think of breaking her bargain with fate. Her father must wake, and when he did, how could she tell him she'd laughed when Rory threw his cell phone in the creek?

*O*n the Monday morning after her father's surgery, Mariah entered the Grant conference room for the weekly meeting. She wore a black pants suit for the appearance of authority and had pulled her hair back as severely as she could manage.

Word about John's illness had traveled through the senior staff over the weekend. Public relations director April Perry had toned down her usually bright clothing, appearing in gray wool gabardine. Her helmet of reddish hair remained motionless when she moved. Corpulent chief counsel Ed Snowden wore a weary expression. Arnold Benton looked shell-shocked, making him seem more beige than usual.

What had her father seen in him, to put him in charge of

the company finances?

Tom Barrett came in with beads of perspiration on his forehead as though he'd rushed to arrive on time. Expecting his effort meant he would chair the meeting, Mariah was surprised to see him sink into a chair and defer to her.

When she moved to the head of the table, Arnold sat straighter and bristled.

Keeping things simple, she made sure all projects were moving forward, but accepted and encouraged a slower pace this week. "Let everyone in your departments know we'll keep them up to the minute on John's condition. And thank them for how well they've avoided the press since the accident."

The team murmured assent.

Looking around at them, Mariah said, "What can anyone here tell me about a missing workman from the Grant Plaza site? I've heard a guy went AWOL after the accident."

Arnold Benton glared at her. "Conspiracy theories?"

Mariah's heartbeat accelerated. How quick he was to attack as soon as he believed her father wasn't able to protect her.

April Perry broke in. "Manuel Zaragoza. Male. Age 28. Five feet eleven, brown eyes, at last report wears his hair in a ponytail."

Mariah frowned.

April went on. "Employed as a welder by a subcontractor on the Grant Plaza project. Rents a room in a private home, answered an ad for it. His things are still there, but he hasn't been seen for a week."

"Missing for a week?" Mariah stared at April. "What are

you saying? That the accident was sabotage?"

"Just stating the facts." April's tone was expressionless. "Though the police and everyone else think it was an accident, of course they're looking to question Zaragoza. I've got a PI trying to find the guy." She tapped a CD case beside her on the table. "I'll give you a copy of his first report."

"A private investigator?" Arnold asked. "Isn't that carrying things a bit far?"

April ignored him. "Zaragoza holds a California driver's license under a defunct address in Oakland, leases a Ford Taurus."

Mariah tried to keep alarm off her face. The description matched that of the man she thought had followed her in traffic. "If he did something to cause the cable to part . . ."

She looked at company engineer Ramsey Rhodes, a studious sandy-haired man who kept his own counsel except when pressed. The fact that he was excellent at what he did more than made up for his taciturn nature.

This morning Ramsey deliberated long enough for Mariah's alarm to escalate. At last, he reported, "The hoist company is studying the point of failure on the cable; we've got an independent lab as well. Anything fishy, which I doubt, it'll turn up."

With a confidence she didn't feel, Mariah said, "It sounds as though you have it covered."

After asking if anyone had other business, she adjourned the meeting. Tom, who had not said a word, came to her. "I'm going to the hospital at lunch. Want to ride along?"

Arnold materialized at Tom's side. "I wouldn't mind joining you." To his credit, he sounded worried.

Tom glanced at her. Apparently reading her expression, he told Arnold, "John's in no condition to have a lot of visitors . . . he wouldn't even know you're there."

"I see." Arnold gave her a dark look that said he blamed her for shutting him off from John.

Her father's words came back to her, how he hoped the two of them would get along. Was there an agenda she didn't understand, some twisted matchmaking or, God forbid, Arnold was being groomed to be her right hand man when John and Tom retired?

The room emptied, but April stayed behind and handed over the CD with the investigator's report.

"Thanks." When April did not turn to leave, Mariah gave her a curious look.

"Did you forget?" she asked. "The *Chronicle* reporter is waiting to interview you."

"I did forget." Mariah had allowed April to make the appointment last Thursday before "On The Spot" broke into Charley's viewing, and before the press staked them out on Friday. "Do you still think I should do it?"

April leaned a hip against the conference table, her slim arms crossed over her simple yet elegant jacket. "It's up to you. The *Chronicle* has run a reasonably fair story every day, all by the reporter waiting for you."

Mariah sighed. "All right, then."

"I think you should do this in John's office, rather than

the conference room," the public relations director suggested.

Having already taken over her father's role in the meeting, Mariah accepted this next step.

In John's corner office one wall of windows faced Market Street, and the other had a filtered view of the Bay Bridge. "Take his chair," April suggested. "Get out some papers and look busy while I fetch the reporter."

Mariah walked into the room, made emptier by the knowledge Dad wasn't down the hall or visiting a site. One of the ficus plants he insisted on caring for himself had dropped leaves since the cleaning crew had been in. On the windowsill, his collection of African violets sported a bottom row of wilting foliage he would have pinched off first thing this morning.

She stopped by the chessboard and noted her last move had not been countered.

With a sigh, she moved on reluctant feet and took John's empty chair. Tall windows framed the building where DCI officed, centered in the view. Mariah had never given it a thought before, but when her father came back — she would not consider an alternative — she'd try and talk him into trading space with Tom on the other side of the floor. It couldn't be good for him to be constantly reminded of his enemy.

The office door opened, catching her without the guise of working.

The thirty-something reporter who entered with April was pretty in a foreign sort of way. Her dark curly hair and skin reminded Mariah of the reddish gold of horehound candy. Her eyes were apple green. "Dee Carpentier." With a butter-soft smile, she put out her hand.

Mariah stayed on guard. This woman might have her claws sheathed, but she suspected they were made of steel. Though Dee's stories about Grant Plaza had been fair to date, under her by-line a lot of reputations had been ruined.

April indicated a wing chair and offered refreshments.

Dee declined. She flipped open a note pad, rummaged in her portfolio, and placed a small tape recorder on the desk. "With your permission."

April reached into her jacket pocket and positioned a higher tech machine alongside. "With yours."

The next minutes were a blur. Mariah tried to keep her thoughts together and answer professionally.

Yes, John Grant was in the hospital.

Dee wished for a speedy recovery.

Certainly, the Grant Plaza accident had been a terrible tragedy.

Dee expressed sympathy.

Of course, the company regretted and mourned the loss of Charley Barrett and Andrew Green. They had no idea what had happened, pending inspections.

Dee crossed her slim and elegant legs, her taupe skirt riding higher as she leaned forward. "What can you tell me about your evading the press last week?"

"I can tell you about that," April fielded. Mariah felt she should be fighting her own battles, but as PR was April's specialty, she let her go on. "It was on my advice as well as our chief counsel that the principals avoid giving indiscriminate statements. Once the facts are in, cooler heads can prevail."

Dee's focus on Mariah was unbroken. "I was referring to you personally. I understand Grant Development and DCI have a bitter rivalry, yet you and Davis Campbell's son drove off Friday afternoon in his Porsche."

April's porcelain brow furrowed.

Mariah swallowed, then wished she hadn't. A good reporter would note that telltale dip of her Adam's apple.

"Where did you get that?" April asked sharply. She did not look at Mariah.

"I sometimes exchange information with Julio Castillo at 'On The Spot.' It works since we're not in direct competition." Dee's smile was no longer soft.

"They haven't run anything," Mariah argued. "They must not be confident of their information."

"They're sure." Dee poised her notepad and pen. "So, where did you and Rory spend the night?"

Their secret hideaway in the Ventana wilderness now seemed like a dream.

Mariah rose and pushed back John's chair. "My private life is not the subject here."

The reporter stared at her a moment longer. "I think your private life will be public very soon." She stowed her pad in her purse, retrieved her tape recorder, and said politely, "Thank you for your time, Ms. Grant."

"I'll see you out," April said coldly. Mariah felt certain that on her way through the doorway the public relations director threw her a look of condemnation.

Late Monday morning, Rory studied computer plots he'd drawn for an assisted living center. His father hoped to use it in a development overlooking the ocean in Daly City, but the tract there was too small without buying an adjoining piece of state land.

This was where Rory's calculated courtship of Sylvia Chatsworth was supposed to come in. The Senator could get the land green-lighted for development, and myriad other future favors, especially if the relationship between Davis Campbell and Lawrence Chatsworth was cemented by their children's marriage.

Rory found he clutched a pencil so hard he was in danger of snapping it. Against his will he found himself comparing the Senator's daughter to John Grant's.

Flamboyant and bold, beneath Sylvia's occasional bursts of temperament was the closely guarded secret of a little girl's heart. He did like her, even if she failed to move him.

But Mariah . . .

A laughing girl feeding the gulls off the stern of *Privateer*, a woman grieving the loss of her friend Charley, an enchantress, sleek and naked in the hot bath at Ventana. His need for her had an edge to it, far different from when their younger selves simply took what they desired.

Friday night at Ventana he'd been transported back to

that state, and in the taking he'd wanted as never before to give. It drove him crazy that she'd insisted on coming home.

Even more so, since she'd not returned the calls he made to her apartment. On the other hand, he'd failed to get her cell number and hadn't wanted to leave a message at her father's. She had wanted to handle John alone, and Rory needed to give her that chance. Perhaps she'd stayed over in Stonestown, or the press had forced them to move to a different hotel.

With regret for their missed Saturday and Sunday, he decided to call her at Grant Development. They'd meet for lunch at a steakhouse on Market, where there'd be lots of opportunity to be seen together during the busy noon hour.

He reached for the phone to call her. It rang, making him jump, but he picked up and tried to sound even. "Rory Campbell."

"Get in here," his father said.

Irritated, Rory replaced the receiver. He'd been pleased back in March and April that things seemed to be going well, but since Davis's abrupt personality change, his patience was wearing thin. He was almost tempted to ignore the imperial summons.

Yet, professionalism demanded that if he was on the company payroll, he must answer to the company chairman.

Taking his time, he went down four doors and paused on the threshold, enjoying the view. The fortieth floor corner offered a panorama spanning the northwest, the Golden Gate Bridge like a child's model. Across the Bay, clouds wreathed the forested shoulders of Mt. Tamalpais.

Ignoring the vista that until recently seemed to please him, Davis glared from behind a gleaming black lacquer desk the size of a queen-sized bed. His decorator had selected shining black wood again in the coffee table and for the frames of silkscreen prints.

Rising with a brisk motion, Davis demanded, "Where were you this weekend? I called your cell a dozen times."

"I went down to Big Sur."

"With Sylvia?"

"No."

Davis's eyes narrowed. "I hope you're not imagining yourself with Mariah Grant again."

It wasn't imagination. Every minute, from when Mariah had come to his townhouse to go sailing, through the incredible heights they had scaled in the king bed at Ventana, had been real.

He straightened his back. "Where my imagination begins, your business ends."

His father came toward him, invading his space. "Don't be flip. That woman is dangerous."

Though shocked, Rory did not retreat. "Dangerous? You think she'll steal my wallet when I'm sleeping?"

A pained expression came over his father's haughty face. "Tell me it hasn't gone that far."

"You're the last person I'd tell."

Davis closed his eyes. "You have no idea," he said in a low and passionate voice, "what a woman like that can do to a man."

"Maybe I don't know, but I'm going to find out," he declared.

His father took several steps to a black leather couch and leaned against its back. Coatless in a starched shirt with one of his two-hundred dollar Italian silk ties, he crossed his arms over his chest. "I should know it's no use telling a child what a father learned the hard way."

Before Rory could protest at being talked down to, Davis spread his hands. "I know, I know. You're a man now. Older than I was when I learned my lesson." His gaze wandered out to where the business district's spires rose to the sky.

"Once, I wanted to marry for love." He spoke in a low tone, reverently. "She was beautiful . . . in body and soul. Even after nearly thirty years, I still believe she could have saved me."

Rory's thoughts whirled. If his mother had been second choice, then perhaps that explained what had always been lacking in his parents' marriage.

"What happened?" he asked softly.

Davis's fist clenched on his thigh, his face contorted. "She died."

"Father, I . . ."

"Mr. Campbell," Davis's secretary announced from the speakerphone, "Thaddeus Walker of First California, line one."

With a swiftness that astonished Rory, his father re-donned his cloak of invincibility and took the call. "Thaddeus!" he enthused.

Rory went to the window. Though it was Monday, a few dedicated windsurfers and sailors had their crafts skimming over the white-capped Bay. He longed to be out there with them.

"The hell you say?" Davis said. Then he listened to the person on the other end of the call for a moment. "Friday night," he mused, then, "All right, thank you for telling me."

Hanging up slowly, he made his way to his black leather throne and sat. "Our fortunes have taken an unexpected turn," he said in a tight voice.

"How's that?"

"John Grant had a bypass operation. It'll be a wonder if he lives."

Rory's heart set up a hard thudding. Mariah's nightmare of her father's body . . . "You call that fortune?" he gasped. "Are you out of your mind?"

"I was speaking of our business fortune." Davis's black eyes were opaque. "Do you really think I'd wish someone dead?"

Only moments ago, Rory had been taken in by a tale of ancient woe. But he must have imagined the vulnerability and pain. "Yes." He put a match to the tenuous bridge between him and his father. "I believe you might be glad your old enemy lies at the edge of the world."

He turned on his heel and left Davis Campbell's domain. And though he phoned Grant Development and identified himself to the receptionist, he was told Mariah was not there. In answer to his query about which hospital John was in, he was told, "I'm afraid that after all the recent negative publicity, Mr. Grant's location is confidential."

Mariah kissed her father goodnight as though he were aware of her presence. The doctors said she should assume he heard every word and felt each touch, a not-so-subtle warning against negative commentary on his prognosis. With a last survey of the onscreen display of his vital signs, she tucked the sheets more snugly around him and left his CCU cubicle.

When she entered her apartment, her answering machine message light once more blinked. This morning she'd erased the ones from the weekend without listening.

Please, she thought, let it be a solicitation from the county Republican Party, a charity with a truck conveniently on her street, anybody except the hospital with bad news about her father.

Or Rory.

She crossed to the phone and pushed the button.

"I heard about your dad," his deep voice enunciated. "Call me, no matter what time you get in."

She stared at the phone as though he might materialize through it. Just the thought of being with Rory made the heavy something inside her chest struggle to lift the weight away.

But what of her father? When he was finally coherent, to him it would be only an hour since she'd told him she was with his enemy's son.

A stab of her finger erased the message.

At ten-thirty, the phone rang. She almost dropped her hairbrush. In the bathroom mirror, her eyes looked enormous, ringed with dark smudges. The cut over her left eye still looked raw and angry.

The phone shrilled again. She padded to the kitchen to listen.

"Mariah?" Rory sounded as close as the next room. "If you're there, pick up."

It was all she could do to stand still, her feet bare on the chill ceramic tile.

"I guess you're at the hospital." He hesitated. "I hope he's okay."

Everything in her wanted to rush across the room and pick up the phone. But, for Dad's sake, she forced herself to walk back to her bath and finish getting ready for bed.

Once there, sleep was impossible.

She found a tapestry of Charley's funeral fluttering on the backs of her eyelids. The incongruous perfection of the blue day, the marble angel dragged to earth by grief. The ache of loss swelled in her throat. How was she going to manage without her sounding board, her class clown, the one who shared her childhood memories of kick the can, hide and seek, and Halloween pranks?

Remembering Charley's love for playing cards, she knew it was all a game of chance. It no longer mattered whether he had won or not; he'd lost the most important lottery when he stepped onto the Grant Plaza hoist. And if fate frowned on her father, by the end of the week she might see him in a real coffin rather than a nightmare one. The doctors had said he reacted badly to the cocktail of anesthesia and drugs and the outcome was still uncertain.

It didn't assuage Mariah's guilt to know that the accident, if it had been an accident, had put him under huge stress. Not an issue that he was taking responsibility for the death of his best friend's son. Useless the words of Dr. Patel, who said family members always worried about triggering a heart attack. Deep inside, she believed she and Rory had pushed him over the edge.

The phone's shrill alarm nearly catapulted her out of bed. Red letters on the clock radio said eleven-fifteen.

Her pulse raced. Terrified that an impersonal hospital voice waited to shatter her, she threw back the covers and went once more into the kitchen.

The answering machine clicked as it took the call.

"Mariah," Rory said fervently. His rough breathing reminded her of being in his arms. "I've called some of the hospitals, but I haven't located where he is."

Her nails drilled crescents into her palms. His ragged uncertainty, the implication that John might no longer be in a hospital but a mortuary . . .

Slowly, she crossed the room and picked up the receiver. "He's in Cal State."

"I tried there."

Twisting her free hand in the phone cord, she felt the ache in her chest start to ease at the sound of his voice. "I asked that the switchboard not list him. Because of the press."

"It wasn't in any news I saw . . . yet." He paused. "I'm coming over."

"No!" she gasped.

"What?" He sounded incredulous. "Don't tell me you don't need me. Christ, I need to see you, hold you . . ."

She couldn't. If he came, her promise to a God or the fates that might be merciful would be broken. "Please," she begged. "Not tonight."

A beat of silence.

"All right, Mariah," Rory said quietly. "Not tonight."

Rounding a hospital hallway corner near the CCU the next day, Mariah found Dee Carpentier of the *Chronicle* standing in the hall. The reporter was jotting notes on her little pad.

Mariah strode forward. "What are you doing here?"

"I came to check out a rumor your father was in there." Dee directed her pale eyes toward the wide swinging doors. "Since you're here, may I assume it's true?"

"Where do you get your rumors? Julio Castillo?"

Dee pressed her generous lips together. "You know we reporters like to protect our sources, but in this case I'll tell you. Davis Campbell phoned to tell me what happened. He thought it would make a good addition to my series on your company's trouble. So . . . is it true?"

"Davis Campbell wouldn't know the truth if it hit him in the head," Mariah blurted. God, Rory must have told him where John was.

"Your father's not listed as a patient," Dee supplied. "Are you saying it's not true?"

Mariah hesitated. If she lied, Dee would find out, making the story even more exciting.

With a sigh, she relented. "He's here."

Another of Dee's deceptive smiles spread over her tawny features. Mariah looked toward the doors about to open for a limited thirty-minute visitation period.

"Please," she said. "Don't go in there." She could imagine the graphic description of John lying helpless with tubes and the respirator, equipment lights blinking. Or, God forbid, the reporter might even take a photo with one of those mini digitals. "What about the healthcare privacy laws?"

"When the unit doors open, anyone can walk in. If I'm challenged, I'm looking for someone who turns out not to be here." Dee gave her a bargaining look.

"If you promise to stay out," Mariah said. "I'll give you some information."

The reporter inclined her head and gestured toward a quiet corner not far from the doors.

A few minutes later, having been told the rudiments of John's condition and about his surgery, true to her word Dee was gone. Mariah turned toward the CCU.

Expecting to see her father lying still as death, she approached his bedside warily. This time, weary gray eyes watched her.

"Dad!" She took his bruised and fragile-looking hand, noting fewer wires and catheters and not as much data on the monitor over his bed.

Pale and drawn, he struggled to speak. "Feel . . . like someone took an axe . . . to my chest." He showed her a button he could push for more pain meds in his IV mix. "Damn thing. On a timer."

"Don't talk," she said.

"Campbell . . ."

Shame heated her cheeks. "Dad, I'm sorry." There was so much more she wanted to say, but she feared upsetting him. "It didn't work out with Rory," she assured.

"Not . . . surprised."

"It was something I had to find out." Now was when she should confirm her promise not to see Rory, but it stuck in her throat.

"Don't want you hurt . . . again," he got out.

It was too late for that, but she managed, "No. It won't happen again."

Trying to regain her composure, she opened her purse and brought out the picture of Catharine she'd brought from the kitchen counter in Stonestown. Knowing John must have willed his wife to stay with him the way Mariah now prayed for him struck fear in her heart.

His exhausted face brightened, and he tried to reach for his wife's photo.

"Rest now," she soothed.

Lapsing into silence, he closed his eyes. A few minutes later, his chest rose and fell evenly.

For the rest of the precious allotted half-hour, Mariah

looked from the photo of Catharine, frozen forever in youth, to the character lines in John's face. Her mother must have been something for a man to love her for so many years.

When the loudspeaker announced the visiting period was over, she looked at the clock with the same reluctance she saw on the faces of other family members and friends. She bent and kissed Dad's cheek and his pale eyelids trembled like a moth's wings. As she had each time she'd been forced to leave his side, she memorized his features in case it was the last time. A snippet of a child's prayer . . . if he should die before he woke . . .

Wiping tears from her cheeks, she went through the wide double doors of the CCU.

Outside, Rory leaned against the wall.

Her fist went to her mouth. She should have expected him, but the suddenness was a shock. He looked as though he'd not slept, bluish shadows beneath his eyes.

Thinking only of protecting her father, she waved him away. "He mustn't see us together," she insisted despite the closing doors. "You could give him another attack."

Rory straightened. "I didn't give him the first one." With a glance at the crowded waiting room, he nodded toward the elevators. "We'll talk over coffee."

She planted her feet. "No."

Rory might attract her with a power that left her weak; the only man who made her tremble with need and fulfillment, but how could she trust him?

"You told your father what hospital Dad was in," she

accused. "Davis called Dee Carpentier at the *Chronicle* and tipped her."

Rory's jaw set. "I swear to God I have neither seen nor spoken to my father since last night."

"How else could he know?"

"He's been closeted in his office making calls. You'll have to blame it on one of his many sources."

Mariah hesitated. Once more, she wanted to believe him, but . . .

Rory took her shoulders, his hands warm against the hospital air conditioning. "Talk to me. Then, if you still want me to, I promise I'll go."

Her determination weakened at the distress in his dark eyes. He deserved to understand. When he realized how direct a role they'd played in Dad's heart attack, he'd see they couldn't go on. With a last look over her shoulder toward the CCU, she let Rory lead her into the elevator.

In the hospital cafeteria, he bought coffee in paper cups, doctoring hers with the precise amount of creamer she'd always taken. When they were seated at a large round table in the nearly vacant room, he looked at her with concern. "How is he?"

"Still touch and go."

"I'm sorry." He glanced toward the steam tables. "Have you eaten anything? Slept?"

His gaze came back to rest on her.

She ducked her head and tried to straighten her hair.

He reached, and took an errant strand between his

fingertips. For a moment he held it, then tucked it behind her shoulder. "I am sorry about your dad. Ever since this morning when I heard, I feared, too, that something we did . . ." He trailed off, then went on, "But we can't really be to blame for John's illness. Did he watch his diet? Did he exercise? Isn't he a workaholic?"

"His work is all that matters to him." She faced the issue that conspired to drive them apart. "And your father is laughing right now, thinking he's beaten Dad. Maybe you didn't tell Davis what hospital, I don't know . . ."

"I did not tell him," Rory said, too evenly.

Once more, despite the damning evidence, her instinct said to believe him.

But not his father. "Davis calling in the *Chronicle* to make matters worse for Grant Development is despicable."

Rory's expression hardened. "I came here for you," he said. "And because I needed to see you. Let's don't fight."

"I'm not fighting. I'm telling you the way it is. I told my father about us, and look what happened."

"He could have gotten sick any time, and you know it." Rory gripped his cup and sloshed coffee onto the table. Looking down at the spreading stain, he reached for napkins. "I've already told my father to mind his own business about us. When we go public, it'll only make it more clear."

She'd waited eight years for him to stand up to Davis and win her trust . . . but with Dad near death, it was too late. "There is no us."

"The hell there isn't." He crumpled the stained napkins.

She shook her head. "When he woke up, the first thing he did was start up about you. Don't you see, every time we try this it goes wrong?"

"You think what we did last Friday was wrong?" His voice rose. "My God, for me there was never anything more right!"

Though she wanted to go into his arms and let him unravel the hard knot of hurt in her, she couldn't shake the image of her father's relief when she had promised not to see Rory. "I can't upset him like this. I told him we wouldn't be together again."

The lines beside Rory's mouth carved deeper; a crease slashed between his brows. With horror, she watched the shutters she knew so well in his father come down over his eyes.

"Very well," he said.

Miserably, Mariah watched him shove his way between tables and pass through the outside door.

*N*ine days later, Mariah's father came home from the hospital. She arranged for Mrs. Schertz, a kindly retired nurse, to take care of him while she spent days at Grant Development. To cover night duty, she moved back home, calling it "temporary."

Though she'd visited often in the intervening years, now she found the bungalow somehow shrunken, as though the walls of her old bedroom were closer together.

On the first Saturday morning after he came home, Mariah dressed in her oldest well-washed jeans and tired sneakers. "I'm going to take care of your plants and get those weeds out of your garden."

"You're a stickler for perfection like me." He moved toward his recliner with evident care for the stitched-up incision down the center of his chest. If she found the house smaller than she'd remembered, that was nothing compared to the way the past few weeks had changed him. At least fifteen pounds lighter, his pajamas and robe hung on him. The furrows beside his nose cut deep grooves.

While he rested, Mariah tended to his houseplants, taking the smaller ones to the sink for a deep watering. She dusted the leaves of his rubber plant and picked fallen impatiens blossoms from the carpet without disturbing John's pile of papers and magazines on the floor. The *Chronicle* stories of Dee Carpentier continued to run as a series.

Though construction was a dangerous business — personal injury lawyers advertised on billboards to handle on-the-job accidents — and fatalities did happen, Dee wrote, the Grant accident was different in its spectacular nature. People related on a visceral level to free-falling from great height. Especially so for John Grant, the paper suggested, who had a heart attack after burying one of the victims.

Mariah wished she could censor his reading material.

The one strange note was that neither Dee nor "On The Spot" had gone public with anything on her and Rory. After the reporter's prediction that her private life was about to be aired like soiled laundry, she read the *Chronicle* each morning with trepidation and watched the news show every evening, expecting images of Rory shutting Julio Castillo down at Charley's viewing, or of her driving into Rory's garage.

She could only hope his threat of lawsuits was keeping them at bay. Yet, there were other possibilities. The most benign was that the media's spying had discovered she and Rory had not seen each other again. For, after he had walked away from her in the hospital cafeteria, she had not heard a word. And, of course, with Dad still so ill, she would not contact him.

The other, more dire scenario was that the reporters were biding their time, following Rory. One of these days, Julio Castillo might get his payback with a juicy story on roving playboy Campbell, using footage of him and Mariah as well as Sylvia Chatsworth, or whatever woman he had now taken up with.

Despite that she and Rory could never be, the thought of him with another woman brought tears, blurring the ivy plant she was setting down near her father's recliner. Quickly, before he could see, she grabbed up an African violet and took it into the kitchen.

On the Monday morning after her father's homecoming, three weeks after the accident, Mariah entered her office early as usual. Crossing to place her purse in the desk drawer, she suddenly stopped and looked around.

Something prickled her skin.

She told herself not to be silly. Just because she was one of the first at work was no reason to imagine she was vulnerable.

The company had cardkey access security; she had presented her own to get a green light onto the twenty-ninth floor.

Mariah stood in her office filled with morning light and tried to breathe normally. Feeling spooky was normal after witnessing Charley and Andrew Green's death, and getting chased by reporters.

Reassured, she walked forward around her desk and nearly stepped on several CDs scattered on the carpet. She recognized them as ones she'd left loose on her desktop last Friday, some plans sent over from an architectural firm.

Opening the side desk drawer, she remembered the Zaragoza CD was in her bag. She stopped, unsnapped a brass clasp and drew the unmarked plastic case from the side pocket of leather.

Looking from it to the mess on the floor, her chill returned. What if it hadn't merely been a bad weekend for the cleaning staff? What if someone had been in here pawing through her things? Looking in particular for a CD that wasn't on the company network.

"Hey, there," said a deep voice from behind her.

Mariah jumped and turned from gathering the fallen discs to find Tom Barrett in her doorway. Although John was doing better, Tom still looked so bad she worried he might follow his friend into the hospital. She wondered if he struggled like her with the recurrent sense of the bottom dropping out, of being poised on the verge of a screaming acceleration.

Leaning a big shoulder against the jamb, Tom looked at the CDs as she placed them on the desk, or perhaps his eyes just followed the movement of her hand.

Despite that they were in the office and should be businesslike, Mariah went and hugged him.

"Ready to face the new week?" he said over the top of her head.

"Ready," she lied.

When the Monday morning meeting began, Arnold Benton gave his usual self-important report. Using a series of number slides, he showed that all was well on the financial front. To hear him talk, you'd think nothing had happened to the company's reputation.

Impatient to hear about the Grant Plaza inspections, Mariah said dryly, "Thank you, Arnold. I'm sure all our loans are being serviced and our bills paid. Let's hear from Ramsey about the accident." She turned to Grant's chief engineer.

Ramsey Rhodes crossed his burly arms over a pocketful of pens and pencils. "I'm afraid I've got nothing new this week. The metallurgy lab is backed up analyzing an oil tanker spill on the north coast, the one that polluted a federal preserve."

"People died at Grant Plaza," she protested with a regretful glance at Tom. "It should take priority."

Ramsey's usually studious look sharpened. "I was told by the head of the lab that Senator Chatsworth contacted them personally to emphasize the priority of the environmental issue."

"Chatsworth?" she echoed, her mind racing. "He shouldn't be able to interfere. Time's wasting, and the police can't pursue a criminal inquiry without lab results saying there was something suspicious about the accident."

Arnold Benton put down his coffee cup with a clatter. "Sounds like you believe in looking for bogeymen under the bed."

Ramsey said in his patient, engineer's tone, "Before we jump to conclusions, we have to wait for test results. The best that could happen for Grant's reputation is to have the investigation point to a design flaw. Unfortunately, that would mean a lot of workers all over the world are at risk using the same model hoist."

Tom looked stricken. "I hate to think of other men's sons in the same peril."

April Perry spoke up. "The hoist company is now pointing the finger at Grant. They want to know exactly how many sheets of glass were on board."

"The last thing we need to find out is that the car was overloaded," Ramsey said.

Charley had stuck out his arm and warned her away. "Weight limit." If it were so close that a hundred-fifteen pounds would have made a difference . . .

Mariah straightened her back and looked around the table.

April brushed a lock of coppery hair from her forehead. "At least we have one thing going for us. The longer it takes, the better chance the press and public move on to other stories."

But, was that true? While Davis Campbell's senatorial chum held up the metallurgy work, the press's interest in Grant Development had not flagged.

That night, Mariah could not sleep. Long days at work, evenings spent cooking homemade soups and baking bread for her father — none of it served to keep her mind off Rory. A month had passed since he invited her to his father's house, and while part of her wished she had torn the invitation to shreds, in every restaurant, on every lunchtime walk on Market Street, her eyes were alert for a dark head that stood above the crowd. Soon it would be June, the time of school's end and looking forward to a new life, the anniversary of a Sausalito Sunday when she and Rory had rushed headlong from strangers to lovers.

For eight years, she'd never forgiven him for caving in to his father and marrying a woman Davis must have thought suitable. Yet, hadn't Rory spoken the truth when he accused her of refusing his calls? And couldn't he now say she'd gone to Ventana, made love with him, and turned away because of her father?

She switched on her bedroom light and took out the ruby ring. Neither had its fire, nor had the ache in her diminished as she remembered him slipping it onto her finger. Turning the gold band in her hand, she knew she should return it. It was far too valuable a piece to keep.

But, as light shimmered in the stone's facets, she knew she wasn't ready yet to part with it. Call her sentimental, but as long as she had it, she felt there was some connection with Rory.

Early the next morning, she went to Grant Development's bank, First California, and rented a safe deposit box.

"Would you like to use the privacy booth, Miss?" asked the older gentleman helping her.

"Thank you, no," she said. "This will only take a minute."

Taking the ring from her purse, she clenched it for a moment in her hand. Then she put it away into darkness.

Tuesday evening Rory drove toward his parents' house, hoping there had at least been a truce in their recent state of war. The part of him that would always be a child longed for them to find peace.

He wished for it, too.

After he had walked away from Mariah in the hospital cafeteria, Rory recalled that the gossip rags said he was good at exit scenes. Maybe they and Sylvia Chatsworth were right, but if he wanted to get technical, his leaving Mariah had not been his exit.

She had sent him away.

In the parking garage, he had jerked open the door of his Porsche and got in. A savage turn of the key and a heavy foot brought the engine from silence to a throaty growl. Gripping the steering wheel with one hand, he shifted rapidly with the other. He was driving on instinct, his old habit of escaping whatever troubled him by clearing his mind.

It hadn't worked. How could he argue with the guilt trip Mariah was on? What if John's daughter joining the enemy camp had caused his attack?

Rory exhaled a heavy breath and parked his car in his father's drive. After suffering the usual indignity of having to knock and be let in by Anna, he started toward the family room. His heel strikes echoed in the tall stone and glass foyer.

"Rory!" his mother called.

He followed her voice to her sunroom on the far end of the house from her husband's room full of trophies. Beyond the wall of windows, the molten ball of sun hung over the darkening sea.

"Hello, darling." Wearing a silk caftan, Kiki rose from an overstuffed armchair and came to Rory with open arms. "Here's my best boy."

He chuckled at the greeting she'd given him since he was three.

Everything in this room was the antithesis of Davis's rough masculinity, from the flowered chintz couches to the collection of china figurines Kiki had collected over the years.

With these most exquisite, intricate, and breakable porcelains he'd ever seen, he wondered how the family and the help had managed to avoid knocking off a shepherd's crook, angel's halo, or a hummingbird's needle of beak. When he was a little boy and was allowed into this room, his father spent the entire time cautioning, "If you break something, you're going to have a talk with me in the library."

That was enough to skewer him to the edge of a white damask chair like a butterfly with its wings pinned.

Now, he reached a hand and stroked the painted head of golden hair on a delicate statue. It reminded him of Mariah, as she must have been as a girl, coltish, kneeling barelegged in shorts and a sleeveless shirt on the beach, a big seashell held to her ear.

From the corner of his eye, he noted that his mother almost cautioned him and then restrained herself. These fragile little figures were like Kiki, Rory thought, although anyone who met his mother casually might disagree. The flamboyant dress and bright hair hid a vulnerable and easily wounded lady.

Reaching to the side table, she refilled her wine glass.

Rory glanced at the tea set on a tray with matching pot and cups that looked like roses and pansies. It wasn't his taste, but usually when Kiki was in this room, she had a pot of aromatic Earl Grey at her side. "No tea today?" he asked mildly.

After a generous swallow of what the wine label revealed to be a Chilean Cabernet, she gave Rory a direct look. "No tea." She drank again, and he checked the level in the bottle, more than half empty.

As he bit back suggesting it was a bit early in the evening, her green eyes filled with tears. "So, he took the call right there at Sunday brunch in the Marin club. It was some goddamn woman, telling him when and where." She rolled her eyes. "I threw my glass of wine at him and said I hoped she makes him happy. God knows, I never have."

Rory's heart went out to her. How dare his father behave so cruelly, flaunting his peccadilloes?

"One of these days . . ." Kiki went on.

"One of these days, you'll what, Mother?"

Her shoulders slumped. "I . . . don't know. Things have been so terrible lately, but I'd never give him the satisfaction of leaving. At least now he has to sneak around."

"If it pleases you," Davis said from the doorway, "I'll stop sneaking and be open about it." Dressed in a black DCI golf shirt and starched blue jeans, his long-limbed body advanced into the room like a big cat's.

Rory scowled.

Davis flung himself down into an armchair that was too small for his frame. "Now I know why I never come into this room." He rose again and glared at his wife's wineglass. "How many of those have you had?"

"Not nearly enough," she replied, taking another long swallow.

"Jesus!" Rory burst out at his father. "You've been a real bastard lately. What in hell's the matter with you?"

Davis stretched his arms over his head and looked bored. Ignoring the question, he turned to his wife. "Are you coming with me to Tanzania in August?"

"Lion hunting," Kiki mocked. "Sleeping out in tents and listening to baboons at night."

"You're just afraid you won't be able to get the red dye number twenty for your hair."

"It's just that I could never imagine taking up a gun and deliberately killing anything."

Davis smiled, a lazy confident expression that said he could more than imagine it. It sent a chill through Rory.

"Why don't you take one of your little diversions to

Africa?" Kiki suggested coldly. "Impress her."

"It worked on you," Davis came back without missing a beat.

Rory's father and mother had met when Gates Campbell and prominent surgeon Carl Mainwearing brought their adult children on safari. The matchmaking must have been effective, for within weeks after the trip, Kiki and Davis were married.

"What about you and Tanzania, son?" he asked. "Why not bring Sylvia?"

"No, thanks." He didn't bother to reveal he'd not seen her since the night of the Senator's fundraiser.

"Speaking of Sylvia . . ." Davis's casual air turned intent. "Wilson McMillan's house party this weekend will be a nice place for you two to make an announcement."

Wilson McMillan, well over seventy years old, was one of the founding fathers of the northern California developer's club. Rory had been invited and planned to go . . . alone.

"I'm not taking Sylvia to McMillan's."

"She'll be there," Davis assured. "She, Larry, and her mother." He frowned. "You're not planning to bring Mariah Grant, are you?"

These past weeks Rory had tried to forget Mariah. A hundred times, he'd played back her hurtful words in the hospital hall, when she'd accused him of causing her father's heart attack. He'd driven his Porsche relentless miles. Yet, each night, tossing on sweat-dampened sheets, he was haunted by her quick intelligence, the soft look in her golden eyes when she came into his arms.

"No," he said quietly. "I'm not bringing Mariah to Mc-Millan's."

Rory noted that at the mention of John Grant's daughter his mother sat straighter and studied him. Perhaps she read the sadness in him, kindred to her own as she said, "Don't settle for the wrong woman, Rory. Even if you have to remain alone."

Turning to her husband, Kiki went on, "I was foolish enough to believe I was the one you wanted."

"I've stayed with you all these years . . ." Davis began.

"You've stayed, I've stayed." She slashed at air with her hand. "But lately, you've been so strange I might surprise you and go."

Rory couldn't take any more. "I hate to give you the satisfaction, Father, but I've had about all of these family values I can take." He bent, brushed a kiss on his mother's cheek where there might have been tears, and left the house.

His mother's suggestion of staying alone rather than being with the wrong woman was exactly what he planned. But why did Mariah Grant, whom everyone agreed was wrong for him, continue to feel so right?

CHAPTER 10

*T*haddeus Walker of First California did not belong at Grant Development unannounced on a Wednesday morning.

With a sigh, Mariah pushed the button on her office phone and told the receptionist that someone would be with him shortly. She rose from her desk, sorting through the possible reasons for the visit, and wished she knew Walker better. The bank representative had taken over the company account last winter when Bill Bryan, Grant's manager of twenty years, had passed away. Not even John had had much time to develop a relationship with the new man. In fact, he had mentioned several times that he was thinking of shopping for another bank.

Although it was nearly nine, a glance down the hall told Mariah that Tom Barrett wasn't in. She thought of asking corporate attorney Ed Snowden or PR director April Perry to join her with Walker, but dealing with the financial side was Arnold Benton's turf, and she knew it. With reluctance, she phoned and asked him to meet her in John's office.

In the reception area, she found the narrow-faced banker reading *The Wall Street Journal*. His close-cropped grayish hair did nothing to hide his prominent ears. His cuffs were shot from the sleeves of his expensive charcoal suit, and his tie depicted money, gold coins on blue silk.

Mariah wished she'd worn something more formal than olive drab slacks and an open-necked khaki shirt, but she had not expected outside meetings today.

She greeted Walker and found out he shook hands like a dead fish. Then she led the way to the corner office while he silently followed. Arnold, jacket on, pale hair neatly combed, had beaten her to John's chair.

"Coffee?" she asked Walker.

He refused with a curt shake of his large head.

Arnold said, "Black," with a tight grin.

Mariah crossed to the door and asked John's secretary to get it.

Taking a seat in one of the chairs across from Arnold, Walker leaned back and made a tent of his fingers. Apparently in no hurry to get to the point of his visit, he proceeded to study his hands as if the solution to a fascinating and intricate problem lay in their proper alignment. Twenty-nine stories below on Market Street, an emergency siren wailed faintly.

At last, Walker addressed Arnold, "Back in May when Grant had those late loan payments . . ."

Mariah almost gasped aloud. She'd worked at Grant the entire month of May and heard nothing about any payments in arrears. She shot a hard look at Arnold and found him avoiding her eyes.

Walker went on, "I was willing to accept your explanation that you were changing software. Now, this accident and the news coverage have spooked our directors."

Mariah got a griping sensation in her gut. Her father had always advised that saying too much was more deadly than too little, but Arnold began babbling about the unreliability of computers. She knew the trouble with that. Computers were built by people, programmed by people, and used by people.

Walker looked at John's desk as if estimating its cost. "After the . . . incident at Grant Plaza, I was willing to give a company with the strength of yours the benefit of the doubt, but with John's health problems . . ."

Mariah interrupted. "His doctors say he should be back at work in a matter of weeks." They had originally projected twelve, actually months, but she wasn't going to tell Walker that or anything about the complications her father had been having.

Arnold joined in. "Grant Development is not about John Grant, or his family." He gave her a disparaging look. "We have many projects and fine people." Though the statement was a backhanded attack, he'd essentially said what she would have told the banker.

"I'm sorry." Walker's tone said he wasn't. "I've got no choice but to call your business loans with First California."

Mariah went hot all over. Two hundred million dollars, all but a few tied up in properties under construction.

"For God's sake," she said, "we haven't even completed our investigation of the accident."

"You know the bank has a perfect right to call your notes." Walker's eyes narrowed. "Your payments were late, and that allows me to foreclose."

She wanted to storm at Arnold, to ask how he had permitted this. All companies borrowed money as their lifeline, but his department had tightened their rope into a noose.

"You know we don't have that kind of money lying around." Her hands started to shake, and she folded them together in her lap. Thank God that Dad wasn't here.

Arnold continued to talk too fast. Walker simply stared at him.

At last, Mariah turned and waited until the banker met her direct look. "Do we have any room here?"

He shook his head. His porcine eyes made her understand why John had wanted someone else to handle their account. It also reminded her with sharp clarity of seeing him cozying up to Davis Campbell at his mansion last month.

"Effective date?" she asked.

"June sixth. Cash."

"It's May twenty-eight. That's next Friday," Arnold blurted.

"The sixth is the monthly payment date on your schedule. Good as any, I expect."

Mariah felt a dizzying sensation. She stayed upright by pinching the soft skin between her thumb and forefinger and telling the black sparks in her vision to go away.

"Shouldn't we have ninety days or something?" She hoped her voice sounded normal.

"Old Bill Bryan and your dad were great friends. Their loan agreements were dirt simple, either party could back out any time. Guess John shouldn't have trusted Bill would always be around."

Mariah rose to indicate the meeting was at an end and let Arnold see Walker out. Left alone, she looked at her father's empty chair. Such a short time ago he'd had been on top of the world, watching Grant Plaza soar toward completion.

Arnold came back with Tom Barrett. The big man looked as rumpled as Mariah felt. "I heard," he said gravely. She waited for him to tell her what to do, but he sank into a chair with a sigh and offered nothing.

"This isn't my fault." Arnold's hands moved restlessly. "We were changing our accounts payable software. Your father did those deals with Bill Bryan, you heard . . ."

"I should fire you right now," Mariah said.

He reddened. "How dare you sweep in here and start running the place? I've been with John for the past seven years and where were you?"

"Arnold," Tom warned.

Though the tirade subsided, Arnold continued to glare

at her.

"As for you, Mariah," Tom went on, "you may be John's next in line, but this isn't the time to go throwing your weight around. If there's any way out for Grant, we need a man who understands our finances inside and out. God knows, I haven't been much help lately."

Without her father, with Tom a beaten shadow of his former self, and the loans due in a matter of days, the future of Grant Development settled onto her slender shoulders.

Driving south from downtown, Mariah tried to think how she'd break the news to her father. Though both Tom and Arnold had offered to come with her, she'd insisted on going alone. John didn't need to see any displays of disunity in his senior staff.

What could they do? Try another bank, but with all the negative publicity, it would be an uphill battle. The most obvious solution, and the one she hated most, was to try and sell off properties prior to their completion. Her hands clenched the wheel as she realized Grant Plaza might have to be one of them.

Arriving too soon in Stonestown, she parked in front of her father's house. Inside, she found him in his recliner, dressed in casual flannel pants and a T-shirt. His legs, encased in elastic stockings, were elevated.

"Where's Mrs. Schertz?" she asked, surmising from the

air of stillness in the house that he was alone.

"I sent her to the grocery store." Something sharp in his tone tipped her.

She met his eyes. "Who called you?"

"Arnold."

"That weasel."

Her father looked reproachful. "The man is as distraught as can be. He said you refused to let him come with you."

"I didn't want you upset."

"You can't protect me from everything. I'm just as disturbed about the threat to the company no matter who brings the news." He patted the hassock beside his chair. "Your attitude toward Arnold is a great disappointment to me."

Mariah ignored the summons to sit. "Can't you see he despises me precisely because I'm your daughter? I'll bet he thinks without me he'd be your heir apparent."

John studied her with steady eyes. "He would. Tom and I aren't getting any younger, and you're not ready to run things alone."

She couldn't argue with that. Now that Thaddeus Walker had pulled the foundation from under Grant Development, she longed for her father to be whole and well, to take the burden from her.

"Rely on Arnold, daughter. He does care for me, even if you can't see it." He nodded toward an expensive carved soapstone chessboard that had appeared in the house a few years ago. "He brought that back for me from Alaska. We play together every Wednesday evening . . . it's time we started again."

It was no use arguing that she'd seen Arnold's kind before, people who sucked up to get ahead.

"About the loans . . ." she said.

John nodded. She would have expected more emotion, but he sat expressionless. Then she recalled his doctor saying the beta blocker drugs used to slow his heart rate kept a person calm.

Trying to keep her own head, she finally took a seat. "Before I came home, I talked to Ed Snowden and had him give a legal opinion on the borrowing agreement. At first, I thought it was impossible for First California to do this, but Ed says it's going to happen unless we do something drastic. Sell some properties."

Her father stirred to life. "Davis Campbell would love that."

He was right. Despite Arnold's accusing her of seeing bogeymen under the bed, she wondered if Davis had influenced the banker's decision by dangling some bait, like sending DCI business to First California.

"Dad," she said. "I saw Davis and Walker together at his party. They looked mighty cozy."

Despite the drugs, her father swore a vicious oath. "I'll have to come back to work."

"No," she argued. "Your sternum won't be healed for another three weeks, and you can't drive or lift over ten pounds until then. Let me take care of things." It was the least she could do to make up for her role in putting him in the hospital.

He scratched at his scar, his angry expression dissipating.

With his ability to read her, he said, "It's time for you to stop blaming yourself."

How she wished she could shed the weight of guilt. "Every time I think of it, I want to go back in time and undo that phone call. Telling you I was with Rory right after we buried Charley was unforgivable."

John reached toward her with a pale hand. Blue veins showed through his skin as though he were a much older man. "Love makes everything forgivable." He smiled gently. "There is no way you gave me a heart attack by letting me know you were with Rory. I'm just glad you figured him out before you got hurt again."

She looked away, hoping to hide how the mention of Rory slashed at her. Her eyes sought a tapestry over the sofa. An elderly bearded man in traditional robes stood on an arched wooden bridge with a young woman. Behind them, the uniquely serrate mountains of Japan strove for the silken sky. When she was a child, she and her father had liked to walk in the Japanese Garden at Golden Gate Park, and she'd imagined the picture was a magic glimpse of them when she grew up.

"Look at me." John put a hand over his chest and breathed a little fast.

She lowered her eyes from the threads, reminded of the complex web woven by deceit. She still wanted Rory and had to hide it.

"Just as I've never been able to care for anybody but your mother, you've never moved on in all these years. I've watched and hoped you'd find someone else, not make work your life the way I have."

His words underscored how the threat to Grant Development cut to the core of everything she stood for.

The telephone rang. Perhaps Mrs. Schertz was calling on her cell to ask what brand of mustard John preferred. On the other hand, it might be Tom with something from the office. Mariah moved to answer it.

"Hello, it's Lyle Thomas," said the assistant D.A. she'd talked with at the Marriott, a blond Norseman tamed into a business suit. "I tried your office."

"I came home to see Dad."

"I was sorry to hear about his health problems," Lyle said sincerely. "Please give him my best wishes."

"I'll do that." She reminded herself that as big a gossip as Lyle was, she must be careful not to let him know about the loans.

"You remember I said I'd introduce you to some people?" He sounded hearty even on the phone. "Well, there's a house party at Wilson McMillan's place in Pacific Grove this coming weekend."

Mariah knew of McMillan well. An attractive offer, but she couldn't see leaving Dad alone overnight. "I'm sorry, Lyle, but . . ."

"No 'buts.'" He chuckled. "If you're worried about sleeping arrangements, this is strictly platonic."

"I believe you," she said, "but with my father's illness, I won't be able to go."

As soon as she got off the phone, John asked. "Was that Lyle Thomas of the D.A.'s office?"

"That's right."

"You said no to what?"

"He asked me to Wilson McMillan's house party."

With a gesture toward a pile of mail on the table beside him, John said, "I was invited." He rummaged, found an envelope and tossed it to her. "That's his house."

Pulling out the creamy paper embossed with a Moorish-style castle, she felt a twinge of regret. It looked like the kind of place where a Cinderella story might come true.

"I was going to suggest you go," he said. "Mrs. Schertz can stay over in the guest room."

He might say he'd forgiven her for Rory, but guilt urged her to take care of him. "No, Dad."

Listen to me," he said. "You have to build your power base in this town. My day is ending."

Mariah wanted to put a finger to his lips and shush him, but she listened.

"With this loan crisis, you've got to find prospects we can sell property to." He sounded as though he'd bitten into a sour fruit. "The last thing I want is a fire sale to Davis Campbell."

"My, God." If Davis had put Thaddeus Walker up to calling Grant Development's notes, he might be waiting in the wings, his goal to take the entire company.

Suddenly, it was no longer good enough not to know what had gone wrong between the two men. "You and Davis have been rivals for as long as I can remember, but it seems to go a lot deeper than that."

John looked through the windows at his beloved garden he could no longer tend. Though he clearly didn't want to talk about it, she couldn't let this go. "Dad, please. Tell me why you despise each other."

"Who said *I* despise him?" His face twisted with what looked like pain.

"Are you all right?" A clutch of fear went through her as she hoped she'd not pushed too hard.

"Fine," he said. "That is, my heart's okay. I'm just thinking how different things would be," he reached to stroke the embossed castle on the invitation, "if I hadn't gone to McMillan's house twenty-seven years ago."

It misted rain all afternoon, but the sun came out when John drove his Ford Fairlane past the big dunes at Fort Ord. He looked out at the wild, foaming surf and wished his friend Davis Campbell weren't on the far side of the ocean hunting with his father in Africa. John could use him along this weekend at Wilson McMillan's.

Oh, John had plenty of confidence in his ability to get a job done; no doubt in time he'd be a most successful builder. It was just that his new partner Davis was better at talk. There was bound to be a lot of social banter along with golf on the world-renowned Pebble Beach or Spyglass Hill courses. John's duffing would be less noticeable if he shared clubs with Davis, who was an excellent player.

The worst of it was that until Davis got back and made the break with his father's company, John couldn't announce that they were going into partnership. Davis had wanted to wait until the hunting trip was over, for he expected Gates Campbell to take it poorly.

After driving the oceanfront route through Monterey and Pacific Grove, John guided his Fairlane over a hill and caught sight of Wilson McMillan's castle. Near the beginning of the 17-Mile Drive, it was set above an emerald fairway overlooking the broad curve of Spanish Bay. Offshore, the surf crashed and careened in a dozen directions off the last rocky outpost before thousands of miles of open water.

Seeing the imposing setting and the thick-walled limestone fortress made John even more apprehensive. Lots of men would bring their wives, and today he wished he had one. Someone sweet and lovely who'd charm everyone into thinking he was a clever fellow to have won her. At thirty, he had yet to meet a woman he wanted to spend the rest of his life with.

Driving under the arched stone porte-cochere, John's palms were sweaty on the wheel. To his relief, a servant welcomed him as if he belonged to the moneyed set. He followed the white-jacketed young man through a glass-walled solarium, down a wood-paneled hallway ornate with carving, and up marble stairs. The spacious room allotted him overlooked the golf course and the sea.

"Cocktails are at six, sir, below." His guide pointed over the balustrade to a larger terrace decorated with potted evergreens and bougainvillea climbing trellised arbors. "We dress."

John resisted the effort to tip, for he'd never had this kind of service outside of a hotel.

True to instructions, he changed from his usual uniform of khakis into a suit. To avoid being conspicuous, he waited until a group gathered before he went down. Even so, as he reached the bank of French doors onto the lower terrace, he hesitated.

"John!" A strong hand gripped his shoulder.

He turned to find Wilson McMillan's bright simian eyes beaming at him. The wiry forty-something developer exuded energy as he offered a crushing handshake.

Wilson gestured to a balding man beside him. "Henry, you must meet John Grant. John's been working with Hugh Vinson, but I think it's time for him to start his own company."

John felt a wave of pride as he shook hands with Henry Sand.

After talking a while with Sand, John wandered, listening unabashedly to snippets of conversation.

"I'm going over to First California for all my construction loans," said a man in a fine cashmere sweater. John made a mental note to check out the bank.

"And if you aren't known at Jack's, you're going to have to stand in the crowded hall for at least half an hour," an older woman's voice rose for emphasis, "even with a reservation."

McMillan had taken John to lunch at the landmark San

Francisco restaurant the day he'd invited him down. At the time, John thought the bright lights and mirrors overdone, the poached salmon in hollandaise too rich, and the prices sky-high. Now, he wondered if Wilson had been telling him where to be seen.

"Trust me, renovation is the key in the city proper." The tall man leaning against the balustrade dipped two fingers into his martini and fished out an olive. He bent closer to Wilson's wife Hilda, a handsome brunette at least ten years younger than her husband. "Those old Victorians that are falling down will be priceless someday."

John wanted to build, not renovate.

Glancing at his Timex, he wondered what time it was for Davis in Rhodesia. Another week before his friend would break the news to his father that he and John planned to compete with Gates Campbell's company. It was a daring move in a city where being a member of the club was everything, but Davis believed he could pull off getting out from under his father's heavy hand. John couldn't wait to reveal the contacts he was making this evening.

Wilson circulated back and gestured at John's half-empty drink. "How're you doing there?"

"Fine, sir."

He felt Wilson's hand on his arm, turning him to look over the balustrade.

"You see that rocky point?" The vibrant developer pointed southwest toward the setting sun, through the salt mist floating above Spanish Bay. The surf boiled, flinging itself against the buttress of boulders. White spray leaped thirty feet and cormorants huddled against the wind.

"That's Point Joe," Wilson instructed. "A lot of sailors mistook that headland for the entrance to Monterey Bay and ended up smashed against those cliffs. You take a lesson and see you don't end up on the rocks in your career."

Left alone again, John surveyed the other guests, many of them older and more prosperous than he. It wasn't long before his eye was drawn to a young woman standing alone, looking out to sea.

She was not tall, about five feet, wearing a simple black dress that emphasized the curve of her waist. A fantastic wealth of flaxen hair tumbled down her back. When she turned, the sun caught her eyes; they might have been made of gold. Lit by the last rays of light that made the sea molten, she was quite simply the most beautiful woman he had ever seen. He looked around to see if she might be one of the older men's trophy wives, but she remained by herself.

Whoever she was, she was certainly not for him. She seemed made to ride in luxury rather than his Ford, to wear diamonds as big as doorknobs and travel regularly to the Continent.

John shrugged and headed toward a group of people surrounding Henry Sand. Before he had gone three steps, Wilson's wife Hilda turned from her conversation and placed herself in his path.

"I happen to have the advantage of you, Mr. Grant," she said, offering a hand that was callused, he supposed, from tennis. "It's a pleasure to have you here."

John thanked her, stealing a glance over his shoulder to see if the blonde was still where he'd seen her.

Hilda's alert eyes followed his. "Ah, I see you've noticed her. As you two were the only unattached young people this weekend, I placed you together at the table."

He had trouble believing his good fortune as Hilda smiled and gave him a nudge. "Go on over and introduce yourself. I'd be in the way."

Hoping his palms would not start to sweat, John moved toward the rail. When his dinner partner turned and faced him, the party's chatter suddenly seemed muted by a roaring in his ears.

"Hello," he said. A brilliant opening.

"If you don't mind my saying so, you seem as much a stranger here as I am." Her voice was low and softly modulated.

"This is my first time down. I'm John Grant."

She extended both slender hands, and he grasped them. "You will take me in to dinner?" she asked delicately. John could not decide if she was a woman who needed a man's protection, or whether she might be made of flexible steel.

"I'd be honored," he said.

He'd never imagined this could happen to him. For the first time in his life, he saw a woman he believed was everything he'd ever wanted, and he knew it went deeper than her breathtaking looks. There was sincerity, a ring of elemental truth in her gaze, and strength in her delicate-looking fingers.

"I'm Catharine Stockton."

John dropped her hands as if he'd been burned. Yet, the

fire in him was not so easily quenched. Last month Davis had told John he'd met someone special. For the first time in his life, he was serious . . .

About Catharine Stockton.

John had found it hard to believe, remembering the swath Davis had cut through the coeds at Stanford. Even now, his best friend never had fewer than three women on a string. He seldom introduced them to John, keeping that part of his life separate from their friendship. When Davis had left to go hunting, John figured Catharine was a memory. Instead, he had received a postcard from Johannesburg, South Africa.

I want you to be the first to know, Davis had dashed in his handsome script. *I've decided to marry Catharine. And before you ask, yes. She is enough to make me give up other women for the rest of my life.*

During dinner, John battled with himself. The prime rib and vintage Bordeaux went down without note as Catharine devoted her attention to him. By the time dessert arrived, he was beyond help.

Late that night at Spanish Bay, the dunes shone whitely beneath a nearly full moon. Catharine's hair shone as she ran ahead of him toward waves glowing with bioluminescence. Holding her skirt above her knees, she danced with the ebb and flow on slender legs like a sandpiper. John watched her with a smile. In her innocent pleasure, she could have no idea what she did to him. It would be folly to let her see, for as Davis's girl, she was merely being polite to a fellow stranger in the gathering.

Feeling dread at the prospect of taking her back to the castle, he called her name. This couldn't be, yet how right the word sounded on the night breeze, a promise instead of a door closing.

Catharine walked toward him across the gleaming sand, looking up at him with golden eyes. She seemed open, not at all like a woman cheating on her lover. Was it possible Davis had read more into their relationship than she did?

Her face changed from innocence to a waiting posture. With her head tilted, her lips parted, she moistened them with her tongue. Now was when he would have taken her in his arms had she been any other woman.

With an effort, John said, "I had a postcard from Davis Campbell in Africa. It was all about you."

Catharine placed a gentle finger to his mouth, her slightest touch shocking him to the core. "No more," she whispered.

He wondered how he could possibly be thinking of pulling her against him. "But, you and Davis . . . He's my friend."

"I know he is your friend. He has told me enough about you that I feel I already understand you," she said steadily.

"I guess I'm the one who doesn't understand." How could she be so guileless if she were truly engaged to Davis? "He said he's going to marry you."

She went as still as a statue. "He never told me that."

"I guess he will when he returns from Africa."

Catharine shook her head. "You and I both know one woman will never be enough for him."

"But his note said you . . ."

"He can say what he wants now. He may believe it." She moved closer. "Could you love someone, marry someone you knew was wrong for you?" She lifted her hands and placed them over John's heart. "I think when the right two people meet, they know."

He thought later of blaming the moonlight, for he was holding Davis's girl . . . no, not his friend's girl. The pounding surf matched the pulse that rose inside him, while Catharine wove her gentle gossamer magic.

It all came clear as Mariah imagined a younger Davis, a handsome kid who looked a lot like Rory. A man without the bitterness and rancor he now carried. Finally, she understood the intense scrutiny he always subjected her to. In her, he must see Catharine.

Sitting in his well-worn recliner, John told Mariah, "I married your mother the next week, while Davis was still in Africa."

She drew in her breath sharply. "You didn't wait for him to come home? You and she didn't tell him in person?"

"Catharine assured me over and over that Davis had never brought up the subject of marriage to her. That she didn't want to wait another day for us to be together . . ." John shook his head. "I could never resist anything she wanted but . . . I did feel bad about springing it on him that way."

"I can imagine." If the youthful Davis had half the

passion she had sometimes glimpsed in his son, he would have been devastated.

"Davis has never forgiven me for marrying Catharine, 'out from under him,' he called it." John said sadly. "Sometimes I wonder if I were in his shoes if I wouldn't feel the same way."

"Did you ever talk to him about it?"

He gave a bitter chuckle. "Are you kidding? The one time I tried to bring it up . . . he showed up at her memorial service . . . I thought he was going to slug me there in the cemetery."

Then he looked thoughtful. "You know, all these years someone has been sending fresh flowers to her grave on a weekly basis. I'm sure it must be him."

Mariah imagined Davis coming to Cypress Lawn, to the hill where Tom Barrett and John both had their family plots. Getting out of his black Mercedes, carrying a sheaf of lilies or a spray of rosebuds still bearing the dew from the florist's bucket, he would walk with bowed head to Catharine's resting place. He'd stand there a few moments, looking at the grieving marble angel in the nearby plot, at the words carved in granite: *Catharine Mariah Stockton Grant*, and then run his eyes over John's name and birth date. All that would remain for him was to fill in the day John died.

"So, you both went at it trying to outdo each other all these years." Mariah's stomach ached at the thought of what could have been had the two men combined their considerable talents. All these years, she'd thought her father hated

Davis. Rather, he had once loved him, might still have loved him except for the way Davis had reacted to the loss of Catharine.

A chill went through her as she realized the true meaning of what she'd learned. Davis's vendetta was not about the testosterone overload that drove him to big game hunting. It had nothing to do with the competitive spirit he showed in sailing and business. Rather, it was a deeply personal quest for vengeance.

This made it all the more important that Grant Development not fail. Time was running out, and if she were going to find buyers for Grant properties by next Friday, she must accept Lyle's invitation to Wilson McMillan's.

CHAPTER 12

$\mathcal{M}$ariah's first sight of Wilson McMillan's castle astounded her. The pale stone fortress crowned an expanse of perfectly manicured golf course, with a view down to Spanish Bay. She saw the rocky point where hapless sailors lost their ships, still a beacon surrounded by the peaks and valleys of churning waves.

"This is beautiful," Lyle Thomas said with appreciation. The weather was cooperating by producing a chamber-of-commerce weekend.

On the drive down, Mariah had learned that the assistant district attorney was more soft-spoken and cultured than his courtroom reputation would suggest. It didn't hurt that with his golden hair, ice blue eyes and perfect features, he might have modeled men's clothing. Because of Rory, she couldn't muster anything other than friendly interest.

It felt good to get out of the city. Somehow safer, though she continued to keep an eye out for the press following her, or, God forbid, someone who meant her harm as Tom Barrett had suggested. She had not forgotten the scruffy-looking man in the Taurus whom she believed had shadowed her into Chinatown. So, every few miles she checked behind Lyle's Mercedes convertible.

Now, he guided the sports car under McMillan's arched stone porte-cochere, cut the engine and looked around. "Gargoyles, for God's sake." Sure enough, carved figures of dogs, dragons, and monsters decorated the eaves and downspouts.

An elderly man in a white jacket ushered them in through a glass-walled solarium. "Cocktails are at six, there." He pointed to the outside terrace, decorated with potted evergreens and bougainvillea climbing on trellised arbors. "We dress."

Mariah smiled at the reception that hadn't changed since her father had been here nearly thirty years ago. The servant led her and Lyle up marble stairs, down a long hallway hung with museum-worthy masterpieces, and showed them to doors on opposite sides.

After admiring the spacious room with marble bath, Oriental rugs, and porcelains trimmed in gold, Mariah went onto the private balcony. No, not private; a matching set of double French doors opened onto the stone expanse fronted by a limestone railing. This pristine retreat overlooked a long green fairway, the beach, and the sun gold of the Pacific. Heady floral scents wafted from climbing roses.

Stretching her arms over her head, she tried to relax and forget her troubles. She was here to help save Grant Development, but the evening reception wasn't for an hour yet. Surely, for a little while she could enjoy this lovely place.

Looking down at the terrace, she inhaled a long slow breath. There was the carved stone balustrade where her mother had been standing when John had first seen her. As Catharine had gazed at the same sea Mariah now watched, what had she been thinking before she turned to John and found her life forever changed?

Mariah had believed in that kind of magic when she'd come upon a lithe, dark youth on the deck of his father's yacht. Now, she knew dreams didn't last, not for her parents, or for her and Rory.

Would he be here? After his swift exit from the hospital cafeteria, she could imagine him revving up his Porsche, pulling out his cell and dialing Sylvia Chatsworth's preprogrammed number. Pain stabbed at the thought of the black-haired siren's manicured nails sliding over Rory's muscled back.

Offshore, the sun silhouetted a sailboat beating to windward over the shining sea. As she watched the prow cutting through the waves, she heard the sound of a door opening from the room next to hers. She remained at the rail with her back turned, to preserve her neighbor's privacy and because she didn't feel like meeting anyone right now. After a shower, she'd put on her company face.

Out on the horizon, the boat changed course, coming up on the wind to tack. She remembered Rory at his boat's helm with the wheel in competent hands, his face intent on their heading.

Footsteps approached her from behind.

The sails flapped as the helmsman turned the wheel.

"Hard alee," said Rory's voice.

She turned to find him smiling, his tousled hair lending a rakish air. Faded jeans sheathed his thighs below a black golf shirt.

The DCI logo over his chest drove her back to reality. "Are you next door with Sylvia?"

"I'm next door," he said with faint emphasis on the first word.

She knew she should stop, but only a moment ago she'd been tormented thinking of them together. "Did you bring her?"

His expression betrayed nothing. "I believe I saw you drive up with Lyle Thomas."

"Eyes of an eagle." Okay, let him think she was with Lyle if he was truly sharing a room with the Senator's daughter.

"Now that we have the table cards arranged, what shall we do?" Rory slid a hip onto the balustrade and cocked a dark brow. "Fight about our fathers?"

His dry tone infuriated her. "It always seems to boil down to that."

"How is your Dad?" he asked in a softer tone.

"Much better." That was relative, but she had to assume

the information would go to Davis Campbell. "Back to work part time in a few more weeks." She hoped.

"That's good." His lips curved into a smile, and he sounded genuinely pleased.

She turned her head away so he wouldn't see her disquiet at thinking of her father's health.

"Hey." Rory's voice lowered to a more intimate range. When she did not turn back to him, he took her arm. "Still feeling guilty?"

How quickly he cut to the heart of what kept them apart. Not Sylvia or Lyle, but the sense of being pawns in their fathers' chess game.

Rory's hand was warm on her. "Look at me."

Wondering if she were playing the fool, she did . . . and the compassion in his dark eyes made her answer. "I suppose I will always feel guilty."

The corner of his mouth went down. "Have you asked his doctors if what you did could have caused his attack?"

The memory of the hurtful things she'd said to him at the hospital hung between them. She stared out over the long emerald slope toward the sailing vessel in the restless sea.

"For God's sake, Mariah." Rory shook her arm, his fingers digging in. "Does John blame us?"

Her gaze was drawn to his wounded look, and she relented. "The doctors made it clear his clogged arteries were a time bomb. It could have happened any time."

His hand relaxed and slid down to hers. "What has John said about it?"

The caring in his tone made her go on, "He told me to stop blaming myself." Then, because Rory seemed to be holding his breath as he awaited her next words, she admitted, "He said people can't always choose the one they love."

Rory exhaled a long breath. "I've missed you," he murmured, lifting her left hand. She saw the question in his eyes when he saw it was bare of his ring.

She could tell him it was some place safe, but realized she was falling into the old trap. All Rory had to do was touch her, and she turned into a marshmallow.

As he lowered his lips and touched them to her hand the way he had at the Italian café in Sausalito, she fought the familiar melting warmth. He probably had come with Sylvia. She was no doubt inside taking a shower or something without knowing Rory was playing both ends against the middle on the balcony.

Yet, his lips persuaded, and the warm tip of his tongue flickered over her skin. She wondered if he could feel the pounding of her blood.

"Rory, I . . ."

From the terrace below, "Really, Davis, I haven't had a drink since lunch."

"You're practically staggering."

Rory gripped Mariah's hand and yanked her away from the rail. His quick movement shocked her.

The fracas below continued with Kiki's strained voice. "I'm entitled to a little fun now and then. God knows you've been a barrel of it this past month."

"Pipe down, will you?" Davis said cruelly.

Rory stopped in the shade of the trellis outside her room, out of sight from below. His face looked flushed.

Her cheeks heated as well. "You still don't want your parents to see us?"

He stared at her without answering, and she challenged him with her own gaze.

"Why, hello." Lyle Thomas stepped out from her bedroom. He cut an elegant figure in his dinner clothes.

Rory dropped her hand. She whirled, thinking she must have left her hall door off the latch. Lyle's eyes flicked from Rory to her.

"You've met Rory Campbell?" she offered. Lame, but it was the best she could do.

Lyle put out his hand. "Sylvia make it?"

Rory shook. "She's probably putting on her face for this evening."

Mariah gasped. He'd been playing word games, sweet-talking her while he never actually said he wasn't with Sylvia.

She tried to control her voice. "I need to dress as well."

Shoulders square, she put a light hand on Lyle's arm and guided him toward her room. When she turned back to close the door behind them, she did not miss the hard look Rory shot her.

"Did I interrupt something?" Lyle asked.

She went to the closet and opened it blindly. While she'd been outside, McMillan's house staff had unpacked her clothes and set out her toilet articles.

"Mariah," Lyle insisted. "You and Campbell looked upset."

She talked to the clothes rack. "I need to dress."

Lyle's heavy tread came closer and stopped a few feet behind her. "After the little scene between you two at the Marriott, I was tipped to curiosity. Now, I guess I know." On his way to the door, he patted her shoulder. "Fair lady, your secret is safe with me."

As he went out Mariah figured she should not be surprised. Lyle, with his incisive courtroom eye, knew raw emotion when he saw it.

With fumbling fingers, Rory shoved a ruby cufflink into his sleeve. The mirror reflected his flared nostrils and the cords in his neck standing out. That Mariah had gone so quickly to another man wouldn't seem possible if he hadn't seen the evidence with his eyes. For God's sake, if Lyle had shown up ten seconds later, Rory would have made a fool of himself trying to kiss her.

He began to insert matching ruby studs in his tuxedo shirt. The stones weren't as large or as fine as the one he'd bought Mariah, but they had sentimental value. He'd inherited them from his grandmother Mainwearing.

Thinking back to when he was a small boy, he sensed that his mother's parents had been happy in their marriage. It tore him up inside that in public this afternoon Kiki and

Davis had been unable to keep from airing their differences. To leap back from the sound of their stridence had been instinctive, both for him and to keep Mariah from being exposed to the unpleasantness.

Now he told himself it didn't matter what she thought about his parents, not with Lyle sharing her bedroom.

Rory brushed back his shower-damp hair and went down onto the main terrace where an array of animated guests gathered. The first person he greeted was the distinguished senator from the state of California.

With a sweeping glance, Chatsworth appraised Rory's tuxedo studs. They must have passed, for the older man offered a firm handshake, "Call me Larry."

Sylvia materialized at Rory's side. As always, she looked stunning. Her shining fall of black hair set off a trademark red dress that hugged her curves. In contrast to the extravagant display of her assets, her face was set in innocence; as though the last time she'd seen Rory, they'd been close as lovebirds. She took his hand, her long red nails garish compared to Mariah's pale pink crescents.

Rory did not immediately pull away to avoid offending the Senator Chatsworth . . . that is, Larry.

"You will take me in to dinner?" Sylvia asked archly, placing her other hand firmly on his chest over his heart.

"Aren't you with someone?" he hoped aloud, trying to take a subtle step back.

"Just Daddy and Mama," she pouted, staying with him and stroking the satin lapel of his tux. Larry smiled beatifically at the two of them.

Thinking how to escape gracefully, Rory suddenly saw Mariah framed in the archway leading into the house. She sparkled in a gold dress he remembered too well, her lips and cheeks pink from rouge or having just-been-kissed. Lyle's arm rested around her shoulders.

Was it Rory's imagination, or was there a subtle clouding of her smile when she saw Sylvia caressing him? He couldn't be sure, but what she did next sent his temper soaring.

Mariah met his eyes for a beat, enough for him to be certain she was looking directly at him. Then she turned into the crook of Lyle's arm, stood on tiptoe and whispered something that made the big blond laugh loud enough to project all over the terrace.

Rory had been a fool on the balcony upstairs. He wasn't about to be again.

Forcing a smile, he bent to accept Sylvia's dinner offer. "Since we're both alone, we must definitely go in together."

She smiled almost shyly. His daughter placed, Chatsworth excused himself to press the flesh.

As if a switch had been thrown, she dropped the little girl act. "So my father says, Sylvia, you could do a lot worse than Rory Campbell." Her laugh sounded victorious.

"He did, did he?"

Thoroughly miserable now, Rory stood beside the wrong woman, while Mariah smiled up at Lyle Thomas.

Lyle led Mariah to Wilson McMillan, introduced her, and melted into the gathering.

"So sorry John couldn't be here." Wilson moved briskly for his seventy-odd years, taking her hand in both of his. Eyes as keen as an owl's peered at her from his golf-tanned, leathery face.

"Dad sends his fond regards," she told him.

"My best to him. And to you, the little lady who is filling his shoes." He made a sweeping gesture to include his guests. "I'll introduce you around."

True to his word, he stayed with her for half an hour, gracefully insinuating his way into conversations and presenting her. With each group, she accepted good wishes for her father's speedy recovery and made her pitch. "With Dad's illness, we're going to have to pull in our horns, temporarily, you understand. We're thinking of selling some properties before they're complete. Just too much on our plate."

She tried to keep it casual, all the while aware of First California's ticking clock. There wasn't time for any sales to close in the five working days before the June 6 deadline. She hoped letters of intent would do.

Takei Takayashi of Golden Builders listened to her presentation with more enthusiasm than most. Once Wilson had left her alone, he came up to her. "I'd be interested in talking. I'm not long on cash, but for the right price . . ."

"We'll have to see," she countered his opening preparation for a low bid. "There's no need for us to rush into anything."

"No rush?" said a deep male voice behind her. Something sinister and memorable in the tone identified Davis Campbell.

She turned to find him looming over her in a black tuxedo. Gold Cape buffalo studs stared belligerently from his crisp shirtfront, his study of her as bold. "I thought you had to raise some major capital in a week or so."

It was a gut punch, but, "I don't know what you mean."

She was afraid she knew all too well. This was not something she'd told Rory, and no one at Grant Development would have broken confidentiality and talked to him. That left Thaddeus Walker.

"Why, I mean those loans you have to retire at First California." Davis looked appropriately solemn. "I know it couldn't come at a worse time, what with John's illness and your safety problems."

Takei nodded gravely. "Yes, the safety problem at Grant Plaza."

"It was an accident," she snapped. A trembling began inside her.

"Of course, an unfortunate accident," Davis soothed.

Any sympathy she'd had when John told her of Davis's love for Catharine evaporated.

People did terrible things for vengeance and what better candidate to have set this terrible chain of events in motion than Davis Campbell?

Staring up at him, she said, "The police have been informed that someone might have sabotaged the cable and the emergency brake."

Davis crooked a dark brow. "Indeed?"

Her mouth half open to accuse him, she noted Takei's listening pose. Anyone who would hire a welder to rig the hoist cable and disappear had to expect that someone would die . . . Tom Barrett had suggested the target might have been her.

She stared up into the coldest eyes she had ever seen and swallowed her words. One did not accuse Davis Campbell of murder in Wilson McMillan's drawing room. Not without some fine evidence.

With a racing heart, she turned to Takei and attempted to sound steady. "Why don't we talk about Grant's properties?"

He inclined his head in a slight bow and preceded her away from Rory's father. She started to follow.

A hand shot out; Davis's thumb and forefinger pressed her wrist. She tried to pull away, and his grip tightened into a vice. "You've always been the image of your mother. The same passion."

With her fingers beginning to numb, she jerked free. "You think you ever really knew her?"

The corner of his mouth went down the same way Rory's had earlier on the balcony outside their rooms. The challenge in his eyes corroborated everything John had told her of Davis desiring Catharine. "Better than you. Do you even remember her?"

Though her palm fairly itched with the urge to slap him, she decided not to make a bad scene worse. Instead, she started away from him as though the back of her skirt was on fire.

A few feet away, she collided with Rory. In a dark tuxedo like his father's, he cut an imposing figure. His ruby studs were beautiful, but nothing like the one in the ring he'd bought her.

He put out his hands and caught her bare shoulders, his touch defining that she was still shaking from her encounter with his father.

"Let me go," she said.

"Steady," he returned softly. "I heard."

"I'm fine," she insisted.

Rory slid his hands down her arms; the caress sent a shudder through her. "You're no more fine than I am. I heard the way he stripped you down and flayed you." He murmured at her ear, but his words had the impact of a shout. "Quite clever, the way he drew blood without touching you." She believed she heard the full force of his battle to be different from his father.

As she dared to wonder if she'd been wrong about his ducking his parents on the upstairs balcony, an acid female voice cut in. "Hey. Dance with the one you brought." Bold as ever, Sylvia Chatsworth pushed close to Rory.

Like the last time Mariah had seen her, Sylvia wore red, clinging stretch velvet that left little to the imagination.

Extricating her hands from Rory's, Mariah escaped down marble stairs onto Wilson McMillan's grounds. The sea air failed to cool her hot face as, heart pounding, she ran until she was out of breath and had to stop with a stitch in her side.

Finally, a breeze started to soothe her brow. Walking more slowly, she wandered gravel paths through a rose garden worthy of a palace. Fountains made music in the deepening twilight, but did nothing to improve her mood. She sank onto a bench, the stone cold against the backs of her legs.

Replaying the ugly scene with Davis Campbell chilled her further. Guilty though he might be of impossible arrogance and dirty tricks, was she truly ready to call Rory's father a premeditated killer? She honestly didn't know, but if Davis had done this awful deed, with a senator in his pocket he would have no trouble with SFPD. He belonged to the elite club of those who might be able to get away with murder.

And Rory. His comforting her in full view of his father had set her heart yearning once more, only to watch Sylvia Chatsworth publicly claim him.

Lyle loomed out of the darkness. "You've been busy working the crowd."

"Yes." She kept her face turned away until she was sure it was composed. "I appreciate your bringing me."

He stopped her with a palm out gesture. "I saw what happened to you in there. Campbell is a piece of work."

"Which one?"

"Which . . . oh, you mean father or son?" Lyle gave a rueful chuckle. "I must admit it sets me back a bit seeing both you and Sylvia Chatsworth hanging on Rory Campbell."

"I was not . . ."

His chuckle became a laugh. "Relax. I'm not giving you

a hard time about wanting him. I'm just saying I think *la* Chatsworth might be worth a second look."

"Thanks," she said. "I'm sick and tired of watching the Senator's daughter snag every man in sight."

Lyle sobered. "I didn't mean to make you feel bad."

The onshore breeze picked up, bringing a taste of salt along with the green scent of fresh-mown golf course. Lyle took off his jacket and draped it around Mariah's shoulders, its folds making her feel like a doll. They sat in comfortable silence for a few minutes

Perhaps to make amends for advertising his admiration of Sylvia, Lyle plucked a pink rose and presented it to her. She planted it discretely in the hollow between her breasts.

"What's the story on you and Campbell?" he asked.

"Rory and I aren't . . ." she began automatically.

"Maybe not, but you sure want to be."

Mariah sighed, for she did not intend to tell Lyle what happened eight years ago. Let him think what he'd seen between her and Rory recently was a passing fancy.

"I know your fathers hate each other." Lyle selected a yellow rose and harvested it. "But it seems to me there should be a way for you two."

On his lips, it sounded reasonable, but he didn't know what it required. Wipe the slate clean of Rory's denying her at his father's behest, of his marrying Elizabeth, dating a dozen women, and never once contacting her in all that time. Inviting her to a party, but secretly, then sneaking away to Big Sur for a fantasy getaway, now hiding out on balconies when he was here with another woman. She was supposed to be satisfied with crumbs when she wanted a banquet?

Lyle fingered the rose stem. "On the other hand, maybe he is toying with you. I keep hearing rumors out of Davis Campbell's office that Rory's going to marry Sylvia."

The aromatic flowers suddenly smelled nauseating.

A chime announced dinner.

They went up the garden steps to find Rory and Sylvia at a patio table. The dark beauty's head was thrown back, laughing at something he said. Mariah turned away before she could fully see and feel the pain.

The evasion was no use. She wanted to rush up and claim Rory, and knowing she could not without making a scene was enough to make her rage.

Taking a steadying breath, Mariah returned Lyle's coat. Rory gave her a disapproving look that deepened into a scowl at the rose between her breasts.

The McMillan dining room was as large as the one at Hearst Castle, the single long table seating at least fifty. Hunting tapestries lined the walls. Place cards at each setting directed the diners to their seats. To Mariah's dismay, she and Lyle were seated across from Rory and Sylvia.

Over lobster bisque, served with a buttery Chardonnay, Mariah became more animated. She flirted unabashedly with Lyle. With the arrival of the main course, medallions of elk with a raspberry Zinfandel reduction, Sylvia fed Rory a taste from her fork. By the time a chocolate crème cake was carried in, Mariah had lost all appetite.

All she could think was that Lyle had to be wrong about them getting married. She couldn't bear to read another of Rory's wedding announcements in the newspaper.

As dessert was served, it was all Rory could do to stay in his seat. Across the table, Lyle acted like he owned Mariah, bending close to hear what she whispered, touching her arm from time to time. Just the thought of him slipping that rose into the neckline of her dress made Rory want to mess up his perfect face.

Beside him, Sylvia burbled on, oblivious to his misery. Once you got past the tough girl act, she was a good person who didn't deserve to be mixed up in Davis Campbell's schemes. Unfortunately, her fate had been sealed when she was born.

Rory looked down the table to where Senator Chatsworth sat next to Sylvia's mother. Publicity had informed him that Laura Cabot Chatsworth had the blueblood background and soft polish that came from a southern education at Sweet Briar. Both the Senator and his wife wore the pleasant, practiced expressions of career politicians.

Toward the other end of the table, Davis held court while Kiki picked at her food. With her bright hair and stylish clothing, she could pass for a younger woman, but only at a distance. Rory searched for the face of his mother, but she'd lost it years ago. In her forties, she'd gained weight, and her chin had bloated. By fifty, she'd dieted and found a stringy chicken neck beneath an angular jaw. Last year she'd had the tuck beside the ear and the eyelids lifted. The well-dressed woman looked youthful, but the mother he remembered was gone. Looking at her sitting miserably beside her husband, Rory couldn't see bringing any woman into the hell his family was becoming.

Mariah had experienced a taste of Father's cruelty this evening, blindly fleeing the field when she ran into him. What he'd overheard when his father confronted her was disturbing, that business of loans at First California. DCI didn't bank there, and Davis shouldn't have known their business. Yet, Thaddeus Walker had been the one to call with the news of John Grant's heart attack.

Worse was the suspicion that had been growing ever since his father spoke to Mariah of her mother. Everything, from the intensity that strung Davis taut as wire when speaking of her mother's passion . . . all of it suggested that John and Davis's enmity might have begun in a battle over the same woman. The only other time in his life his father had been this unreasonable was the first time Rory had taken up with John Grant's daughter.

Across the table, Mariah looked as miserable as he felt, prodding listlessly at the chocolate crème. Eyes that Rory knew could be fantastic lacked luster.

On impulse, he slipped off one of his patent leather tuxedo shoes. Reaching carefully with his foot, he first encountered the table leg and then explored further. His sock-clad toes touched the top of her sandal.

He felt her flinch. With a glance at Lyle, she appeared to rule him not guilty. She didn't appear to consider Henry Sand, the retired developer who sat at her other elbow.

She looked at him; their gazes locked. He expected her to pull away, but she did not.

Sliding his toes up the silky slick surface of her pantyhose to her calf, he explored. How was it possible that just this forbidden touch tightened his groin, while Sylvia no longer excited him?

The color in Mariah's cheeks rose, along with a pretty flush on her chest above her low cut gold dress. Her lips parted.

Wilson McMillan's wife rose to signal that dinner was at an end. Rory knew he shouldn't risk it, but on the way out of the dining room, he caught up with Mariah and bent to her ear. "You're with the wrong man."

She speeded her steps and kept up with Lyle.

With dinner ended, one man called for a poker game in the library. Wilson McMillan announced a movie in his entertainment center. Davis and Kiki started a table on the terrace that quickly filled.

Rory sidestepped the group and let Sylvia lead him toward the cool retreat of the rose garden. He didn't miss that Lyle took Mariah in the same direction. She might be with the wrong man, but she made it clear she was staying with him.

Feeling the need to move, Rory said to Sylvia, "Let's walk on the golf course."

"You walk," she snapped, shocking him. "Or go take a cold shower."

Rory stopped in the middle of the path. "What are you talking about?"

"I'm talking about playing footsie with Mariah Grant." Busted, he stood silently while Sylvia ordered, "You stay away from her!"

She was getting cocky, first talking about how Senator Chatsworth approved and now asking for a ball and chain. Well, no matter that Davis, "Larry," and Sylvia all thought he should conform to their expectations, he couldn't go along.

"I'll think I'll take that walk," he said.

Sylvia stormed off toward the castle. He was glad to see her go, relieved of the pressure to keep up his act.

On the way out of the garden, he passed an alcove with a stone bench. Mariah and Lyle sat with their heads close together. Rory hurried his steps, swearing under his breath, not stopping until the Pacific lay at his feet.

His anger at Sylvia began to cool when he realized she was another pawn in the game of powerful men and their offspring. To be fair, he had led her on this evening.

As for Mariah, he didn't know what to think. When they were younger, there had been no push-pull kind of games. It had been everything, then nothing, when she refused to communicate with him and he . . . looking back he could see how he'd taken the immature way out in turning to Elizabeth, who'd loved him since their sandbox days.

He backed away from the surf and turned his steps

parallel to the steep berm glistening in the moonlight. A walk beside the ocean had always been his release. From his parents' Seacliff mansion down the steep road cut out of the side of the cliff, he would go down to the sand on China Beach and strike out, walking against the wind. Big combers rolled in and broke, leaving patches of pale foam that looked like ice floes in the chilly breeze. Turning back toward the house where he'd grown up, he'd see the mansion crowning the misty bluff, a castle on a pedestal. Reminding him of the Campbell dynasty, that someday he was expected to rule.

During the summer of Mariah, as he'd come to think of it, he had walked and wondered what he would do with his life. Despite that he'd told her he would as soon run whitewater raft trips as work for DCI, he did know that he loved building.

As the months of June and July slipped sweetly into August, and he and Mariah drew closer with each passing day, he had formulated a plan. Despite their fathers' enmity, he was going to ask her to marry him. That fateful night on *Privateer*, he had planned candlelight, champagne, and to surprise her with the question. After college, they would each work for companies other than their family one, training toward the day when John and Davis, out of the same class at Stanford, would both turn sixty-five. Then, the way clear, he and Mariah would merge the companies and command them together.

How had it gone so wrong?

In the peaceful cove at Spanish Bay, Rory walked too close to the surf and got his feet soaked in a foaming wash of wave. After, he was less careful, getting his tuxedo wet to the knee.

He had to admit to his share of the blame in their break-up. The threat of having to drop his education as he was learning the magic of architecture, the specter of not being able to work in the industry he had come to love . . . But could he have fought harder, called his father's bluff?

Remembering the implacable look in Davis's eyes upon finding his son with John Grant's daughter, he did not think so. He'd never seen his father like that before, and not again in the past eight years . . . until recently.

No, it wasn't possible . . . had Davis's new vendetta against John Grant begun at about the time Rory had heard Mariah was back in town? Had his father been so worried Rory would fall for her again that he'd taken new and aggressive steps to vanquish his old foe?

*C*onfused and chilled, Rory climbed with wet, sandy shoes toward the castle, intent on getting a stiff jolt of Wilson McMillan's best brandy. A private gate marked the edge of McMillan's grounds; he entered and ascended through tiers of garden. Ahead of him on the path, a couple meandered toward the terrace, a blond woman tiny beside a bear of a man.

With an effort, Rory slowed until Mariah and Lyle were up the garden steps and inside. He didn't want a confrontation, for in his present mood he was likely to make a fool of himself.

Once in the castle, he entered the great room where a party was in progress before the ornate bar. The sight of his mother and Sylvia on adjacent saloon stools decided him to skip the drink.

Halfway down the second floor hall to his room, he realized he had not dawdled long enough. Mariah and Lyle were outside her room next door to Rory's. The big man looked relaxed, one hand on the wall above her head, the other hooking his jacket over his shoulder. Rory nearly retreated down the marble stairs to avoid a scene, but his shoes squished on the Oriental carpet.

Lyle turned and met his eyes. With a smile that challenged, he murmured something, bent and kissed Mariah.

Rory had always thought the expression "seeing red" was a joke.

Lyle drew back, opened the door, and watched Mariah go inside. A nod to Rory, "G'night, Campbell." On his way down the hall, he began to whistle.

Rory almost stopped him, but it was Mariah who had made her choice. He watched until Lyle opened another door and went in as though settling for the night.

Once in his own room, Rory kicked off his ruined shoes and socks and dumped them out on the balcony. Next door, a light came on, spilling illumination onto the terrace.

Still heated, Rory took off his tuxedo jacket and pants. He released his ruby cufflinks and dropped them in a porcelain dish. The studs followed. Moonlight from the skylight over the bed struck fire in the stones, reminding him of the exquisite perfection of the Burmese ruby.

When she'd agreed to go to Big Sur with him that

weekend, he'd been as high as a man could get without a flying machine. He'd stood on the brink of a brand new world, slipped the ring onto her third finger, left hand; damned irrational behavior for a born-again bachelor.

Where was the ring tonight?

Stripping to his skin, Rory went onto the balcony.

Mariah stared at her face in the bathroom mirror. When Lyle had whispered, "Let's make him think," she had not realized he was about to kiss her. His lips had toured hers, warm and leisurely, and though he was a catch by any woman's definition, he had evoked no fire.

Only one man had ever been able to do that for her.

Slipping off her golden gown, she hesitated over the velvet robe Rory had bought her in Carmel. The ring might be in the safe deposit box, but she'd refused to allow herself to be soured on the beautiful, soft wrap. Crimson silk glided over her skin.

Coming out of the bathroom, she noted the drapes stood open, as she had left them.

She went to the French doors and reached for the cord. Through the glass, she saw that Rory leaned on the balustrade, staring out to sea. A silver wash of moonlight defined the long bronze line of his bare back, tapering to pale globes of buttock. Strong tan thighs and calves led to sinewy feet. Looking at him, her head was suddenly filled with the scent of the gingered oil he'd poured on her at Ventana. An olfactory hallucination, made more vivid for seeing Rory naked and vibrant. Her palms felt full with wanting to slide them over his skin.

A small moan escaped her. She didn't believe he could hear it, and he did not look her way, but she thought his profile changed in the moonlight. It was all she could do not to open the door.

But though he'd gone into the room alone, she had seen Sylvia downstairs talking with his mother. The two women had been laughing together as Mariah and Lyle passed the door of McMillan's bar. If she went out to a naked Rory and a senator's daughter found them on the balcony . . .

Her face flaming, Mariah grabbed the cord and closed the drapes.

Hearing a faint sound, Rory spun and caught the swirl of settling brocade at Mariah's door. He glimpsed her hand on the drawstring, pale against a dark backdrop of sleeve. Did she still wear the velvet robe, even as she had stripped her hand of his ring? Had she seen him before she withdrew?

When there was no further sign of movement in her window, he looked back toward the ocean. With the party sounds diminished, he could hear the sibilant resonance of surf, a restless cadence pulsing with his blood. He stood for a long time until the night chill drove him into his room.

The click of the latch sounded final.

Shivering, he turned on the shower full and hot. Beneath the flood, he washed salt spray from his hair and skin. As falling water pounded the tension from him, he looked forward to sleep shutting out the constant images playing in his head . . . Mariah naked in the Japanese bath at Ventana, her hair streaming over her shoulders, lying on the bed while his oiled hands defined the curve of her back and buttocks.

He soaped his arousal and groaned aloud . . . Pressing his lips to her rosy nipple, burying himself in her moist heat . . . If he were smart, he'd finish the job solo and go to bed.

But she was right behind that wall, through the thickness of marble and sheetrock. Alone, for Lyle had gone to another room. He splayed his fingers and pressed them to the warm, wet stone.

Rory turned off the taps and toweled dry. The last he'd seen of Mariah, she'd accepted Lyle's kiss. Yet, he could not forget the softness in her eyes this afternoon on the balcony. A heartbeat away from kissing her himself, he could have sworn he was the one she wanted. That is, before his parents showed up to spoil it.

Yet, truth to tell, hadn't he been the one to ruin it by dragging her back and making her think he was ashamed to be seen with her? And after Lyle came out of her room, hadn't he spent the better part of the evening making public love to Sylvia to throw it in Mariah's face?

What if she was also playing both ends against the middle, putting pride above truth?

He slammed his fist onto the bathroom counter. To stay or go was the same kind of no-win chess he and Mariah had been playing since their first meeting. He pulled on his sweat pants and looked out the glass door into the night.

Next door, Mariah lay naked between expensive, soft sheets, feeling as though she were about to jump out of her skin. Thoughts whirled, images of Sylvia with Rory, real and imagined. She saw them next door, playing like puppies in the sheets, along with tortured dreamscapes of surf smashing her father's house and swirling the lovers away. She strained her ears, but no voices came from his room, though the audio of a TV late movie seeped through from the neighbor on the other side.

The moon sailed in the ceiling skylight. Had Rory seen her close the drapes? Did he suspect she'd seen him standing like a Pagan god, limned in silver radiance? Her hands spread wide on the mattress, her pulse throbbed in her palms. An ache spread like warm honey through the rest of her.

Even as she formed the thought of going to him, she knew she could not. That was Sylvia Chatsworth's kind of brash action. What kind of woman would be with one man in public and sneak under cover of darkness into another's room, taking the risk he might not be alone?

Nonetheless, she drew back the covers and reached for her robe.

Moving silently, Rory went back onto the balcony. The stone lay cool beneath his bare feet as he padded toward Mariah's door.

She would scream. Rouse the household. Throw him out.

He needed to get back to his own room. At breakfast, shake Lyle's hand and smile.

He turned the knob and, finding it unlocked, opened the door a scant two inches. "Mariah?"

All was quiet within. He dared to push the door farther open, fumble for the edge of the drapery and pull it aside.

She stood at the foot of her bed, a shadow in black. A paler seam within revealed the robe was open. In the skylight illumination, her hair shone silver.

For a long moment, they looked at each other. Then she sighed, a soft sound that set his heart hammering.

To stop the wind billowing the drapes, he came inside and pulled the door shut. She did not protest. He began to walk toward her, waiting for a sign, for her to draw the robe closed.

He reached her. Her hands came up in the dim light, one to cradle each side of his face. Her touch, exquisite as a feather, coursed through him like liquid lava. "I take it this means you're not going to throw me out?" he whispered.

She rose on tiptoe to kiss him, a bare brush of lips that nearly shattered him. "I was about to come to you."

Though he longed to crush her against him, he held

back. "I want to be with you without words or thoughts of the past or future." Yet, even as he spoke, he knew the time for such fantasy was past. He placed his hands on hers and gently lowered them from his cheeks. "I want to, but we can't escape that way anymore."

She drew the robe together and belted it. "No." Her gaze sharpened. "What about Sylvia?"

He answered with a direct look. "What about Lyle?"

Mariah turned away, climbed onto the king-sized bed, and settled against a pile of pillows. He sat down cross-legged, at least four feet from her.

"Lyle," she said, "is a friend who brought me along as a favor. When he saw you and I on the balcony, he figured us out and played along all evening to make you jealous."

Rory's back muscles begin to relax.

"Sylvia?" Mariah gave him a steady gaze.

He tensed once more. "Since I saw you again, I haven't wanted her."

"Then, what are you doing with her?"

"I'm not. Father wanted me to bring her and when I refused, she came with her folks. When I saw Lyle come out of your room onto the balcony, I saw red and starting playing the same stupid jealousy game with Sylvia." Recalling his father's credo of never apologizing, Rory decided that while it might work at the negotiating table it had no place in the bedroom.

He leaned toward Mariah. "Forgive me for trying to make you jealous."

With those simple words, a weight lifted.

"Forgive me," she returned.

Feeling even lighter and curious as to what other miracles could be wrought, he took a fortifying breath. "While we're on the subject of forgiveness, there's something I need to say. You must be having a difficult time trusting me after the way things ended eight years ago. You could so easily despise me for caving in to my father."

She started to speak, but he held up a hand. "Let me do this."

With a nod, she settled back.

"I was young," he went on, "but I'm not hiding behind that excuse. I do want you to know that when Father caught us on the yacht, he threw up walls in every direction you can imagine. He didn't just offer to get a judge to annul it if we married. He threatened my education, promised to blackball me from working in the building industry."

Mariah sat straighter.

"To see me parking cars."

"Oh, Rory, no."

"He asked if I wanted your father to support me."

"I had no idea . . ."

Rory lifted an index finger. "Don't forget, I'm not making excuses. I should have tried harder to find a way for us."

Mariah looked stricken. "I should have, too, instead of refusing your calls."

He moved close enough to grip her hand and forged on. "As for Elizabeth, our relationship was completely different from what you and I had. I was so battered by the rough seas we went through that she seemed like a haven from the storm."

Mariah moved closer and put a gentle hand on Rory's bare arm. "I've often wished I could have found solace in someone else."

He glanced toward the doors that shut out the world and back to her lying in the moonlight, her pale hair spread over shoulders covered in black velvet. "I'm glad you haven't."

"So am I," she whispered.

Awareness flowed between them; the comforting warmth of her hand changed and sent a tingle up his arm. Her lips parted, beckoning.

"We're all alone," he said. "Nothing to stop us but our demons."

"Nothing to stop us at all."

In the moonlight, she crawled across the mussed comforter to him. Her robe gapped, revealing small perfect breasts. Across a tangle of legs, they managed a dry peck on the lips. Not much of a kiss, but he felt it deeply.

Mariah lowered herself to her back on the bed, and he went down beside her. Propping his head on one elbow, he looked at her half-covered body. The memory of her skin, hot and slick beneath his hands, tormented him. He kissed her again, this time fully, and the sweetness of her mouth was different from the way he remembered it. Her embrace was about passion and the flesh, yet more.

Gradually, the pressure of desire built in him until it was all he could do not to roll her over and bury himself in her moist heat. Her hand found its way below his waist and closed over his aroused sex. He kicked his way out of his pants.

Pushing up to her knees, Mariah replaced her stroking fingers with lips and tongue. He gasped at the heat of the inside of her mouth, for she'd never done that for him, not during their long-ago explorations, or at Ventana.

"You're going to make me lose control," he warned.

She lifted her head and said fiercely, "I want to make you lose control; I want you to forget everything else."

He did. Let go of all except her and the coil winding tighter in him. Each time they were together, it made him hotter and took him higher than the last.

Filling his palm with her breast, he hoped to incite her to greater heights. He tugged at her hair that spilled over his stomach and gasped, "Let me . . ."

She sat back on her heels. By the time he donned the protection he'd brought along in his pants pocket she was watching him with eyes like coals in the moonlight. He reached between her thighs and found her ready, her moan all the encouragement he needed to slide his fingers into her silkiness.

"Rory . . ."

He couldn't tell if she wanted more of his touch or . . .

"I want you," she said, her voice black velvet as her hand once more found him.

He moved over her, his chest brushing soft breasts, and then her impossibly hot flesh enveloped him. It was all he'd dreamed of since their night at Ventana, more, as she wrapped her legs around his back and rocked him ever closer.

As she had desired, he lost control and went over the edge. Her cries answered his.

The delicious euphoria beginning to subside, Mariah felt herself settle back to reality. Though this glorious taste only whetted her appetite for long luxurious nights, all of them spent together, she knew their safe haven could not extend over this room's threshold.

"Rory," she said, "What have we done?"

He brought her fingers to his lips. "Given in to forces we can't resist."

"But, what's going to happen now? Do we go down to breakfast together and shock everybody?"

He bent and brushed a kiss on her cheek. "It would get the job done."

Could it be that simple? Rory said he wasn't with Sylvia, so she had no claim on him. She and Lyle were friends and after the role he had played last night, he couldn't be too surprised to see them together. Davis Campbell would be livid, but she and Rory were both adults now. They could take whatever tantrums he threw.

Rory's expression turned thoughtful. "Although that could be tricky."

Her stomach clenched. Was he still afraid of his father?

He propped on an elbow. "This little shindig is going to be written up in the Sunday gossip columns. You've already weighed in for the weekend with Lyle Thomas. Though I didn't ride down with her, I've been paired with the Sylvia. Do you see where this is going?"

"I'm afraid I do." Lyle was too nice a guy for her to publicly dump him as her date. Not that she cared about Sylvia; humiliating Lawrence Chatsworth's daughter would make the bombshell of Grant and Campbell all the more sensational. If her father read about her and Rory in the Sunday paper when he thought she was down here with Lyle, he might have some kind of relapse.

Much as she hated the idea of a secret affair, Mariah nodded. "We have to keep this quiet, at least until we get home."

CHAPTER 14

*R*ory breathed the bracing salt of morning air on Wilson McMillan's main terrace. Offshore, the sun was burning off the last traces of ocean fog. He had hated to leave Mariah's side, but after last night, he believed things were clearing for them like the weather.

Looking around the breakfast crowd, though, he found his euphoria threatened. After the way Sylvia had stormed off last night, he'd expected her to avoid him. However, at a table set for four, she shared breakfast with his parents. Dressed in demure navy slacks and a matching sweater, with her hair brushed smooth like a child's, she called, "Come and join us."

He smiled, for he could afford to be agreeable. Once home on Sunday, Mariah would tell her dad that she and Rory were determined to see where a renewed relationship led them. And though the idea of it turning into something more permanent had Rory a little scared, he planned to tell his father about them. He would wait for Monday morning at DCI, where the expected scene could not disturb his mother.

Rory worked his way between the breakfast tables and approached the little domestic tableau.

"Did you sleep well?" Father asked with the slightest insinuation. For an instant, Rory wondered how he knew about Mariah. Then he realized the innuendo might refer to Sylvia, who cast down her eyes, her wide mouth managing to look both innocent and corrupt.

Rory sat, poured coffee from a pitcher, and reached for a slice of melon. "I slept like a stone." Truth, for after he and Mariah had wrung each other out, he'd gone down into a deep and dreamless slumber, interrupted several times by more lovemaking, and then more restful sleep.

Waking around dawn, he'd kissed the somnolent Mariah and gone onto the balcony to find the world newborn . . . fresh mist rising from the golf course, the distant boom of surf a revelation.

Tasting his melon, he found it tart and delightful, the coffee strong without being bitter.

Davis wore golfing clothes. "You playing a round?"

"Not this morning," Rory replied.

As soon as he spoke, he wondered if he made a mistake in

letting Sylvia think he was unscheduled. With relief, he saw her check her watch. "I'm going into Carmel to shop with the golf widows," she told Kiki. "Want to come?"

"No, thank you, dear." His mother sipped a tomato drink Rory figured for a Bloody Mary.

Sylvia rose and leaned over to kiss him. He turned his head to the side so her lips barely grazed his cheek.

Kiki smiled after her. "Such a lovely girl. I had a nice talk with her after dinner."

Rory pushed his plate away. Last time she and Sylvia had a powwow, his mother had spilled the story of him and Mariah during that distant summer.

Davis rose and checked his watch. "Tee time in twenty minutes." He and Kiki wandered into the house behind Sylvia.

As Wilson McMillan's guests headed out to enjoy the day, Rory saw Lyle and Mariah near the stone rail. Despite the way last night had ended, he suppressed a twinge of jealousy.

The big man, dressed for golf, left her and stopped by Rory's table. "Morning, Campbell." He gave a co-conspirator's smile. "Mariah said something about wanting to take the 17-Mile Drive."

She stood with her back to Rory, looking out to sea. Though it had been only a few hours since he'd made love to her, her snug white shorts gave him ideas.

"I'd better go or I'll miss my foursome." Lyle left him and Mariah alone.

Rory went to her and clowned, "Good morning, miss, I understand you're looking for a car and driver."

The prospect of a day with Rory stretched before Mariah as an impossible luxury. The valet brought his Porsche, and they set out together.

At Point Joe, they watched the turbid mix of ocean currents. Bird Rock, a small island festooned with white guano, harbored thousands of sea lions, harbor seals, and cormorants competing for space. In the parking lot, a flock of gulls with two-inch beaks dogged Mariah and Rory's heels for handouts.

Farther along, they drove through Crocker Grove, a forest of native pine and cypress. On a winding stretch overlooking the ocean, Mariah pointed out an "Open House" sign. Before she could suggest stopping, Rory pulled into the steep drive.

Down the forested brick lane, they found a secluded retreat. Unimposing from the front, the squat brick chalet had a slate roof and narrow windows. When a middle-aged woman in a red suit opened the front door, they found a different story. Two stories of glass made up the rear wall.

With a glance at Rory's Porsche, the Realtor qualified them as potential buyers. "Welcome to your new weekend home, Mr. and Mrs. . . ."

"Campbell," said Rory.

Mariah's blood began to pound the way it had in the Italian grocery in Sausalito when he failed to deny they were married. In the house's sunny dinette, she dared to imagine them breakfasting on flaky pastry and cold, tart juice. In the library, she saw them curled on the big sofa reading. On a cold day, they'd build a fire in the grand hearth and watch a veil of storm sweep in off the Pacific. She dared not speak her dreams, but didn't Rory's eyes also light when he pointed out features he liked?

Their tour complete, they left the house and drove to the famous lone cypress on a rugged point. Below the cliffs, the ocean churned a clear blue-green, alive with seals and otters fishing the kelp forest. Yet, as Mariah and Rory took in the scenery together, holding hands, a cloud came over the sun. Though she wanted to believe that this time everything would work out, she knew they were a long way from home free.

"Rory," she said. "Before you talk to your father about us, there's something you should know. Why he hates Dad, other than their business competition."

"I think I've figured it out," he said. "Father told me recently about a woman he once loved . . . in the same breath he warned me off you."

"Davis wanted to marry my mother. She chose Dad."

Rory eyes went wide. "I thought I was prepared to hear something like that, but God . . . At the reception last night he said you were the image of your mother . . ." He walked away to stand beside a stone wall at the lip of the sea cliff. "I suspected, but this is worse than I imagined."

Mariah followed him. "If Catharine had lived, maybe she could have patched things up between them."

Rory shook his head. "Who knows what would stop them? In the past few weeks, Father has stepped up his efforts. It's as though something new has set him off."

She thought. "Maybe it was over one of the tracts Grant outbid them on this spring."

There had been a few of those, but it didn't seem like enough provocation.

"Perhaps. If Father has his way, Grant Development will be wiped out."

From the worried look on Rory's face, she wondered if he were also thinking that their fathers' mutual bitterness was the kind of mess where people ended up committing crimes of passion. She thought about bringing up her suspicions about Davis playing a role in the accident, but remembered how Rory had reacted when she'd mentioned it in the funeral home chapel the night of Charley's viewing.

"I won't let Grant be wiped out," she settled for saying.

"I know you won't," Rory agreed. "If I can help it, I won't either."

She realized that this was the first time they had spoken of their fathers in a way that had them both on one side. Even though he still worked at DCI, she began to feel a tide had turned.

"Maybe we could bring them together," she hoped. "They could forgive and forget."

He shook his head. "I'm afraid Father isn't big on forgiveness. And as we've been discussing, he can hold a grudge for thirty years."

Rory drew Mariah against him, and she felt his hands warm on her back. She pressed her head against his chest and heard his heartbeat. There had been no talk of love, and she wasn't entirely sure about that aspect of it yet, but somehow she believed that together they could defy anything.

After lunch at Pebble Beach Club, and a few hours driving down Big Sur and back, they turned back toward Wilson McMillan's. Because the sea fog began to come in, or perhaps because their idyll was ending, Mariah could see tension in Rory's jaw as he drove.

They both seemed to have run out of talk, but she imagined he felt the same frustration at knowing they must part at the door to the castle. It made her wish they'd decided to say the devil with convention and appear together at dinner, instead of with Lyle and Sylvia.

Rory must have heard her thoughts, for he said, "Maybe we should fix Sylvia up with Lyle."

That sounded good, but when he pulled up beneath the portico with a jerk, she saw retired developer Henry Sand standing beneath the overhang. Wearing red trousers, a windbreaker, and golfing cap, he was talking with a similarly attired Takei Takayashi.

"Oops," Rory said as he set the brake on his Porsche to account for the downhill slant of the driveway toward the sea.

Though Mariah had planned on at least walking inside

with Rory, perhaps using their private balcony as a means to an afternoon interlude in one of their rooms, she put her hand on the door latch. "I'll get out here, then."

Rory looked ahead instead of at Mariah. He gave the Porsche some gas, and it growled as though impatient to be on its way. "I'll ignore the valet and park it myself."

She opened the door and got out quickly. Her cheeks hot, she managed to get abreast of Henry and Takei before they noticed her.

"Miss Grant," Henry said.

"Gentlemen," she murmured.

Takei peered down the drive with alert brown eyes. "Wasn't that Rory Campbell?"

"Why, yes." She tried to sound casual while her mind raced for a reason she would be with him after the scene Takei must have witnessed with her and Rory's father last evening. Gesturing to the thickening fog, she said, "Rory was kind enough to give me a ride in out of this."

Not exactly a lie, but it carried the implication she'd been out walking.

Takei glanced at her dry clothing and hair, but though he could surely tell she had not been out in the weather, he said nothing.

As she hurried in the heavy wooden door, she felt both embarrassed at the subterfuge and angry that it seemed necessary. She and Rory should be proud of what they had, and they would be, as soon as this weekend was over.

CHAPTER 15

*A*t dinner, Mariah and Lyle were seated away from Rory and Sylvia. On the one hand, she was pleased not to have to watch Sylvia beside him, but she also recalled the illicit thrill of his touch beneath the table.

Her hopes of her and Rory managing a rendezvous in one of their rooms this afternoon had been dashed as they had returned from their drive with barely time to dress for dinner.

The dining table was so large that she had trouble in locating Rory. Finally, trying not to be too obvious in her bending over and staring, she made out that he was near the end of the table. He and his father sat side by side across from Kiki and Sylvia, with Wilson McMillan between them at the head. Senator Chatsworth and his wife Laura were also with them, making it look enough like a cozy family group to set Mariah on edge.

It got worse when Sylvia caught her looking and gave her a gloating look. The black-haired beauty's burgundy silk was more tasteful than her usual garb, and it made Mariah feel plain in her black-jacketed dinner suit with ice blue satin blouse.

The meal seemed interminable: endive salad, French onion soup, salmon in dill butter, and fresh asparagus. Mariah sipped little as the wines progressed from crisp Sauvignon Blanc to a big, oaky Cabernet. She made small talk with Lyle, who knew she was floating after her outing with Rory, and charmed Henry Sand with whom she had scarcely spoken the evening before. Thankfully, he did not mention seeing her with Rory this afternoon.

As the help cleared dessert, Mariah noticed them setting out tall flutes at each place setting. They opened bottles of expensive champagne and poured, while a murmur went through the guests.

Wilson McMillan rose from his place, dapper and smiling. "Everybody, if you would pick up your glass . . ."

The buzz escalated. Wilson bent to Sylvia and said something that made her laugh. She turned to Kiki and hugged the older woman.

Mariah's mouth went dry.

Wilson lifted his glass.

Sylvia fixed Mariah again with her snapping dark eyes.

"Ladies and gentlemen," Wilson called, "it's my honor as your host to propose a toast."

"Uh, oh," said Lyle.

Wilson finished, "Miss Sylvia Chatsworth has consented to become Mrs. Rory Campbell."

At first, Rory thought he was hearing things. One look at Sylvia's smile told him he had it right. The dinner party burst into oohs and ahs. Glasses clinked, snippets of conversation rose.

"A lovely couple."

"Wonderful match."

"Now Campbell will be pulling strings in Washington."

Sylvia knocked her flute against Rory's with a ring. Kiki beamed at him and drank off half her champagne. Wilson McMillan thumped him on the shoulder, bent spryly and bussed Sylvia. She rushed around the table and hung on Rory's arm.

My God, what must Mariah be thinking? He tried to see her, but too many people blocked his view. Setting down his glass, he shook his arm free, waving it in the air. "Folks," he called.

His father, seated to his left, dug his fingers into Rory's leg above the knee.

Pain radiated from the pincers-like grip. To keep from sprawling face first on the table, Rory clutched his chair back.

"I'm damned if I'm going to let you do this."

He knocked the hand off his leg, jumped up, and gritted in Davis's ear, "Don't even think about it."

And through it all, Davis smiled, a man exchanging a private pleasantry with his son. "You'll not spurn a lady in public. Or make a fool of a United States Senator."

"If that's what I have to do, I'll do it." Rory felt like throwing up. "Hey, everybody!" he shouted.

The crowd clapped as though his exclamation was one of joy.

Davis raised his arms and called, "No speeches now."

At his words, people began moving out of the dining room.

Rory pushed into the crush to find Mariah.

❧

Mariah clutched her glass. If she'd been holding the stem, she might have broken it.

"Let's get out of here," Lyle said at her elbow.

"No," she hissed. She must never show the depth of her humiliation.

Lyle set his champagne flute on the table and took hers from her. "Smile . . . and come with me."

With an effort, she stretched the corners of her mouth into what she hoped did not look like a grimace.

Lyle winked and grinned at the couple across the table. "I don't think Mariah and I will stay any longer." His blue eyes conveyed his interest in getting her alone.

"Have a pleasant evening." Henry Sand nudged Lyle's ribs.

"Will do," the big man boomed, slipping a supporting arm around Mariah. Amidst the blur of approbation and clinking glasses, he manhandled her through the nearest door, the servants' entrance into the castle kitchen.

"Some water here," she heard him direct as though from a distance. The racks of pots and pans spun and, but for Lyle, she would have fallen. A cold cloth draped her neck, soaking the collar of her satin blouse.

The clatter of dishes came to a halt. Curious men and women in caterer's black and white stared. "She needs air," Lyle said.

Mariah trembled. Chill water dripped down her sides.

He hustled her through the kitchen and down the back stairs. As the cool freshness cleared her head, numbness gave way to disbelief.

"I'm sorry." Lyle patted her shoulder like a big bear pawing.

"I've got to get out of here," she said. "I can't stand this place another minute."

They walked downhill toward the sea. The fog hung thicker over the lawn and contributed to her sensation of dreaming. How was it possible Rory had gone from her arms to toasting his engagement to another woman?

Her heels kept sinking into the turf, so she kicked off her evening sandals and carried them. Dressed more warmly this evening than last night, she refused Lyle's offer of his jacket. But as the chill from the fog cooled her heated brow, she threw the damp rag onto a bush and went with him down to where lawn merged with fairway. Her pantyhose grew wet from the dewy grass, but she kept moving as though distance could insulate her.

It didn't help. Rory's engagement couldn't be real, but she had seen it with her own eyes. How could she have been so stupid as to believe in a Campbell?

The answer was clear. Rory had gone to great lengths to earn her trust. One step at a time, from his party invitation, to running "On The Spot" out of Charley's viewing, and promising his father could go hang. The final degradation was making love to her so passionately she'd believed his fervor.

She and Lyle reached the highway and she put on her shoes to cross the pavement. Once they passed over to soft sand, she took them off again. On the way down to the water, on the same beach where her mother and father had come together and alienated Davis Campbell, agony metamorphosed to fury.

Had the stepped-up campaign to take down Grant Development kicked off when Davis heard she was returning to San Francisco? Rory had "warned" her, but what if he meant to put both Grants on notice of precisely which family was winning the war?

Lyle walked with her a while in silence. "You were with him all day and he didn't say a thing?"

"He said a lot of things, designed to set me up for a fall." She reached the smooth wet sand near the water's edge and felt the Pacific's chill on her bare soles.

"You really think this thing between your families has gone that far?"

The jury was still out on how far they had gone. First California, Zaragoza . . . sabotage?

"There's nothing else to believe. Years ago, Rory chose his family over me, made a marriage his father wanted. Now he's gone to work for him."

The pieces continued to fall into place. It made sense that he'd toyed with her emotions and she'd been the same kind of fool she'd been eight years ago, falling for a man whose acting skills were worthy of the stage.

She had no choice but to conclude the goal was not only to destroy Grant Development, but also to gain retribution by breaking the heart of a woman who was "the image of Catharine."

Revenge was, indeed, a dish best served cold.

On swift feet, Rory searched the marble halls and rooms. He ducked out onto the empty terrace and checked the garden, calling, "Mariah, Lyle, you out here?" On his way up the wide staircase toward the guest rooms, well-wishers ambushed him. Sylvia led the pack. "I've been looking all over for you."

Rory steered her outside to a private corner between moss-covered stone walls. "What were you thinking, pulling a stunt like that? You know I'm not going to marry you."

Sylvia's smile faltered. "Last night I talked to your mother. She said you needed the right woman in your life, but you're cynical about getting burned again." Her lower lip trembled. "She thought if we made the announcement you'd come around."

"I can't see Mom suggesting a circus like this evening." Rory bent closer to see Sylvia's face in the light from a small iron wall sconce. "Think now, did she really say that last part?"

Her eyes filled with tears. Dark hair swished her shoulders as she shook her head. "No. Kiki just agreed when Davis came up with it at breakfast."

The rage he'd felt at his father in the dining room resurfaced. "This time he's gone too far." After he found Mariah, Rory was going to tell him what to do with his money and his company.

Sylvia's mascara ran. She dashed at her eyes and smeared it further.

It made Rory feel like a bastard. Though Chatsworth and Campbell might push an alliance between their families, she had nothing political to gain. No doubt, she truly wanted him.

She gulped back sobs and he glanced around to see if anyone observed. Fortunately, they were alone in the dimly lit alcove.

He let his voice soften. "Did you really think I'd marry you?"

"Kiki said with time you could learn to love me."

"If that worked, I'd still be married to Elizabeth."

And if time brought relief, he would not still want Mariah. He should be upstairs right now explaining things to her, but only a man as cruel as his father would shove Sylvia aside at this moment. For all her boldness, she was no match for Davis's dirty tricks.

"I've been unfair to string you along," he told her, "but I'm not free to care for you."

"Mariah Grant." Another tear rolled and made a wet mark on her silk-clad breast.

"That's right," he said evenly. "I've got to find her and sort this mess out."

Sylvia clutched his arm. "What will I tell my parents?"

"The truth. It'll be public knowledge soon enough."

He went into the castle and ran up the marble steps. The long corridor was deserted.

The door next to his stood closed. He knocked and wasn't surprised when she didn't answer.

"Mariah?" Trying the knob, he found it turned smoothly.

Still silence, so he pushed open the door. Inside, a stained-glass lamp beside the bed was the only light. An air of stillness said no one was there. Still, he moved to the bathroom door, noting the clear countertop. The closet was empty save for a nest of bare hangers.

He reached for his phone, but she had never given him her cell number. Hell, she'd know better than to answer even if he could call.

Poised on the edge of rushing into the foggy night, driving his Porsche to the limit to catch her and Lyle, he knew he couldn't do it. Since she and Lyle weren't sleeping together, the only logical place she'd have him take her was her father's, where she'd been staying. And much as he'd like, Rory could not storm the home of a man recuperating from open-heart surgery in the middle of the night.

As he moved to leave the bedroom, he saw something dark draped over on a pale chaise lounge near the balcony door. Going closer, he recognized the black velvet robe he'd chosen for her.

She must have known he'd find it.

Catching up the cloth, he crushed it against his face. It still bore her scent, and he inhaled deeply, vowing this was the last time his father would interfere in his life.

CHAPTER 16

Sunday morning Mariah lay in her childhood room surrounded by the blue dotted Swiss she'd selected in high school. She'd passed a quiet existence in this house, dated uncertain boys, saw movies where things happened to other people, until Rory had blown into her life like a Pacific typhoon.

Last night when Lyle had brought her home, she'd tapped on her father's door, told him she was there, and fled into her room without discussing why she'd cut the weekend short. Now, she wondered if telling him about Davis Campbell and the loans would be sufficient to explain her pallor. She certainly couldn't reveal what had happened with Rory without looking brainless.

Avoiding the moment of reckoning, she decided to take a bath. Her terry robe, soft and floppy as a well-worn stuffed animal, was far more practical than black velvet trimmed in crimson silk.

As she started to open the bedroom door to head for the hall bath, the pale blue phone on her antiqued white and gold nightstand rang.

Mariah's breath caught, but it couldn't be Rory; he must be breakfasting with Sylvia. Nonetheless, she stood frozen through the second ring.

It stopped then, and she realized John must have picked up the cordless extension he kept by his recliner in the living room.

A moment later he called, "Mariah! Phone for you."

Her heart raced. It could be anybody, most probably Lyle wanting to know how she was holding up. She knew her father would stay on the line until she made the connection, so she picked up.

"Mariah," Rory said in a drawn voice.

On instinct, she slammed the phone down and stomped toward her door.

From the living room, she heard John. "Who's there?"

Her steps slowed.

"Certainly," he went on in an oddly formal tone.

She tiptoed into the hall.

"I'll tell her." His tone softened. "I take it this is important to you?"

Mariah closed her eyes and put a hand on the wall. She alternated between rage at Rory for disturbing her dad and wondering why he would call. In the other room, she heard the portable phone replaced in its cradle.

Her bare foot managed to find one of the creaky boards in the hardwood floor. Her father's hearing wasn't as good as it once was, but he knew his house. "That was Rory Campbell," he said at normal volume. "I suppose you knew that when you hung up."

She went slowly into the living room. John reclined in his pajamas, a lock of his silver hair standing straight up. Pieces of the Sunday paper lay scattered.

Mariah wrung her hands. "I swear I tried to stay away from him."

"Do you remember what I said last week about me never getting over your mother and you never getting over Rory?"

She nodded miserably.

"Much as I might condemn you, I can't. Or him."

"Dad, it's over," she insisted. "He was just using me because his father wants us both hurt. Last night at McMillan's Rory announced his engagement to Sylvia Chatsworth."

Thoughtful gray eyes pitied her as John reached for a section of the paper lying open and handed it across. Rory wasn't in the picture the way he had been with Elizabeth, but even so, Mariah had a sickening feeling of déjà vu. Sylvia's photo showed her looking fresh and lovely, a white day dress setting off her black hair and eyes.

Miss Sylvia Elise Chatsworth, daughter of Senator and Mrs. Lawrence Arthur Chatsworth III, to wed Rory Davis Campbell, son of Mr. and Mrs. Davis Gates Campbell.

Mariah let the paper fall. "So, why would he call?"

John nodded toward the phone. "He said to tell you this is one of Davis's tricks. He's not going to marry her."

She shot to her feet. "I can't take any more of this."

"Maybe he can't either. He sounded like hell."

On swift feet, she fled to the bathroom.

With meticulous care, she turned the taps and waited for the tub to fill. Testing the water with her toe, she dumped in a load of lavender salts. She had ginger-scented crystals, but she couldn't bear being reminded of Rory spreading Ventana's aromatic oil over her body.

Sliding into water as hot as she could stand, she submerged everything except her face. It was quiet save for the occasional gentle splash as she moved an arm to adjust her bath pillow or reached with her toes to let water out and replenish it with a fresh flood from the tap.

Tears welled in her eyes, broke the dam, and ran down her wet cheeks. It had all felt so real; Rory accepting a share of blame for their first breakup, the electric intensity in him when they made love, walking through that open house masquerading as husband and wife.

Yet, he must have been faking. She'd seen him toasted and congratulated in McMillan's dining room. She'd seen the newspaper.

No, it couldn't be true. He'd just called and talked to her father. John thought he sounded sincere.

But Rory always sounded that way. Listening to him speak, she never detected the dissimulation or evasion she'd heard from people in business and in some of the men she'd dated in the past eight years. Yet, he must have been lying with both his lips and his body, stripping away her defenses even as he removed her clothes. Mariah hoped both he and his father were happy this morning, as Rory achieved the Campbell's objective of vengeance. For, while her tears mingled with bath water, she knew . . .

She had the supreme misfortune to have fallen in love with Rory Campbell.

Again.

The first time, she'd been a starry-eyed innocent. This time it came with the exquisite pain of knowing they had no chance for happiness.

From the front hallway, she heard a rasping. Gripping the side of the tub with shriveled fingertips, she pushed upright. Another knock came louder. She sat motionless, listening.

A pounding set up, accompanied by a faint shouting.

From the living room, Mariah heard her father call her. He sounded alarmed.

She jumped up, and water sheeted off her nude body. Wrapping herself in the terry robe, she went out with her hair in damp strings. Beneath her wet feet, the hall floor felt slick.

She skated with care to the front door, rose on tiptoe, and used the peephole.

Rory stood in the rain on the small brick stoop, his shoulders hunched against the downpour, droplets beading the ends of his hair and trickling down his face. "Mariah?" he peered at the peephole. "If you're there, open up."

She pressed her palms against the wood. Everything in her said to walk away.

Dark stubble shadowed his jaw. "I wanted to call or come after you last night, but I waited until a decent hour because of John's illness."

Was it possible he'd not spent the night with another woman?

"Please. Did he tell you I'm not going to marry Sylvia?"

She opened the door a wedge. At least the screen was still latched.

"He told me you're playing cruel games." She wanted to hurt him the way last night's announcement had plunged her into despair.

"This isn't a game," he said grimly. "The whole thing was a mistake."

"If it wasn't true, how could you let it happen?"

He put his hand to the rain-beaded screen. "They sprung it on me. I knew nothing until McMillan stood up. Father convinced Sylvia I would go along with his dynasty building."

"From the way he's always controlled you, he had good reason to think so."

Rory tried to pull the screen open against the latch. "I told you, it's off. It was never on. Sylvia's telling her folks I'm not going to marry her."

Despite her anger and disbelief, the look of pain on his face tore at Mariah.

Rory yanked at the knob so the screen door rattled. "If you can honestly tell me what's happening with us isn't real, that it's not the best thing that's ever happened to either of us, then I'll go."

"I don't know what's real anymore."

He slammed his fist against the jamb. "Open this door!"

How she longed to believe he wasn't involved with Sylvia, but Mariah could not trust him. She shut the door in Rory's face.

At nine that night, Mariah stared at the chessboard, unable to care that her father had her in check. She'd only agreed to play for the distraction.

"Come on, daughter," he goaded. "Arnold played a better game when he was over this weekend."

She shoved at the board, wanting to suggest he play with Arnold exclusively from now on. Instead, she made a deliberately obtuse move.

Without his usual victory smile, John moved another piece. "Checkmate."

Mariah rubbed her arms while he began to set the pieces for a new game. "I'm sorry I'm not better company, Dad."

"It's just that your mind is elsewhere," he finished.

He must have discerned her thoughts of Rory, but she refused to acknowledge the lead-in. With a glance at her watch, she said, "I need to get in to work early tomorrow. Hopefully, the bait I put out at McMillan's will start to get some bites."

Her father turned one of the stone pawns in his hands.

She leaned forward. "I know you don't want to sell anything to the Campbells, but Takei Takayashi was the only one who seemed serious about any of the properties. And he prefaced it by saying he was short on cash. If Davis's campaign to scare people over safety makes them hold back . . ."

John sighed. "I keep hoping we can get out from under this without losing Grant Plaza."

"We'll try." Mariah wished she felt more confident.

The chess pieces in place, he inclined his head for her to make the first move.

"I don't feel like another game," she said. "As you said, my mind is elsewhere."

"I'd say that's also true of your heart." His gray eyes watched her alertly.

She rose. "We've been over all that, Dad. Rory and I might have enormous chemistry, but as long as he works for his father, it can never be."

Rory sprawled on the leather sofa in his townhouse, wearing his oldest sweats. He stared sightlessly at the TV, where John Wayne pulled his gun with a practiced draw. The Sunday paper, another failed attempt at distraction, lay strewn over the Berber carpet and his ship's hatch coffee table. The image of Mariah closing the door in his face seemed more real than anything else.

He had an inkling how stalkers felt. No matter the

downpour, he wanted to wait in her yard until she ran out of milk or eggs and had to leave the house.

The closing credits of *Rio Lobo* gave way to the trailer for "On The Spot." About to jab his thumb onto the "off" button of his remote, Rory was shocked to hear his own name.

"Stay tuned for this evening's exclusive exposé of one of San Francisco's most eligible bachelors. Has Rory Campbell's engagement to Sylvia Chatsworth settled him down? We don't think so, and we have the tape to prove it."

Rory had been expecting something virulent from Julio Castillo ever since he beheld the reporter's angry countenance looking up from the funeral home floor. Still, it shocked him to be the lead feature.

First, he watched a clip of him and Sylvia at a restaurant back in April. "Old news," he told the screen as she fed him tiramisu from a spoon.

Then he saw himself at Charley Barrett's viewing in a flurry of shouting, Castillo going down in a windmill of arms and legs. The voiceover made it sound as though Rory had acted on Mariah's behalf rather than through common decency.

Next was a clip of him leaving his townhouse in the Porsche with Mariah, the day of Charley's funeral. Castillo said smugly, "Miss Grant's car remained in Campbell's garage until they returned together the next day."

Rory muttered an oath at them saving up clips to use when the story got juicy enough.

The farce went on. "The engagement was announced at retired developer Wilson McMillan's palatial Pacific Grove mansion Saturday night, and in the San Francisco Sunday morning *Chronicle*."

Rory started scrabbling through the newspaper. Underneath the sports and world news he found what he called "the women's section." Mrs. Chatsworth must have phoned it in so it made the final edition.

The photo of Sylvia was years old, from a debutante ball. Daughter of blah, son of, more blah. Campbell attended Stanford University, Kappa Alpha, and his business fraternity. And the clincher . . . being groomed to take over Davis Campbell Interests.

He crumpled the paper and sent it flying into a corner.

Back on TV, there was this morning's footage of him standing in the rain before John Grant's front door. A zoom in and he stood with his hands spread on the screen. Mariah could be seen through the door in her bathrobe. Audio from one of those long-range microphones, "Sylvia's telling her folks I'm not going to marry her," he said. "If you can honestly tell me what's happening with us isn't real . . ."

His face flamed.

And finally, "Open this door!" He sounded like a fool. Looked like one hitting the doorjamb with a manly fist.

He'd go down to the station and smash Castillo's face, but that would make the reporter's day. He'd call a lawyer and sue for defamation . . . but everything on the tape was real.

For the second time that day, he watched Mariah shut the door in his face.

His phone shrilled again. Caller ID said his parents. He

let the answering machine roll.

"Pick up, or I swear to God I'll come over there . . ." his father threatened.

Lifting the handset, Rory clicked on, then off to halt the call. The phone started to ring again. Angrily, he answered, "What do you want?"

"Get over to the house," Davis snapped, "now."

Despite that his father's tone meant there would be hell to pay, Rory decided, "No."

"What do you mean 'no'?"

"Just what I said." He gathered courage. "If you come over here, you'll have to break in. And if you try that, I swear to God I'll call the cops." He hung up.

If Father came, Rory would call 911, not so much for protection, but to keep him from taking his own anger at everything out on the older man. Maybe he should go to a hotel and hide out like John Grant had. Yet, that was sure to backfire, for somebody from "On The Spot" must be waiting outside, a minimum wage clod dozing in a vehicle littered with fast food wrappers.

Determined to sleep on his rage before confronting his father, Rory put on his burglar alarm and went to bed.

CHAPTER 17

When Mariah entered the Grant conference room for the Monday meeting, a lively buzz of conversation cut off. Taking John's chair at the head of the table, she sipped coffee and hoped the caffeine would rejuvenate her. Despite going to bed at nine-thirty when her father had nodded off, she was exhausted. Nonetheless, she pulled her notes toward her, raised her head and looked around the table.

Arnold Benton stared at her with revulsion. She met the challenge in his eyes and felt a ripple go through the rest of the watchers.

Before she could ask what his problem was, he shoved back from the table. "If you're planning to chair this meeting, maybe you should talk about the conflict of interest with you and Rory Campbell."

If Arnold had thrown a cup of coffee, she could not have been more shocked. A look toward Tom Barrett found his tousled head bent. April Perry, dressed to kill in a red designer suit, wore a grim expression.

"You must be hallucinating." Mariah kept her voice controlled. "Rory is engaged to Sylvia Chatsworth."

"Mariah." April's voice bore the quiet of command as she pushed the black plastic rectangle of a VCR tape across the table. "Maybe we should postpone the meeting until you look at this."

As if April were in charge, the staff filed out except for Tom. Mariah remained in her father's seat feeling like a suspect under interrogation, while the PR director started the tape on the big-screen TV.

When the "On The Spot" logo appeared on the monitor, Mariah groaned aloud.

"I take it you and John didn't catch this last night," Tom said.

The opening scene of Sylvia feeding Rory a bite of dessert curled Mariah's fingers into fists. The footage of Charley's viewing made her cringe and cast an apologetic look at Tom. He watched with stolid interest.

Seeing herself at the front door in her bathrobe, Mariah knew how celebrities must feel when they saw their face in grainy newsprint that made them look their worst. Rory tried to force the locked screen.

"Is nothing too low for these people?" she said.

Neither Tom nor April answered. She had the feeling they were thinking, like Arnold, that she had betrayed the company.

The final scene was of Rory after she closed the door. He leaned his head against the screen door and rolled it from side to side like a wounded animal. Mariah gasped and heard it come out as a sob.

April pointed the remote to rewind the tape. Tom kept staring at the TV as though the show still played. It was time Mariah needed to compose her face and choke back the hard ache in her throat.

At last, Tom looked at her. "You told me it was nothing."

With an effort, she met his disappointed blue eyes. "You saw the tape. It's over."

He shook his big head. "You probably even believe that." At the conference room door, he turned back. "Why don't we skip the meeting this week?"

Trying to maintain a shred of dignity, Mariah nodded. There was only one thing that mattered any longer, to sell properties and prevent foreclosure. Failing that, Grant Development would need no more meetings.

April's eyes were on her. In the older woman's expression lay fierce loyalty to John and censure for the wayward daughter she'd never met before this spring. "Your father doesn't know about the show?"

"Not unless one of you, maybe Arnold who loves to carry tales, called him after I left for work."

Feeling the weight of the chore ahead of her this

evening, that of showing the footage to her father, Mariah
went to the VCR and extracted the tape. "I'd like for this to
come from me."

April nodded, her arms crossed over her chest.

Mariah went on, "Since the meeting's been tabled, does
Ramsey have anything new from the metallurgy lab?"

"Chatsworth's project should wrap soon," April assured
her. "Then they'll start running our samples."

Four blocks down Market Street, Rory stood outside the
closed door of his father's office.

The secretary was not in sight. After sleeping on it, Rory
had wakened determined to have it out. His father could no
longer match-make for profit, or keep him from Mariah if
she'd have him.

He took a deep breath and, without bothering to knock,
walked in.

Thaddeus Walker of First California sat opposite Davis,
who was behind his lacquered desk. The banker turned with a
furtive look on his narrow face, reinforcing the distrust Rory
had instinctively felt upon meeting the man years ago.

Davis shot up with the air of a king interrupted by a
serf. "Don't you know better than to walk in when my door
is closed?"

Rory flushed.

Walker checked his watch and rose. "I need to go anyway.

I'll let you know about that line of credit."

"Do that." Davis sounded as though he was doing the bank a favor.

Rory went to the window while the guest was escorted to the door.

"I'll make the offer as soon as I hear from you," his father said in parting to the banker.

A moment later, a heavy hand clamped his shoulder. Rory jumped, for he'd not heard footsteps in the thick carpet.

"You see Grant Plaza out there?" Davis asked with a pleasantness that rang false. The forty-story edifice dominated the area near the convention center. The glazing was almost all in place, making it look close to completion.

"What about it?" After hearing the byplay with the banker, Rory was afraid he knew what was coming.

"It's going to be mine."

Even with advance warning, it felt like a blow. "I'm not surprised a man as small as Walker fits in your pocket."

"For God's sake, learn to run with the big dogs," Davis sneered. "Thaddeus is looking after the best interests of First California by calling Grant's loans. After the accident, there's the safety issue."

"An accident can happen on any site in town. You're the one playing it up with anybody who'll listen."

"You take advantage of opportunity where you find it," Davis instructed.

"And of course, First California fronts DCI when you try and buy Grant out."

"You learn fast."

"I have a good teacher," Rory said bitterly.

His father's handsome face twisted. "Then, why haven't you learned a damned thing? You looked like a fool on television. When Larry Chatsworth called me he was livid."

"I don't care."

"Your prospects are limitless here." His father waved his arm to include the city skyline. "I don't understand why you seem determined to sabotage them."

Rory saw the ugliness: the scheming with the bank, the senator, and God only knew what else. In contrast, there was the clean beauty of Mariah. And there was John Grant, a good man whose greatest sin had been to fall in love.

He glared at his father. "I don't suppose you'd understand."

Leaving the office, he moved automatically through the halls of DCI. Men and women smiled with the deference given the owner's son. He left the building and walked the city streets.

If Catharine Grant had lived to develop a thick waist and a crop of lines around her eyes, would Davis still be obsessed with vengeance? Rory had always known his father as hard driving and competitive, in sailing and hunting as well as business, but this was beyond the pale. The premeditated destruction of Grant Development, John, and Mariah sickened him.

People on the crowded sidewalk must think him mad, a tall man striding fast to outrun his demons. What twisted the knife of pain was the memory of a hard hand covering his on the tiller of his first small sailboat. Riding on tall shoulders, Rory had visited construction sites where workers crowded around and called him Davis's little man.

His mouth pressed into a line. If Rory stood by and watched Grant Development go down, he would indeed be a little man.

At three o'clock Rory presented himself in Grant's outer office. The receptionist behind an impressive circular desk looked like a pro football cheerleader, with round breasts beneath a snug knit.

"Mariah Grant, please," he asked, more intent on his mission than the girl.

"Sir, did you have an appointment?"

"Look, tell her it's Rory Campbell . . ." He cast about for something business-like. "On a matter of extreme importance to Grant Development." Boy, that was special.

She murmured into her headset, and then listened for a minute. "Please be seated."

He folded his long frame down onto a couch and looked around the lobby. Whereas Davis had called in the decorators and given them a blank check, Grant's waiting room looked like a moderately successful doctor's office. Dark green carpet accented soothing, color-coordinated landscapes on the walls. The exception was the fine trophy case in gleaming mahogany. It held a collection of the awards the city's developers regularly passed among themselves. John Grant had won Developer of the Year for three of the past seven. Rory knew that DCI had won twice, as had Golden Builders.

He wondered if there would be a Grant company to compete this time next year.

The door to the inner workings opened to reveal a woman whose red tailored suit complemented her hair. Rory recognized her as the public relations director who'd been on TV in the days following the accident.

"Mr. Campbell," she said coolly. "May I help you?"

He rose and tried to look professional. Anybody in PR would have seen "On The Spot" by now. "I asked to see Miss Grant."

"She's not here. I came out because of the . . . ah . . . importance to the company? Won't you come back to my office?"

He felt like a double agent on enemy turf, but once past reception, he'd have a better chance of finding out if Mariah really was here and avoiding him.

The farther they walked down the hallway, the more he wanted to turn around and leave. In one office, a bland man with thinning hair looked up from his desk. His jaw dropped in apparent recognition. Next door, Tom Barrett, whose son had died at Grant Plaza, was coming into the hall.

"Campbell," he said coldly. "What are you doing here?"

From behind Rory, he heard another man say, "I was wondering that, myself." Turning, he saw the fellow who'd apparently recognized him and gotten up to check him out, someone he was certain he'd never met. No doubt, he had

"On The Spot" to thank for that.

April led the way into her corner office and the two men followed. Everyone stood as if waiting for Rory to conjure a rabbit.

"It's pretty simple, really," he said. "I came to see Mariah."

"She's not here," Tom replied.

"So April tells me."

The public relations manager gave a tight smile. "Mr. Campbell told reception he wanted to see Mariah on a matter of grave importance to the company. I thought someone should see him."

A knowing look broke out on the bland guy's face. "More like a matter of personal importance."

"Hold on, Arnold." Tom turned to Rory. "You know I helped John found this company over twenty-five years ago. Suppose you tell me what you've got."

His soft words were persuasive, but it wasn't even tempting. If Rory were going to blow the whistle on his own father and on the company he owed loyalty to . . .

"I really need to talk with Mariah. It's a follow-up to a discussion she had with my father in Pacific Grove over the weekend."

Tom raised a brow. "About property sales?"

"Have you come to make an offer on something?" April pressed.

Surrounded by people certain that he bore them ill will, he shook his head. If he told of his father's treachery, they would think it some kind of Trojan horse trick.

Without waiting for escort, he walked.

Bayview Townhomes overlooked the west shore of San Francisco Bay. Though the smooth curve of the San Mateo Bridge arched gracefully nearby, the highway noise did not sound excessive to Mariah. Jets on the southeast approach to San Francisco International were still high enough not to disturb the peace. Waves lapped at the newly built bulkhead.

Skirting a patch of mud, she dropped her laptop case, purse, and cell phone into the back seat of her sedan. There had been no good reason to visit the site this afternoon, but after watching "On The Spot" with Tom and April, she hadn't been able to stay in the office. How could any of Grant's senior managers ever take her seriously again? No one would be able to meet her without seeing her in a rumpled bathrobe.

She wasn't sure if the Bayview construction manager had seen the show, for he had maintained a dignified demeanor, answering her questions. The men were another story, jostling each other with elbows, grinning, and making commentary in Spanish too rapid for her to catch.

When there had been nothing more to do outside, she'd spent time in the model unit writing memos on her laptop, putting off going home. In her purse, she carried the "On The Spot" episode on tape. To say she dreaded showing it to her father was too mild, even though he'd no doubt heard most of what she and Rory had said at the door yesterday morning.

Even so, seeing his daughter dragged publicly through the muck would be tough. Especially with him recovering so slowly she wondered if he would ever be back to work full time.

Mariah leaned against her car in the softening afternoon. The laborers had driven away in their pickups and panel trucks, their passage marked by a litter of taco wrappers tumbling toward the water. Her soft black dress, cut full and flared at the bottom riffled in the wind.

A faint sound came from the construction entrance. It grew louder, and when she recognized the feral growl, her heartbeat accelerated. Squinting into the sun, she made out a black car speeding over the ruts toward her. It braked, nose down, and pulled up beside her.

With a smooth purr, the passenger window slid down. Rory leaned across the console and looked at her through opaque sunglasses. "Get in."

At the tightness in his voice, she took a step back. "No."

He removed the glasses and revealed his eyes, dark pools of hurt. He rubbed his chin, speckled with the bluish note of five o'clock shadow.

"How did you find me?" she asked.

He cut the engine and got out. "When I was leaving Grant, your receptionist told someone on the phone where you were." His cobalt silk tie snapped in the wind and hit him in the face.

"What were you doing at Grant?"

"Looking for you." Rory loosened the knot, slid it hand over hand from around his neck, and slipped it into the pocket of his charcoal wool suit jacket. "We have to talk," he went on, placing his hand palm up on the Porsche's roof.

She wrapped her arms around herself.

With long strides, Rory came around the hood to her. "You've seen that inexcusable piece of TV trash?"

"I've seen it. As far as I know, my father hasn't. I get the pleasure of playing the tape for him this evening."

"Those bloodsucking leeches. Your dad doesn't need any more trouble." Rory captured her, his hands on the car roof on either side of her. His voice softened. "I'm sorry I got you into this. If the press weren't always after me, you might have been left alone."

"It didn't hurt that you were supposed to marry a senator's daughter."

"I already told you the announcement wasn't true."

Mariah brought up her arms and knocked Rory's away. "If it wasn't, you should have told the whole room it was a pack of lies the minute it happened."

"I tried to. Didn't you see me waving and calling for order?"

"Didn't you see me leave?" She walked toward her car.

"I was so livid at my father I was lucky to see anything." Rory followed her across the broken ground. "For God's sake, how can you stand there and keep telling me what's going on with us is nothing?"

He grabbed her arm and turned her to him.

She gave him an icy look, and he removed his hand.

"When are you going to learn to trust me?" he asked. "I've been looking for you all afternoon to tell you Thaddeus

Walker is loaning DCI the money to buy Grant out."

Though she had suspected something of the sort, she was still shocked. "You came out here to tell me that?"

"I went to Grant to tell you as soon as I heard. The line of credit is waiting for Father to make his move on John."

She studied Rory with dawning wonder.

"Trust, Mariah." He looked exasperated. "It's time."

"I want to believe you," she said slowly. She couldn't think of how Davis might benefit from Rory bringing her this piece of news, so it didn't sound like a trick. And as always, Rory looked and sounded completely sincere.

"Then do believe me," he said. "And believe Father was behind that fake engagement."

"I'm trying." How she wanted to set aside everything that conspired to keep them apart.

"Don't try. Do it."

He took her by the arm again, his hand sliding warmly up beneath her sleeve. She felt the deep insistent pulse that had started the moment he took off his sunglasses. Too aware of him, she noted his long thighs inside pleated pants, the span of his shoulders.

"Let's go into the model home," he suggested.

The evening chill was coming down. Soon fog would begin to condense from clear air.

Still uncertain, she led Rory across the rutted earth toward the new construction. A neat stone path crossed an emerald jewel of lawn, colorful flowers banked against brick walls. With her key, she let them into the sales unit where mingled smells of fresh carpet, wallpaper, and paint met them.

Rory sniffed. "Some folks like the smell of new car. I think this is the best." She followed as he wandered through the model, nodding. "Efficient square footage." He looked up at high ceilings and skylights. "Good illusion of greater space."

The tour complete, he turned his elegant head toward a decorator display on the counter between the kitchen and living area. A vase of silk flowers sat beside a marble cutting board with a plastic wedge of Brie. Plucking out the only genuine item, a bottle of Napa red, he reached into his pocket and pulled out a knife with a small corkscrew.

"Eagle Scout," he said.

Leaning against the counter, she watched him pull the cork with deft hands and pour wine into the glasses rounding out the tableau. He passed her one, sipped, and swished the liquid in his mouth. "Not bad."

She tasted and found it tart, with an undertone of dust. She considered what if, for the sake of argument, he had gone against his father this day. "What will Davis say if he hears about your coming to Grant Development?"

"Not if. With his spies everywhere it's a matter of when." Raising his glass, he clinked it against hers. "Here's to burning bridges."

Puzzled, she studied him. "I can't drink a toast if I don't understand it."

"I'll make it clear." He smiled. "I'm leaving DCI."

Joy surged and spread to the tips of her fingers and toes. She clinked her glass against his and swallowed wine that now tasted a lot better.

Rory set his drink down, took hers and placed it beside his on the counter. Throwing back his head, he laughed.

Mariah laughed, too, and loved it when he put his hands on both sides of her, pinning her against the counter. The urge to shove his jacket off and put her hands inside his shirt seized her. She'd feel the beating of his heart.

Rory, too, seemed to sober and held her gaze with his. Ever so gently, he lowered his head until she raised her lips to meet his. He moved his hand to cradle the side of her neck, his thumb stroking the hollow at the base of her throat. With her pulse pounding beneath his touch, she gave up all thought of denying him.

For no matter what happened to Grant Development, Rory was leaving DCI to be his own man.

He'd only had a few swallows of wine, but Rory felt high. Buoyed by the decision he'd made to break with his father, he reveled in the touch and taste of Mariah. On this roller coaster ride, the lows were dark valleys, each new summit more spectacular than the last. With an exuberant flourish, he lifted her as if she were a feather and deposited her on the smooth granite counter. Her brows lifted, and her eyes went wide, but she laughed again, a clear peal that made him believe in magic. Somehow, despite Davis's designs on Grant Development, everything would be all right.

They could be together, the way they had been the last two Friday nights.

He bent to kiss her, and she met him with the sweet strength that always surprised him in a woman so small. Drawing her closer, he sensed the breadth of his own chest against her compactness. Her pumps clattered to the tile floor, and her legs wrapped around him, bare feet pressed to the backs of his thighs.

The sound of his name on her lips had him thinking, "This was a model home, right? There ought to be a bed here somewhere." The way Mariah was holding on to him had him thinking she would find that an excellent idea.

He pulled away, went to the door in the entry hall, and engaged the dead bolt. Swiftly, he closed the living room drapes and the kitchen shutters, holding his eyes on hers as he moved about. When he put a hand to the light switch, she shook her head.

He wanted to see her, too, to slick that little number of a black dress off and throw it as far as he could.

Mariah waited impatiently. When Rory returned to her, she spread her thighs to accommodate his body between them. It felt so right, with his fingers digging into her backside and sliding her forward on the counter. Her dress slid up high so that her cleft, clad in a scrap of crimson silk from the Carmel lingerie shop, cradled the swelling at the front of his trousers. He pulled her closer and pantomimed what they both needed, pressing his hips into her.

"You have too many clothes on." He skimmed her dress up over her head to reveal her undergarments. "Too damn many clothes."

With a slow smile, he released the front clasp of her lacy crimson brassiere. A tug at the straps, and it followed the dress to the floor.

For a moment, she sat before him without moving, while his gaze traveled over her taut breasts, down her tummy to the triangle of silk, and back to her face. "That's better," he murmured.

The heat reflected in his eyes leaped to her.

She fumbled the buttons of his starched shirt open, shoving it and the jacket off his shoulders into a heap on the floor. He bent his head, his parted lips claiming her beaded rose nipple and tugging strings deep inside her. She wanted him, hot and tight in the most secret part of her.

Rory knelt before her and slid both hands up her legs. Lifting her weight, she helped him strip her panties down and over her ankles.

She sat naked before him and reached for his belt buckle. He pushed her hands away and knelt before her. Instinctively, she pulled her legs together, but he caught her knees. "Let me." It wasn't a question.

Still, she hesitated.

"You're beautiful to me, there and everywhere," he promised.

How could she resist a man with mental telepathy on his

résumé? With a sigh, she parted her thighs.

When his breath stirred the golden tendrils, she appreciated the contrast between his dark head and her blondness. Her head fell back, and she braced herself as his fingers parted lips already slippery with moisture. Her hips bucked against him. With a soft chuckle of pleasure, he replaced his touch with the impossible heat and softness of his tongue.

Shock waves shimmered through her, radiating from his mouth that must surely scorch her skin. Moments before she'd felt shy, but arousal made her shameless. Raising one of her hands, she ruffled his hair. He ignored her, still intent on laving her with his lips and tongue. Digging her fingers in, she tugged.

He lifted his head and looked into her eyes. She could see in his what he must be finding in hers, a kind of glazed intensity. He moved then, getting up and pulling her tight against him. His bare chest pressed her breasts, and she loved the feel of their naked skin together. With eager hands, she unbuckled his belt and shoved his trousers over his hips.

With Mariah spread before him like the most exquisite smorgasbord, Rory realized the bedroom was too far away. With her hair backlit from the kitchen, she wore a halo effect that definitely did not make him think of an angel. She was, rather, a siren who had cast her spell long ago and never released him. Tasting the tang of her on his lips, he brushed his mouth against hers and made a mix of her essence, sweet and slightly salty.

How was it possible that this was so much better with her than with any other woman? The same mechanics, the same breathy exertion, but with Mariah he felt closeness and comfort. A sense of belonging that threatened all the barriers he had up against letting anyone into his heart.

When she took his sex into her hand, he gasped and nearly lost himself. Perhaps she sensed it, for her fingers danced over him lightly, careful not to go too far.

Yet, despite her care, pressure built in him like a wave streaming toward the shore. It rose steadily, until it towered and curled toward its crest.

Mariah looked down and saw the length of him, more clearly now than in the subdued light on the patio at Big Sur, or in the moonlit bedroom at McMillan's. Rory's sex was beautiful, rising powerfully out a thicket of close black curls. In her hand, that flesh felt far hotter than the rest of him, as he fumbled for his wallet condom and rolled it on.

Before she could finish the thought, he arced up between her thighs and filled her. A groan escaped him.

For a long moment, he remained motionless, pushed in to the hilt. "That's fantastic."

Daringly, she clenched her inner flesh around him. "Better?"

"Do that again and I'm gone," he promised.

Cupping her breasts, he lowered his mouth and captured a nipple between his lips. She closed around him again, this time involuntarily.

He began to move, carefully slipping out, then back in. It wasn't possible, but it was even better than the last time. Clutched tight against him on the counter's edge, she felt his hands set the rhythm. He thrust in deeply, enhancing her sensation of being stretched to the limit. Yet, when he pulled back, she longed for more.

The mirrored wall in the living room reflected his muscular bare backside, his trousers around his knees. Mariah saw her own face, golden eyes wild, her hair spilling over his shoulders. She'd never seen herself like that before, wanton and wanting with a high flush and her mouth panting open. He turned his head, and their eyes met in the glass, widening with the enhanced pleasure of seeing as well as touching.

He moved faster, she moaning her assent. Her crescendo spiraled, rising.

Hot light leaped, and he was in her more deeply than she'd imagined possible. With a hitch in his breathing, he went still. "Don't move."

She obeyed, but with a smile at her power over him, she once more tightened her inner muscles. The feel of him, along with his elemental shout, sent her over the edge. With an answering cry, she watched herself, falling and falling into the eyes of the man in the mirror.

Still sheathed in Mariah, Rory lifted her from the counter and carried her into the ground floor master bedroom. Without breaking their connection, he let her down onto the bed and propped on knees and elbows to avoid crushing her.

The faint flowery scent of her hair mixed erotically with the musky smell of sex. Her eyes looked dark in the light that came in from the living room, misty and soft.

Rory rolled over to lie beside her, one hand propped beneath his head. It had always been this way for them, from the day that had met on Davis's boat, from their first touch.

The memory of that night on *Privateer*, the exotic feel of a woman's flesh surrounding him naked for the first time . . . In the midst of it, Davis had dragged him off Mariah. A scene Rory had kept in a dark corner of his mind, now the disaster came flooding back with all its present implications. He'd told her he was going to leave DCI, but he had yet to actually make it happen.

Soft fingers stroked his cheek. "Don't think about your father."

"How horrible that in the midst of something so wonderful, he can still intrude." Rory had risked a lot going to Grant Development today, and Davis would certainly find out about it through his ubiquitous channels.

No matter. Tomorrow morning Rory would see Takei Takayashi at Golden Builders and get his old job back. Time spent doing architectural design, working with the pure lines that transformed space, would set him back on the road he'd once chosen.

With a plan in place, he smiled. "I don't know about you, but sex makes me hungry."

She arched a brow. "I don't think the plastic grapes and Brie are going to hold us."

They got up from bed and Mariah went into the bathroom. He used some Kleenex from a decorative box, got his pants up, then brought her clothes from the other room and straightened the covers for model home viewings.

Back at the kitchen counter where the storm had struck, he finished tucking in his shirt and tossed off the rest of the wine in his glass. In a few minutes, Mariah came into the living room with her soft-looking black dress askew, her hair scrabbled into a hasty knot at the back of her head. With an apologetic glance, she asked to borrow his cell phone.

Rory poured more wine and watched her pace the tile barefoot. She looked so delicious, with one shoulder bare and whisker burned, that he wanted to drag her back to bed.

"Hello, Dad?" She stopped pacing. "Mr. Pappas?" As she listened, Rory didn't like the grim look that came over her face. "I'll go right to him."

She punched the button to end the call. "That was our neighbor, waiting for me at our house. Dad's back in the hospital."

CHAPTER 18

$\mathcal{F}$ear gripped Mariah's chest as Rory's Porsche streaked up 101. He drove with both hands tight on the wheel, his eyes alert for openings in the stream of traffic. On the southbound side of the freeway, it was gridlock, a river of oncoming headlights. Rory switched lanes a dozen times, but so smoothly she never felt he was reckless.

She'd had to think twice about leaving her car at Bayview, but if she needed wheels, she could have Rory drop her by the house and use her dad's. He hadn't driven since his heart attack.

"You holding up okay?" Rory pulled off the freeway and sped toward the hospital at Cal State.

"I'll be all right if you stay with me." She waited for the familiar guilt at being with Rory to resurface, but it did not come.

After what felt like an interminable time, they arrived at the information window in the ER. "John Grant?" Mariah said. "I'm his daughter."

The woman behind the desk looked motherly enough to bake homemade cookies and her voice was chocolate milk. "Jes' a second." She consulted her monitor and lips rouged with red-brown stain curved into a smile. "He's been taken up to 904."

Before Mariah could voice her fear, Rory spoke. "Is that the CCU?"

"No, sir. Just a regular private room."

Mariah leaned into Rory and felt his relief as he hugged her. "Thank you," he told the receptionist as though she were responsible for their good fortune.

On the upper floor, they found John's name on a card outside a closed door. Rory's arm dropped from around her. "I'll stay out here."

She pushed open the portal with care. Inside, her father lay propped on the hospital bed. He looked the same as he had when she'd left for work this morning, pale and drawn, but not that sick. Above the bed, a monitor showed his EKG, his heartbeat peaking and falling regularly.

A woman in a loose blue shirt and pants had her back to the door, making an adjustment on an IV. "Now, you ring if your chest pain gets any worse," she said brightly.

John's eyes met Mariah's and her heart clutched at the

eager look on his face. "Daughter."

The nurse turned. "He's doing fine right now. The doctor will be in to talk with you shortly." Briskly, she left the room.

"What happened?" Mariah went to the bedside and took his hand.

"My chest felt tight and I had trouble breathing." He tried a shrug. "Wouldn't you know, soon as I get here I feel better."

"That's good."

"Since I couldn't reach your cell I left Pappas at the house to tell you where I was."

He coughed and grimaced. "I called Arnold and he was here for a while."

Mariah's teeth caught her bottom lip. With an effort, she said evenly, "I'm sorry I missed him." Try as she might, she couldn't think what to say next. Rory waited in the hall, wondering about his condition.

John squeezed her hand. "Do you remember when I told you about meeting your mother? How I tried to deny my feelings because of Davis?"

She nodded.

"You were with Rory this evening." It wasn't a question.

"Yes." She didn't even try to blunt the implication of why two people might turn off a telephone.

He gave a faint smile. "After he came by the house yesterday, I thought that was probably where you were."

The mention of Rory on the stoop in the rain made her wonder when she would get the chance to tell him about "On The Spot." Or had Arnold beaten her to it?

She didn't think so, for surely he would have mentioned it by now.

"You and Rory . . ."

The look of empathy in his eyes made her bold. "There's someone outside who needs to hear this." She went to the door.

Rory turned quickly to her from where he stood with feet planted apart as if to ground himself.

"He's okay," she told him. "Come in."

Rory looked uncertain. "Are you sure?"

"I am. Are you?"

He hesitated.

"You don't have to." Rory had been okay talking to John on the phone, but maybe he wasn't ready to face the man.

As she turned to go back into the room, rapid footsteps sounded on the linoleum floor. "Wait for me." There was time for him to drop a swift kiss on her cheek and then they were inside together.

John didn't act self-conscious, not even in a gown everybody knew left his behind bare, with a tube running into his arm, and his heart's behavior on a monitor for everyone to see. "Hello, Campbell," he said, then amended, "Rory."

"Sir," Rory answered. "How are you feeling?"

"Better, but they're talking more tests." His apparent attempt to sound casual came out flat.

"Well, I hope they all turn out for the best."

An awkward silence fell.

Mariah had an idea of something that could ease the men's discomfort with each other. "Rory is leaving DCI."

John gave a low whistle. "What did Davis have to say?"

Rory glanced at Mariah. "I thought I'd line something else up before I told him."

"I'd offer you a position at Grant," John went on, "but it might not last past the end of the week."

"I'll find something."

John gave him a smile Mariah found fatherly. "Before you came in I was talking about her mother. Catharine will always seem superhuman to all of us who knew her, like everyone who dies young. Davis loved her first, but I won her . . ." He looked sad. "It destroyed the best friendship I'd ever had in my life. Only Tom Barrett has stepped in to fill that role." He paused and rubbed his chest.

"Are you in pain?" Mariah looked for the call button.

"Not so much." His gray eyes settled on Rory. "In the beginning, I nearly turned away from Catharine because I loved your father. Davis and I were going into business together, but of course that never happened." John sighed. "For a long time, I told Mariah she should avoid you. Now I know you can no more stay away from each other than I could from Catharine."

The door opened to admit Dr. Patel, the surgeon who performed John's bypass. With a smile for Mariah and a nod for Rory, he went to the bedside, drew down his patient's gown and exposed his scar.

Beside her, Mariah felt Rory turn away from the sight of the angry red slash adorned with side stitches. "Looking good," Patel said, bringing out his stethoscope. "What's this about chest pain?"

John ducked his head. "Just enough to get me in here. Then it stopped."

Patel completed his examination, asking more questions. He lifted the phone and made a call.

When he hung up, he said, "Your cardiologist, Dr. Hanover, is not on call this evening. Though your EKG looks fine now, I'd suggest you be our guest for the night and consult her in the morning."

As the doctor opened the door to leave, he let Arnold Benton in. Mariah almost didn't recognize Grant's financial VP in casual khakis and a ball cap. He carried a sack from a fast food restaurant that gave off the unmistakable smell of beef, onions, and French fries.

"There you are," John said warmly. "I was about to faint from hunger."

Arnold dumped the sack on the bed tray in a familiar fashion and pulled out a pair of wrapped bundles labeled as cheeseburgers.

"Dad, you aren't supposed . . ." Mariah began.

"Now, daughter, I missed my supper at home and got here after the hospital served their rubber chicken. The nurse offered me fruit juice or gelatin." He made a face.

Arnold brought out biggie fries, sticking every which way out of the top of their cardboard container.

John snagged one, ate it, and gave Mariah a reproving glance. "After all that boring food you've been making me eat, it's time I had something tasty."

Mariah wanted to snatch the high fat treats and dump them in the trashcan. "It's for your own good, Dad." She pointed at Arnold. "You should know better."

He lifted a shoulder in a dismissive motion. "You heard the man. He's been on the straight and narrow ever since his heart attack. He's feeling all right since his chest pain went away and he wants real food."

Mariah looked at him standing beside her father's bed as if he were family. Before she could think of something rude to say, Arnold crossed his arms over his chest and surveyed both her and Rory. "You and Campbell still at it, then?"

Rory took a half step forward. "What's it to you?"

"Benton," Mariah put in. "This is Arnold Benton, our financial officer who's responsible for the trouble we're in with First California."

Arnold also moved a step toward Rory, but it was not to shake hands.

"Stop it, all of you!" John's voice cracked with the power she remembered in him.

Everyone froze.

Her father went on, "Now Arnold and I are going to eat what he brought. Then we're going to have a game of chess." Putting out his hand, he encouraged Mariah to come to his other side away from Arnold.

She went to him.

He pulled her down and hugged her. "You go along now. I'll be all right tonight . . . leave your number and the hospital will call if there's a problem."

She straightened. "Dad, I want to stay." But did she if Arnold was going to exercise squatter's rights?

"It's better if you and Rory go," he urged. "I don't need him and Arnold at each other's throats."

Rory cleared his throat. "I can take off."

John smiled at him. "Buy my daughter dinner." He squeezed her hand. "Arnold will stay a while and go home."

"But what if you get worse during the night?" She tried to tamp down the sense that John was favoring Arnold.

"You didn't spend nights the last time I was in," John said.

Much as she hated to admit it, he was right. She had slept at home, even during the worst of his recuperation from surgery. The medical staff had encouraged her to get enough rest, and she had the company to run.

"Come back in the morning and hear what Dr. Hanover has to say," he suggested.

Arnold chomped a French fry and smiled as Rory led Mariah out the door.

Once in the hall, she vented. "I can't believe Dad lets Arnold near him! It's all his fault the company is being threatened and he brings cheeseburgers."

Rory paused with his finger halfway to the elevator button. "Arnold doesn't like us being together."

"He probably came in disapproving because he thought Dad was."

Rory raised a brow. "John did disapprove until recently."

On the way down the hall toward the exit, she was struck by how fast things were moving. Her father had looked at

Rory with a new trust, had clearly seen the two of them standing together as a declaration.

How did Rory feel about that?

As if he heard her thoughts, he put an arm around her and snugged her against him.

"With your Dad on our side, all we have to do is win over Father."

They went out through the hospital's automatic door into the parking lot. In a pool of orange light beneath a pole lamp, a dark Taurus sat in the drive.

Mariah felt a clutch of alarm as a man inside watched them approach, raised a camera, and started filming their walk toward the Porsche.

"Dammit." Rory ducked his head and tried to shield her. "That must be 'On The Spot.'"

She recognized the black-haired, hawk-faced man as the one who'd been following her when she left Rory's townhouse after returning from Big Sur. While it was a relief to know he hadn't been out to do her physical harm, she didn't want to see her position at Grant undermined further. And Rory didn't need more press about being a shiftless playboy, not when he was going to be looking for a job.

He opened the car door and held it for her. As she turned away from him to get in, he detained her with a hand on her shoulder.

She looked up and found a boyish grin spreading over his face. "What the hell. In for a penny . . ."

Before she could figure his intent, he brought his mouth

down on hers.

She gasped and tried to push him away. "This is for TV!" Mortified by their first appearance, she couldn't imagine what he was thinking.

Rory drew back and she saw determination in his eyes. "Let my father see this. Let the whole world."

With a nudge of his thigh, he moved her against the side of the car. Her arms went around his back and one hand slid up into his hair, pulling his mouth down harder on hers. He loosened the silver clip in her hair and let her curls tumble around her shoulders.

She sighed, almost a moan, and capitulated. There'd be no more wondering if Rory had told Davis about them.

With the knowledge and joy swelling in her, she lifted her hand and placed it in his hair above his collar where it grew a little long. Her fingers combed through, teasing the back of his neck.

Let everyone see this and know. Now and forever she wanted Rory, to let the swift current that flowed between them sweep her away. She heard his ragged breath as his promise to take her someplace she'd never dreamed of reaching, a place where they might be joined at the heart.

$\mathcal{S}$everal hours later, Mariah wasn't feeling as confident. Sitting cross-legged and naked on the bed with Rory in her apartment, she watched the opening for "On The Spot" come up.

"Here we go," said Rory. He lounged against the headboard, eating a bowl of spumoni ice cream he'd brought from their dinner at Little Joe's on Broadway. Mariah shot a glance at the VCR, where she'd inserted the infamous tape to add this to the Sunday night story.

When the hospital parking lot filled the TV screen, Rory sat up straighter.

"This evening, an update on the Grant-Campbell story," said the voice over. "It looks as though there may be a happy ending after all, as Mariah and Rory visit her father in the hospital. The elder Grant checked in late this afternoon, complaining of chest pain, but is reported to be resting comfortably in a private room."

"How do they do that?" she asked.

"They're snakes."

The commentary continued while the video showed Rory shooting a dirty look at the camera. "It appears the lovers aren't happy with our roving eye." The film showed them beside his car on full display for the metropolitan viewing area. The kiss began.

When Rory had taken her in his arms, it had been beautiful. In grainy, poor quality night video, they appeared cheap and shoddy. Like one of those late-night shows where the host wandered the seamy side of the city after the bars closed.

With a sinking feeling, Mariah wished they'd had more sense.

By morning, she was even more upset. "When will this publicity end?" she asked Rory as they dressed, he in his clothing from the day before. Her Victorian bathroom was crowded with the two of them vying for space with a huge bathtub on claw feet.

He paused in the act of buttoning his rumpled dress shirt and looked at her in the mirror over the sink. "It never ends, but I suppose it might ease up when things get settled one way or another."

She hoped the settlement he spoke of meant some kind of permanent arrangement between them. Last night in bed,

Rory had touched her with an intensity that matched her own. More than once during the night, she had nearly told him she loved him, but had held back. As passionate as he was, she sensed some darkness in him; a reluctance to give everything she sensed was inside.

Though they needed to get moving, she to the hospital to meet with her dad and the cardiologist, she wanted to put her arms around Rory and have him hold her once more.

She did not because he was tucking in his shirttail with brusque efficiency, annoyance over the press coverage in his expression.

"This is only the start," he said. "My leaving DCI will be a bombshell."

Not just "On The Spot," but the business sections of several papers and magazines would no doubt run stories on the rift between father and son. Mariah was sure she'd be named as the cause of their estrangement.

Rory borrowed her brush to tame the waves of his hair. She smoothed her black pantsuit that served as armor when she had a tough day planned.

They left her place around six and drove through gray dawn to his townhouse. Mariah made coffee and brought a mug to his home computer, where he was adjusting his résumé to reflect the work he'd done for DCI.

While it printed on thick, creamy paper, Rory sipped from his mug with a thoughtful look. "I didn't think I'd need another one of these lists of my qualifications, not after I went into the family company."

Mariah figured that no matter what Davis had done, it must be difficult for a son to make a break with his father.

Rory changed into a gray double-breasted suit and they set out. Running fast against the traffic into the city, they arrived back at Bayview. The sun was fully up, sparking diamonds on the water to the east, and the site was already bustling. Mariah's car was surrounded by contractor's vans, pickups, and the small, worn econoboxes the workers afforded on hourly wages. Rory got out of his Porsche and kissed her in front of a group of men who catcalled and whistled.

"Wish me luck." He held up crossed fingers.

Mariah straightened his bright red interview tie. "Call me as soon as you know something."

"No matter what, I'll see you this evening," he promised. "I hope John's doctor has good news."

An hour later, Mariah entered Dr. Heidi Hanover's office with her father. The stout woman built like a fireplug inspired confidence with her no-nonsense manner. "I'm sorry I was out of pocket last night when you threw us a scare," she told John.

He gave a tight grin and a shrug. "I got bored sitting around."

Mariah heard in his voice how he longed to do something useful.

At their last visit, Dr. Hanover had expressed hopes for a complete recovery. This morning she was more guarded.

"John, I know you're raring to get after it, but I'm afraid you're in for a deal more rest before that happens."

Mariah put a hand on her father's arm and felt the muscles tense beneath her fingers. His ears reddened. "I've got a company to run!" At least he did until the end of the week.

"This is never easy." Dr. Hanover spoke in a gentle tone. "Do you think I've ever seen a patient who thought it was good time for them to slow down? Now, if you want to get back on your feet, you'll have to be patient and keep out of the office."

"I've been staying with him," Mariah put in.

Her father shifted in his seat. "She's been counting every fat gram that goes into my mouth."

Dr. Hanover smiled at them both. "One thing for you both to remember. When John decides he's ready to take care of himself, I think it's safe to let him. Independence is a crucial issue for him now, especially since he can't make a contribution in the workplace." She gave him a serious look. "Just keep your emergency call button close at hand."

After driving her father home later in the morning, Mariah settled him into his living room recliner and sat down opposite, where she could see the Japanese tapestry that spoke to her of father and daughter. "Do you need me to stay with you?"

"No," he said irritably, fiddling with the string of the call button around his neck. "You heard the doc and you've got work to do saving the company. Without me there, you'll have to keep in charge."

There was one trouble with that, and it was in her purse: The tape with the "On The Spot" footage from Sunday, along with the Monday night segment she'd taped while she and Rory sat on her bed. Strange, she thought, that Arnold hadn't said something when he confronted her and Rory last night at the hospital. Or told her father after they'd gone. But, if he had heard about Sunday night or seen last night's episode wouldn't he have mentioned it?

She could go along to the office without revealing her shame, but the time had come.

"Dad . . . I need to tell you something before I go to work." Mariah rummaged in her bag for the tape. "Tom, April, none of the managers respect me anymore."

"Nonsense." Still restless, John jerked the lever that readjusted the height of his feet.

"No, it's true. Because of this." She held up the VCR tape. "Didn't Arnold tell you about 'On The Spot?'"

John frowned. "No."

Mariah set up the tape and pressed play. When the show's logo came up, her face flushed and she closed her eyes.

Yet, she must face this.

She opened her eyes, but tuned out the TV and watched the drama unfold on her father's face. First disbelief, then shock registered in his gray eyes when he saw Rory standing in the rain outside his front door. Mariah gave the show a single glance and then looked away from the sight of her closing the door in Rory's face. When it reached the part where he rested his forehead on the screen door, John motioned

Mariah to the hassock beside him.

She sat, her heart pounding.

As the Monday night segment began, John scowled. The kiss in the hospital parking lot once more came across as tawdry and she bowed her head. How could she explain that it had felt so right after believing she and Rory had his approval?

When the segment dissolved, she felt a hand on her shoulder. "Daughter." He massaged in small circles over the tightness in her muscles.

Mariah lifted her head and searched his eyes. "You're not angry?"

He moved his hand to chuck her under the chin as he had when she was small. "You heard what I said about you and Rory. If you love each other . . ." He paused, and though she had come to know she once more loved Rory, she could not speak for him.

When she did not reply, John went on, "You may have to fight Davis, but not me." He nodded toward the TV where the screen had dissolved into a snowy pattern at the end of the tape. "As for being angry, it's time someone put a stop to those buffoons. They destroyed Charley's viewing, and now they're trying to ruin you and Rory."

He squared his jaw and lifted the phone, selecting a pre-programmed number. "Ed?" She guessed he was speaking to Grant's corporate attorney Ed Snowden. "Have you seen this 'On the Spot' crap?"

A pause while Ed apparently admitted that he had.

"I want you to call their studio and put the full weight of Grant Development behind getting them to cease and desist. Threaten them with DCI, too; Davis can't want his son dragged through the dirt like this. No more harassment of Mariah," he glanced at her, "or young Campbell. No quiet settlements. Ask them if they want the whole expensive jury trial circus in a city where they can't beat Grant and Campbell."

Although relieved by her father's support, Mariah went to the office with a sense of dread. She called the managers of all departments to the conference room and while she waited for them, she wiped her sweaty palms on a paper coffee napkin.

Tom Barrett arrived first. The bags beneath his eyes looked deeper than ever. With a brief nod to Mariah, he busied himself pouring decaf from a silver pitcher on the sideboard and seemed to have trouble getting the right mix of cream and sugar. She wanted to go to him and tell him John was on her side, but Arnold Benton entered.

Giving her a dark look, he started to speak, then bit it back and pulled out a swivel chair. One thing she could not figure: If he despised her so, why had he not taken the opportunity to sully her by telling her father about "On The Spot?" He could not have known the older man understood falling in love with the wrong person.

April Perry came in looking camera-ready in a tailored teal suit with black braid trim. Rather than meet Mariah's eyes, she settled into a swivel chair and aligned her Waterman pen and pencil set perfectly beside her black leather organizer.

When the rest of the group had gathered, Mariah rose

and made her announcement. "Last night John went back to the hospital."

A murmur like a low wind moved through the room.

"This morning his doctor indicated his recovery is going to be longer than expected."

"How long?" Tom growled.

"I wish I could say." She watched them all take it in and could see the moment when concern for their boss gave way to doubts of her leadership ability. "In the meantime, he has asked me to continue to act for him."

"That's a joke," Arnold leaped in. "Sunday night's 'On The Spot' was bad enough, but did you all see it last night?" He looked around the group.

A few people nodded. Tom looked embarrassed.

Ed Snowden put up a hand for order. "I saw that piece of trash," he said in his deliberate manner. "John has, too. This morning he called to have me threaten them with a lawsuit, putting the complete power of his company and his name behind stopping the harassment of both Mariah and Rory Campbell."

The room grew still and she watched the staff digest the news. It was clear most of them had thought she was estranged from her father over Rory.

After a few seconds that felt interminable, Tom was the first to meet her eyes. He gave a nod.

April picked up her pen. "All right. I'll call a press conference and publicize our position."

"Don't." There was no way Mariah was going to have more

publicity if she could help it. "Let Ed call them and see if it does any good. I'd as soon this died down without more . . ."

Arnold leaned forward. "Without more muckraking? If you had stayed away from your father's enemies, none of this would have happened."

Mariah could tell him Rory was not her father's enemy, but what good would it do?

To change the subject, she turned to chief engineer Ramsey Rhodes. "Is there a status report on the accident?"

He consulted his notes. "It now appears that heat stress on the cable is a possibility."

Sweat broke out under Mariah's arms. A welder, gone up the hoist just before the accident, and now no one could find him. Davis Campbell's saturnine countenance appeared in her mind's eye and what Rory had said at the Lone Cypress overlook echoed in her head. "The past few weeks . . . stepped up efforts. If he has his way, Grant will be wiped out."

"Ramsey," Mariah said. "Does that mean the welder Zaragoza, or someone, did something to the cable to weaken it?"

The engineer gave her his usual calm look. "You're jumping to conclusions there. We'll need scanning electron microscope pictures of the cable break to say for sure if the heat was due to something like a welding torch."

Mariah looked at April Perry. "This makes finding Zaragoza and questioning him more important than ever."

The public relations director fiddled with her pen. "Our PI is still looking, but the trail is cold. He thinks Zaragoza may have left the country."

"What if someone paid his way to cover both their tracks?" Mariah said.

Arnold Benton shot to his feet. "That's the most ridiculous thing I've heard. You can go on investigating all you like, but the company's reputation is in ruins and John isn't coming back. We've got exactly out four days to get out from under the loan problem, and the only way I see is for all of Grant Development to be sold."

CHAPTER 20

Just before eleven a.m., the time of his appointment with Takei Takayashi, Rory pulled his Porsche into the familiar campus-style complex of Golden Builders in Menlo Park. It was like coming home, for two years ago he had drawn the design. He set his car alarm and strode toward the octagonal center building, faced in gold glass to match the company name. In the courtyard, brick pavers formed a matching eight-sided spiral. He could still remember the pattern in a plot from the design software spread out on his drafting table.

The place looked and felt good. Low buildings sprawled, surrounded by open space and gardens that invited one to contemplate. It matched owner Takei Takayashi, deliberate and thoughtful.

Golden's reception area was an extension of the exterior decor. A mural of aluminum, copper, and brass depicted the skeleton of a skyscraper under construction against a sunset sky and the Golden Gate Bridge. Usually Rory saw the promise of completion in partially finished structures, but today the mural reminded him of the accident at Grant Plaza.

Pushing open the copper-clad door to the inner offices, he saw his reflection in the mirrored surface. His best suit set off his silk tie. Takei liked red.

Rory brushed back an errant strand of dark hair that had fallen onto his forehead. Though he tried not to look apprehensive, his heart started to slam and he told himself to calm down. Inside a black leather folder, he carried his résumé.

In Takei's office the décor was traditional Japanese, with a gravel garden accented by bamboo along one wall of the room. Rory accepted green tea from his host in a tiny translucent cup. California-born Takei did a lot of business with Orientals and his parents had been immigrants. Taking tea together had been a midmorning ritual for him and Rory before green tea was supposed to be healthy.

In traditional Japanese fashion, Takei made small talk for several minutes. It was considered Western bad manners to get to the point too soon. Rory made his replies, speaking of golf and both local and national sports. Finally, Takei set aside his teacup and placed his palms on his desk.

Rory swallowed and willed his antiperspirant not to fail him. He drew out his résumé, placed the paper in front of

Takei and looked the older man in the eye. "I came to see if I could get my old job back."

Silence gathered, and Rory's dread grew. Despite his father's claims that no one would hire him, he'd seen Golden as a safety net.

"I am sorry," Takei said.

Despite the negative answer, Rory recognized the remembered kindness that had emboldened him to come.

Takei's expression softened. "You know I miss having you here. You could have been my right hand man some day."

Pride swelled Rory's chest. "I'd like the opportunity for us to see if that could still work. I see myself in a hands-on role; my goal is to see my ideas take shape."

"That's a reasonable aim for you to have had, once." Takei frowned thoughtfully. "I think now your job is to rise above breaking-in projects like this building. It's time for you to get the overview of the development business, what your father's got you doing on the executive floor."

When Takei described Rory's ideal career managing DCI, it sounded infinitely reasonable. How could he get across that he would never succeed if Davis were giving the performance evaluations?

"I don't fit in with my father," he confessed. "I need a place where I can be me, not the owner's son."

"You'll be the owner."

"The man's fifty-seven and healthy as a horse. He won't let go the reins till he's at least seventy, if then. To him, I'll never grow up."

"You now know the inside secrets of DCI. Even if you don't talk about them, they're in your head. You come back here awhile and then decide to make up with your father . . ."

Rory's face got hot. "You think this is a little family quarrel?"

"It's not just that. When I saw you with Mariah Grant at McMillan's, I thought there was something between you. Now with the 'On The Spot' publicity, there's no doubt you've got a conflict of interest."

How utterly stupid he had been, flaunting Mariah before the camera. "She and I don't talk shop. I'd like to think you know me well enough to trust my word on that. And to believe I never talked about what we did here at Golden after I left."

Takei nodded. "I do trust you, Rory."

"Then understand that I need to leave my father again to make my own way . . ."

Golden's chief looked mournful. "If it were up to me, I'd take you back, but any of our directors who saw last night's TV piece would think I was crazy to take the risk."

Rory sat behind the wheel in the parking lot with no destination in mind. The peaceful campus atmosphere he'd help to create and believed he could come back to mocked him. He'd planned that by now he'd be calling Mariah to tell her he was free.

He started the car and drove west, down the long tree-shaded avenue that led to Stanford. When he met Mariah for the first time, he'd been a student here. That fall when they broke up his grades had been the worst of his life. He pressed the accelerator, speeding as he left the university for Interstate 280. Passing through seventy-five on a straight stretch of highway, Rory tried to formulate Plan B.

At his desk at DCI that afternoon, he sat behind a closed door and tried to implement it. Using his cell phone, he didn't risk anyone listening in on a landline. At the end of five hours, he'd talked to at least twenty company managers in the Bay Area. All were friendly and apologetic, but none were willing to discuss employment with Davis Campbell's son.

When he'd been through the list, he sat back and stared out the window at the skyline. If he wanted to be a design architect for a firm with deep pockets, he would have to look outside San Francisco, possibly even the state.

Suddenly his office door opened with a bang and his father glared at him from the doorway. "You didn't believe what I told you."

Rory rose. "Believe you about what?"

"About finding another job."

His chest tightened. He should have known one of Davis's spies would phone in a report.

"Tell me it wasn't Takei who told you."

"Not Takei." Davis seemed to consider for a moment. "Actually, it was the man I've got inside Grant Development."

Rory knew there had been leaks about John's company

but assumed they came from someone like Thaddeus Walker at First California. An insider, someone close to John. That Arnold guy had been at the hospital, but John could have spoken by phone to anybody last night and passed on the story of Davis's son as gossip. He and Mariah had not told him it was a secret.

"Who do you have in Grant?"

Davis crossed his arms. "If I told you, you'd just run to Mariah with it. Then he would be of no further use." He came farther into the room and gave Rory a curious look. "So, are you going to leave DCI without a safety net?"

For a moment, Rory thought he sounded as though it mattered to him at a level other than exerting his power. Nevertheless, John and Mariah were being destroyed. "I'll have to."

Davis's expression hardened. "Don't try it. You know Chatsworth can pull strings all over the country."

"I'm sick and tired of that one," Rory said. "You said he was livid after I jilted his daughter in public. You think he'll stay bought?"

Davis slammed his palm on the desk. "Of course he will. This is business." Without warning, he smiled. "You know there's still plenty of time for you to make up with Sylvia."

"That will never happen," Rory answered automatically.

But it was as though no time had elapsed in eight years, his father still trying to block all escape routes.

All that Tuesday, Mariah waited for Rory's call. She tried his cell a dozen times but it rolled over to a mailbox. Finally, after another day in which nothing surfaced to stave off the company's foreclosure, she drove to Stonestown in the rain.

For dinner, she prepared her father's favorite pasta, but a low fat vegetarian version. It took a lot longer with one person cooking. After dinner, he sat in his accustomed place in the recliner. When he reached absently to massage his chest, Mariah resisted asking him if it was chest pain or merely a muscle ache.

"Everything seems to be winding down. My heart . . . Losing the company." She could almost hear his thought that death was not far behind.

"You mustn't talk that way. Things will get better." If only Rory would call.

John looked doubtful. "Have you heard from anyone about our properties?"

"No, but it's only been a few days since I spread the word at McMillan's."

He squared shoulders that were thinner since his illness. Losing a few pounds was probably good for him, but she longed to see him full and hearty again.

"We've only got a few days," he said. "Tomorrow, I'm coming to work. It will help morale, and I'll make some calls. Find out the lay of the land."

She put up a hand, but he said, "Just for a few hours. And I'll take it easy."

Despite her concern for his health, she realized it would be useless to argue. He needed to see for himself that nobody was coming to his company's rescue.

"All right, Dad."

He brightened and gestured toward the chessboard. "How about a game?"

She didn't feel like it, but agreed to pass the time while she itched with curiosity about what was going on with Rory. At nine o'clock, after declining to play a second time, she casually left the living room and used her blue Princess phone to call his townhouse. She turned her purse upside down on the bed, but she could not locate the card with his cell number and realized she had left it at the office. God, she should have programmed it into her phone.

She sat on the edge of the bed and tried to remember it, then dialed and got his voicemail again. This time, she didn't leave a message.

By ten, John was asleep in his recliner, snoring lightly.

Mariah shook him awake and saw him to his bedroom, bending to help remove slippers and socks. Since she'd been away overnight at McMillan's he'd been more vocal about doing things for himself, so she left him to undress. This insistence upon going to the office fit the pattern.

She had refused to agree with his doom scenario, but that had been the sheerest bravado. He'd aged at least ten years in a few weeks, going from a reasonably healthy, if not youthful, fifty-seven, to a man who appeared to be around seventy. Even though he dressed each morning in street clothes on the doctor's orders, he looked as though he belonged in bed.

Out on the front stoop, she found the rain had stopped. Fog rolled past, the drifting tendrils wearing an orange cast beneath the streetlights. Up the way, Stern Grove rested in forbidding darkness.

The stand of redwood held a memory of Rory, for Sunday morning had not been the first time he'd come knocking on John Grant's door. One summer night when she should have been planning her future at UCLA, she'd been trying to watch a TV program through flickering mental images of Rory. It had been exactly a week since she'd gone to Sausalito on a Sunday morning mission. As she stared at the TV, her first awareness of a visitor was that her father stood in the archway to the hall with his mouth set in a hard line. "Someone for you."

She'd gone to the screen and found Rory leaning against the jamb. Even better on the eyes than she'd remembered, he stood hipshot in snug jeans and a Stanford Kappa Alpha T-shirt. Without telling John, she opened the door and disappeared. A block up to Stern Grove; the stand of redwoods preserved as a city park provided twilight shadow.

"I tried to stay away." Rory tipped her face up and the heat in his eyes melted away the lonely days and nights.

Where was he this evening?

About to go inside and try to sleep, Mariah suddenly heard the familiar growl of a Porsche turning off Sloat Boulevard. She leaped to her feet and by the time Rory pulled to the curb, she waited on the sidewalk.

He got out of his car in jeans, rain parka, and running shoes. Looping two fingers into the waistband of her jeans, he tugged her toward him.

"Where have you been?" she asked. "I thought I'd hear from you sooner."

Rory's arms wrapped her. She'd been with him only this morning, yet it seemed like an eon. The rain started again, steady and dismal, but it took a long moment before the cold dripping registered.

He snuggled her inside his coat and pulled up the hood. Against her mouth, he murmured, "Come with me, we'll go somewhere."

She wanted to drive back to her apartment, or his townhouse, and make long, slow love. She needed to taste the salt of his skin while they lay spent and rubber-limbed. Yet, what if her father woke and needed her to take him back to the hospital? The thought of him calling into the darkness gave her pause.

"Come inside," she told Rory. To his questioning look, she said, "I don't want to leave Dad alone."

Rory went with her across the lawn and up the front steps. In the entry, he twined his arms around her and kissed her until his support was the only thing that kept her upright.

Despite the familiar rise of passion, she detected something different about him. This morning he'd been full of hope while he printed a copy of his résumé on his home computer. "Dirt simple," he'd said. "Golden Builders, DCI, and back again."

Rory continued to kiss her as though a great void had opened inside him and he needed her to fill it. She wanted to ask what was wrong, but he held her fast. Her arms went around him underneath his coat and she stroked his back. Tenderness for his dark mood, and the desire to draw him closer made her hands urgent.

A drip of rainwater spilled from the hood of his jacket into her eye. She shoved his wet parka off his shoulders and it landed in a heap on the hardwood floor. The zipper thunked on landing.

Her father called, "Mariah?"

Reluctantly, she slid out of Rory's embrace and went down the hall to open the bedroom door a crack. "Rory's here."

"Fine," John said mildly.

When she returned, Rory was studying the chessboard in the hall. He picked up a pawn and turned it in his hands. "This past month, I've been thinking that to my father I'm no more than one of these." He picked up two more. "Here's you and Sylvia Chatsworth." He replaced the pawns. "All of it so he," Rory touched the black king, "can checkmate," he moved his finger to tap the white one, "your dad."

Mariah stood for a moment looking at the board. Somewhere there in the bishops and knights were men like Thaddeus Walker and the senator.

With a shake of her head, she led the way to the kitchen. Rory picked up his wet parka and followed, draping the dripping coat on a kitchen stool. He grabbed paper towels, wiped the hall floor, and laid more towels out beneath to catch the drops. Mariah watched his domestic skills with a smile.

"Something to drink?" It was warm and stuffy in the kitchen, even with the window open. John's house had never been air-conditioned, and most of the time it was not needed.

"Glass of milk?"

She poured for him and got herself a Diet Coke, feeling that the counter looked unusually bare since John had taken the picture of Catharine to his bedside.

Rory sat at the kitchen table and she took the chair opposite. "Where have you been?" she asked again.

He swallowed milk. "Driving . . . thinking. This afternoon Father bragged of having a spy inside Grant. It wasn't just Walker who told him your loan payments were late."

"I suppose I shouldn't be surprised," Mariah said bitterly. "In fact, I should have known." No one new had joined the company since she'd been there. Therefore, it must be somebody entrenched in the developer's community and playing both sides.

Her first instinct was that it must be Arnold, but she hated to jump to conclusions. If he wanted to be groomed by John to head up Grant Development, why would he work against him?

She thought aloud. "Public relations director April Perry is a single mother. Maybe Davis somehow got to her." The thought of them in bed together sickened her, but it could have happened.

"He did say it was a man," Rory offered.

"Chief engineer Ramsey Rhodes has money troubles

with both his parents in long-term care, but I can't see him taking a payoff."

Rory drained his glass and wiped away his milk moustache. "Let's think this through. If your dad was in the hospital all night, whom could he have told I was leaving DCI? That's what Father said the spy passed along."

"It must be Arnold." She hated to think of John's trust being so badly misplaced. It was one thing for Arnold to be jealous of her, but another for him to betray her father. She envisioned him jollying his way into the hospital room with cheeseburgers and leaving with information. Long exchanges of confidence over the chessboard, and pretending to take the high road by leaving Mariah to reveal her and Rory being featured on TV.

Icy fingers plucked her nerve strings. Arnold, Davis . . . If Davis really had worked a deal with First California, and planted his spy in Grant, where might he draw the line? The elevator plunged in her mind and she dove away from it, as she'd imagined doing so many times since it happened. "It was almost you," said Tom's voice in her head.

Mariah slid her hand over Rory's. "How did your father take your quitting DCI?"

He drew away and brushed back the errant damp curl that had fallen over his brow. "I haven't yet."

"You're kidding." Uncertainty replaced the feeling of freedom she'd had knowing Rory was going to resign. "Takei didn't jump at the chance to have you back?"

Rory's shoulders lifted disconsolately. "He, like everybody

else in town, saw 'On The Spot.' Said his directors would never let me come back after working at DCI and being involved with you. Too much conflict of interest." He fiddled with his empty milk glass. "My father told me long ago never to try finding another job, not in this city. I called everybody in the region this afternoon and no one will talk to me."

When they'd been young, she'd thought nothing could ever be as painful or as serious as Rory leaving her. Now she knew she'd been naïve.

He hesitated. "I'm going to stay at DCI a while."

"Stay?" Her voice rose. "You promised me you were leaving!"

"Actually, I promised me that."

"Don't you see that if you do that, you'll never be free?"

"Mariah." He gave her a steady look. "I'm doing this for us. Until things are settled with Grant, this week if that's all it takes. If I can find out who the spy is, look around for other evidence of dirty tricks . . ."

"It'll still be too late to save Grant." She was certain Davis was behind a calculated plot to incinerate her dream of carrying on her father's tradition and became more certain he must have resorted to sabotage at Grant Plaza.

"Think," she told Rory. "If he's got a spy, what else might he have done? What if he hired that welder who disappeared to disable the elevator Charley was on?"

Rory pushed back his chair with a scrape. His face turned tense. "You hinted at that at the funeral home. At the time I thought you were overexcited, but now . . ." He seemed to catch himself and shook his head. "No. Can you, can I . . .

believe Father is capable of murder?"

"I don't know." The memory of that night on *Privateer*, his eyes hooded like a cobra's . . . "When he caught us together that summer . . ."

Leaning against the counter, Rory crossed his arms over his chest. "That was a long time ago."

The wavering candlelight had made things surreal in the yacht cabin; she and Rory naked, his sex shriveling, she trying to cover her breasts and pubic hair while Davis raged. His fist drawn back and she knew he was about to smash Rory's face. "When he dragged you off me," her voice raised, "I thought for a minute he was going to kill you."

From the rear of the house, John called out weakly.

She went to his door. "It's all right, Dad."

When she came back to the kitchen, Rory was putting on his parka with jerky movements.

"Where are you going?" He couldn't leave now.

"I need time to think." He gave his attention to joining the zipper and pulling it up with a rasp. At the front door, he paused and looked back at her with a distant expression. "I'm not sure I can accuse the man who raised me of such a thing."

CHAPTER 21

On Wednesday morning, Mariah woke before six. Truth to tell, she had never really slept, pummeling her pillow and kicking the covers away from her feet every few minutes.

In her comfortable old bathrobe that had been seen on a million TV sets, she ran water into the kitchen kettle and put it on for tea. Outside the window, a gray dawn came late as the continued rain sheeted down the glass.

Yesterday she had been so full of hope that things were working out at last. Yet, Rory had not yet left DCI, albeit he couched it in terms of helping save Grant Development. And when she dared to accuse his father of plotting the Grant Plaza accident he had not only refused to consider it, he had walked out of the house.

She busied herself with the blue ceramic teapot she'd chipped when she was eight. Last week Dad had confessed he'd kept the pot all these years because the little white mark on the rim reminded him of her. From the healthy products she'd introduced to his kitchen, she selected white tea reputed to be high in antioxidants.

Warm smells of steeping tea leaves and lemon soon filled the room. Morning finally brightened the windows and Mariah turned off the overhead light. Taking her cup to the kitchen table, she settled into the chair Rory had taken the night before. Outside the window, tired and sodden flowerbeds surrounded a patch of ragged lawn. She'd have to insist on a hired gardener to do what John could not.

She felt torn about letting him go to the office. He wasn't strong enough . . . if he got sick again . . . Did she dare tell him there might be a corporate spy in-house?

Assuming so many things, that Davis had told Rory the truth about the spy and that he had repeated it with accuracy, that it had not been some kind of planted story — by father or son — a lie designed to create discord in the already disordered ranks of Grant . . . there were a lot of "ifs."

If it were true, who could it be but Arnold? And if that were true, could he have used his position as financial vice-president to torpedo the company with late loan payments?

"How about some eggs?" John spoke from the doorway. His business suit hung loosely on his diminished frame.

Mariah gestured toward the counter where a loaf of

whole grain bread sat beside the toaster.

John sat and pulled the teacup she'd poured for him closer. It rattled against the saucer. "So, I'm still living with the diet police." He sipped and flashed a look of irritation that was a lot like his old self. "This heart healthy tea tastes like a boiled dishrag."

She drank some. "It's not so bad."

John shoved the cup away. "Did you mean what I heard you tell Rory last night? That Davis would resort to murder to get at me?"

In the daylight, she was less certain. "I don't know how I'd ever prove it."

He sighed. "I want to think you're mistaken."

Mariah shoved back from the table. "Believe it or not, for Rory's — for all our sakes — I want nothing more than to be wrong."

Two hours later, the stormy morning threw back her windowed reflection from the darkened canyon of Market Street. Her pale hair was pulled starkly back from her face, a tailored navy suit severe on her small frame.

Her father sat in his accustomed place for the first time since his illness. With a trembling hand, he reached for a Styrofoam cup of black coffee.

Mariah resisted the impulse to go and steady his hand with hers.

"No creamer, no fat," he groused.

She forced a smile, remembering Dr. Hanover's verdict that if he could complain he was getting better.

He leaned toward her with a more serious expression. "The other thing I overheard last night was something about Davis having a stooge in the company."

"Rory reports his father bragged on it to him yesterday." She braced herself for a fight. "My money's on Arnold."

John shook his head. "After working with him, being friends with him, I find that hard to believe."

"Then you tell me who the spy is. Did you tell Arnold that Rory was leaving DCI?"

Her father looked miserable. "I did tell him. I hoped it would soften him toward you if he knew there would be no more conflict of interest."

"Did you talk to anybody else at the company last night or this morning?" She hated hammering at him, but they needed to know who had betrayed them.

John set down his cup unsteadily. "Only Arnold."

"What if he's lying about software being the cause of the late payments? He's the one who suggested the entire company would have to be sold yesterday."

"He's probably correct, from a business standpoint," John argued.

"Why don't you ask him whom he has in mind for a buyer? If he says Davis Campbell, would you change your mind about him?"

"If I confront Arnold, he will no doubt suggest it is

Davis's son feeding you false information."

The silence would have been absolute but for the distant rumble of thunder. She remembered cowering beneath her bed covers as a child, believing that thunder was the devil rolling empty barrels down the stairs of hell.

She'd been ready to trust Rory again with her heart, with her very life . . . "Is that what you think?"

"I said Arnold would say that." John made an impatient gesture. "We've got an accident that might not be an accident, a banker and a senator in Campbell's pocket, reports of a spy in-house. I have no idea what to believe, but I know one thing." His voice firmed "I cannot see this company taken away from us."

Thunder rolled louder down Market Street as he reached for the telephone. "We have to raise the money and pay off the loans." He waited while a number rang. "Hello, Takei. I was wondering if I might expect an offer from you on any of our properties."

Mariah watched her father's face fall as the head of Golden Builders explained politely that he was overextended.

For the next few hours, she listened while John called all the major developers. A man in Oakland offered to "take a property off their hands" for less than half what Grant had just paid for it. When John told him that would not service the debt, he said he was sorry, but he was committed to other things. Another owner mentioned she'd like three small properties for around forty million. John gave her a verbal acceptance, for the price was fair, their contract people to get together in the morning.

By one o'clock, he had phoned L.A., Seattle and Vegas. It sounded as if they could raise around a hundred million. The foreclosed loans were twice that.

Going back to the window, Mariah searched the dark day.

At two-ten p.m., Rory opened the door to Davis's office and went in. He'd been careful this time that the richly decorated Oriental domain had no visitors.

Mariah had unsettled him with her accusation that Davis had committed what was at the least manslaughter, but during the night, he'd weighed her words. Much as he wanted to believe it was impossible, he was no longer certain of anything.

Davis raised his dark head from studying his computer screen. "I thought you were leaving DCI."

Though it ate at his pride to stay, he reminded himself it was for Mariah. "I decided I'd better have something set up before I go."

He passed his father's lacquered desk and his pant leg brushed a folder off the corner onto the floor. Bending to retrieve the well-worn manila, he found a sheaf of photos with yellowed edges spilled out onto the carpet.

A look at the one on top, and he nearly dropped it again. She was beautiful, slim and elegant, and smiling so boldly at her photographer that Rory wished he could join Catharine on the rock-strewn beach. Davis must have taken the pictures with his old Yashica, down the coast at Monterey. The tide was out, leaving the crystalline granite bare, the tidal pools drained to a few feet of the clearest water. Orange starfish and dark green sea cucumbers lay among piles of purple mussel shells. Sea anemones feathered their glassy tentacles and the kelp lay limp, waiting for deeper water that would allow it to float free like a woman's long hair. The camera had captured Catharine's silvery tresses, whipped into sensuous disarray, and her golden eyes beckoned endlessly. Rory wanted to know her.

He raised his eyes and found Davis watching him. Slowly he got to his feet with the photos and folder in his hand.

"You curious about that?" Davis shoved to his feet. "About why I despise John Grant? Look at the rest."

The envelope beneath the photos was lavender, clearly a woman's stationary. Impossibly, it seemed to still bear a faint perfume.

Davis,

There will never be a good time for what I have to say. I have fallen in love, so deeply and perhaps foolishly that I can barely believe the earth is the same planet I inhabited before. There is no help, and all I can tell you is that I am sorry it could not have been you.

John and I were married last week.

Please do not blame him. He tried to be a valiant friend to you. If only there were some way, that I could do this without hurting you, a solution where I could live out separate lives as two women, one for each of you.

   Catharine.

Rory flipped through the rest of the well-thumbed photos. "I understand how painful it must have been to lose her, but . . ."

"I didn't lose just her. Catharine could have been the love of my life, but it was my best friend's betrayal . . ." Davis's voice choked. "John and I were friends all through Stanford, roommates, drinking buddies . . ." He raised a fist. "God, how we dreamed of being the best building team in the state, hell, in the world."

As he saw a suspicious sheen in his father's eyes, Rory felt a sting in his own.

Davis turned away and walked over to load a tape into his office VCR. "Have a look at this." His voice was back under tight control.

For a moment, Rory thought he was going to have to watch his "On The Spot" appearance, complete with scathing commentary about how he was no better than John Grant for taking up with his daughter. With relief, he saw it was merely a clip from the local TV news.

A young Chinese newswoman spoke energetically into her microphone. "This morning, Field Incorporated, the Seattle-based company who built the Grant Plaza construction hoist, has categorically denied that any mechanical weakness or flaw on the part of their equipment contributed to the accident. Rather, they have pointed the finger at Grant, claiming that unsafe installation or usage must be to blame."

Rory stood straight and watched without expression.

When the video ended, Davis turned off the TV. "That's not all. My source at Grant tells me John is in his office right now, calling everybody he can think of to sell properties."

Rory was surprised that John had gone in, but the clock was running out on the loans.

Davis opened the door of his adjoining private bath and went in. Through the open door, Rory saw him wash his hands, straighten his expensive silk tie, and smooth back his wings of sleek hair. "John's not having any luck, so we're going over there now."

The idea of walking into Grant Development with his father made Rory's stomach ache. "You don't need me."

Davis's toilet complete, he grabbed his cell phone off the desk. "We're going to buy out Grant. I thought you'd like to see this."

There was no way Rory would join in humiliating John and Mariah. He imagined the disbelief and horror on her face and knew he couldn't be a part of it. He had to refuse or phone ahead and warn her.

"I'll get my jacket," he agreed.

As soon as he escaped, he hurried down the hall. His own cell phone was in his office, so he went around a corner and down thirty feet to a closed door. He went in, shoved the door shut behind him, and headed for the desk.

The Grant operator was ringing Mariah when the door opened. Swift footsteps crossed the carpet and Davis depressed the button. "I'm not letting you call your girlfriend and warn her. This is going to be a surprise."

Rory straightened. "Get away from the phone," he said evenly.

Davis studied him with eyes of obsidian, while he wondered if his father's obsession with Catharine, rekindled by Mariah's appearance in the city, had truly sent him over the edge.

Nonetheless, Rory stood his ground and redialed. While the phone rang, he watched his father as though waiting for a lion to spring.

With Grant Development once more on the line, he said, "I'm sorry, I was holding for Mariah Grant and got cut off."

The receptionist, the young girl whose voice he recognized from the day he'd gone to Grant came back at him. "I checked and she's in a meeting. They've given orders not to be disturbed."

"This is urgent. Couldn't you . . .?" He was talking to a dial tone.

"She'll know soon enough," Davis said.

Rory replaced the receiver, tensed for an explosion.

Instead, Davis smiled. "Let's get over there." It seemed Rory's failure to get through to Mariah had him pleased.

Refuse, or go? Walk into Grant like his father's lackey, or stay here while God knew what went on? There was no good decision. All he knew was he couldn't stay behind and wonder what was happening. When they got there, he'd try to speak to Mariah alone. Failing that, he'd find a way to let her know he wasn't behind this.

Rory looked toward the window where the building with Grant's office was usually visible. Today, it was obscured by black rain streaming down the darkened glass.

Mariah sat at the conference table with her father and a handful of the other Grant managers. He looked exhausted, but had insisted on having his first meeting in weeks before he went home to his recliner.

April Perry pointed out that the morning's press release from the elevator company would have a negative effect on their already reduced ability to sell properties. Head Counsel Ed Snowden reported that Field's denial of responsibility was merely spin, and not relevant when a lawsuit was either settled or tried before a jury.

"Andrew Green's widow has filed suit asking for twenty million dollars." Ed spoke in his usual laconic manner, but he twisted his silver Cross pen up and down with restless energy.

"And put those adorable fatherless babies on television," April added dryly, referring to another recent "On The Spot" feature.

Tom Barrett sat stolid and silent. He looked terrible with huge bags beneath his eyes, but despite the crushing blow his son's loss must be, he'd never mentioned filing suit.

Mariah looked around the room, wondering if Davis's spy was present. Her eyes lingered on Arnold Benton. Though she hoped she was wrong about Rory's father engaging in a criminal act, she could not sit by without at least trying to find out.

"April," she said. "I wonder of you could have the PI look into any potential connection between Davis Campbell and the welder Zaragoza . . ."

Arnold snorted. "There she goes again, coming up with things that can't make a difference in our predicament. If you can't pull together enough money to pay the loans, the only logical thing is to try and sell the entire company to Campbell . . ."

"What did I tell you this morning?" Mariah said to her father.

John skewered Arnold with a sharp look. "That's enough."

She leaned forward, hoping Arnold would further give himself away. Pleading the case for a Campbell buyout was a start.

Tom Barrett shifted in his chair. "Maybe he's right. If First California would accept a merger agreement between Grant and DCI . . ."

Mariah stared at Tom. "You can't be serious."

Arnold tried again, flushing to the roots of his hair. "He's right, and so am I. Just because you don't like the man is no reason not to see what has to be done. Campbell is the only one with both the means and the desire."

Mariah's father shot her a despairing glance, drew a long breath, and turned to Arnold. "It has come to my attention that Davis Campbell has someone working for him inside our company."

Arnold leaped up as if the chair were spring-loaded.

"This spy," Mariah elaborated, "tipped Campbell about the late loan payments."

"You know Walker must have done that."

She went on as though he had not spoken. "In fact, this man — and I have it on good authority that it is a man — could have arranged for the loans to be late. Do you have any idea who might have done that?"

"No!" Arnold shouted. "I've told you over and over we were changing software. It was a mistake and you keep blaming me." He was so agitated Mariah almost believed him.

Turning to John, Arnold pointed at her. "How does she know what Davis Campbell is up to? More nighttime secrets passing from his son to your daughter?" To Mariah, "How do you know he's telling the truth? Why are you so sure he's not poured from the same mold as his father?"

Though her father had warned her this would be his response, her hand went to her throat.

"I'm not selling to Campbell," John told Arnold. "You can assure him of that."

He spread his hands. "I hardly know the man. Whatever you're talking about, it wasn't me." He gave Mariah a look of pure hatred. "You're behind this. You've never liked me and you've turned your father against me."

It was a convincing performance, but she still believed that if anyone in Grant had turned traitor, it was Arnold. "The other night Dad told you Rory was leaving DCI. You were the only one who could have passed that to Davis yesterday."

"Me and the six or seven people I told in the company over coffee before eight in the morning. Rory Campbell leaving DCI is big news." He turned on John, his spine erect. "I've never been anything but loyal, but I won't be accused of lacking integrity. As of today, sir, you have my resignation."

The conference door opened to admit John's secretary. When Arnold shoved past her, her composure frayed, her usually porcelain cheeks pink. With a confused glance over her shoulder, she turned her attention back to John. "I'm sorry to disturb you, Mr. Grant."

"I gave orders we were not to be."

"I'm sorry," she repeated, "but Davis Campbell is here to see you, and I thought . . ."

Mariah imagined Davis pushing past reception, intimidating staff all the way down the executive floor, since the managers were all in the conference room.

"Don't see him, Dad," she advised, forgetting her vow to call him by name at the office. A confrontation could put him back in the hospital.

John sent a sharp glance at the door Arnold had walked out, and Mariah thought he must also wonder how Davis knew he was at work.

"There's no sense putting this off." With his hands on the table edge, John supported himself on the heavy mahogany and got up.

"No, Dad."

"Bring Campbell to my office," he ordered.

Davis strode into John's domain like a conquering general.

Mariah and John posed as if for a family portrait, he in his high-backed leather chair, and she with her hand on his shoulder. It wasn't business-like, but she had the feeling it was about to get personal.

When she saw Rory, it got damned personal. Only last night, he'd told her he was on her side, bringing information about a spy in Grant. Yet, as soon as she accused his father, Rory stood with him.

Davis moved, catlike, and stopped before the desk. Physically beautiful, with slashing dark brows, straight blade of nose, and lips as full as a youth's, he was the perfect picture of a man who had lost his humanity. He didn't reach to shake hands.

John did not rise.

Though watching the two rivals, Mariah saw from the corner of her eye that Rory gestured to attract her attention. Her own hands trembled with rage that he'd come; she lowered them out of sight behind John's chair back.

"Mariah," Rory said quietly.

She met his intent gaze. He jerked his head to the side, indicating for her to come to him. Though her heart was thudding at the troubled expression on his face, she stayed where she was with her father.

John looked at up at Davis. "Remember how we used

to plan for the day we'd be in business together?" His voice was mild and non-threatening, the last thing Mariah would have expected.

Davis's expressions had never given her a clue to what thoughts were in his head. Now, for the first time, she saw the mask fall away. His eyes were no longer fathomless, but windows onto a world of pain. He stood motionless, his sharp chin high.

John went on. "We'd sit in that little pub off campus, the Sherwood Forest. Other kids organized the weekend beer bust, but we drew plans on paper napkins. None of them ever got built."

"Thanks to you," Davis shot back.

The color drained from John's face. Mariah wanted to caution him to take it easy, but the two men faced off like mongoose and cobra.

"For God's sake, why can't you let it go?" John cried. "She's been dead for over twenty years."

"Have you let her go?" Davis's voice was a handful of gravel thrown and scattered. "You never remarried, because she's there to remind you." He fixed on Mariah and she knew he was seeing Catharine.

Davis moved slowly around the desk until he stood a few feet from her. She resisted the urge to run. His hand came up, as if he were unaware of it, and touched her hair. Then he cradled her cheek and looked into her eyes as if searching for something that could never be.

"She's not there," Rory said loudly. "See for yourself."

Davis dropped his hand and turned away. Mariah realized that every muscle in her was drawn taut as a bowstring, and she took a breath.

For another long moment, Davis stood silently.

"Mariah," Rory said again.

It seemed to galvanize his father. Pulling himself together, Davis reestablished his bravado and turned to John. "I've come to buy Grant Development, for the loan payoff plus one million dollars," he said in a cold and carrying voice.

Mariah gasped, as if she hadn't known it was coming. "That's a ridiculous lowball."

Davis nodded. "I happen to know John's called everybody else in the industry and I'm the only taker."

"You learned that and found out Dad was here today because your spy told you," Mariah said.

"It never hurts to have an inside track," Davis agreed.

Her rage rose. As long as he was confessing, no, bragging about his power, she would goad him further. "You hired Zaragoza to sabotage the hoist."

Davis's dark brows knitted.

"Perhaps you wanted to kill someone at random; maybe you wanted me to die, to quit reminding you of Catharine . . ."

"You go too far!" He skewered her with a look of hatred. "You aren't like her at all."

She nearly stepped back, but stood her ground. "No, I'm my own woman, but ever since you saw me and dredged up your old memories, you've been plotting to take us down. You can forget it!" She included Rory in her fury, throwing him a look of defiance.

Davis's black eyes widened. He took a step toward her.

Rory moved swiftly and put his body between them. "Back away."

For a long moment, father and son faced each other. Both men were breathing quickly.

Then Davis stood down.

Gathering dignity, he glared at the man who was once his best friend. "The offer on the table for you is a million, to set you up for life. In your present circumstances, you'd better take it."

An insult, a fire sale, but Mariah feared John would end up doing it. It would allow him some money to retire, and enough for her to make a new start in life. The trouble was she didn't want to start over. The only dream she'd ever hoped to achieve was being trampled.

John shoved back his chair, and she had to move fast to get out of the way. He was pale, yet determined, with hands clenched into fists. Mariah had visions of the two men slugging it out.

Before she could move, Rory put a hand on the sleeve of both men. "Leave it," he said sharply to his father. "He's a sick man."

John and Davis stared at each other. The silence was so thick Mariah could hear the ticking of a clock on the side credenza.

Then Davis gave a curt nod and retreated. John's fists opened, but when he spoke, his voice was still taut. "I'd always hoped someday you'd find forgiveness in your heart for me and Catharine, but I can see it's not to be."

"You've never asked forgiveness."

"Nor will I. Catharine and I could no more help loving each other than any poor human souls." John sent a significant glance at Mariah and Rory, and then looked back at Davis. "You came to buy Grant Development . . . I'll give you my answer. If I have to dismantle every project brick by brick with my bare hands, if I must go into bankruptcy, you will never see your name on anything of mine."

Mariah inhaled sharply.

Davis gave a curt nod. "So be it." He turned toward the door.

Rory hesitated.

"Are you coming?" Davis barked.

Despite that Rory had twice intervened to keep the meeting from becoming a brawl, Mariah still couldn't believe him representing DCI in dealing the death blow to Grant. "He's right at your heels," she told Davis.

Rory gave her a last look, then followed his father out the door.

When they were gone, John looked as though he'd run a hard race. He moved unsteadily back to his chair and massaged his chest.

"Did you mean that about bankruptcy?" she asked.

Sitting down, John's voice firmed. "I'm not letting him win."

Mariah's mind raced. "There has to be another way. We'll get a business broker, have them auction the company on the east coast."

"You're welcome to try, but don't forget that with the Grant Plaza construction note, we were temporarily upside down on our loans. The sales at Bayview were going to turn things around within a month."

"I've been wondering about that, Dad. I'd have thought you too conservative to let that happen. Did Arnold talk you into it?"

"It was his idea, but I would never have done it if Tom hadn't agreed."

Out on the street, the rain had let up. Instead of hailing a cab like they had on the way down, Davis struck out walking fast on the wet sidewalk. Rory had no trouble keeping up with his stride, as angry as he was.

"I can't believe you went in there like that, Father," he burst out. "You had to know he'd never sell his life's work for a lousy million dollars. Your house cost three times that!"

"He'd better take what he can get!" Davis raised his voice as well, drawing curious glances from people outside the building where Grant officed. "On Friday the company will be worth nothing to him."

Rory grabbed his father's arm. When that didn't slow him, he speeded his steps and blocked his path. "What did you expect? That he'd roll over and let you cut his throat, maybe lie there on his back with his belly exposed and whimper, 'I'm sorry I fell in love with the same woman you did.' People can't help things like that!"

Davis shook his head. "One way or another, I'm going to bring him to his knees."

Stares gave way to pedestrians giving them a wide berth.

"Why can't you leave it?" Rory lowered his voice. "John is old before his time, and sick. If he dies, Mariah won't rest until she sees you in your grave."

"She won't fight me."

"The hell she won't. Catharine may have been sweet, but as you've just seen, John's daughter is tough. She'll fight you, and I'd bet she's going to find out whether you had anything to do with the Grant Plaza accident."

Rory looked into his father's eyes and saw pain.

"You believe that of me, too?" Davis said with what appeared to be dawning wonder. "I've done things you don't approve of, but I'd never compromise the safety of people on the job."

Without warning, Rory's eyes misted. "I want to believe you," he said thickly.

"But you don't," Davis cut in. "When you made that call, trying to warn the Grants, you went over to their side."

Rory envisioned the chess pieces in opposition. "I'm sick to death of people expecting me to take sides. It's past time this feud came to an end."

He drove into the June twilight to release the tightly wound spring inside him. Punishing the Porsche, he crossed the Golden Gate, took the exit for Shore Highway, and put the car through its paces on the winding road that flanked Mount Tamalpais. The afternoon's rain had given way to a perfect gem of an evening, but its beauty was lost on him.

He'd told his father people couldn't help whom they cared for; John had said that, too. Well, Rory cared for Mariah and the cold look in her eyes when he'd come into Grant with his father had cut deep.

Yet, how could he be upset with her for defending the company? It was her father's life's work and she had the same drive to create and transform space. Her vehicle to do that was Grant Development just as he had naively imagined DCI would someday be his when he'd come into the company. Some might say a gift like theirs was wasted on commercial ventures like Grant Plaza or Bayview Townhomes, but he didn't see it that way and knew she didn't either. They each knew that the product was not merely metal, glass, and plaster, but a space designed for people to work and live.

That French country chateau on the ocean between Pacific Grove and Pebble Beach had beckoned them both. He'd turned in to look merely because he enjoyed real estate, but it had quickly become more personal. Mariah's shining eyes as they went from room to room told him she imagined the two of them together. He'd done the same, seeing them sunbathing poolside, casting off in a small tight sailboat, and returning home at dusk to prepare a meal in the brick country kitchen.

But how could any of that happen? John's refusal to roll over would only make Father more determined to make him bleed. After Friday's inevitable foreclosure, he'd probably talk First California into going after John's personal accounts and his house. It might not end until John was dead.

Then Mariah would have lost everything, and in her mind, he would share the blame.

The thought made Rory feel like a foot-wide hole had been kicked in his chest. He had to go to her, explain . . . for God's sake, if he showed up at John Grant's house, no one would open the door. And he didn't relish the idea of a repeat of his "man locked out" performance for TV.

With his headlights making ghosts of hulking redwoods, he forced his reckless energy through the gas pedal. The mountain road wound down to the ocean at Muir Beach. Rory pulled into a parking lot to watch the sunset. Usually he enjoyed the spectacle of the orange orb sinking into the windswept navy sea.

Tonight he stared out at the restless swells. What he was going to do with the rest of his life? One thing he did know was that as long as DCI was in the hands of his father, he would have nothing more to do with it. It was too late for him to find out anything that would save Grant Development from the inevitable foreclosure, so there was no excuse to remain.

He got out of the car and leaned against it while the ochre horizon faded to crimson. The first cold bluish star might be Venus or Jupiter; he wasn't up on his astronomy.

He wished on it anyway. Like a superstitious fool, he asked for an insight on getting outside the box.

Looking for work was a dead end in the city, impossible anywhere if Father's buddy Larry Chatsworth took it out on him because he'd publicly left Sylvia at the altar. And, say he found a post somewhere else, moving would mean leaving his unhappy mother behind. Despite her threat to leave Father, he thought she was too much a prisoner of feeling to walk away. Even if he could get to Mariah, she would stay behind; she would never leave John in ill health.

Leaving town was no good. Neither was selling used cars or carrying a sign that said, "will work for food" and hanging out under freeways.

The last time Rory had driven and ended up at the sea, back at the beginning of May, he'd struggled with the same demons. He'd been jousting those devils since the rainy day in Sausalito when John Grant's daughter came into his life and changed it forever.

Below on the rocks, the surf made a white explosion. Wind whipped at his shirtsleeves, but he bore the cold without reaching for a jacket. If Mariah were here, he'd put his arms around her, pull her against him to keep her — and him — warm. Once more, he marveled at how he could feel alone in a crowd, but never when she was with him.

There had to be an answer for both him and her. It was out there in the gathering night, hiding in the fogbank rising as the air cooled. Something that would not merely rearrange the kings and the pawns, but sweep away the pieces and break up the board.

CHAPTER 22

*T*hursday morning Mariah awakened in her dotted Swiss bedroom and felt that nothing had been accomplished in all the years since she'd slept there as a child. It was all she could do to make it out of bed. Once she did, she put on her terry bathrobe and followed the aromas of perking coffee and toast to the kitchen. Her father, already dressed in his khakis and blue shirt, stood at the stove overseeing poached eggs.

"First, fast food Monday evening with Arnold . . ."

John turned and gave her a hard look. Last night, she had watched him try to phone Arnold a dozen times, to no avail, each time hanging up with silent grief and disappointment in the man he'd trusted with his finances, and ultimately, his life's work.

The subject of Arnold was clearly off-limits.

"My cholesterol is one-forty-five." John said, lifting the pan from the burner. "Besides, eggs, poached without butter, are off the blacklist."

Mariah closed her mouth and went to the cabinet for a cup, noting that the can on the counter was labeled decaf. She poured and took her coffee to the table, torn between wanting to mother him and knowing he'd lived nearly sixty years on his own.

He pulled down two plates, arranged the dry toast and placed the eggs with care to avoid breaking the yolks. She liked her yolks runny. Though her impulse was to jump up and help, she let him bring the food to the table, go back for silverware, salt and pepper, and fetch his own coffee, black.

They ate in silence for a few minutes. When both had sopped up the last of the eggs with toast and settled back into their chairs, he placed his hands on the table, palms down. "I think it's time you moved back to your apartment."

"Are you kidding?" She pushed back her plate. "You were just at the hospital Monday."

"Dr. Hanover said it was up to me if I needed you hovering. She said as long as I keep my call button handy for emergencies, I should do fine on my own." He gestured at the dishes. "I can keep myself fed and watered. Mrs. Schertz will come in and do the housework and shopping until I can drive."

"You're not coming in to the office today." She prepared to do battle.

"No. After yesterday, I think I'll take Dr. Hanover's advice and rest." From the scowl on his face, she thought he was thinking of Davis.

Mariah looked at the sensible breakfast he'd cooked; perhaps she had been too harsh about a single cheeseburger. It had to make him nervous when she rearranged his magazines and tended his houseplants. With his company being taken from him, his sense of pride demanded at least that he have personal independence.

The difficulty lay in her. If she left her dad's companionship and moved back to her place with Charley forever gone, and no chance of being with Rory, she'd be more alone than ever.

On the drive to Grant Development, Mariah plotted one last move to make before the company was in checkmate. It was a long shot, as John had indicated, but she wanted to see if a business broker might be able to auction the company or its major assets online. She thought she could find the appropriate appraisals and descriptions in the company files and email them in time.

Once she was in her father's office, she went online and found the name of Eli Roggen in New York. She dialed his number, her stomach queasy.

Broker Roggen acted interested until she told him the loans were due in less than two business days. "Well, now, Miss Grant," he clipped out in his Manhattan accent. "This is a bit unusual. Why do you need to have the company auctioned on such short notice?"

She explained about the software problem and the late loans, using the terms Arnold had used to defend himself. "The bank is planning to foreclose and we haven't been able to raise the loan amount selling properties piecemeal."

"Still, it seems highly unusual that First California would be in such a hurry."

Mariah let the silence lengthen, following her father's rule of not saying too much. She heard a faint clicking and guessed Roggen was using his computer mouse to work while they talked.

"Say," he said with the air of a cat pouncing on a mouse. "This the same Grant Development that had a fatality accident? May fifth?" He continued to read, she presumed from a story on the Internet. "The deceased, Andrew Green and Charley . . ."

Mariah's nails dug into her palm. "That's the one. The accident investigation is still pending."

"Sorry," Roggen said, "but I can't take this on, especially with there being no consensus between Grant and," he paused, evidently still reading, "the hoist company, Field. We still don't know who was at fault."

Mariah bit her tongue to keep from airing her suspicions about it not being an accident. There was no use. This man had said "no" and there were others to call.

"Before you ask," Roggen sounded eager to get her off the line, "I can't think of anyone else who'd want to get involved."

In an even tone, Mariah thanked him for his time and

put down the phone. She imagined putting her head down on the desk and crying, but of course, she didn't. She sat dry-eyed and faced the calendar page turned to Thursday, June 5.

All her life, Grant Development had been her inspiration, the way some people loved art, music or another person. Each day when she was a schoolgirl and John got home from work, she'd ask about his day. Rather than answer in generalities, he had regaled her with details of the progress of a model home, a new branch of the public library, or the student union at a local college. Each night she had lain in bed dreaming of the day she would grow up and run the company.

Today, it felt like a dead weight.

Someone knocked on John's office door, and Mariah tried to compose her face into placid lines. After a moment, she called, "Come in."

April Perry entered, wearing her muted gray suit as though already mourning the company's demise. She carried a CD case, which she tapped with a fingernail. "Zaragoza has been located in El Salvador. Apparently, his green card expired and he left the United States the day of the accident. When the hoist fell, he might have been afraid he'd be blamed; probably bolted for the border, figuring he'd get deported anyway."

Mariah's eyes narrowed. "Or, he didn't want to answer any tough questions. Like, who wanted Grant Development to go down?"

"There's no telling if anything like that happened." April brought the CD to John's desk and gave it a little push toward Mariah. "You asked about Davis Campbell being involved, but the PI turned up nothing connecting him with Zaragoza."

For Rory's sake, Mariah hoped the PI was right. She wasn't convinced. "Have him track down Zaragoza and talk to him. Put on some pressure and he may finger Davis."

April hesitated. "I'll do it, but it will take us past Friday."

"I don't care. After the way Davis treated Dad yesterday, I won't be satisfied until I know how far he was willing to go to bring Grant down."

April nodded, empathy in her eyes. "I suppose there's nothing to do now but wait for the foreclosure tomorrow."

"Don't say that." Mariah got to her feet. "We can't just sit and watch it all go. I've got to think of some way out."

"I don't see how." April looked bleak. "The mood downstairs . . ." She referred to the floors below the executive offices where more than a hundred Grant employees had their offices. "The best word for it is 'grim.' Nobody believes they'll have a job come Monday." She started to leave and then turned back. "I know I was tough on you about Rory Campbell, but I didn't have any idea your father approved."

Mariah shrugged. "That's all moot. Yesterday, Rory showed where his loyalties lie."

The older woman nodded. "For what it's worth, I'm sorry we won't be able to work together any more."

"I'm sorry too, April."

Alone, Mariah sank back into her father's chair. She wished she'd had the chance to rightfully take her place there, but Grant Development was being delivered to First California, and, no doubt, ultimately to Davis Campbell.

She clutched the leather armrests and held back tears once more. The years ahead without her dreams looked like a wasteland. Find a job somewhere, enough to pay the bills and take care of her and Dad. If his health continued to improve, he might be able to do some consulting, unless Davis tried to blackball her and her father the way he had his son. With a sigh, she realized she had to expect he would.

She got up and turned her steps toward the coffee bar. Four doors down, she started to walk past Arnold Benton's office, but on impulse she stopped and opened the door.

A carved stone chess set remained on the side credenza, the pieces matching those he had given her father. A game was in progress, but only a few moves had been made, too soon to establish an advantage.

Though her father had trouble with Arnold being Davis's spy, Mariah had to assume that her joining the company had been the catalyst for his betrayal, much the same as her return to the city had set Davis on the road to revenge.

With a sigh, she went back into the hall. The next closed door was Tom Barrett's, who must have called in sick again. In a few days, it wouldn't matter.

The coffee bar was empty and she was glad she didn't have to see anyone. A half pot of stale coffee sat on the burner, and instead of waiting to brew fresh, she poured and heated a cup in the microwave. How terrible that it had come to hiding out at Grant, but she couldn't face another employee who depended on her to save the company.

Before she made her escape, Amy, the very young woman who served as secretary to both Arnold and Tom, came in. "Mornin', Miz Grant," she said without her usual chipper attitude.

Recalling that Amy had liked Arnold, Mariah returned her greeting neutrally and turned to leave.

"Mr. Benton," said Amy, "did he say where he was going to work?"

Mariah decided not to reveal how sudden Arnold's departure had been. "No, he didn't. Did Tom call in this morning?"

Amy fingered her bottle blond hair. "He's here, Miz." Her dire delivery suggested another officer might be about to abandon the deck.

Mariah went back down the hall and rapped on Tom's door. If she managed to salvage the company, she was going to need him more than ever. If they sank, she counted on him to the end.

"Tom?" She twisted the knob and opened the door.

Her father's old friend and partner, the man who'd been like an uncle to her, stood at his desk putting a framed photo of his wife Wendy into a cardboard box. At the sight of her, his big shoulders slumped and he shook his shaggy head.

Mariah went inside the office and shut the door.

There were no words. He might have been packing some items he wanted to take home, but that wasn't the way it worked. She crossed the carpet and put her hand on the arm that had lifted her high, given her hugs, and tucked her in when she slept over at his and Wendy's house. "Don't. Dad and I need you."

Tom trembled beneath her touch and she let him pull away. He busied himself putting another photo in the box, this one of Charley and Mariah playing when they were about eight. In the picture, she was wielding a garden hose. The vividness of pale limbed, tousled-haired Charley jumping beneath the spray made her expect to see the image move. A far away echo of children's high-pitched giggles was almost audible.

"When were you going to tell me?" Mariah tried to keep her voice steady.

"I wasn't." Tom's normally bright blue eyes looked dull.

"You were going to call Dad?"

"I'm afraid not."

A creeping cold took hold of her. "Tom, I need for you to tell me what's going on."

He dropped the pretense of packing. "I was going to slip out at lunch. I've written a note." From the desk, he picked up a white number 10 envelope with *John* scribbled on it.

She took it and turned it in her hands.

"Go ahead and read it," Tom said. "I owe you that." He came out from behind the desk he no longer claimed and lowered his body into a guest chair.

Mariah took the one opposite. Her heart beat hard as she slit the envelope and removed the paper.

Dear John,

The message began in Tom's familiar scrawl. She'd seen his handwriting on everything from her sixth year birthday card to the proud letter he had written for her college graduation. Lately, she'd seen his scribbled notes on the conference room white board.

There are no words for me to tell you how sorry I am, for making fatal mistakes that have spelled the end for Grant Development. Now that Arnold has gone, I can no longer hide behind my sheep's clothing among the flock. I should have spoken up during the meeting, but I was a coward.

The prickling premonition that something had gone terribly wrong chilled Mariah as her eyes flicked to the next line.

Arnold was not Davis Campbell's man.

Mariah closed her eyes. She could still see the slanting ink stark against white paper.

The root of my downfall was my gambling problem. In the old days, I'd play the horses, or phone my bookie and bet on ball games. When it got to where I was spending our retirement money, Wendy laid down the law. Quit, or lose her.

Mariah raised her eyes from the page and took in the misery of a man who looked utterly broken.

I quit.

Until the Internet made gambling as easy as the press of a mouse. I'd sit behind my desk and feel the computer calling me, whispering that there was margin left on my credit cards. At first, I won big, but then, as it inevitably does, it *turned against me.*

I tried to borrow against our family IRAs at First California without Wendy's authorization, and Thaddeus Walker caught me out. He suggested I go to Davis Campbell and, God help me, I asked him to square my debts in exchange for certain information. I knew it was a pact with the dark side, but I didn't see any way out. I was forced to choose between the certain loss of my wife's trust and the chance that you and Mariah would learn of my betrayal.

She should be red with rage, yet all she felt was emptiness. "Was it you who dropped the CDs on the floor in my office?"

He nodded. "Campbell asked for information on the accident investigation. I figured the PI's report on the missing welder would be a sensational tidbit, but nothing that would compromise the company."

He could have inadvertently been helping Davis cover his tracks.

Tom rubbed his face with both hands, then ran them up and tousled his hair as though unaware of what he was doing. "Arnold surprised me in your office on a Sunday. I let the CD's fall and asked him about a financial on Bayview Townhomes, as if that's what I'd been looking for. We walked out together."

"Arnold didn't do anything wrong," she realized aloud.

Tom shook his head. "He would have walked through fire for your dad."

The chess games, the hospital visits . . . "Oh, God."

"Don't beat yourself up," Tom said. "You had no way to

know I was the traitor." His bitter tone brought her attention back to the letter.

Tell Mariah I am sorry to leave her to fight the battles that lie ahead, but I can no longer face either the mirror, or the sweet sight of Wendy's trusting face, knowing that I betrayed you, the people I loved most in the world.

Gooseflesh prickled her scalp, and she looked at Tom. "This is a suicide note."

He stared at a spot on the carpet.

Flinging the paper to the floor, she leaped up and knelt before him. Picking up his heavy, lifeless arms, she dragged them around her neck. "No," she cried, "Dad needs you. I need you. With Charley gone, Wendy couldn't take another loss."

How close she'd been to not even coming to the office today. Thinking that she might yet be in bed feeling sorry for herself . . . "Please, Tom. Whenever you think there's no place to turn, and that nothing can get worse, there's always hope." She tried to believe it was true for her and her dad as well.

Slowly, beneath her embrace, she felt Tom come back. First, he inhaled a ragged sob, then another. She held him as tightly as she could, wetting his shirtfront with her tears. "Please, please, stay with all of us," she begged.

Tom's arms came around her, he squeezed so hard she feared for her ribs.

"We can get through this," she said, "if we all stick together."

"But Wendy," he sobbed, his big chest heaving.

"She'll understand if you join Gamblers Anonymous and stay with it this time."

Gradually, the storm subsided and they held each other, rocking gently back and forth.

At last, Mariah pulled back and stared into his eyes. "Promise," she ordered. "Promise you won't do anything foolish."

After a long moment, he nodded. "I'd hate to miss seeing that bastard get his."

She scrambled on the carpet for the suicide note and tore it. First long ways, then across, she kept on shredding until there was no piece large enough to read. Then she grabbed a china bowl full of paper clips, emptied it, and dumped in the confetti. Knowing that Tom smoked, she held out her hand, "Lighter."

"Let me." His hand trembled as he pulled out a Bic and flicked it with his thumb. The paper caught slowly at first. Then it blazed up and cast a flickering vermilion light over the desktop and the side of the cardboard box. Within a minute, it had subsided into charred wisps of black ash.

"I didn't read that," she announced, "and Dad will never hear of this from me. What you tell him is up to you."

"I want to tell him everything," he said. "I'll drive out there now."

"Do you want me to come?" She still feared for him.

Tom patted her shoulder. "I reckon there's things a man has to do for himself."

In the ladies' room, Mariah dashed cold water on her

face. While she dabbed at her swollen eyes, it occurred to her she might have been foolish to let Tom go alone. If he had been acting, helping burn the evidence of his intent, he might still do something like crash his car. The insurance company wouldn't know it was suicide.

Though she found it almost impossible to believe her well-loved friend had manipulated her, Mariah stopped in the middle of repairing her makeup. While she'd been pulling herself together, enough time had elapsed for Tom to get to Stonestown. She had to check, and if he didn't show soon, she'd have to break her promise not to tell her father what had happened.

Mariah rushed back to her office and dialed the number at home. As she listened to the ringing tone, fear clutched at her.

On the sixth ring, her father answered.

"Is Tom there?" She gripped the phone.

A moment of silence. Then, "He's here," in an infinitely weary voice.

She let out her breath. "Dad, I want to come over."

"Later. Let Tom and I talk."

She didn't want to hang up, but he was right. Though she had known about Tom's gambling in the past, she wondered if she would have been so quick to cry in his arms and offer forgiveness had she not feared he was suicidal. And now, how John dealt with his best friend's betrayal was between the two men.

"All right, Dad. I'll see you this evening."

As she replaced the receiver, one thing puzzled her. Tom had suggested he offered to spy for Davis Campbell, rather than Davis overtly attempting blackmail. Of course, no matter how it had started, the result was the same. Davis had known he was buying one of Grant's men by paying his gambling debts.

Had Rory been aware, or was he as uninvolved in his father's chicanery as he claimed? Though her love wanted to declare him innocent, she was bone weary of trying to decide whether he truly cared for her or had been playing an elaborate charade. If he were the flame and she the moth, then her wings were damned near burned through.

Slowly, Mariah slumped forward until her head rested on her folded arms on the desk. Pain lanced through her, and she closed her eyes.

"Well," said an acid male voice from her doorway.

She opened her eyes to find Arnold Benton watching her with an ugly expression. Jeans and a T-shirt had replaced his usual neat suit and the skin around his eyes looked sallow.

"Arnold." Her cheeks flushed, for no matter his acerbity, she had falsely accused him. His walking out on the job now seemed the act of honor he had declared it to be.

"I came to see if John was here, but with you at his desk . . ."

"No, he's home. Yesterday turned out to be too much for him, in a lot of ways."

"I can well imagine," Arnold said bitterly. "You all believe you found your spy and are well rid of him."

"Arnold, I . . ."

He put out a hand to stop her and cast his gaze upward as though thinking. "And no doubt Davis Campbell arrived with the merger offer to keep Grant out of the bank's hands."

Yesterday, Mariah would have suspected him of being on the inside track with DCI. Today, she figured he must have seen Davis and Rory while storming out.

With a sigh, she pushed to her feet. "Dad turned down Davis's offer of the loan value plus a million. He says he'd rather go into bankruptcy than sell to the Campbells."

A surprising smile played at the corners of Arnold's mouth. "Good for him."

Mariah's brow furrowed. "You were the one pushing a sellout to Campbell yesterday."

"Of course I was. From a business standpoint, it's the right thing. But on a personal level," his tone softened, "I know it would destroy John's spirit to go down that way. He would rather be in the poorhouse than take Campbell's money like a handout thrown to a sick and pitiful creature."

Mariah turned to face Arnold. "That's exactly what he said."

"I do know your father." He sounded sad. "Very well."

"We . . . I was wrong about you. I know now that you're not the spy." She did not intend to reveal that Tom was. "You must know that Dad never could believe it was you. He tried to call you for hours last night."

Arnold grimaced. "I listened to the phone ring, but I was too angry to talk. This morning I woke up and knew I had to come here. To try, in the name of our friendship, to convince him I would never have betrayed him or Grant Development."

"He knows that." She had been too caught up in her feud with Arnold over which of them would be favored to see the man clearly. "I understand that you care for him."

Arnold looked over his shoulder toward his office. "I also came by to pick up my things."

"But, aren't you going to stay until . . .?"

"Until the end?" He shook his head. "Mariah, it's over tomorrow. I may as well get my chessboard and the like."

She wanted to cry out, as she had to April, that there must be something they could do, someone Arnold knew in the financial community to call, but his slumped posture told her it was no use. In that moment, she knew that if her father thought there was any hope of saving the company, he would have insisted on coming in today.

Arnold gestured toward the desk she had been lying across when he arrived. "I always thought I'd be happy to see you in despair, but somehow I'm not."

"Perhaps because you know my loss is also Dad's."

"And mine."

She looked into his pale eyes and saw they shared the same frustration at a dying dream.

Arnold straightened his shoulders. "I'll get my things and catch up with John later."

Seeing him walk out made the end of Grant Development even more real. She supposed she should start gathering up her and Dad's items so there would be no confusion as to property.

The phone on the desk rang.

Rory . . . no, not Rory. She would have to stifle this knee jerk reaction to every call.

As she reached to answer, she noted her bare left hand. Only two days ago, she'd planned to visit her safe deposit box at First California and get the ring as a surprise for Rory. Now she resolved to sell it at the first opportunity.

The phone rang again.

Not Rory, but someone with good news, a big deal. Even the sale of Grant Plaza would now be acceptable if the company could be preserved. It made her ache to see the spire from the window, glowing in the perfect morning that mocked her troubles.

On the third ring, she managed to break out of her reverie. "Mariah Grant."

"Glad I caught you in," Lyle Thomas said, so warmly she could almost see his thousand watt grin. "Whatever plans you had for lunch just changed."

All she wanted was to go home, climb into bed, and pull the covers over her head. Except that she would not be doing that, but making more calls. She could not give up the reins of Grant Development until they were torn from her hands.

"Lyle, I can't have lunch with you."

"You have to eat."

"It's a long story, but things couldn't possibly be any worse right now."

"Trust me, it'll be worse if you don't go."

When things had fallen apart at Wilson McMillan's,

Lyle had been on her side, but she couldn't go off on a noon-time jaunt. "Time is of the essence on the foreclosure. It all ends tomorrow."

"Heard it on the street." Lyle's voice firmed. "What if I told you I could solve that?"

CHAPTER 23

$\mathcal{T}$en minutes later, Mariah stood on the curb while Lyle pulled up in his Mercedes. He had the convertible top down and his Viking looks had both male and female heads turning on the sidewalk.

She opened the substantial door and got in.

Lyle guided the car into the lunchtime traffic on Market Street. "Tough day?"

"The pits." Mariah twisted in her seat to look at him. "What did you mean about something that could save the company?"

He put on his turn indicator and headed west on Geary. "Could I ask you to wait until we get where we're going? What I have to show you is important, and I don't want to louse it up."

A few blocks later, Lyle took a right onto Van Ness.

"Where are we going?" Mariah asked a few minutes later, as he took Lombard west toward the ocean.

He gave his most attractive smile. "I thought Sausalito."

Sausalito was the last place she wanted to go. Memories of Rory haunted every waterfront shop, the marina calling her to step onto the dock and see if his boat was there. A vision of the sailboats, the music of their shrouds . . .

"Can't we go someplace else?" At least in his trousers and fine silk shirt, Lyle wasn't dressed for boating.

"Not for the meeting I've set up."

All right, then it would be Sausalito, for anything that might save the company must be considered. Though impatient to know what Lyle was up to, Mariah settled back into the luxurious leather seat.

A few minutes later, he drove up the approach to the Golden Gate. They passed through the tollbooth and he accelerated onto the bridge.

"How are you holding up?" he asked kindly.

"Don't ask. I'm at wit's end trying to think of a way out of this." As he had refused to enlighten her before they got to Sausalito, she changed the subject. "What's been up with you?"

"Let's see." His tone was teasing. "I've been watching 'On The Spot' quite a bit."

Her face went hot. "How can you joke about that?"

"How can you not?" he countered.

She couldn't smile about anything, especially not since

she and Rory had been the topic of the video mag. "Just thinking about it makes me feel like I've got a stone on my chest."

Lyle gave her a sidelong glance. "Is the stone for the show or for Campbell?"

The weight got heavier. "It's over with him."

"You satisfied with that?" This time his blue gaze skewered her, reminding her of his reputation in the courtroom.

She crossed her arms over her chest. From the high bridge, the Bay appeared and disappeared between the rapid-fire strobing of openings in the rail. The far tower rose in salmon-tinted majesty, supporting the huge conduits that swept up from the center of the bridge.

When she did not answer, Lyle's attention went back to the road. The wind ruffled his blond hair. Another minute passed and they were in the middle of the bridge.

"If I play my cards right, I can make 'On The Spot' next," he said with a casual air.

"Have you landed a high-profile case?"

"No such luck." He gave an exaggerated grin. "I figure 'On The Spot' will have me on with Sylvia Chatsworth, since I'm planning to take her to dinner tonight."

Mariah burst out laughing. "You and Sylvia?"

Lyle's expression shifted to a pout. "You don't approve?"

Her laughter died. For all his mugging, he was apparently serious.

She looked out at a container ship piled with cargo boxes. If Sylvia took up with Lyle, she wouldn't be with Rory anymore.

Tamping down a ridiculous surge of joy, Mariah focused on Lyle. "You and Sylvia could be a wonderful political move."

His jaw clenched enough for her to know she'd struck the wrong chord.

"You've really fallen for her," she amended.

"I have fallen for her," Lyle agreed. "She puts on a tough act sometimes, but underneath there's a woman who could be for me."

Better Lyle under Sylvia's spell than Rory . . .

Had she said that out loud? No, for Lyle continued to drive with hands relaxed on the wheel.

It was past time to stop this. Rory would never leave DCI. He'd remain a single playboy or get into another bad marriage, if not with Sylvia, then with someone of whom Davis approved. Imagining herself scouring the papers and watching "On The Spot" for news of him, she wondered what it was going to take to get him out of her mind.

After the end of the bridge, the Sausalito exit came up fast. Lovely steep hills with secluded homes clinging to their sides passed in quick succession. Before she knew it, they were in the picturesque village overlooking Richardson Bay. Paintings in the local galleries played up Sausalito's Mediterranean flavor, portraying the often fog-shrouded town in brilliant sun-washed color. After yesterday's black rain and overnight clearing, today had turned into one of those picture postcard images.

Despite the town's placid beauty, Mariah's apprehension grew as they approached the waterfront. There was the market where she and Rory had bought lunch supplies and had coffee after their memorial sail for Charley. The proprietor had thought they were married.

"Lyle . . ." This was a mistake.

Then her heart started to play timpani, for three cars over sat a black Porsche.

Lyle took her arm in a gentle grip. "Mariah."

"No."

"Yes. There's somebody here who needs to see you." He nodded toward the head of the pier.

Rory looked snappy in black slacks and an open-collared blue shirt. In the crook of his arm, he carried a sack bearing the logo of the Italian market.

She pulled away from Lyle. "This is too much." He thought Rory "needed" to see her? What were the two men doing, deliberately deceiving her by the lure of something to save Grant?

Mariah slammed out of the car and rushed toward the dock. Rory's dark eyes flashed at her approach and his lips lifted in a smile. It died when she scowled at him. "You've got a lot of nerve getting Lyle to trick me."

Rory shifted the groceries from one arm to the other. "Better hear what I have to say before you start yelling at me."

"There's nothing you could say after you came into Grant yesterday afternoon. Haven't you and your father hurt my family enough?"

"There's been too much hurt." He bore her anger with an oddly placid look. "It's time to start the healing."

Lyle caught up with her. "Rory phoned me last night and brought me up to date. He asked if I'd help."

Rory shifted the sack again. "This is getting heavy. Let's go out to my boat and I'll put it down." He turned and walked away, his long legs taking easy strides over the boards.

"Take me back to the city," Mariah told Lyle.

He smiled down at her from his great height. "Do you trust me?"

"You, I trust," she said with a baleful look at Rory's receding back.

"Then, believe me when I say you should listen to him."

Rory reached his boat and disappeared on board. The little ache in her chest when he went out of sight once more betrayed her. "What can he say to make anything different?" she asked Lyle.

"Remember what I told you at McMillan's? That there ought to be a way for you two to work things out?"

"Idle talk. What can Rory do to save Grant Development? He's a DCI man to the bone."

Lyle's hand at the back of her waist gave a little push. "I can go out to the boat with you and referee, but I'd rather not."

Going to Rory, after he had stood with his father against the Grants was against everything in her. "I can't."

"You can," Lyle said. "It's time to end this Grant versus Campbell thing."

Of all the dreams she'd dared since she and Rory had been reunited, that was the most dear. If he were still standing before her, she'd challenge how he expected to accomplish such a goal.

"You decide to stay, wave goodbye and I'll drive off." Lyle turned away, his steps crunching on the gravel.

To go or stay? She did trust the burly D.A., but how could he vouch for Rory? The two men scarcely knew each other.

Torn, she considered that ultimately it all did boil down to trust. She had to believe that whatever Rory wanted to discuss was vitally important or Lyle would not have consented to get involved. And, he had indicated in good faith that it had something to do with saving the company.

Yet, it went deeper than that. Lyle said Rory needed her, and Rory had spoken of healing. If there were the smallest chance to alleviate the agony that threatened to cut her in half, she must go to him. If she did not, she would continue to wonder "what if" for the rest of her life.

With a deep breath, she moved forward, forcing her steps to be slow and deliberate. The salt breeze riffled her blouse and the familiar tune she'd remembered in the shrouds made something twist inside her. Passing Davis Campbell's *Privateer*, huge and shiny with mirror-like teak and fresh white hull paint, she found her heart pounding. It wasn't difficult to picture a younger, more timid version of her creeping along the dock in tennis shoes.

Four slips farther on, Rory's smaller, less pretentious vessel had been backed into the slip. On the bright blue stern, fresh white letters a foot high proclaimed her the *Mariah*.

She gasped as she had that long-ago rainy Sunday morning when the sight of Rory had taken her breath. Today was no different as he waited for her at the head of the companionway ladder. She approached; he came to the rail and offered his hand.

"The *Mariah*?"

"I finally figured out her name."

They touched. His palm felt smoother than it once had, now softened by office work. His eyes were the same intense gems, but surrounded by tiny lines that spoke of living. Slipping off her dress shoes to come aboard, she felt the silky black slacks she'd worn to work drag the dock. Her wardrobe had improved from when she was eighteen.

Rory's clasp was firm as he helped her step over the rail. Just as she had eight years ago, she felt she left her world behind.

He brought out wineglasses and began laying out lunch in the cockpit. The familiar repast was of crusty bread, assorted cheeses, and a straw-bottomed bottle of Chianti. When all was ready, he turned and handed her a glass of wine.

She was tempted to give in to the sensuous atmosphere and the entreaty in his eyes but first she needed to know. "What am I doing here?"

He gestured at the bench covered with food. "Having lunch with me."

The roller coaster she'd ridden ever since she met Rory took another dip. She waved her free hand at their surroundings. "Paint my name on your boat, a loaf of bread, a jug of wine, and what?" A penetrating gaze designed to seduce her? Then back to DCI for him? "It's not that simple."

He spread his hands. "It can be, if you want it badly enough."

"What are you thinking? What was Lyle thinking to bring me?"

Rory raised his glass. "You're here to drink to us."

"There is no us."

She wanted to stamp her bare foot on the deck, to slosh the contents of her glass in his heartless face for toying with her, but most of all she craved for him to contradict her.

"You said that before." Rory lunged to his feet and dragged her up beside him. "I've told you before and I'll tell you again . . . the hell there isn't." His mouth descended to hers, his arms dropped to pull her against him. Heat was instantaneous and incandescent, a brushfire out of control.

There was no denying she wanted him in the most elemental way, no mistake in her sensing his instant arousal. In a heartbeat, she could go below with him, fall into the berth as she had on his father's boat . . .

She shoved at his shoulders until he lifted his head.

"You're thinking again, Mariah. We always get in trouble when you think too much."

She tried to think, but he made her feel. It was like this with them every time, and as he held her, an insidious little voice whispered that what she felt was the purest truth she had ever known.

His kiss softened, an entreaty that spoke to her parched and lonely places. It was as though he meant her to know this wasn't about the gut level animal magnetism between them. No, it was more, an end to the credo she'd subscribed to in L.A., the fantasy that she didn't need anyone in her life.

Rory raised his head and his expression sobered. "When I phoned Lyle, it took some pretty powerful persuading to get him to ask you out here. He would never have helped if he hadn't believed . . ."

She wanted to believe, as never before in her life, while Rory studied the bay beyond the stern like a diver deciding whether to plunge.

At last, he said, "Marry me."

Mariah leaped to her feet. The boat gave a little dip. "Are you crazy?"

Rory captured both her hands. "Go easy on a man's ego, will you?"

She stared down at him and kept shaking her head. If a tidal wave had swamped the marina, she could not have been more surprised.

"I am asking you to marry me." He wasn't exactly on one knee, but he gazed up at her from the cushioned seat.

The tilt on her world dizzied, while flashes of a future she'd only dared to imagine strobed; dinner with him at an intimate candlelit table, loving together late on weekend mornings, or rising early to catch the sunrise.

"Listen to me," he insisted. "You said we needed to bring our families back together. This is the way."

"After what we saw of our fathers yesterday, it's impossible."

Yet, he looked serious. And there was Lyle, a perceptive

man, trained in the nuances of human behavior for the courtroom. He'd believed Rory was sincere or he would never have brought her.

After years of agony, when she'd believed in Rory's betrayal, after her lack of trust had made her believe he was carrying information to his father, every act of perfidy had been traced to Davis, Senator Chatsworth, Thaddeus Walker, and even Tom Barrett. Since they'd met again, Rory had been nothing but straight with her.

"You're not joking." Her voice sounded far away and she stopped trying to get her hands free. Remember this, she thought strangely. Always see how the sun played on his hair and remember when the gray threads through it.

He turned her hand over and kissed the palm. "We'll go to Lake Tahoe this afternoon."

Just like that, they could be married this day. Her head spun with the wildness of it.

"Now?" She was more organized than that. "Things like this need planning."

"You went to Big Sur without planning. We have to do this the same way."

The same treacherous temptation that had swept her off to a weekend seized her now. This time it could be for keeps.

When she did not speak, Rory went on, "The loans are due tomorrow."

Mariah felt as though she'd been struck in the chest. Here she was thinking romance, while he and Lyle had been covering the business angle.

Her face heated with embarrassment, for this was not the proposal she'd dreamed of, one accomplished with declarations of love and promises of fealty. Except for his tacit acknowledgment of their undeniable sexual chemistry, not one word of devotion had been exchanged.

"DCI and Grant merge," Rory said.

"Dad swore he would never sell to your father."

"I said merge, not sell. Once we're married, both men will have to see there's no more sense in keeping the companies separate. Tomorrow, we'll get Father to call off First California and tell them to hold pending the merger . . . our merger, Mariah."

The offer on the table was that of a corporate union, to save the assets of Grant from liquidation because John refused a straight sale to Davis.

"What do you think?" Rory still held her hands, but there was no fire in her now.

Pride made her want to pull away and tell him she wasn't for sale. It was all very well for him to guard his heart by not giving all of himself, but what about her? She loved him with the kind of desperation she had sensed in Kiki Campbell's unguarded gaze at Davis. If she married Rory, would it be her fate to end up in the same hopeless circumstance?

She could jump up and rush down the pier away from Rory's boat and his father's *Privateer*. How aptly named that blade-like vessel, whose owner stabbed at the heart of all she stood for.

Yes, she could refuse Rory. See Grant dismantled and

both her and her father destroyed.

Put like that, it was a no-brainer.

"All right, Rory. I'll marry you."

CHAPTER 24

The decision made, Mariah went to the bow of the boat and waved Lyle back to the city. He raised a big arm and even at a distance, she saw the flash of white teeth as he grinned and turned away.

From the excellent repast Rory had laid out, she managed to eat bread and cheese and sip a little wine. Their picnic complete, they packed up the trash and put away the cockpit cushions. Rory shut the companionway hatch and locked it.

Mariah thought of them sailing together, spending weekends on the boat. Waking up late and making slow love before a late breakfast on deck . . . She tore off the thought and trashed it along with the lunch sack.

Rory steered the Porsche over the Golden Gate to the city and parked in front of her apartment house. Once inside, he sat on a stool at her kitchen counter and talked at her while she went into her bedroom to pack, innocuous statements with no bearing on the serious step they were about to undertake.

"What do you wear to get married in Lake Tahoe?" she called through the doorway.

"Your gold dress," Rory said. "I've got my tux."

Her hands went still in the act of tucking a hairbrush into her makeup bag. She went to the doorway. "You must have been pretty sure of my answer."

Fishing in his pocket, Rory brought up the knife with the corkscrew he'd used at Bayview. "Eagle Scout," he told her again, sticking with banter. "Were you ever in Scouts?"

She shook her head and gave him a serious look. "There's so much we don't know about each other." During the quick passion of their youth, they'd spent a lot of time necking, but in the way of the young, not much time talking. Even now, despite his dear familiarity, she had to admit Rory was a stranger.

"Did you pack to . . . stay the night?" she asked.

"I did," he replied in an even tone, "but we'll have to get up early to get back in the morning to talk with Father. I assume once he agrees to a merger without having to pay your Dad any front money, he can phone Thaddeus Walker and tell him foreclosure's no longer part of the plan. DCI — that is, whatever we call the combined company — can pick up on the loan payments."

Mariah went back into her room to pack the gold dress. For staying overnight, she put in underwear, her black pantsuit for the drive home and tomorrow's meeting with Davis, and extra toiletries. She hesitated over her bathrobes. Her favorite worn terry one was still at Dad's, and it wouldn't do for a bride. If only she hadn't left the black velvet at Wilson McMillan's. As a compromise, she selected a blue silk kimono, closed the lid, and took her bag into the living room.

Rory rose to take her burden. "Did you bring your ring? I thought . . ."

If this had been a wedding in the true sense of the word, she would have wanted to wear the ruby he'd bought her in Carmel.

"I don't . . ."

His look of disappointment was so sharp it sent a slam of excitement through her.

"I told you when I bought it that you should have had a ring eight years ago. Now that we're finally getting . . ." He paused.

Despite that this was not going to be the wedding she'd imagined for them, she nodded. "It's in the safe deposit."

The next stop was First California, where she told them she wanted to close out her box.

"No sense giving them any more business," she said in an aside to Rory.

For the attendant, she signed a card and proffered her key. In a small private booth, she opened the box. There was only one thing in the small metal container.

Mariah brought out the velvet case and offered it to

Rory. He lifted the lid to reveal the ruby and pair of flanking diamonds sparkling even in the bank fluorescents. For a long moment, he studied his gift to her before snapping the top shut and slipping the case in his pants pocket.

Back in the car, Rory turned the Porsche's nose toward the Bay Bridge that would take them to the mainland and toward the Sierras. Yet, a funny feeling told Mariah there was something more to do before leaving town.

"I know we can't tell your father until after we're . . ." she skipped the word "married" as Rory had done, "but do you think we could stop by Dad's? He'll keep our secret until tomorrow."

In answer, Rory made an immediate U-turn through a break in the median and aimed the Porsche south toward Stonestown. When they pulled off Sloat Boulevard onto her father's street, Tom Barrett's car was at the curb.

"Company?" Rory asked.

"It's Tom, Charley's dad." She hesitated. "There was some trouble this morning." For a moment, she wondered whether to tell Rory, but it would be nice not to have secrets. "I'm afraid your father was paying Tom's gambling debts in exchange for him spying on us at Grant."

Rory shut off the ignition and stared at her. "What next?"

The hurt in his eyes made her put a hand on his arm. "You said he wasn't always this bad. Until he saw me again and got upset over Catharine."

"He's distinguished himself this time."

Unspoken between them hung her charge of attempted

murder.

Rory looked at John's house. "Do you want me to come in with you?"

Just as she and he had stood together before Dad in his hospital room, today she felt they should both announce their marriage, unconventional as its reasons were. "Of course."

The front door was unlocked. Mariah went in ahead, calling, "Dad, Tom?"

The sound of serious male voices came from the living room.

She stopped in the archway from the hall as her father's gray eyes and Tom's blue ones fixed on her. "Dad, I know you said not to come over now, but I've got something to tell you." She swallowed beneath their scrutiny. "I know it's kind of sudden . . . You both already knew we . . ." She trailed off and reached behind her to draw Rory into view. "The two of us are going to Lake Tahoe to get married."

Tom swore.

Beside Mariah, Rory flinched. She understood that Tom was no doubt reacting to who his father was, but it didn't make it any easier.

She looked at her dad. On the drive over, she had played out a range of reactions, from disbelief to anger, but she had not even considered what happened next.

His gray eyes twinkled. "Whose idea was this?"

"Mine, sir," Rory spoke up.

"Have you told Davis?"

Remembering what Rory had told her about his father's

old threat to get any marriage annulled, Mariah lifted her chin. "We thought we'd wait until we get back."

As if he read her thoughts, Rory took her hand. "This time I think we're a bit too old for Father to find a judge to set it aside."

Tom still looked dumbfounded.

John struggled out of his recliner and shook Rory's hand. "You're a chip off the old block, kid, and I mean that kindly."

"Thank you," Rory said, "I think."

John appeared to note Tom's ambivalence. "Look here, this is a brilliant stroke. I suppose tomorrow we . . . or you two, explain to Davis that a joint family company is the only sensible thing."

Tom shifted in his seat. "He'll never go for it. Just up and merge with his enemy because you kids went out and defied him?"

Rory frowned.

"Believe me," Tom went on, "he plays hardball."

"I always knew he pushed the envelope, but I thought he stayed within bounds." Rory said. "Now Mariah tells me he blackmailed you."

Tom put up a hand. "I went to him, son. That puts a little different spin on it, but you still can't underestimate his vindictiveness."

John looked dejected. "This has to work. We've only got till the close of business tomorrow to get him to call off First California."

They had been naïve. This was too simple to possibly

outflank Davis.

"There could be another way," Tom suggested.

John snapped his fingers. "You mean, what if I call Davis and accept his buyout."

"Dad, no." Yet, Mariah suspected what he was thinking. Take the deal and the million as his revenge, along with the knowledge his daughter had married Davis's son against his will.

She turned to Rory. "If Dad agrees to the sale, there's no reason for us to get married."

Rory's eyes searched hers. "No?"

Hope filled her chest at the fervor in his voice.

He went on, "It's insurance that a Grant is in the family and can't be bought off or forced out."

Mariah wished he would speak of love instead of real estate. Yet, he was right again about their strategy. "Let's get on the road, then."

The Nevada shore of Lake Tahoe was lined with casinos, but Rory didn't want to stop at one. He imagined Mariah didn't either after learning Tom Barrett's downfall had been gambling.

A twinge of guilt went through him that on the drive up his thoughts had been on his father instead of Mariah, but it was difficult to deal with his new knowledge of how far Davis was willing to go to get at John. Rory had wanted to believe his chicanery of spreading rumors, making political contributions for favors, and paying off First California with new business had been the extent of it. All somewhat distasteful, but legal, even acceptable to many in a city where hardball was played. But blackmail?

Rory steered through the resort traffic. "Mariah, what did Tom mean about going to my father for the money?"

"Apparently Tom got into trouble at the bank and Thaddeus Walker suggested Davis as a way out."

"That doesn't change what he was doing." Rory's knuckles whitened on the steering wheel. He found it difficult to swallow that the man he'd seen almost in tears over the betrayal of his best friend kept lashing out like this. "It was blackmail, pure and simple."

Mariah touched his arm. "I'd say pure, but not simple."

He tried to hold on to his father's expression of horror when Rory said he might have rigged the Grant Plaza disaster. No, it wasn't simple, not when a son had to wonder whether his father had two deaths on his conscience.

Mariah's hair brushed her shoulders as she looked to the right and left of the busy street. "So, where do we . . .?"

"One of those wedding chapels, I suppose." He'd seen a few already and thought them either garish or tawdry.

"Will we change clothes there?"

He hadn't thought of that, though he'd packed his tux. At the look of uncertainty on Mariah's face, he trashed the thought. She — and he — deserved to do this right.

"Let's find a quiet place to stay away from the crowds and

clean up. After we get . . ." He paused again over the word "married." "Later, we'll have a nice dinner and . . ."

Sitting close in the bucket seats, he thought Mariah might have flushed at the subtle mention of the night ahead.

He'd botched asking her. It had started out fine, a romantic picnic with a kiss that scorched them both, and then he'd managed screw up the mention of Grant Development. Sure, that was the reason for the urgency, but no woman would want a proposal couched in commercial terms.

Rory turned onto a mountain road that led up to a ski resort. There, as it was the off-season, he and Mariah had their pick of picturesque condos. After checking in to a two-bedroom, they went out onto a high wooden deck overlooking a densely forested valley. It was early, a few minutes past five, and now that he no longer had driving to focus on, the awkwardness between them hung heavier than the scent of pine.

"Do you want to change your mind?" he asked carefully.

Her slender hands gripped the porch rail. "I'm scared to death."

"I'm pretty shaky, myself," he admitted.

Last night when he'd thought of getting married, everything had fallen into place. It was not only the best solution to their problems with Grant and DCI, but once he'd determined to go through with it, a weight had lifted from his chest. After phoning Lyle and testing it on somebody else to good advantage, he had slept through the night with a calm sense of certainty.

Now, he wasn't so sure. Questions roiled in his mind,

and, he was sure, in Mariah's as well. Would they get back the sense of intimacy that had been building between them at Ventana, at McMillan's, and the night he'd stayed over at her apartment? Were either of them prepared to make their marriage a serious one, or was this going to be a corporate merger? Though she had assured him Lyle was a friend, and the big man had assisted in getting them together, Rory was reminded that, single or married, Mariah could have her pick of men.

Standing with the backdrop of sky and forest, Mariah looked so lovely it sent a shaft of longing through him. He wanted was to take her in his arms and pour out his jumbled thoughts and feelings, to find out what was in her head.

Before he could move, she turned to him. Her expression was direct. "So, are we going to do this thing or not?"

He put a hand on her arm, but her gaze did not soften. With a sense of opportunity lost, he drew back. "Put on your gold dress, Miss Grant," he made his tone light, "and prepare to change your name."

Rory took his bag into the spare room, leaving the master to Mariah. He showered and when he heard the water running behind the wall, his imagination took over as it had in the marble shower at McMillan's. Her blond hair darkened and streaming, her breasts and stomach sheeting water that ran down into her golden thatch. If not for his awkward proposal, he could be in there washing her back.

He sighed.

Maybe he should have said he loved her. Would that have

put a light in her amber eyes instead of this determination to go through with it to save her family legacy? Yet, so many folks bandied those three little words about cheaply. As an untested young man, he'd pledged himself to Mariah and then broken his vow. At the altar with Elizabeth, he'd given a promise of love when he should have known what he felt for his wife was a deep and abiding friendship.

Of course, Mariah had not said she loved him.

Though he could have gotten by without a shave, he scraped a blade over his chin. The spicy cologne he'd packed was not his usual and he hoped she'd notice. He brushed his damp hair and left it curling above his collar. Before he went into the living room, he opened the velvet box and looked at the ring. It had been an extravagance when he'd forced it on her in Carmel, a guy throwing his money around. But hadn't there been a crystal of truth when he slipped it onto her left hand?

On this perfect blue day, Mariah was to be married. At seven o'clock in June, nearly the longest day of the year, the sun still rode high over the Sierra Nevadas. Ringed by mountains studded with virgin forest, the cobalt lake rippled with whitecaps. Along the roads that rimmed it lay the evidence of man: houses, hotels, and ski runs, paler green slashes against the verdant slopes.

Cruising past the more gaudy marriage mills, Mariah

was turned off repeatedly. She wondered if her reluctance was due to the butterflies in her stomach.

Stop it, she thought. This had been her dream, to become Mrs. Rory Campbell. She should be delirious with joy, for she was in love with him again, as though their years apart had never been. Unfortunately, this was a new Rory, more complex, darker, and conflicted even now over his father.

Truth to tell, wasn't she also changed, embittered by their past and the lonely years in between? Even as she went to the altar, wasn't she holding back because she sensed that he was?

"There." Rory pointed toward the blue lake.

The small wedding chapel on the shore occupied a rustic log structure, somebody's ancient summer cabin turned commercial. Behind the quaint structure, a wooden pier jutted over the water. As he pulled the Porsche up and gave the chapel a scrutiny, Mariah's nervous stomach tried to perform a back flip.

"What do you say?" Rory asked.

She took a long breath. "This should do."

On the way into the chapel, he held her hand. His palm was dry and his grip firm.

Despite the quaint exterior, inside they found marriage mill kitsch. A churchlike foyer with dark wood paneling and a guest register overlooked the main chapel. Faded red carpet, worn pews and a bare altar did little to recommend it. Dust motes slanted in the sun through painted stained glass flowers.

Rory spied a bell and rang it. A moment later, they were in the motherly hands of Reverend Molly Sparks. Blond and bespectacled, she wore a knee-length black robe over her sturdy body. Her Reeboks matched her robe. She consulted a checklist on her clipboard, information for the license, ID, did they want music . . .

Rory cast what Mariah interpreted as a distasteful look through the archway. She didn't know what she'd been expecting, but this wasn't it. Sure, they had eloped and were here for the quickie version, but this place made her feel sad, with its dark, claustrophobic walls. With a feeling that she couldn't breathe, she nearly rushed out the door. Maybe they could find someplace else, but the last one they had passed advertised you could be married by Elvis.

What about a nice Justice of the Peace? But it was after hours and they couldn't afford to wait until tomorrow.

She spied the sunrays at the window.

Rory squeezed her hand. "Do you think we could do this outside?" he asked the Reverend. "Maybe on the pier?"

Whatever they wanted. Did they want it videotaped?

"No," said Rory, while Mariah said, "Yes."

A smile broke over Molly's plump features.

"No video for 'On The Spot' to get hold of," he insisted. "I've had enough of those guys."

Mariah looked at Rory with his crisp jaw line and ink-dark hair, at his tuxedo with the ruby studs, and wanted the tape with an ache that matched the feeling she'd had on the dock when she had looked at his hair and thought of gray there. In the years to come, they'd be captured as they were today, rather than with the fading tinge of memory.

"We might want to show our folks," she said, "or our . . ." She broke off before the word "children" formed, but she heard her voice say it inside her head.

Perhaps Rory understood, for he told Molly, "We'll have video."

"Got rings?"

"Yes," Rory replied, showing the velvet box.

"No," Mariah said.

They looked at each other.

She hadn't thought to ask him if he'd even wear one. "Do you . . .?"

"All right." His face bore a noncommittal expression, as though he were wondering if he wanted to advertise his marital status.

She wished they were alone so she could ask him what he was thinking.

Maybe all weddings were like this. Her friends who had gone through the ceremony had spoken of pre-wedding jitters and how they felt alone in the back of the church, even with their fathers at hand to walk them down the aisle. If only Dad were here to give her away, and Rory's father stood by, an accepting — no loving — smile lighting his black eyes.

Some things were not to be.

Reverend Molly went to a panel in the wall and lowered it. "Men's." She pulled out a rack of rings.

Mariah looked at the confusing array. Even the plain

bands came in different widths and textures, along with more intricate styles set with diamonds. In deference to Nevada's gambling, there were even golden horseshoes.

Rory selected the widest of plain gold bands.

The Reverend did not offer a box, so Mariah clutched it in her hand. The gold warmed against her skin.

"That should do it," Molly said.

"Not quite." Rory bent to a bucket of roses. He bypassed the red ones like he'd given her in Carmel and chose a single white bud on the end of a long stem.

As they walked out onto the pier, the wind caught her hair that she'd spent such pains with. Rory's bow tie flapped.

He held her arm in a protective gesture. "Will you be warm enough?"

Though the breeze was cool, she couldn't imagine going back and being married inside the dark little chapel.

The ceremony was short and surreal. The video camera wielded by Molly's pimpled nephew made Mariah nervous. The lake wind raised gooseflesh on her bare arms and she pricked the sensitive tip of her index finger on a rose thorn. In a voice that sounded remarkably steady to her, she promised to love, honor, and cherish Rory for as long as they both should live. He recited the same.

Prompted by the Reverend, Rory brought the ruby from his pocket and slipped it onto her left hand where it glowed in the sun-washed light. She slid the wide gold band onto his finger, and they clasped their ringed hands between them.

A wave of elation lifted her and she clung to him with a

grip so tight she wondered why he didn't ask her to stop. He could have stayed at DCI without challenging his father and let her and Dad both go down the drain. He could have married a senator's daughter.

Yet, he was marrying Mariah and the sight of him beside the cobalt water with his tuxedo snapping in the breeze was the most beautiful thing she had ever seen.

"And now, by the power vested in me by Almighty God and the State of Nevada," the Reverend intoned, "I pronounce you man and wife."

It was done. For better or worse, and now that Rory had stood with her in the sun and promised everything, Mariah wanted it all.

❧

At a restaurant on the mountainside overlooking Lake Tahoe, where the last light of day had an ethereal quality, they toasted with champagne and ate briny, yet clean-tasting, Puget Sound oysters.

Though Mariah deplored the reason they'd been forced into a hasty elopement, when their talk turned to business, she was surprised to find she welcomed it. It was the first time she'd felt free to speak with Rory without wondering what his father would do with the information.

She took a bite of crusty French bread, savored it, and swallowed. "What shall we do with Grant Plaza? Dad and I were planning to office there, but now maybe we should lease it out."

"Hell, no. It's a great plan." Rory raised his flute. "Let's move our joint offices to the top floor."

"Even after . . ." Despite her hopes for the skyscraper, seeing Charley die there had her feeling superstitious.

Rory gestured with a forkful of oyster he'd dipped in a horseradish sauce. "Especially after the accident." He looked at the mouthful of food and set it back on his plate.

Pain knifed through her as when her friend had fallen to his death. These last weeks had been filled with so much that she'd been repressing her sense of loss.

"Charley was such a darling cut-up." She imagined him and Rory joking together as they had on that long-ago day on the Bay. Charley hauling on the jib sheet while she cranked the winch, Rory manning the wheel with his legs braced against the seas. "I wish you'd known him better."

"I knew him enough to understand how you cared for him," Rory answered. "You remember when I said we should have a memorial sail for Charley?"

Mariah nodded.

Rory leaned forward and put his hand over hers on the table. "Since he died working on Grant Plaza, that whole masterpiece of edifice, complete and filled with tenants going about their business and their lives . . . that will also be his memorial."

Though Charley had accepted that his limited abilities precluded shining in the boardroom, he'd been happy as part of the Grant Plaza crew, his contribution to the company his father helped build. With Rory's words, Mariah realized she didn't want to give up on the building, either.

"You're right." She turned her hand over and twined her fingers with Rory's. "I couldn't see it."

Their synergy made her see she and Rory could be a team, designing and implementing projects even more spectacular than Grant Plaza. Working together through the years began to seem real.

It was on the tip of her tongue to say something about it, but a fear of jinxing the situation kept her quiet. For, as night fell over the Sierras, she wondered if their marriage would be enough to make Davis stand down.

On the drive up the mountain to their rented condo, Rory was amazed at how he felt. Perhaps knowing Mariah's friend Charley was gone, while the blood continued to flow through his veins, was what made Rory so glad to be alive. He hadn't been this happy in . . . God, it was eight years and that meant the source of his joy was sitting beside him in the front seat.

He reached for Mariah's hand and pressed her wedding ring. It didn't matter that his feet had felt a little cool before the ceremony; that happened to most guys.

As he negotiated the winding road, she asked, "Where should we live?"

"How about my place for a while?" he said easily. He'd

never had a woman there, keeping his social life separate from his home. Even so, the townhouse wasn't the kind of place he wanted to live with Mariah long-term.

He shook his head and chuckled. It was exactly like some of his married buddies had said. If you married the right woman, the minute the wedding was over, you felt different. You suddenly thought ahead to things like houses and hearths.

That house off the 17-Mile Drive . . . Rory made a mental note to call and find out if it was still on the market. If it were, he'd pack them for a weekend down the coast and present the key as a surprise wedding present. That is, if he had the funds after the chips finished falling with his father.

The driveway for the condo came up, and he turned down the steep hill to the complex. Lights twinkled from windows and balconies, welcoming. He imagined bringing Mariah here during snow season, building a fire and taking off her clothes in dappled light beside the hearth.

When they reached the top of the stairs and he unlocked the door, he pointed down at the threshold. "See that?"

Her brow furrowed prettily. "What?"

He scooped her up and carried her inside, depositing her on the kitchen counter.

Mariah put her hands up and twined them in the hair at the back of his neck, sending goosebumps down his spine. "I seem to recall a prior countertop experience." Her voice went husky.

Though his body urged him to take her up on what sounded like an offer, he bent and kissed her earlobe. "Tonight, I think we'll use that king-sized bed. But first . . ." He lifted an index finger and went back to the car for an extra bottle of champagne.

On his way up back up the stairs, he found himself whistling. A pulse in him spoke of having all night. All of many nights.

When he came in, Mariah had disappeared and the master bath was closed off. From his suitcase, he brought out the black velvet robe she had left at McMillan's. It felt soft in his hands, as he tapped on the door panel.

Mariah opened up a crack and peeked around. "It's bad luck to see the bride."

"You're not a bride anymore. You're my wife." After all the negative noises he'd made about marrying again, he did like the sound of it. "Slip into something more comfortable?" He held out the robe where she could see it.

She took it with a smile he thought promising and closed the door again.

The urge to whistle came back as he iced the champagne and brought it to the bedside. He turned back the comforter and plumped the pillows, like room service in a five-star hotel. Remembering the candles they had lit aboard *Privateer* long ago, he found one in the living room and lit it, turning down the other lights. From his kit, he brought out a bottle of the ginger massage oil he'd taken home from Ventana.

There were aspects of being married to Mariah he was going to like very much.

In the bathroom, Mariah put on the robe. The lining matched the center stone in her wedding ring, and seemed to cast a warm light onto her skin. In the other room, she heard Rory whistling. She'd never heard him do that before.

With a deep breath, she opened the door. He stood at the foot of the bed, jacket off and shirt open, removing his ruby studs. His hands stilled when their eyes met.

She went to him and pushed his hands aside. Gently, she took the stones from his shirtfront, placing them one by one on the dresser. The mirror reflected the scene of domesticity. She shifted her attention to his cuffs, loving his fine-boned hands, from their clean, square-cut nails to the sprinkling of dark hair on the backs. When she reached to push the shirt off his shoulders, he helped her, shrugging out of it to reveal his bare chest.

Planting an open-mouthed kiss in the hollow where her shoulder met her neck, he let her strip him down until he was as bare as when he'd been born, with a notable exception. The gold ring branded him as hers.

She took his hand and looked at it. "Are you still afraid?"

He gave her a steady gaze. "I'm sure there will always be something to fear. Right now I'm not." He slipped his hands inside the robe she'd left loose and circled her waist. "You?"

"No."

Rory's eyes seemed enormous, drawing her as if she might

float off the floor. She let her palms take in his skin's texture, smooth in places, in others hair-roughened, like reading Braille. He kissed her and she realized she was crying from the salt taste of tears at the corner of her mouth.

He urged her down on the bed and began to make slow love with his hands and lips. The clean geranium smell of his cheek mixed with the spice of an aftershave she hadn't noticed on him before. She lay taut and proud, the hand wearing her wedding ring cradling the back of his neck.

Impossible, but it was once again better than she remembered, for this time they were one, at least in the eyes of the Reverend Molly and the State of Nevada.

"When we were younger, you said you would always love me," she dared through a languorous haze.

Rory raised his head and stopping caressing her.

She felt like curling up and pulling the comforter over her. Instead, she waited.

He pushed up on an elbow. "I didn't know what I meant by 'love' then."

Mariah maintained her silence.

"I thought we settled this at McMillan's." Rory pushed up and sat on the edge of the bed. "Neither of us had the gumption to fight for each other, so was it really love or were we enamored with the idea of it?"

Perhaps he was right and her younger self hadn't understood the full meaning of the word. She'd been a kid with no idea how deeply she could need this man who was now her husband.

He ran his hands over his chin "If I'd loved you the way you deserved, I'd never have let you go."

She looked into his troubled brown eyes. "I'm here now."

"When I think of the wasted years we should have been together . . ."

Mariah scrambled up and knelt before him, a hand on each of his thighs. "Don't go back there. Even after we talked about our breakup, I was still hung up on the past. I believed the worst when you decided not to leave DCI and when you came with Davis to Dad's office. God, Rory, let's be done with the past and look forward."

He took her mouth with a desperate tenderness she had never felt in him. "I do want us to have a future," he vowed. "I want that with all my heart."

Her pulse thudded as she weighed pride against this man who still wrestled with their past breakup, his failed marriage, and his parents' rocky relationship. She could walk away because Rory could not or would not say certain words, but the ones he'd just uttered meant even more than the rote ritual of their wedding ceremony.

"I want our future, too," she whispered against his lips.

CHAPTER 25

*R*ory awoke in a cocoon of covers with Mariah's arm around him. There was no instant of wondering where he was or with whom. Just a slow drifting up from sleep to a place that felt safe. He'd slept restlessly, sometimes pushing her away, at others holding her hard against him. Now he breathed deeply and evenly, as though in some dream of her he'd found peace.

Last night he and Mariah had left the drapes open, letting in a rose dawn light that fingered the nearest mountain peak. Not yet ready to face Grant Development's last day and all the uncertainty it brought to both him and his wife, he closed his eyes and pressed his back to her warmth.

"You're awake," he whispered.

"How did you know?" She shifted slightly and curled her legs so they spooned snugly.

"I sensed you there."

He turned over to face her and kissed her neck softly. His hand on her side moved to beneath her breast. His breathing became more deliberate, as images of last night readied him for more lovemaking.

For, it was love.

How utterly stupid he'd been to hesitate over the word. After the jubilation he'd felt as soon as they were married, he should never have suffered the old knee jerk reaction against giving a woman the ability to hurt him. Those days were past, and as Mariah had said, neither of them must ever go back.

He brushed her hair back from her face. "Last night . . ." he whispered.

The pealing tones of a muffled cellular phone began. They both jumped and he swore.

"It's mine," she said, gesturing toward her purse on the nightstand.

Mariah was closest, but he cleaved up, reached it, and handed it to her.

"Hello." She threw back the covers and sat on the edge of the bed. "Dad?"

On the drive down from the mountains, the soaring

heights of the Sierras gave way to the broad San Joaquin valley. Summer row crops and fruit trees brought forth bounty, but the optimism Mariah had felt at their marriage saving Grant Development had blackened on the vine.

Her father's terse words, "You'd better get down here as soon as possible," had been a rough wakeup, but then he'd said, "Don't ask for details now, but Davis knows what you and Rory did."

"How?"

"I'll explain when you get to the house, Daughter." The weariness in his tone made her accept the wait.

Just before ten a.m., Rory steered his Porsche onto her father's street in Stonestown. She jumped out, ran up the walk, and used her key to let them in.

John wasn't in the house; the back door stood open. Bougainvillea on a trellis was in full bloom, cascading tiers of bright fuchsia and coral.

"Out here," he called.

Mariah and Rory went through the kitchen and stepped onto the patio. She bent to kiss her father's cheek.

He held out a hand to grip both hers and Rory's. "Congratulations, you two."

"Thanks, Dad."

"Thank you, sir," Rory said. "Now, what happened with Father?"

The pleasant set of John's face turned sad. "I'm afraid I made a huge mistake. Instead of calling and accepting DCI's offer, I decided to tell Davis the truth. That you had gone to get married and that it was time we buried the hatchet."

As Mariah formed the same thought, Rory said, "Bad idea. What happened?"

John's expression hardened. "He buried it in my back." He shook his silver head. "His offer is no longer good. After Grant goes under, he'll cherry pick the properties at the foreclosure auction."

Rory slammed his hand against the post that held up the bougainvillea. His ring glinted, mocking her with the futility of what they'd tried. "Let's go."

"What are you going to do?"

"We're going over there and confront him with his blackmail of Tom Barrett. He's going to by God stand down as head of DCI or I'll drag his name through the dirt. Lyle Thomas would be happy to prosecute."

The sight of Rory's rage brought John up straighter in his chair. "Hold on. Tom made it clear he approached Davis. There was no extortion involved."

Mariah found her hand on Rory's arm. "He's right. There's nothing to be gained by going over there and starting a brawl."

"You always wanted me to stand up to him," Rory told her. "Now you don't?"

Before she could speak, John said, "I've been sitting here thinking about what Wilson McMillan once told me about winding up on the rocks. Well, I'm there now, and you don't need to join me."

"McMillan!" Mariah snapped her fingers. He'd been a

friend to John through the years, and she'd been impressed with his wisdom. "He's rich as Croesus, but we didn't think of calling him about the property sales because he's retired."

"What could he do?" John did not look hopeful.

"We won't know until we call him," she said.

An hour later, wearing her favorite black pantsuit as armor, with an emerald silk blouse, Mariah waited for an opening onto Sloat Boulevard. She'd pulled her blond hair back as severely as she could with not a stray curl, wore gold hoops at her ears, and pale porcelain makeup, no blush.

Rory had taken his Porsche and planned to meet them at DCI. Though they had only been separated for a few minutes, she already missed him.

"What's wrong?" John asked from the passenger seat of her sedan.

"Nothing." She kept her eyes on traffic.

"Call it a hunch, but you don't seem as radiant as I expected."

Mariah fiddled with the radio dial, thinking of turning up the news. Her father waited in a listening posture, following his own advice that patience reaped reward.

She thought it was going to sound silly in the cloudless morning sunshine, but she decided to tell him. "Rory hasn't said he loves me."

"He may not have said it, but he does!" John's voice sounded stronger than it had since before his heart attack. "I know a man in love when I see him. I imagine he's skittish of the trappings of commitment because Kiki and Davis exist in a state of war, and because his first marriage failed."

Almost noon according to her dash clock, and there wasn't time for this. They had a plan to execute. Yet, she said, "I know why Rory's like this, but that doesn't change it. When we were younger, he said he loved me. Now he says he doesn't know what he meant by that."

John mused for a moment. "Of course, it's possible he may have mistaken infatuation for love the first time through. For about ten minutes I was afraid Catharine and I were doing that."

"That's what Rory says we did." Mariah changed lanes. "But I'm sure now that I love him. What can I do?"

John shook his silver head. "I don't know. Although you barely recall, you saw me with Catharine, and you want nothing less."

"That's right." Her desire to have a marriage as lyric as her parents warred with her love for Rory. Last night he'd declared his desire for them to be together, but would that be enough for her as time went on?

Mariah steered the car toward the heart of the city. Market Street wound past Twin Peaks and then settled out into a straight run toward the skyline. In minutes, the tall buildings closed in.

The sight of Rory waiting in the building lobby threatened to burn a hole in her chest. Once more, he'd dressed in his best suit, the one that he'd worn to see Takei Takayashi.

His appraisal of her was swift and hungry, darting from her coiled hair to the hem of her pants, but he greeted John first.

A handshake turned into the awkward half-hug of men who are extended family. "Sir," Rory said.

"Call me John."

"All right . . . John." Rory broke into a grin.

He bent to brush a kiss onto her cheek. His hands gripped hers, the touch of his wedding ring both tormenting and reassuring.

Tom Barrett arrived next, with his hair tamed as neatly as Mariah had ever seen it. Since his confession the other day, he moved like a man ten years younger. "John, Mariah," he drawled, drawing her into a bear hug that almost lifted her from the granite floor. "Campbell."

"Call me Rory."

Wilson McMillan joined them.

The grand old man of the Northern California developers stepped lively, sharp and ready for anything. "John." He gripped his hand. "We'll get this thing sorted out directly."

Rory thought the group stood in the awkward pose of people outside a courtroom. Underlying tensions masqueraded beneath a veneer of normality, with nothing to be decided until they went inside.

An elevator arrived and they ascended to the executive offices on forty. The receptionist in the palatial anteroom to DCI looked up in alarm at the six striding purposefully toward the inner sanctum, but she did not challenge Rory. Guarding Davis's entry, his secretary wore a blue-blood expression, but Rory brushed aside her exclamations. He opened his father's office door.

Davis stood at the window, looking out in the direction of Grant Plaza. Only a few holes remained in the glazing on the top floor, the custom panes broken in the accident. He turned toward the sound of the latch with a look of surprise that quickly shifted to shock.

Rory confronted his father. "A group of us have come to tell you how things are going to be from now on. You know Mariah and I are married and since you've chosen to ignore the implications of that, we will have the board vote you out as Chairman."

Davis gave a mirthless bark. "How do you propose to accomplish that?"

"Once they hear of your backing Tom Barrett to spy on Grant Development, it should be no problem."

Davis shot Tom a disparaging look. "You don't have the nerve to accuse me. You came to my office with your hat in hand." He focused back on his son. "Rory, you know what that would do to your mother."

Though it pained him to see his mother cast onto the board as a game piece, he kept his gaze steady. "It will be tough on her, but I think she'll understand. Especially after the way you've been lately."

Casting about, Davis focused on Wilson McMillan.

"What's your role in this?"

"Young Rory tells me you've used your weight with Senator Chatsworth and others to keep him from pursuing other opportunities. I came to tell you two can play that game. I may be an old man, but I've still got some clout."

Davis lost a bit of his bravado. "I know you do, Wilson."

"I saw you baiting John's daughter about the bank loans at my house party. At the time I didn't realize how serious the situation was." Wilson moved closer to Davis. "I've known you and John a long time." The elderly developer sounded almost kind, his usual megawatt energy reined in. "And I knew Catharine."

Davis's eyes flicked to Mariah at the mention of her mother's name.

"It's time all this came to an end," Wilson declared, "especially now you're all family. I've spoken to the chairman at First California. He's holding Thaddeus Walker up on the Grant foreclosure, pending a merger agreement between these two." Wilson indicated Rory and Mariah.

Rory took her cold hand and they faced his father.

"You have this all figured out," Davis temporized. "I get dragged through the mud, along with your mother, while you," with a hard glance at Rory, "and your new family come out smelling like petunias in the park." Proud and stubborn, he drew himself up. "Walker will never admit what happened for the sake of his own career." He looked at Tom Barrett. "It's my word to the board against a man who works for Grant, is in gambling trouble, and has just lost his son."

Mariah cut in. "He lost his son, or you took him away. I'm still waiting for the final report on the hoist cable, and we're sending a PI to El Salvador to interview the welder who was up there that morning. When we find him, I imagine he'll have a story a lot like Tom's."

Davis dropped back a step.

She kept hammering. "What did you offer Zaragoza?"

Wilson McMillan joined in. "I imagine a call from me to Dee Carpentier at the *Chronicle* would put you as a suspect on page one. She's a bit more credible than 'On The Spot.' "

"This is ridiculous." Davis's eyes met Rory's with a question in them.

Rory remembered his father's apparent disbelief when he'd accused him on the street after meeting with John. He looked into his heart, and at his father. Could he publicly accuse him of attempted murder? See it in the headlines?

"I didn't do it!" came the sharp cry from the man who'd given him life.

The silence following Davis's outburst was absolute. Then Rory heard Mariah's ragged breath and knew his own was as erratic.

Davis gave a last look around the room for quarter. McMillan's face was granite, Tom guilty yet unyielding. Mariah met him stare for stare, Catharine's daughter, but her own woman. He lingered on Rory. "My own family turned against me."

John spoke up. "There's an alternative to any ugly business."

As much as Rory knew his father had to go, it didn't feel like victory to watch him close his eyes and rub the bridge of his nose, weighing the odds. At last, Davis turned to the man he'd both loved and hated in equal measure.

"All right, John." His voice was that of a marathon runner who'd hit the wall. "What do you suggest?"

John moved forward and put an arm around Rory and Mariah. "I say we both retire and let these two get on with their life, and their business."

He and Mariah had engineered this coup, but all Rory could feel was sick inside as the arrogant man whose profile might have crowned a Roman coin, bowed his head. "I'll draft a letter to the board."

~∙~

The abdication should have been a triumph, but it didn't make Mariah's chest lift the way she'd expected. Instead, she watched Davis walk out of his own office with an unexpected ache. The door closed behind him with a snap that sounded final.

As soon as his rival had left the room, her father sighed. She met his eyes and the sheen of tears there made her own throat grow tight.

"That's that," he said. "I suppose we need to inform the staffs."

Rory put up a hand. "Yes, but we need to check in with First California."

McMillan clapped a hand on his shoulder. "What say you and I go over there while Mariah and her dad take care of Grant Development?"

John nodded. "I suppose we can't call it Grant anymore."

The end of what she'd always believed to be her heritage made her look to Rory. "I'm a Campbell now, but I'd hate to see the Grant name go away."

Rory frowned.

McMillan smiled. "How about an honorable compromise? CGI, Campbell-Grant Interests?"

"Only because Campbell comes first in the alphabet," Rory agreed. "Mariah, John?"

They exchanged a glance and nodded.

"One more thing." Rory pointed out the window toward the skyscraper nearing completion. "I'd like to keep the name Grant Plaza. We're going to get past this accident and make it the finest address in the city."

Now Mariah was sure she saw tears in her father's eyes.

"Thank you, son." He moved to clasp the younger man's hand.

Once she and John got to the their offices, he called a general meeting of the company to be held in half an hour. While they waited, he telephoned each manager and gave them a thumbnail sketch of what was happening.

When he hung up for the final time, he stared at the receiver. "I wish Arnold was here."

For the first time, Mariah did not cringe at the mention of the financial manager's name. His affection for her father seemed nothing but genuine. In fact, he would be a good man to have in the new company. "Do you think he'd come back to work for Rory and me?"

John smiled. "I talked to him about that last night. He came over and we had a game of chess."

"What did he say?"

"I think you must ask him yourself. I already apologized for doubting him . . ." He trailed off and she understood his meaning.

As the hundred or so employees crushed into the executive conference room, Mariah could see on their faces that they believed the foreclosure had happened. John's somber expression didn't encourage them and she expected he was having second thoughts about the deal he'd made with Davis to retire.

When everyone had gathered, with the exception of Arnold Benton and engineer Ramsey Rhodes, who was out, John rapped on the table for order. "Folks, I've got some news that means a lot of you will keep your jobs. There will be no foreclosure."

Smiles broke onto faces. Exclamations of surprise and delight drowned out his attempt to go one.

John held up his hands for order but it was a while before quiet was restored in the conference room. "Hold on, everybody. There will be a lot of changes. Grant is merging with DCI . . ."

"What the . . ." An oath broke from their lead draftsperson.

"Davis Campbell?" John's secretary shook her head.

"How's that going to work?" called a young man who'd joined the company only last week upon his college graduation. Even he knew of the legendary rivalry between Grant and Campbell.

John waited until curiosity got the better of them. When the group settled, he went on, "Both Davis Campbell and I have retired." Murmurs and whispers broke out, but at a level he could speak over. "Mariah and Rory Campbell will be running the combined company, to be called Campbell-Grant Interests." He glanced a question at her.

She nodded and stepped up beside him. "You all may have seen some confusing things about Rory and me this week on TV."

The speculation grew louder so she raised her voice. "Yesterday afternoon, Rory and I were married."

Silence greeted her last word. She stared at the assembled company and they back at her. She realized she was holding her breath.

Pandemonium erupted. Mariah's eyes stung while applause and cheering went on and on. Why was everyone so excited about her marrying Rory?

April Perry jumped up from a front row seat and embraced her. "Congratulations. I think having your story on TV turned you and Rory into celebrities."

Tom Barrett grabbed her into a bear hug and spoke into her ear. "Everyone believes you and Rory can make things right."

People surrounded her, laughing, and offering best wishes. All the while, she wondered how she and Rory could make things right between them when his father might have tried to kill her.

$\mathcal{A}$s the lunch hour had been taken up by the meeting, Mariah suggested they order in pizzas for the entire company. The staff all stayed to await the tower of boxes, filled with crusts smothered in tomato and cheese and topped with everything from olives to anchovies.

Just as Mariah grabbed a paper plate and started eating, her cell phone rang.

She chewed and swallowed a mouthful of pepperoni and cheese. "Mariah Gra . . . Campbell."

"Now you've got it," said Rory warmly.

His voice sent a little shiver through her and, still giddy from the reception of their news, she laughed. "Everyone here is celebrating."

Because of the noise level, she went out into the hall and stepped into her old office. It seemed unfamiliar since she'd been working out of her father's on the corner. "Now I can hear you."

"McMillan and I are finishing up at the bank." He paused for effect. "The threat of foreclosure is officially off, pending the legal creation of CGI."

"We did it." Mariah felt the final knots loosen in her shoulders and back. "I can say it now without worrying about a jinx. We really did it."

Rory sobered. "I showed them Father's letter of resignation and First California's chairman called Thaddeus Walker on the carpet."

She imagined the long-faced banker's usually dour expression growing even darker.

"It'll be a wonder if he keeps his job."

She almost said that was great, but why celebrate misfortune? Instead, she said, "We're eating pizza here. You want to come by?"

"McMillan and I are having lunch to discuss some innovative financing for the new company. Also, he says he wants to invest in us. We'll meet with him together next week."

A nice vote of confidence in her and Rory, but it was a shame her dad was cut out of it.

"Funny," Rory mused. "The chairman at First California expressed regret at the developers' community losing both Father and John. He knows about your dad's health, but I couldn't bring myself to tell him the reasons we forced Father out."

Another pang went through her. Davis Campbell, ever proud, with a spring in his step and a gleam in his eye, brought down in disgrace. She still had the PI looking for Zaragoza and Rory didn't know that.

"Are you coming by after lunch?" she tempered.

"I thought I'd go back to the office and talk to the DCI staff. They haven't heard about the merger yet . . . or about us."

"It's probably better coming from you than from the press," she agreed. "What if both our PR folks send out a joint release?"

She and Rory arranged to meet at her father's house after work.

Mariah returned to the conference room. A thinning crowd stood around a litter of empty pizza boxes. Soft drink cans were scattered over every surface, and a few folks were bringing out trash bags to manage to mess.

John buttonholed her. "We can't visit all our sites, but I think we should go over to Grant Plaza."

"I should have thought of that." The site boasted the largest group of employees outside of the main office.

He patted her shoulder, and she didn't even mind some of the staff seeing. "As time goes on, you'll think of the right things yourself."

They excused themselves and left the building. As she drove them to the site, she dwelled on her inexperience. "I've only been with the company a short time. I wish you hadn't made that deal with Davis to stay out of the business."

From the corner of her eye she saw a muscle twitch in her father's jaw. "I do too . . . now."

Yet, she knew him to be man of honor, who would not break his word unless faced with a compelling reason.

At the site, Mariah parked her sedan alongside the trucks and trailers. She and John got out of the car, and both of them raised their faces skyward. The glass spire sparkled in the afternoon sun like a perfect crystal.

Onsite, the bustle of the crew and the sound of a generator spoke of the work and energy that went into building. Mariah's chest swelled with pride, because even though Charley was no longer with them, Grant Plaza was being completed and her family name would live on in it.

Supervisor Cassie Holden greeted them in the main trailer. "John, Mariah. I'm glad you're here." Her cheek bore a healing scar where flying glass had struck her, a little more prominent than the one on Mariah's forehead. "Ramsey Rhodes is touring the site with the OSHA rep. Said they've got the final results of the investigation."

Mariah's pulse accelerated. "What caused it?"

"He didn't want to tell me before he had a chance to talk with you and John." Cassie opened the trailer door and yelled to a man in a hard hat standing near the base of the replaced hoist. "What floor is Ramsey on?"

"Top," came the answering shout.

"Let's go." John's expression suggested both determination and wariness.

Mariah headed for the hoist with him, suspecting he was thinking about Davis. Cassie discreetly stayed behind.

The metal cage waited at the base of the tower. Normally, Mariah loved the sensation of ascending a structure that only existed from hard work and imagination. Today, her stomach fluttered as she and John rose into the sky. The closer they got to the top, the less she wanted to hear what Ramsey had to say. If her suspicions were correct, the heat stress already found on the cable held the evidence of sabotage. There might not be any way to pin it on Davis, but for the sake of Charley and his family, she had to try and find justice.

If she, if her PI, found evidence his father were guilty would Rory want to divorce her?

The hoist reached the top floor. Though the view of the city, Bay, and bridges was spectacular, she turned without savoring it and went into the building.

Afternoon light grayed in the center away from the tinted windows. Bits of paper and other debris littered the concrete floor from one side of the building to the other. The only breaks in the space were the central elevator shafts and stairwells. Ramsey stood at the north windows talking on his cell phone.

Mariah headed for him with slow dread. How was it possible that after the long wait for answers, she no longer wanted to hear? With all her heart, she wished that Davis had nothing to do with Charley's death.

As she approached Ramsey, she heard him say, "She and John are here now. I'll tell her you're waiting on the okay for a press release." He pressed the "end" button. "That was April. Ready to give out the good news."

"About the foreclosure?"

Ramsey shook his head. "No. She's already sent that one."

Mariah replayed what he'd said about good news and her steps slowed further. The knot in the middle of her stomach twisted. "It wasn't sabotage?"

Completely out of character, Ramsey grinned from ear to ear. "A design flaw, the best possible outcome for us. The hoist company is calling a warning for all of their leased equipment to be inspected before tragedy strikes anywhere else."

"Thank you," Mariah said. "Oh, thank you."

Near the end of the arduous day, Rory was left alone, sitting in his father's chair. His tie had been put aside, his collar loosened. It was all over, as that tired saying went, all but the shouting. Father wasn't going to take this quietly, even if he had left the building as soon as his letter was signed.

Just after six, Mariah called Rory from outside the locked lobby doors, and he went to meet her. She looked beautiful; a few strands of her hair wisping around her neck, and he wanted to take the rest of it down. To run his hands up her arms and pull her against him.

Because John stood beside her, he did not.

"The accident report is complete," she said. "We got it and came straight here."

Sweat broke out on his palms and under his arms. His heart set up a rough and heavy beat. Not Father, oh, not Father. "What caused it?" he asked in as normal a tone as he could manage.

John answered. "The hoist cable showed metal fatigue caused by the heat of vibration. A gear misalignment."

Rory's eyes closed, and he let out his breath. No matter what else his father had done, he wasn't a murderer.

"The cable was past due for replacement from a work standpoint, but not according to hours," Mariah said. "Only under the scanning electron microscope in a metallurgist's lab could the problem have been detected. And the fact that the emergency brake failed to arrest the fall is a one in a million piece of bad luck."

"He didn't do it." Rory's voice rose. "He didn't do it."

Mariah looked at him with somber eyes. "I wish I could jump up and down and be happy. I am happy . . . but what I did was terrible, jumping to conclusions."

John put a hand on his daughter's shoulder. "You have to admit Davis pulled some pretty low tricks this spring."

"Yes, but whatever else he may have done, I owe him an apology," Mariah said.

Rory felt as though there were a weight on his chest. "He won't take it. He'll never want to see either of us again."

"Don't you see, we have to try?" she insisted. "He was making the same mistake so many of us do, dwelling on an old hurt."

John rubbed his chin. "You know, that makes me think.

The other day Davis said I had never apologized for taking Catharine from him."

"You told him you never would." Rory didn't see where his father deserved an apology for John loving Catharine.

The older man looked chagrined. "I said I'd never apologize for loving her, but what we did, getting married while he was in Africa . . . that's always set heavy on my conscience. Maybe what I need to do, what we all need to do, is accept blame for our own part in all that's happened."

Thirty minutes later, Rory turned into the cul-de-sac at Seacliff. He was driving Mariah's sedan carrying the three of them, as his Porsche did not have a back seat big enough to accommodate anyone larger than a preschooler.

Rory got out of the car, chimed the doorbell, and knocked. An inquiring glance from Mariah reminded him once more of the ignominy of a son not having a key to the house he'd grown up in. His "Halloo!" echoed off stone and glass.

Anna came to door, moving slowly as usual.

As soon as she opened it, Rory pushed past her, leaving Mariah and John on the threshold. He went into the kitchen where the Sub Zero threw back his reflection, along with the rest of the ultra modern stone and stainless room. In a ceramic bowl on the counter, he found the spare keys.

Mariah caught up with him. He recognized the extra door keys, selected one, and twisted it off. He put the key in his pocket. "I should have done this years ago."

Together, they returned to the foyer. His mother's sitting room and the library lay in darkness.

"Mr. Rory." Anna twisted her hands together and he hated that he was making the well-loved housekeeper nervous. "Your mother is in the family room."

Her eyes avoided his and Rory's scalp prickled. What if Davis was taking his anger at being ousted out on Kiki?

Once more leaving Mariah and the slower moving John behind, he raced across the foyer and into the trophy room.

His mother sat slumped on the slate floor. An Alaskan brown bear on its hind legs towered over her. Rory wondered that she wasn't freezing, sitting on the chill stone in a thin dress. Tears ran down her cheeks to join the others that had splattered her red silk like raindrops. He surmised now that Anna's nervousness had been because of her following the family rule that servants didn't see certain things.

Like the half-empty brandy bottle atop the bar.

But the family rules were being shattered, and Rory had a sense that something irrevocable was about to happen.

Kiki struggled to her feet and went to the wet bar, where she stared at her reflection. Raising her hands to her cheeks, she kneaded the skin with fingers that clutched, then grasped. Her sharply manicured nails produced a line of blood that welled beneath her left ear.

"Mom," Rory cried.

She turned and saw him. He moved toward her, but he was still fifteen feet away when she grabbed and swung the brandy bottle. The mirror disintegrated into crystal shards. Liquor fumes fogged the falling glass. She stumbled back from the wreckage, clutched the edge of the granite bar top for a second, and then dropped out of sight.

Rory rushed to her, fragments of mirror and bottle crunching beneath his shoes. He slipped one arm beneath her shoulders and the other behind her knees, carried her to a leather couch, and laid her down. Swiftly, he checked her back and bare feet for cuts. Thankfully, there were none.

He became aware of Mariah beside him, her fist pressed against her mouth.

From behind him, John said, "My God."

Rory heard Mariah's footsteps and the gurgle of running water as she wet a bar towel with cold water and brought it to him.

He wiped the smear of blood from Kiki's cheek. "Mom."

She stirred and opened her eyes. "Rory."

"You have to leave him," he said.

"Leave me?" Davis said from the door to the interior hall. Still wearing his European cut suit and Italian silk tie, he surveyed the wreckage. A hundred tall men seemed to march off in all directions where the remaining bar mirrors faced against one on the other wall. To Rory's relief, he sounded sober and he looked as though he'd just gotten home.

When Kiki spoke, Rory realized she wasn't drunk, either, as he'd thought. "Yes, leave you." She pushed herself up to a sitting position on the couch. "I always stayed, because I thought someday you'd get over your precious Catharine, that no living woman could ever hope to equal." A fat tear streaked down her cheek, leaving a darkened trail in her face powder.

Rory got between his father and his mother, a deep trembling in his chest. From the corner of his eye, he saw that John had his arm around Mariah as though to insulate her.

Kiki's voice gained strength. "I got a call from a florist today, one I've never used. It seems that Chez Paris has a new employee, one who made the mistake of calling your home instead of your office to ask about your weekly order. My God, you've sent flowers to her grave every week for nearly thirty years."

"Respect for the dead," Davis replied.

Rory wanted to slug him. "Show some respect for the living. Mom and I have been here for you, all those years."

"Haven't I been there for you?" His father pointed an unsteady finger at him. "I taught you to sail, to build . . . I wanted you on the executive floor with me. If I was tough on you, it was because I wanted you to do well."

"You mean all the times you've given me a hard time, you thought you were being a stern taskmaster?" Rory raised his voice and felt a hand on his shoulder.

John restrained him. "Davis always has been a perfectionist. Whether he was sailing," he pointed to a shelf of prominent gold cups, "hunting," he gestured to the world record trophy animals, "or working, he has to have things just so." He looked at Davis. "Am I right?"

"You're right," Davis said with a trace of wariness.

"And isn't it true," John went on, "that you love your son?

From the time he was a kid on that sailboat and you taught him how to steer?"

Davis made a gesture of impatience. "Of course I love him."

Rory went still inside, but he couldn't help his reply. "Your delivery could use some work."

Kiki pushed up from the couch and faced her husband. "I always dreamed someday you'd come to love me. Do you have any idea what it's like to go on living day after day, without hope?"

The silence that fell seemed as vast as the Pacific outside the wall of windows.

Rory developed an urge to clear his throat and suppressed it.

The moment lengthened, while his parents searched each other's eyes in a manner he suspected they had not for years.

Finally, Davis spoke in a voice that sounded thick. "I love you, too."

"Then why can't you let go of the past?" Kiki's voice cracked.

Davis glanced at Mariah. "Whenever I see her, looking so much like Catharine, it brings up the possibilities I dreamed of and never had." He took a step toward his wife. "But that doesn't mean I didn't choose you. I remember how the setting sun caught fire in your red hair on the banks of the Zambezi. How . . .?"

"Ancient history," Kiki drilled. "What about that bitch that called you on the phone in the Marin Club?"

"I swear to God it was Thaddeus Walker's assistant Louise arranging a meeting. I would have told you, but after you threw your wine at me I didn't even try." He drew a shaking breath. "As for the stories about women, the paparazzi make things out to be more spicy than they are."

"Amen to that," said John.

Davis shifted his gaze to him. "You were right that seeing Mariah grown dredged up a desire to make you pay for stealing Catharine . . . especially when you knew I loved her."

John left Mariah's side and took a step toward Davis. "You know very well that I couldn't steal what you never really had. The other day I said I would never apologize, but I was wrong."

Davis cocked an eyebrow.

"I am sorry for the way things happened. If I had it to do over, I would never have married her until after you came back from Africa. I'd have insisted Catharine meet with you and tell you in her own words what her desires were. Then, maybe you could have found a way to remain my friend, perhaps we could have worked together instead of at cross purposes."

Davis strode toward the bar, sidestepped the mess of glass and liquor and took down a bottle of scotch. He pulled down a glass, poured two fingers and tossed off one.

"You're apologizing to me?" he said in disbelief.

"Not for loving Catharine, not for marrying her," John said firmly, "but for doing it in a way that inflicted maximum pain."

Davis stared at him for a long time. The silence was once more absolute in the great, high-ceilinged room. Rory watched the two men and realized he was holding his breath.

Finally, his father nodded. "I suppose that's as good as I

can expect."

He reached to the bar shelf and took down another glass. He poured scotch into it, picked it up, and gestured with it toward John. His arrogance had been replaced by what looked like regret.

John took three steps toward the bar and stopped.

Davis brought both glasses and met him halfway. "We could have made a hell of a team."

John took the drink and knocked it against Davis's. Both men drank.

"Of course, that will never happen after this morning," Davis went on.

"What happened this morning?" Kiki asked sharply.

He turned to her. "It was on the news. I thought when I walked in that you'd heard."

"Heard what?"

"Rory and Mariah got married yesterday in Lake Tahoe."

Kiki gasped and swiveled her head. Her green eyes glinted at Rory and then shifted to Mariah.

"And they found a way to pressure me out of the company." In a transparent effort to save face, Davis went on, "John's out, too and the kids are going to form one company."

She looked from Rory to Mariah. "They're married?"

"It was a sound business strategy, so I suppose I did teach him a thing or two," Davis said grudgingly. "And I guess you taught your daughter well, John."

Mariah moved, her heels rapping the slate floor. "Business strategy?" she echoed. "Business strategy?" She came to

Rory's side and took his hand. "I'll have you know I happen to love your son."

Though Rory had hoped she loved him, and been ready to tell her himself this morning, her words sent him spiraling. Hoping and hearing it were two different things, and the roller coaster they'd been on hit a new high.

Before he could tell her and the whole room he loved her, Mariah focused on Davis.

"The reason I came here this evening is to apologize to you as well. We found out today that the hoist fell due to a design flaw. I was wrong to believe you were behind the accident."

"I'm sorry about that, too, Dad." Rory used the name he'd called his father when he was a boy.

Davis drank off the rest of his scotch, set down the glass with a clatter on an end table. He sighed. "Thank you for that much."

Kiki got to her feet. "I don't understand all this. You and John, Rory and Mariah taking over . . . are you talking about the accident at Grant Plaza?"

"I'm afraid we are," Davis replied. He turned to the others. "I think my wife and I need some time to sort things out."

"Of course," John said.

Rory looked at his mother to gauge her reaction. Her tears, that had dried, once more brightened her green eyes.

He went to her, bent and kissed her cheek. "Is that okay with you, Mom? Should we go now?"

Davis had said he loved her, and Rory wondered how long it had been since he'd told his wife that.

Kiki put her arms around Rory. "Go ahead," she whispered. "And remember he said he loved you, too."

Despite that his father's delivery needed work, the content sounded like a good start.

At nine that night, Mariah sat beside Rory in his Porsche as he pulled into his townhouse garage. They'd left Davis and Kiki alone and had dinner with her father. It had not taken much persuasion on his part to convince them to go to one of their places for privacy.

"I'm glad we came here," she told Rory. "I don't want to spend another night in my apartment." Though it was not time to forget Charley — that would never happen — she needed to move on.

Inside Rory's home, her home now, they passed through the kitchen and living room and took the stairs to the second floor. Dusk was falling outside his bedroom and when he reached for the switch, Mariah stayed his hand.

"The view is beautiful." She was glad he'd left the drapes open.

They walked past his king-sized bed to the window. From their vantage point high on Vallejo, the vista was of the higher Telegraph Hill to the northeast and the slope down to the Embarcadero and the Bay.

Rory stood behind her and slipped his arms around her. "I don't know about you, but I'm exhausted."

"It's been a tough day, well, more than a day."

"Do you think there's any hope for our fathers?"

Mariah's eyes filled with tears. There was no telling how a truce might work, but this first step made her feel that mountains were not too much to scale.

She stroked Rory's hand on her waist. "I hope they can put some things behind them."

She and Rory needed the wisdom of both these men if they were to make a go of CGI. "You remember telling me the chairman of First California said it was a shame John and Dad would be lost to the developers' community."

"Hmmm," he murmured at her neck.

"What if they're not lost? What if they both sit on the CGI board of directors?"

Rory straightened and pondered. "I know I could use the help."

"Let's ask them." The idea of their fathers finding reconciliation might be too much to hope for, but she dared to wish they'd made a start.

"I just hope my folks . . ." Rory broke off.

"Maybe they can work something out. He did say he loved her."

"She's pretty upset over Catharine and those flowers," Rory countered.

Mariah pulled away and turned to face him. "It's not just the flowers. She's a woman who feels beaten out by a ghost. It's amazing how they all act as though she died only yesterday."

He was silent for a moment. "Think about it. It was eight

years ago when we met, and I can see you on that dock in the rain as if it were this morning."

He took her hand and tugged her toward the French doors to his balcony. Outside, the June air was soft.

"There's something I need to tell you," Rory said urgently. "In a lot of ways, I've been as big a fool as Dad was."

She put her fingers to his lips. "You don't have to . . ."

"Shhh," he caught her hand and kissed it.

His warm mouth sent a melting feeling through her. Her heart set up a deep pounding that she felt whenever something important was about to happen.

She looked up at him, at his familiar tall frame and warm brown eyes that promised everything he had when they were younger, yet so much more.

"Mariah, I know now I was afraid to let myself feel. I don't know why I've held back and lied to myself about it. You've been a part of me all these years, but I buried it. It all came back the day I heard about the accident and ran down the streets looking for you."

Putting her hands into the silky hair at the nape of his neck, Mariah whispered his name.

It reminded her of the first time he'd held her, but there was so much more. Instead of the tremulous passion of discovery, there was her deep and complex caring for the man she'd married.

"I love you," he said close beside her ear.

A floodgate opened, a willful desire to be swept away if Rory was truly no longer afraid of commitment. "Oh, Rory,

I love you, too."

He pulled back and smiled at her. "I'll never let you forget you told my father before you told me."

She tapped his breastbone with her index finger. "Don't give me that. You knew I loved you last night after we got married."

His grin widened. "Busted. I was going to tell you this morning, but after your dad called, the mood wasn't right."

He dragged her back against him and she felt a shift in him, to awareness that her body was against the length of his. She felt it, too, as the banked embers of their last love-making began to smoulder. Soon, those sparks would flare into a conflagration.

She turned her eyes toward the sea. The Golden Gate spanned the narrows, a ribbon studded with the lights of people going places. It reminded her of the evening she'd stepped out onto Davis's terrace, just before Rory and she were reunited. Oceangoing ships headed out to sea, but Mariah no longer wanted to escape on one.

She was where she belonged, as she and Rory set their sights on the limitless horizon.

Christine Carroll writing as Linda Jacobs

SUMMER OF FIRE
LINDA JACOBS

It is 1988, and Yellowstone Park is on fire.

Among the thousands of summer warriors battling to save America's crown jewel, is single mother Clare Chance. Having just watched her best friend, a fellow Texas firefighter, die in a roof collapse, she has fled to Montana to try and put the memory behind her. She's not the only one fighting personal demons as well as the fiery dragon threatening to consume the park.

There's Chris Deering, a Vietnam veteran helicopter pilot, seeking his next adrenaline high and a good time that doesn't include his wife, and Ranger Steve Haywood, a man scarred by the loss of his wife and baby in a plane crash. They rally 'round Clare when tragedy strikes yet again, and she loses a young soldier to a firestorm.

Three flawed, wounded people; one horrific blaze. Its tentacles are encircling the park, coming ever closer, threatening to cut them off. The landmark Old Faithful Inn and Park Headquarters at Mammoth are under siege, and now there's a helicopter down, missing, somewhere in the path of the conflagration. And Clare's daughter is on it . . .

ISBN#1932815295
Gold Imprint
Available Now
$6.99
www.readlindajacobs.com

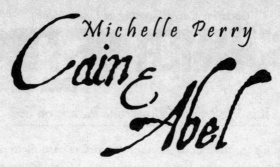

Michelle Perry
Cain & Abel

She fooled him once . . .

In Los Angeles an unexpected pregnancy sparks a daring plan of escape for a brutally battered wife. Jessica Ramsey fakes her death and flees to Tennessee to build a new life for herself and her unborn son.

But nobody fools Cole Ramsey twice . . .

Five years later, a chance encounter has destroyed Jessica's carefully cultivated anonymity. She thought at first Cole had found her, but it was his twin, Alex, who unwittingly unmasked her charade. Now she must trust him to save her from Cole's wrath. But the twins are bound by blood. Will it prove stronger than the fragile relationship building between Alex and Jessica? Or will a third time be a deadly charm?

ISBN#0932815031
Jewel Imprint: Emerald
$6.99
Romantic Suspense
Available Now
www.michelleperry.com

The Keeners
Maura D. Shaw

The rough beauty of County Clare is seventeen-year-old Margaret Meehan's whole world, and it is nearly perfect. Her family is well and thriving, farming Ireland's staple crop. She expects to marry handsome Tom Riordan, raise their children, and live in a cottage across the lane from her best friend, Kitty Dooley. She has found her calling and is apprenticed to the old keener Nuala Lynch. Together they keen for the dead, wailing the grief and pain of the bereaved in hopes of healing their sorrow. Margaret's life is full of hope, full of purpose.

But the year is 1846. The potato blight has returned. Pitiful harvests rot overnight and the people are dying. Ireland is dying. And Margaret cannot keen for an entire country.

Out of devastation, Margaret Meehan's tale begins. Leaving her decimated family, the tragic Kitty, and the death of dreams behind, she flees with her husband, now a wanted man, to America. In Troy, New York, where pig iron, starched collars, and union banners herald the success of Irish immigrants, Margaret discovers something even more precious than a new life and modest prosperity. She finds the heart and soul of Ireland. And she finds it in the voice of . . . The Keeners . . .

ISBN# 1932815155
Platinum
$25.95
Historical Fiction
March 2005
www.mauradshaw.com

KEY OF SEA
MARY STELLA

In her youth, Dora Lee Hanson set her dreams on distant goals. A more exciting life waited, if not over the rainbow, then at least somewhere out of the quiet Florida Keys. The twenty-something beauty left home for a modeling career, but a wealthy magnate swept her off her ostrich-plumed mules. Unfortunately, after more than a dozen years of marriage, the wicked wretch kicked her to the curb. Facing a very uncertain future, she returns to her beloved grandfather and the home she eagerly left behind all those years before.

Successful Keys fishing guide Bobby Daulton has the life he always intended, with one notable exception. He never caught Dora Lee, the love of his youth. After all these years, he never expected her to blow back into his world with tornado force, but he's a far cry from the kid who once let her slip the line and escape.

When an ex-trophy wife with a mid-life crisis hooks up with the hot guy whose heart she unknowingly broke years before, the passionate pair rock more than the romance boat. Dora Lee has her eye on a brand new dream. Bobby has his eye on Dora. He's fallen for her again, hook, line and sinker, and this time she won't swim away.

ISBN#1932815406
Jewel Imprint: Ruby
$6.99
Available Now
www.marystella.com

Jinxed

by Beth Ciotta

Since the day beautiful socialite Afia St. John was born, her life has been plagued with bad luck. After losing her father and two older husbands in "freak" accidents, Afia now discovers her business manager has absconded with her fortune. Vowing not to rely on another man to guide her life, Afia refuses her godfathers' help, and jumps at an unexpected job with the Leeds Investigations.

With a pregnant, broke, sister, and an investigation agency in the red, control-freak Jake Leeds can't turn down the hefty but secret retainer offered by Afia's godfather for hiring her. Quickly seeing beyond her poor business skills, wacky superstitions and sensationalized personal history, he realizes Afia is as generous in the heart as she is misunderstood. But life is never easy for the woman born on Friday the 13th. Will the sexy PI be the good luck charm that puts her on a winning streak or, like everything else in her life, will their relationship wind up Jinxed?

ISBN#0974363944
Jewel Imprint: Ruby
$6.99
Available Now
www.bethciotta.com